Keeper of the Mythos Gate

Published by Winterset Books
www.kaykenyon.com
Hardcover ISBN: 979-8-9884011-3-1

Published in the United States of America

Cover by Deranged Doctor Design

Visit www.kaykenyon.com and join the author's newsletter for a free short story and find out about new releases and reader perks.

Don't miss the first three books of this series: *The Girl Who Fell Into Myth, Stranger in the Twisted Realm,* and *Servant of the Lost Power.* Available in print and eBook.

Also by Kay Kenyon

Fantasy Novels

THE ARISEN WORLDS QUARTET

The Girl Who Fell Into Myth, Book 1

Stranger in the Twisted Realm, Book 2

Servant of the Lost Power, Book 3

Keeper of the Mythos Gate, Book 4

STAND ALONE FANTASY

A Thousand Perfect Things

Queen of the Deep

THE DARK TALENTS TRILOGY

At the Table of Wolves, Book 1

Serpent in the Heather, Book 2

Nest of the Monarch, Book 3

Science Fiction Novels

The Seeds of Time

Tropic of Creation

Rift

Leap Point

Maximum Ice

The Braided World

THE ENTIRE AND THE ROSE QUARTET

Bright of the Sky, Book 1

A World Too Near, Book 2

City Without End, Book 3

Prince of Storms, Book 4

Collections

Dystopia: Seven Dark and Hopeful Tales

Worlds Near and Far

KEEPER
OF THE
MYTHOS GATE

BOOK FOUR OF THE ARISEN WORLDS

KAY KENYON

WINTERSET BOOKS

The Nine Powers

Foreknowing
Manifesting
Creatures
Warding
Healing
Verdure
Aligns
Elements
Primal Roots

PART I
THE WOLF KEEPER

Chapter One

Yevliesza walked through the dark woods with her *sympat*, a gray and graceful companion. Now, as always with Kiya, the world grew quiet, the only sounds those of crickets and other insects. In the wild, small animals crouched low, unmoving when the wraith wolf padded by.

In the weeks since they had formed their bond, she had grown close to Kiya, but could only expect him when few people were around. Tonight Rusadka and one of her guards stayed at the campfire and, once she had gone off by herself, Kiya had found her, crossing over from the otherworld where spirits dwelled. His appearing and disappearing trick was one she wished she had. Then she could freely enter the crossings and disrupt Volkia's hold on the place. As it was, the gates were guarded by the enemy.

Numinat was at war with the twisted realm, and since Yevliesza was always in danger, she was seldom truly alone. Some thirty yards behind her, one of her guards kept watch. Kiya's ears sometimes flicked back; he knew the man was there. Her guards knew that if the wraith wolf came they should fall back. Far enough that Kiya's back fur settled.

A shadow passed over the moon. A dactyl. Yevliesza watched as it glided into the night, riderless, heading for its unknown destination. Osta Kiya used the dragonlike creatures for surveillance, seven of them. The army's dactyls had taken thirty years to train, and, despite the training, some of them would not accept a male rider. The one she had just seen bore no rider; it lived in the wild. She envied its freedom.

Her own life was saddled with duty: to find a way to use her primal root power to attack and weaken the Volkish. But strike at them in a measured way, measured enough to weaken their army but not the Mythos. She must be a saboteur, destroying some things. But not all things.

Her daily task was to help Janov manage a camp with a hundred seekers and more arriving every day. In the Haiga marshlands, her camp for the past month, she had an obligation to those who had gathered, welcome or not: the curious, the seekers. The ones that came to see her though she had nothing to give them. They needed food and supplies. It helped that Anastyna had sent Lord Kirady to her, bringing more of his men-at-arms to stiffen her protection and keep some order at the camp.

She paused on a small rock outcropping to gaze at the ravine in front of her, softly lit by moonlight. Nearby, an align creased the land. At night, such power threads were especially beautiful.

The fiery line appeared to split the forest floor, a stream of molten light, narrow but deep, maybe endlessly deep. Ahead, a rock formation jutted from the hillside. The align pierced it like a flaming arrow, disappearing. The align must burrow deep into the hill. She felt its pull and its path.

Turning around, she walked back toward Zander. Kiya waited for her.

"I'll walk toward the hill," she told the guard, his tall form unmistakable.

"Keeper," he said in acknowledgement. "There is a cave up there."

No reason why an align should not go through a cave. Aligns were like rivers, following some feature of landscape or threads of power. Zander had manifesting, not aligns, and could not see the vivid line.

She turned back to join Kiya, but he had vanished. Gone to the next realm, so it was said. She had always taken that as truth because she wanted to believe it; wanted to know that there was life after life. However mysterious that realm might be. And if Kiya lived half in that land, it must be a wondrous place.

With Zander, she climbed up the scree slope to the cave. "I will go in first," he said.

She stood aside for him, and he drew his sword, entering the gap. His manifested light flickered off the cave walls, revealing a cavity cluttered with pine needles and a scattering of small bones.

"Nothing here," he called to her.

She entered, her attention still drawn by the align. The bright shaft headed straight into the back wall. As Zander approached, bringing a nimbus of light with him, she noticed a series of rings. She squinted at them. Where had she had seen such markings before? Small whorls, such as a pebble produced when thrown into still water. The align passed through the markings.

During her flight from Volkia, when she was in the backways of the crossings, she had learned that whorls of this sort indicated the best place to break through to a nearby path—a shortcut instead of taking a longer route to connect. But how could there be a pattern like this in a remote cave? She wondered if such a mark signified the same thing.

Closing her eyes, she gave herself to the perception of the align.

"Oh," she breathed. A stitch of shock flared in her chest. Behind this wall . . . a path.

The idea blossomed in her mind: she stood just outside of the crossings. If this was an entry point, then it was, in essence, a gate. An unopened one.

"Keeper?" Zander's voice, though quiet, broke her concentration. "A difficulty?" he asked, always alert for danger. Warden Kirady had told him to guard her with his life.

"No," she answered. "A possibility." She turned to meet his gaze. "A good thing, Zander."

He looked doubtfully at the jagged wall, not seeing the featherlight etching in the rock.

Her heart stuttered in her chest at this discovery. The crossings were near. She could see them with her mind's eye, and not only the paths, but if anyone was on them. The nerve endings in her left hand zinged. Her primal root power moved through her body, seeking an outlet, or so she had come to believe.

Once before she had created an exit from the crossings. Into Alfan Sih, when she unlocked a way for Prince Tirhan to return his beleaguered kingdom. This time, it would be different.

She had found a way *into* the crossings. And she was going to open it.

Chapter Two

Volkish Captain Arman Brandt and his men slogged through the muddy field. Less of a field than a bog and becoming more so as the rain fell in unforgiving sheets. They had left the horses behind, afraid to risk them in the swampy terrain near the Volkish capital city.

The men grumbled, hunkered under rain capes that did little to keep them dry. They had left dry behind an hour ago.

"Over by the trees, Captain," Vogert said, pointing at a mist-shrouded manor barely visible in the fog.

Arman's unit of four was assigned to the far outskirts of Hapsigen, one of many search parties assigned to hunt down the notorious traitor Duke Tanfred. He was known to have ties to the primordialists, a group on which the army's intelligence corps had been keeping tabs. When they captured the duke, any citizens who sheltered him would meet the same fate as their hero. Roundups of the disloyal were frequent now, and gallows stood in public squares. In Hapsigen, of course, but smaller towns, too.

"We should just hang them in the yard," Vogert said. "Save the trouble of transport."

Vogert looked forward to finding traitors. "If he's there," Captain Brandt said. "There is still the law."

"We are still at war," Vogert muttered, then averted his gaze as his captain jerked a look at him. He would pay for that bit of impudence.

In front of the manor, a courtyard, muddy as the field, containing only an empty hay cart with a couple of hounds sheltering under it. Arman gestured for one his men, Stohl, to rap on the door.

A strongly built and bearded man opened the door, squinting at them, unhappy to see soldiers, but trying to hide it.

"Keller?" Stohl asked. "This is the home of Danzman Keller?"

A small girl peered around the man's knee, staring at the men with their wet capes, uniforms, and swords.

"I am Danzman Keller," the man said, nodding gravely, noting Arman's officer uniform.

He had no choice but to allow them into the hall, muddy boots and all. They quickly determined that the Keller household consisted of Keller, a wife, two servants, the wife's mother, and four children.

A servant brought an old rug for them to wipe their boots on since the house had polished floors and old, but fine rugs. Only Arman bothered to use it. Another child stood at a door leading from the hall. A pudgy girl no more than four years old.

"How many floors?" Arman asked. "Out buildings?"

"There is only the upstairs, but a small attic, then the cellar. Also shed and barn. Who are you looking for?" When Arman did not bother to answer, he went on. "As I have said, there is no one else here."

Arman smirked. "Of course not. But now we will see for ourselves. Wait for us in the kitchen."

"I can show you the house."

"The kitchen," Arman said again.

As the homeowner retreated, Arman sent Vogert into the rain to search the detached buildings as a punishment for talking back. Stohl accompanied him.

He turned to Corporal Gertz. "Make sure everyone is gathered in the kitchen, and tell them to stay there."

When Gertz went off, the little girl, who had been hiding behind the door to what might be a parlor, peeked out again. "No one ith ever hiding here," she said, lisping.

Arman cocked his head. "Not even for fun?"

She shook her head solemnly. "No one ith in the cellar, Mama thays. No one." She looked at the floor, biting her lip.

"Anna, come!" her father called. The girl ran to obey.

Arman now looked at the hall with new eyes: the polished wainscoting and threadbare, but expensive rug. He would have liked to own such a house. But this one was hiding someone. If it was the duke, the occupants were doomed, even the children. His search would get ugly very quickly. He went to the kitchen where the family was gathered and asked for a lantern.

"You take the upstairs," he told Corporal Gertz. "Overlook nothing."

Gertz climbed the stairs, his boots leaving a mud trail that for a moment looked like gouts of blood.

Finding the door to the cellar, Arman held the lantern in front of him and descended into a musty twilight space. He found washtubs and shelves with glass jars of preserved food. Spanning one end of the cellar, lines had been strung to dry clothes.

In the back against the wall, a large, covered bin. Arman put the lantern on the floor. Lifting the tarp, he found only potatoes. Some of the tarp draped to the far side of the bin. He drew his sword and kicked a boot against the tarp, feeling it thump against a body. Pulling the tarp free, he found someone hiding.

The man, dressed in peasant drabs, slowly stood. He had a round, aristocratic face, looking to be in his early thirties. Though he had been discovered by a Volkish soldier, his face held an expression of disdain.

"Please spare these good people," the man said in a cultured northern accent. "They did not know I was here."

Dear God, it was Duke Tanfred Wilhoffen. "Keep your voice down," Arman snapped.

The duke lowered his voice. "They are loyal Volkish. I beg you to spare them."

Spare them? If he did, and it came to light, Arman would hang. He had long known that might be his fate. But malignant beliefs infected his country, beliefs embraced by Marshal Reinhart and the witch Nashavety. These ideas had led to acts of butchery, enslavement, and diabolic machines. He did not recognize his land anymore, and, to free it, he would give his life.

"I beg you," the duke said.

"You should not be here, so close to Hapsigen," Arman said, speaking low. "The capital is closely guarded. Search parties are everywhere."

By his expression, the duke thought his captor might be a friend. "I was here to meet with a rebel group, but I have not heard from them."

"A rebel group?" Arman asked in surprise.

Thinking Arman doubted him, Duke Tanfred said loftily, "I know of many such patriots who do not accept the war and the sorceress who commands us. I hold their hopes."

Arman listened for any noise of his soldiers returning from their searches. "If you speak of the St. Eustus group, they are all dead." The army officers who had tried to kill Marshal Reinhart and his sorceress. "The members are hanging on the walls of the crossings."

The duke's expression faltered.

"They are all dead, my lord. All except me. I was a member."

Tanfred ran a hand through his hair as he absorbed the news of the cabal's demise.

Arman despaired of the duke's chances, hiding next to a potato bin, waiting for an insurrection that would never come. "Some people thought you had escaped to Numinat." Would that he had never come back.

"I returned to help."

"You must go back. Reinhart will not rest until you are captured. Be the leader in exile."

Tanfred looked like a man defeated.

"My lord," Arman urgently said, "you must find a way."

As Arman turned to leave, Tanfred said, "Perhaps—" Arman turned back. "Perhaps there is someone who could help. The woman who escaped Volkia with me."

"The woman Yevliesza?" Everyone in St. Eustus had heard the story of her escape. "You can contact her?"

"She is in Numinat. But she knows a path through the tunnels, or could find one."

A strange thing to say. No one could get past the boundary gate guards. "If she can help, you must get word to her."

"I have no means to do so. She is in hiding."

"Where?"

"I do not know," Tanfred said. "At first it was Zolvina Sanctuary, but now . . ." He shook his head. "Can you not find a way to reach her?"

Arman shook his head. "Messages cannot be sent." It sounded impossible, but he had to try. He picked up the lantern. "My lord, I will do my best. Do not leave here. Stay, and I will try to send help."

The sound of someone at the head of the stairs. "No one in the outbuildings, Captain!"

Arman gave Duke Tanfred a last, urgent look and then walked to the bottom of the stairs. "Nothing but potatoes down here."

He tramped up the stairs and closed the door behind him. He was sweating, almost trembling. He told Corporal Gertz, "Tell Master Keller we are sorry for the mud."

Anxious to be gone, he led his men from the house. The rain still fell, threatening to create a lake in the field. As he walked, he wondered greatly at what the duke had said about the woman of Numinat. That she might find a way through the crossings. What way that might be, he did not know. But Arman believed him. With that, his trepidation fell away, and a cleansing hope began to fill his mind.

He looked into the rain-darkened sky, murmuring thanks to God.

"Captain?" his corporal asked.

"I think the storm clouds are moving on."

The men looked at each other, but Arman did not care. A weight had been lifted from him. It was not wrong to survive if you had a purpose. There might be a reason he was the last man standing from the St. Eustus group.

To save the future prince of Volkia.

Chapter Three

The morning following her discovery in the cave, Yevliesza and Rusadka gazed at the cave wall, Zander and Ostov standing with them. Rusadka, with her gift of aligns, could, of course, perceive the vector of light disappearing into the wall.

"This one is important?" Rusadka asked.

"I think it means we can get in." With one finger, Yevliesza traced some of the concentric rings. "Because of these." She realized Rusadka could not see the rings. "In the crossings, they mark places where it's easy to break into an adjacent path. When I escaped from Volkia, I found I could use them to connect with nearby tunnels."

Rusadka's eyes narrowed at the implications.

Yevliesza nodded. "The backways are just on the other side. And I might be able to push through."

"You could go in and damage things, to a degree," Rusadka said.

Yes, *to a degree*. Small strikes would be possible if she could get into the crossings. She and Rusadka exchanged a look that said it all. *Now we can hurt them.*

"Shall we test it?" Yevliesza asked. Excitement fought with anxiety. The Volkish were on the other side.

"What we need are the backways," Rusadka cautioned.

"I know. But I can *see* the tunnels, and these are the backways." Rusadka knew that Yevliesza had the ability to discern the labyrinth of the crossings, though most people had trouble imagining that she possessed such an internal map. One that showed figures occupying it at any given time.

"So are we going in?" Yevliesza asked.

"First we think this through," Rusadka said.

Zander and Ostov were watching all this, wide-eyed. They stood by while Rusadka and Yevliesza agreed that if they got in they would reconnoiter, discovering the present uses of the crossings and the enemy vulnerabilities.

"But if you open a gate," Rusadka said, "it could give the enemy access to Numinat."

Yevliesza looked back at the wall with its whorl. "I can make a small entry point, one that's only large enough for one person to pass through at a time. And when we're done, I can close it." Close it without the severe damage she feared would happen if she destroyed the three great gates.

"Good," her friend said, working it out in her mind. "So each time we go through, the access would only be open for a short duration." Rusadka's eyes were alight. She smiled. "Is it empty? On the other side?"

Yevliesza smiled back. "Yes. Right now, no one is there. No one is even close."

They were going in.

Yevliesza wore good boots, a knife at her belt, wool leggings and shirt, tunic, and cloak. She undid the ties and laid the cloak aside. It would be warm in the crossings.

Rusadka was ready. She laid a hand on the pommel of her short sword.

The girl and the warrior. A strange pairing. Rusadka just a few years older, body and mind honed for battle. And she herself . . . Well, what was she? The Keeper. Not only of a wolf, but maybe now a gate.

Zander and Ostov stepped back, giving Yevliesza room to do whatever she did with her primal root power.

She faced the wall, touching it with the side of her hand, trying to focus on the penetration she desired, setting her intention to establish an entry, envisioning the small backways that budded off from the major ways. She concentrated.

Nothing.

"Steady," came Rusadka's voice.

Then the cave wall showed a small crack. As it widened, it sliced the wall open in a harsh crack of parting rock and an explosion of dust. The humid, yeasty smell of the crossings came to Yevliesza.

"By the Mythos," Rusadka whispered.

Yevliesza stepped forward, willing the crack to bore large enough for them to pass.

"Watch for us," she told Zander, unnecessarily. He nodded. Then she looked at Ostov who, obedient, said "Keeper."

They entered one at a time, she and Rusadka, moving into a narrow, faintly glowing tunnel, familiar, but always strange. Soft in her ears, the clicking sounds that she always heard in those regions.

Taking her bearings, she closed her eyes and let the network of ways come to her, the maze of all the paths, great and small, and if anything moved within them. And forms did move. People—presumably soldiers—with concentrations near the great gates.

"The backways are empty," Yevliesza said, "but there are figures in the main tunnel."

They walked on, into the enigmatic, yet familiar, terrain. The backways were smaller than the main ways and, like the main ways, were composed of a tough substance that gave slightly when pressed upon.

"A journey without a distance," Yevliesza whispered.

"Without a distance?" Rusadka asked.

"Something Prince Tirhan once said to me." Yevliesza remembered when he had tried to explain how close Earth was to the Mythos. These ideas were always difficult to hold in her mind. But she wished she better understood it. She was the one mucking about with the fabric of the place.

Rusadka stopped. She cocked her head, concentrating. "Something . . ."

Yevliesza strained to hear past the intermittent crinkling sounds, sounds that Rusadka could not discern. Rusadka had heard something.

Yevliesza had noted before that they were close to the main route between Volkia and Numinat. Bringing the map in her mind into awareness, she perceived something moving. She led the way toward it, passing through several tunnel branches until they reached the wall separating them from the moving forms.

Touching the wall, Yevliesza created a small hole, barely the size of her fist, and peered through.

Battle wagons. She turned back to Rusadka, whispering, "Machines. Wagons with guns protruding."

"Guns?"

"Tubes that can spit out projectiles." She had seen such metal carriages in Hapsigen. "We should stop the wagon." *If I can,* she thought.

"Any soldiers?" Rusadka asked.

"Six. They're walking beside the wagon."

"Do it."

Yevliesza turned back to the wall and brought her goal into focus. She intended for the main tunnel to grow small, to become a constriction too small for the passage of the wagon. But this was a major path, one that had grown in size and stability for ages. When she looked through the spy hole, nothing had happened.

She gathered herself, precisely aiming her concentration, but the crossings resisted. The walls would not bend, would not grow inward. Rusadka took a position to watch out the spy hole. She shook her head. Nothing yet. The machine drew close. Yevliesza leaned into her task, releasing everything in her heart and mind but the will to block the pathway.

Then Rusadka whispered, "Ceiling matter is flowing down! The wagon is mired in it." Through the hole they clearly heard shouting and a grinding sound that might be from tunnel matter shifting.

Rusadka traded positions with Yevliesza. A great sloughing of the tunnel ceiling had pinned down the wagon. Soldiers' frantic voices.

They climbed over the machine, trying to release the elementalist who empowered it.

"Collapse the ceiling," Rusadka hissed. "Bury them!"

Before Yevliesza could try, a jolt of the tunnel matter passed under their feet, sending the two women staggering. In another moment it spread to the walls, visibly rippling them. Trying to remain upright, the two women held on to each other. Yevliesza's heart pounded in her chest. What had she done?

After a few moments, the shaking faded and died away.

When Yevliesza looked through the gap once more, she saw soldiers climbing over the hardened slag of the tunnel walls trying to free someone buried in the twisted battle wagon. The path was hopelessly clogged.

Before anyone might notice the viewing hole, she closed it.

Through her boots she felt the ground tremble. Another quake rumbled, feeling and sounding like a train approaching a station. A Mythos quake. And, she thought in dismay, it was her doing.

"Let's get out of here," Yevliesza said.

They retreated, making their way in the direction of the cave where Zander and Ostov waited. They had damaged the war machine. But what else?

On their way, Yevliesza saw very faint flickers of aligns. At first she thought it was because of the Mythos disturbance. It might be. The crossings were alive with these cracks of light. Had they always been there?

She and Rusadka reached the cave, leaving the backways through the new doorway.

Yevliesza's left hand throbbed as she used her root power to close up the gate. Slowly, the gap began to close, the rock melding together, becoming solid wall.

In the distance, a faint rumbling. And then louder. Zander and Ostov looked about them, anxious. But the trembling quickly subsided.

As they left the cave, Rusadka mentioned the quakes. "I do not like this."

"I don't either," Yevliesza said, trying to come to terms with what had happened.

"But there was no shaking when you opened the tunnel."

Rusadka's observation jolted her. "Maybe disabling is different from opening."

"That is what I am thinking," her friend said.

As they made their way down the slope from the cave, the thought solidified. Creating a gate or a tunnel in the crossings didn't result in quaking. The First Ones had created them all, presumably without ill effects. Creating was not a problem.

Destroying was.

☙❧

Outside Rorrs Gate, Nashavety's pavilion was not the grandest. A humble tent suited her, large enough for a cot, a small trunk, and a cage. In the army encampment, however, her tent was right next to the marshal's. Let it be clear to all that she and Marshal Reinhart spoke often and wished for none to come between them.

As the morning light crept over the camp, she found herself still unnerved by the previous night's event. The loss of an elemental machine, twisted beyond recognition. The driver, crushed to death. And worse, the quaking of the tunnels. Alarms had spread through the crossings, with soldiers cowering lest the walls collapse. Rumors saturated the camp: the machines were to blame; the Mythos itself destroyed the battle wagon, they said, closing the route from Volkia to Numinat. The Mythos was displeased.

What utter nonsense.

Machines had been in the crossings at the battle of the Nubiah gate and no quakes had occurred. The facts made no difference to the rank and file. They knew that machines were inimical to the Mythos. But this was so only for machines with offensive powering. The powering by elementalists was a natural process.

Or natural enough.

Still. The quake had been so profound she had felt it in her tent.

The ground under the whole encampment had trembled. What had caused it?

The collapse would have to be scraped back, and that was not an easy thing, with the material nearly as hard as rock. But the army with its machines must pass through. That time was imminent. For some time the new cohort of elementalists had been in training with their metal cladders, their standing shields that delivered volleys of iron pellets. The invasion was set to begin.

A moan from the cage in the corner of the tent.

She had forgotten to feed the beast. It would not do for it to become aggressive. Also, she was hoping to bond with the creature. It had, after all, lost its close human. In truth, the *strigoi* had killed its human and made a meal of him. A prince's blood, at that.

Nashavety opened the tent flap, telling the guard to bring a fresh bowl, a warm bowl, of blood.

Strigo smiled past a strand of drool. At least, she thought it was a smile.

"You see how good I am to you," Nashavety crooned.

"Huuungry." Its speech was slowly improving. How could this blood demon have learned to speak? It now had rudimentary Volkish, learned from Albrecht, and a smattering of Numinasi from her. It would come in handy when she sent Strigo to find the girl of the mundat. Albrecht had learned that the girl had created a new path from the crossings to Alfan Sih. Such a useful power. The girl must be found and her powers confined. Or, indeed, used toward new goals.

Delightfully, Strigo knew her by smell. By this means, it might well be able to find her. But the beast must understand orders and must transmit those orders to the rest of its horde. Strigo's fellow demons had followed it to Rorrs Gate, but kept to the surrounding forest, feeding on deer and birds and, so far, not soldiers.

"Huuungry," it moaned again.

She crouched in front of the cage and locked its movements down using creature power. No longer able to swallow, it drooled.

She stared at it. "Strigo. You do not need to say that more than once. More than once annoys me." When she released it, it looked up at her with half-lidded eyes and a beguiling—or, more accurately, a pathetically hopeful—smile.

"Permission to enter, madam," came a guard's voice outside the tent.

She gave it, and the soldier entered. Receiving her nod, he opened the cage door wide enough to place the bowl inside. Strigo dipped its fingers daintily into the blood and sucked them clean before stooping to lap up its meal.

As the soldier left, he held the tent flap for Marshal Reinhart. As the military ruler of Volkia, he wore his tailored black uniform bedecked in rather more silver and braid than before. The effect was to heighten the contrast between the elaborately decorated uniform and the slight build and pinched face of the wearer.

He greeted Nashavety and turned his attention to the cage, watching as the blood demon noisily consumed its meal. "Amazing creature," Reinhart said appreciatively. He was looking forward to loosing the swarm of *strigoi* into Numinat. After they had taken care of Yevliesza, the beasts would be available to take part in the invasion. A small terror, but Reinhart was set on it.

"How fare you this morning, madam?"

"That depends, Marshal Reinhart. How fares the tunnel?"

"We have freed the wreck of the machine," Reinhart said. "In two days, the path will be open."

"Then our way is clear. Let us set the date for conquest."

Reinhart's expression was grim. "But before we risk the army, we must prevent such a collapse from reoccurring."

"Prevent?"

"The quake did not cause the tunnel to collapse," he said. "I have personally debriefed those who were present and survived. In the confusion, we assumed the quake brought the ceiling down, but those who were present are certain of one thing: first the tunnel caved in on the battle wagon. Then came the quake."

"Curious."

"You might say so." His face grew pinched, drawing his mustache closer to his nose, narrowing his hatchet face even more. "It was sabotage, madam. From the only person who is known to manipulate the walls of the crossings."

He had not said the name. But he did not need to.

If it was she . . . The thought spread out in her mind, a dark chasm. By all the hells, if the girl had struck at them! Anger coiled in her stomach. And worse than anger: envy. Why should the girl be so endowed, a foreigner, of no noble heritage? So young and brazen, when Nashavety had spent many years in service to Numinat. Then to find she had primal root power, as Strigo had reported. The power he had smelled on her in the maze. And now using that power to attack her soldiers! Her breathing had gone shallow considering the *wrongness* of it all.

"We once had her in our hands, madam," Reinhart muttered. "And lost her because Albrecht wanted her for his pleasure." His mouth quivered on the brink of a sneer.

Finding Yevliesza was now of the utmost importance. Why had Sofiyana not found her yet? Likely she had fled to Anastyna's redoubt. Sofiyana's people knew of Anastyna's new position in the Stora Hills and could have easily taken the girl.

But Sofiyana would not be her only asset in the search for the girl. "We will find her," she told Reinhart. "And soon." She looked at the caged creature, which had finished its bowl and was listening to them. "Strigo, listen to me. I have decided you will kill the girl with primal root power. Not disable. Kill."

"Ohhh," it moaned, swaying from side to side as though considering its answer.

"Do you understand?"

"Ohhh, kill she with roooots."

Yes, kill she with roots. Nashavety looked at the blood demon and imagined it jumping on Yevliesza and ripping her throat out as it had with Albrecht. They must get rid of her before she came into the crossings again.

But if the saboteur was Yevliesza, Reinhart must accept his part of the blame. His defenses had failed.

"How did your people not discover her? One *presumes* your sentries are watching the gates."

"Madam, she did not come in through the gates." He let the statement hang in the air, large and fetid.

The girl knew a way in. Or might she even have created it? What, by all the miserable hells, was the nature of her power?

"My soldiers cannot be everywhere," he muttered. "If she accessed the crossings somehow, we have seen no evidence of the . . . door."

The girl's awful power loomed in Nashavety's mind like an approaching storm. The first curtains of rain had come. Worse would follow. The hateful girl was going to die, and soon.

Strigo was staring at them intently. "Strigo find! Strigo waaant she."

A stream of blood actually fell from its mouth. Nashavety would have laughed, but the picture was too ghastly. Then it cinched its wings close to its body and crouched on its skinny knees, placing its forehead on the floor.

Nashavety watched this act of obeisance. Through her creature power, the blood demon was chained to her, would obey her and, as well, direct its fellow demons.

Reinhart went on. "We have arranged for the body wagon, madam. In four days we bring the wagon to Lowgate."

Getting the *strigoi* past one of the fortified gates of Numinat had taken a good deal of negotiation. Now the operation must be put in motion quickly, before the girl could strike again.

And before Strigo forgot her smell.

Chapter Four

"We have one polity," Anastyna said, coldly looking at her advisors. "One." Valenty and Captain Lysandry attended her outside her hut on a ridge above the camp. She gazed out at the morning cookfires, frowning at the few spots of flame, the flickering support of merely three hundred troops.

They were encamped in a more secure location than their old one along the Yanuri River: the Stora Hills, with its many vales folded among the hills.

Valenty knew that Anastyna was keenly aware of the weakness of her forces. She had Warden Kirady's contingent of two hundred that had been with them since his escape from captivity. But with Anastyna's original sixty, and with the addition of a sizable unit from one of the polities, she still had only three hundred and seventy-five fighters. And they had been recruiting for a full month.

"The city of Tanaya sent men, my lady," the captain reminded her. A handful of fighters.

"And so? The town master sent them. Not a polity. Where is the answer for our call to arms?"

She had hopes of Dorodna Polity under Prince Fadimir. He could bring twelve hundred fighters. But he was waiting to see if Sofiyana had a firm hold on the army and if the rumors of sorcery were true. Even if his troops came, many owed only a set number of days to their lord and would trickle away to return to their farms if the invasion did not come soon. Overall, it was clear that the polities were uncertain who was the rightful princip and where arms were owed.

Anastyna paced along the ridge, head held high, dressed in a plain woolen skirt and a belted smock that had been sewn by the camp cook. Over this, against the cold morning air, a cape given her by Warden Kirady, rabbit fur at the neck, but plain enough. Her boots were the worst of it: a soldier's ordinary leather, hard to walk in with her small feet. Still, she managed to pace with authority.

The men paced with her. Walking on the uneven ground, Valenty winced from the wound in his side. Healed, mostly, but at times reminding him that it was still there.

Anastyna turned to him. "Where, by the Nine, is Elivasa?"

It was going to be a bad morning, with Anastyna counting up all the failures. Elivasa, who could testify to the presence of sorcery in Osta Kiya, had been traversing the outlands, meeting with the princes and wardens. So far, she had scrounged up only the soldiers from nearby Tanaya.

"Elivasa will stay out as long as it takes, my lady," Valenty answered.

She waved this away. "And the Keeper has, what, two hundred? Nearly equal to ours?"

"One hundred, my lady," Lysandry said. "Only spiritual seekers and the infirm seeking healing."

"She puts herself forward as a *providez*?"

Anastyna's mood was not improved by having superior numbers to Yevliesza. In her frustration, looking for slights everywhere.

"No, my lady," Valenty quickly said. He disliked this turn in the conversation. Yevliesza could be in danger if Anastyna turned against her. Their reconciliation rested on the shifting grounds of the princip's moods. "These are merely the superstitions of outland villagers."

Anastyna was not listening. "I sent Lord Kirady and fifteen men to her for her protection. Now it seems I could ill afford it."

"These are early days, My Lady Princip," Captain Lysandry made bold to say, trying to bolster her confidence and not experienced enough to realize that she would take it as a contradiction.

She turned on him. "Early days? Osta Kiya has a standing army of two thousand. They can march against us at any time and will want to do so before Volkia comes. After which they will turn the realm over to Nashavety. Who is, I assure you, coming."

Coming with an army of some ten thousand. More, if they took fighters from occupied territory in Alfan Sih and Norslad. And they would be aided by their diabolic machines. They had reason to doubt that Osta Kiya's army would even fight. Sofiyana would likely surrender.

From this low hill, Valenty could see the army in exile beginning their drills under the Urik's direction. First, sword practice, then a morning meal.

Anastyna pulled her cape more closely around herself in the crisp morning air. "And for all this *Keeper's* abilities, she has done little."

But what did she expect Yevliesza to do? Enter at Lowgate and face hundreds of enemy soldiers on their side of the boundary gate?

Lysandry ventured, "If Nubiah comes, their forces can make all the difference."

A stony silence met this comment. King Jawara, with his large army, was the great hope. But the pinch point was the crossings. Nubiah forces entering at one of their gates would be picked off one at a time in the narrow confines of the tunnels.

The same was not true of breaking *out* of the crossings into Numinat. When Volkia came through with overwhelming force, no garrison could withstand them. They would strike at whichever boundary fort they chose, opposed by Numinat forces that were divided between Lowgate and Causeway Gate, supposing that they fought at all.

Alfan Sih's position was no better than Nubiah's—in fact worse. They were an occupied, defeated land. And Prince Tirhan, though the clear successor to succeed his father, had failed to unite the clans.

Still, when the invasion came, Nubiah and Alfan Sih could enter the crossings and encounter merely a caretaking force. At that juncture they stood a chance of overcoming the Volkish positions. But everyone knew, Anastyna knew, that by then it might be too late. They could not count on foreign allies. They needed the polities.

Anastyna did not answer Lysandry's remark about Nubiah. She was looking out to the soft green knolls and vales spread out before her, the great hill country where their small force had dug in. Here, the heights gave them a view onto any enemy approaches, and the crags provided uphill fighting positions. Strangely, it might be the army of Osta Kiya that she would fight. But when Valenty looked at Anastyna, he saw an expression of longing. When Nubiah was the subject, her thoughts likely went to Prince Chenua, the former envoy of the Lion Court, and her lover.

For all Anastyna's concerns of war and state, she had room to long for him. As Valenty longed for Yevliesza. With Volkia poised to strike, there were many losses to come. Some of them would be unbearable.

Below in the valley, Urik, amid his contingent of *harjat*, looked up at the hill crest where Anastyna conspicuously stood. He raised his sword in salute.

⚜

THE WORST THING ABOUT WAR WAS THAT ONE HAD TO RIDE A HORSE. But there was no help for it—a princip could not appear in front of the troops in a wagon, and a carriage was out of the question in this wilderness. Sofiyana wiped a hand on her indigo-blue velvet cape, trying to clean the horse sweat off after she had patted the creature's face in an attempt to be friendly. The horse had put its ears well back, in what she took for a frown.

Her army leader, Commander Ilyan, sat on his horse beside her, his beard flattening in the wind. His belly distended his red tunic, and his sword belt rode below the bulge. On his left shoulder, a white circle, symbol of the royal torc.

Sofiyana walked her horse to a position next to Ilyan. The second-quarter-day sun threw a glaring light on the plain before them. They occupied a slight rise, giving them a view of the mustering grounds and beyond. In the wind, wisps of Sofiyana's hair escaped from her netting and lashed at her face.

"If they come," Sofiyana observed, "we will have plenty of warning. Unless they come at night."

"Dark does not help. You cannot move ten thousand men without everyone knowing." He glanced at her, adding, "My Lady Princip."

"If they have so many, what good are these three thousand, Commander?"

His expression darkened. "More polities must come with their swords. We have only three so far." That cut. She had sent out the call to arms, and most had ignored the summons.

From her saddle, she looked out on the gathered troops, tents laid out in rows for the officers, and cookfires in their thousands for the common fighters. She held their fealty. She hoped she did, but doubts circled her like gnats. Ilyan had a way of looking at her sideways as though watching her for outbursts of sorcery. She vividly remembered that night in the palace courtyard with everyone gathered around the great circle. The sudden appearance in the tower door of the woman calling, *Save us from sorcery!* A manifesting, of course, but the charge lingered: sorcery. Her secret exposed if they dared believe it. Many of the soldiers did, by their expressions.

The memory of that night of the Blossom Moon festival roiled in her thoughts. Yevliesza striking her, killing her soldiers, snatching Valenty away. The time would come when Yevliesza would pay for this. For now, she hid, and Sofiyana's spies had not yet found her. Rumors had made their way to the palace that she styled herself a visionary, claiming to have spent time in arcane planes of being and in company with some kind of seer from the Agarvesky Forest. The royal spies heard such rumors in several small northern towns like Branova and Vrall. It seemed a strange claim for Yevliesza to make, and Sofiyana could not grasp what advantage that gave her, unless by surrounding herself with followers, she hoped to avoid capture.

"Commander, still no news of Yevliesza? The Keeper, as she styles herself?" They had been searching for her since she had broken into

Osta Kiya and spirited Valenty away. Yevliesza deserved to be punished. When Nashavety had her in hand, it would be an ugly fate.

"We comb the outlands, My Lady Princip, but we cannot spare many men. The Volkish could come at any time."

"But we are still watching Anastyna's camp?"

"We have scouts who watch, my lady. But no one has caught sight of Yevliesza. She may not be in the Stora Hills."

Osta Kiya would not waste its time attacking the camp. Anastyna had fewer than four hundred men; she was not a threat.

A messenger approached Ilyan. He read the message and, giving instructions, sent the man off again.

"Strengthen your efforts, Commander," she told Ilyan. "I would not want to judge you lax." He nodded, acknowledging the order. During the winter she had hoped to capture Yevliesza. But now—now she worried about such a venture. If she was holed up with large group of followers, there could be a fight to bring her out. If many died, Sofiyana would be blamed for the bloodshed. People would say that in time of war, instead of preparing to fight Volkia, the army fought its own citizens.

"How soon will we move camp?" she asked.

"We have word from several polities that they are joining our forces. When they arrive, we will move to a battleground of our choosing."

"Which battleground?" Nashavety would want to know.

Ilyan glanced at her. "I am still considering."

He would not say. The man did not trust her. The army did not trust her. Even feared her.

"Would it not make sense, once our polities have come, to assemble at Lowgate and meet the enemy at the choke point? Lowgate is closer to Osta Kiya, and the Volkish will want to march on the city-palace."

"As you say, lady. But they might defy our expectations and enter at Causeway Gate. We have reinforced the garrison at Lowgate, and they will do damage to the Volkish if they come through there. But we should be prepared that the enemy will overwhelm the garrison of either of the gates. And we must meet them on their way after they have tired themselves from a long march."

Nashavety would be pleased to hear of this plan. Sofiyana thought she had skillfully drawn out the commander without seeming too obvious.

Ilyan pointed out at the great flats. "Our dactyl units patrol constantly and will alert us when they break through. We will be prepared to intercept them."

He looked forward to a great battle. But Nashavety had promised her that no Numinat blood would be shed. When they came, Sofiyana would observe their overwhelming force and ask for a parley. During which she would surrender. It would be her prerogative. The army fought at the princip's command. Or did not fight.

"I approve your plan," she said, "until we have better intelligence of their position. So I leave you to your work." She got the horse started down the slope in the direction of her pavilion. Her back ached, and she stank of horseflesh and dust. She was no soldier.

Nor princip for long, either. Once Volkia had peacefully taken Numinat, Nashavety would assume the role. And Sofiyana would be at her side as her closest companion.

It would be so easy to dispense with the silver torc. She had hated the exalted role from the moment the silver cuff had been fastened around her neck. The horrid obligation to keep the *fajatim* leashed, the extermination of the traitors after Anastyna's defection, the people's growing mistrust after the debacle of the Blossom Moon. The night-time visits from Nashavety . . .

She looked out at the plains before she ducked into her tent. For a moment she thought she saw a dark line on the horizon: the massing of the army that would rescue her from the misery of leadership. And reunite her with her mistress. But it was her only her imagination.

Soon, however. Soon.

AT DUSK, ONE OF ILYAN'S OFFICERS CAME TO HER TENT WITH NEWS. Their patrols had found Yevliesza. She was encamped in the Haiga River region, a day and a half from their position on the plains. Sofiyana's chest tightened. It was time to decide.

The officer reported that Yevliesza was camped with a group of over one hundred and fifty followers. Most of them were peasants without weapons. She had fifteen trained soldiers from Eiger Polity, along with the polity's warden, Lord Kirady, who appeared to have taken her under his protection. She had a devoted gathering who believed she possessed mysterious powers: nonsense like entering the Mist Wall, contact with spirits. Peasant beliefs.

At the Haiga, Kirady's soldiers would fight, and they might draw in the peasant followers. Facing off with the trained men of Osta Kiya, it would be a massacre. When word of it reached the army bivouacked here, it could further divide loyalties. Until now, all Sofiyana had to do was keep things reined in until Nashavety arrived. And now a confrontation at Yevliesza's camp could inflame things. With so much at stake, Sofiyana could not understand why her mistress was making Yevliesza a priority.

"Commander Ilyan seeks to know your wishes, my lady," the officer said, impatient.

Facing the decision, Sofiyana cowered.

"My Lady Princip?"

"I will decide, Captain. I will let you know when I have."

With the arrival of the Volkish imminent, surely sending troops to the Haiga was not of utmost importance. Nashavety would understand, she thought. Would she not?

Chapter Five

When Yevliesza and her group neared their camp at the Haiga marshes, Rusadka rode ahead to alert Warden Kirady of her approach and make known to him their discovery of the gate, a thing they must keep secret, especially in a camp full of strangers.

Yevliesza was glad to have good news for Kirady. He had risked everything to side with her and with Anastyna, and even through the past month of inaction and growing logistical problems at camp, he had remained unshaken. The newly found gate was a stroke of good fortune, but the quaking raised an ugly prospect. Was it proof of the very thing she had worried about from the start? How fragile was the Mythos? And how fundamental were the crossings to its structure?

Mitri's pace freshened now that they were close to camp. Unlike the other horses, he was not much bothered by the boggy terrain of the marshes. Mitri was steady, almost unflappable, and, like her, loved a good run. For a moment she imagined Valenty riding at her side. His strong face. His strong passion.

She shoved the thought away. He'd had his chance to be there.

Ostov, who had the keenest sight of the group, pointed ahead at a someone on horseback coming out from the camp. "Janov," he reported.

The former village master was in charge of camp logistics, a job he took to easily, making decisions she always approved for their good sense. He had been with her since the day she had emerged from Holdfast—that place she had gone under Isha's direction, or thought she had gone. There she had committed to her role. But her ninth power was as ambiguous as ever.

Janov joined them on his mount. "Keeper," he said with affection. He had heard of her success from Rusadka but refrained from mentioning it until they were alone.

He told her that during her two-day absence, a group had come in from the Olyma region west of there. "Thirty people, including four children."

She sighed in resignation. A small number, at least.

"And twenty-two from the small holdings around Vraal," he added. "But they brought a wagon of potatoes to share. And we have had good fishing in the river. Eels aplenty."

Janov was optimistic, and she nodded approvingly, though she disliked eel stew and longed for bread and butter and apples, however wizened this time of year.

"All the newcomers healthy?" Some of the camp followers came because they thought she had great powers of healing.

Janov quirked a look at her. "Well, healthy."

"No?"

"Two of the children are on crutches. I think that is why the Vraal folk came, or some of them."

Fifty-two more to feed, so now, close to two hundred encamped in the marshlands. How had these people even found her, any of them? She and her few companions had been at some pains to remain unobserved. But rumors of her being a *providez*, a seer, had carried far, widening out from Branova. Isha had said people looked for miracles and saw them whether true or not.

Janov went on. "As well, two have come from the *satvary*."

"Zolvina?"

"Aye. You know them, so they said. Lady Dreiza and a young woman. Too young to be a *satvar*."

Kassalya. With her painful gift of foreknowledge. Yevliesza liked the girl, but having her close by could be emotionally fraught. She wasn't sure if she wanted the distraction of foreknowing. Since Kassalya's futures sometimes weren't quite what happened. But she was eager to see Dreiza again.

"Lord Kirady gave them his tent."

That was a rare gift. The marshlands were barren of trees, and most people slept without shelter, or had erected makeshift sleeping quarters in or under carts. Other people's generosity shamed her. Here she had been thinking of how much she disliked eel soup and how hard it would be to have disabled children in camp.

"I don't know what I would do without you," she said as she looked at Janov, broad-chested, broad of mind. He faced every setback with confidence, and she had set herself the goal of being more like him.

"You would do fine, mistress."

Janov had confidence in her, as did Lord Warden Kirady and Rusadka, her closest advisors. Maybe today she had earned that confidence. The new gate. Arrow Shaft Gate, she called it. The discovery altered everything, or could. If she managed to sabotage weaponry without undermining the Mythos.

Drifts of smoke met them from the peat cookfires. Supplies of peat were one reason they'd chosen the marshlands for their encampment. Another was that the many potholes of standing water would slow down any soldiers Sofiyana might send. Yevliesza and her core group could retreat into the wetlands with their barriers of streams and ponds.

Coming into camp, they headed for one of the two tents, with the larger, Yevliesza's, spacious enough for three or four to meet. Kirady, her most powerful supporter, waited for her outside the tent. He was of wiry build, with a trim white beard and wore simple leathers and a drab green cloak. Drab, because he had given his fine one away somewhere. He looked pleased, having heard the news of the new gate.

Kirady and she first met when she had traveled with Janov from the village at the edge of the Agarvesky Forest and journeyed to Anastyna's camp. Where she'd finally told Anastyna of her primal root power. And where she'd asked her for a few select manifesters from the princip's followers who could help her rescue Valenty from Osta Kiya.

"Keeper," Kirady said, as she dismounted and gave Mitri over to one of his men.

Kirady, Janov, and Rusadka were soon gathered inside with her and found seats on the cot, her storage chest, and her tent's only chair. Yevliesza's young maid, Lura, brought in steaming drinks prepared at the embers of the cookfire. Her curly hair escaped from her bun as she handed around the cups.

Yevliesza thanked her, folding her hands around the hot cup and inhaling the fragrance of the blueberry infusion, comforting after the two-hour ride from the cave.

When Lura left, Rusadka set her cup aside to tell the story of the gate and the destruction of the Volkish battle wagon. And the aftermath: the quakes.

Kirady's gaze brightened as she spun the story. It was a small victory, but spoke of things to come.

Yevliesza explained how she had identified the gate by the presence of the rings, or whorls, and how she had recognized them from the time she had been in the backways and had wounded Prince Albrecht.

The mystery of the aligns was growing deeper. Aligns were in many places: in the landscape, of course. But also within the crossings. The tunnels were built along them. The first people to cross over from Earth had been following aligns, creating pathways along their trajectories. Since then, the power to create and dissolve the crossings had faded from the world. Until now. Today she had learned that aligns sometimes appeared as tangents to the paths, crossing them. Slowly, she was learning more about both aligns and the crossings. But she felt there was more to be discovered.

"Arrow Shaft Gate," Kirady was saying, liking the name. "This is a gift of the Mythos."

Rusadka raised an eyebrow. "Keeper's gift, more like."

"It is that," Kirady agreed easily. "Now we will strike them where it hurts."

"Yes," Yevliesza said. "Except for the tunnels shaking. Did you feel it here?"

Kirady shook his head, while Janov said, "The horses in the corral became skittish. I wondered why. They might have felt something we could not."

"What do you make of it?" Kirady asked her.

She voiced her fear: "I worry that collapsing parts of the crossings is dangerous to the Mythos. Structurally dangerous."

Kirady rubbed his chin through his beard, frowning. "But now, small actions, too. That is troubling."

Rusadka saw her struggling with the issue. "But we must go on, yes?"

"Unless we find that I'm doing more damage than good." She returned Kirady's gaze and saw his disappointment.

"If we cannot attack Volkia in the crossings," he said, "we lose a great advantage."

She would try again—she had to. "Maybe the quakes will lessen. Let's see."

Rusadka nodded. "We can test how far to go."

At some point, she left off saying, she might have to stop. People would surely resent her for it. If Numinat was invaded and she did nothing, Valenty would never forgive her. Maybe no one would.

She changed the subject. "What if people in camp get curious about where I'm going? They already think I go into the Mist Wall. They might follow me."

"No one will leave camp," Kirady said. "I will see to it."

Lura entered. "Mistress? I have a hot stew ready."

Yevliesza held up a hand for her to wait a moment. She was starving. But first, looking at Janov, she had to ask, "What are we to do with the children?"

"Their parents want to bring them to you. For healing." Janov shook his head. "Ryura up to her mischief. Saying you are a *providez*."

Ryura had been the first to arrive at Haiga camp, bringing a crowd with her. Now rumors spread like pollen in the wind.

It had started in the Agarvesky Forest, with Isha leading Yevliesza into the woods in the middle of the night, and Ryura and a few others following them, imagining things. "Ryura claims to have my ear," Yevliesza said. "People think she knows things."

Kirady shrugged. "You *did* meet with her a few times."

"Just to convince her to stop." Unsuccessful as that had been.

"Let me speak to her," Rusadka said, looking as though she would make short work of the woman.

Kirady interjected: "Some of these people would fight if attacked. They are further protection to you."

"But still, we can't feed a hundred fifty for long."

"A hundred seventy-five," Janov murmured. "But we have assigned individuals to fish at specific potholes, the larger, permanent ones. The harvest is improving."

Yevliesza was grateful for Janov, for everyone who had come to her side. Rusadka, Kirady, and, farther away but not forgotten, Dreiza and young Pyvel. Adding in Mitri and Kiya, she had the closest thing to a family she could imagine.

Family. Once, she'd had the dream of being with Valenty. But he was bound to Anastyna in service. *I will find you again,* he had said as he lay wounded from the fight at Osta Kiya. *I will find you again.*

Kirady broke her reverie. "We must tell Anastyna about the gate."

Yevliesza hadn't made up her mind whether to make Arrow Shaft known to the princip. If they told her, then, when the princip was desperate enough, she'd come after her. Demanding that she collapse the boundary gates.

Kirady pressed on. "She is our princip."

She looked at Janov, always her touchstone for how the common folk would see things. By his expression he was with Kirady on this. Rusadka as well.

"All right, let's send word to her." She looked at the three of them in turn. "But she doesn't control me."

No one argued.

Lura handed around portions of soup. She had a way with savory stews made from fish, wild onions, and cattail roots. They drank straight from the bowls. Eel soup again.

YEVLIESZA PAUSED AT THE TENT FLAP, HESITATING TO GO OUT. IT WAS a short walk to Warden Kirady's tent, the one he had vacated for Dreiza and Kassalya, but she didn't have the energy to deal with the commotion it might cause.

The peasants kept a watch on her tent and often tried to intercept her, though Zander and Ostov would hold them back. People should be able to talk to her, but they mistook her for a *providez*, and so it was not really her they sought. She had had a better understanding now of why Isha had avoided people: not because of the inconvenience, but to discourage false hopes. However, if parents were bringing youngsters on crutches, she didn't know what she would do.

The unworthy thought came that if they were on crutches, she could get to Dreiza's tent before they could hobble the distance. God, what was she turning into?

Add to those misgivings, she found herself tired from the crossings event, the first time she had experienced any after-effects from the use of her power—either of her powers. The thought came that the Mythos was sending her a penalty. But the Mythos wasn't directing anything, despite how people sometimes talked about it in semi-religious terms.

After today, she couldn't ignore the fact that the Mythos was adversely affected by her actions. She wondered what would happen if the crossings ruptured. Would it mean calamity, or would the realms simply be cut off from each other? For that matter, what were the crossings, exactly? She often thought of them as being in a different dimension. Of course, that must be true of the entire Mythos. Still, the crossings were connections, and they might be more fragile.

She was no closer to leaving the tent and walking thirty paces to visit Dreiza.

Eight hells.

Pushing aside the tent flap, she stepped outside. If she saw Ryura, she would have words with her about this latest rumor. *Providez.* The woman was highly annoying and doing damage as well, if children were being uprooted and made to live in this makeshift camp.

She looked around for Kiya, but he seldom came into camp. Just as well. Once, he had brought his pack with him. It had only been a brief appearance, but it was enough to indelibly affix the name Wolf Keeper to her. Prior to that, she had not been in the presence of Kiya's pack, nor had she been near them when they appeared on the outskirts of the camp. She assumed Kiya would have protected her from the other wolves. He wouldn't have brought them had they been a danger to her.

Someone stood nearby waiting for her. A round-faced woman, close to Yevliesza's age, wearing her hair in a long, single braid. Ryura. Ostov stepped between the two of them.

"It's all right, Ostov."

He stepped aside, and Ryura brightened as Yevliesza approached. She had taken to wearing leggings with a shirt tucked in and a belted tunic over it, the same as Yevliesza. It was a more practical way to dress in camp, but it seemed designed to copy Yevliesza.

Once they were eye to eye, Yevliesza said, "I hate to think that it's your fault that sick and hurt children are coming here. We don't have tents for them, or food. I hate to think they came because of you." She fixed Ryura with a cold look. "But they did."

Ryura widened her eyes. "They did not! I did not invite them."

"But you spread the rumors, and they come. Now you're causing real suffering, not just my own."

"Your suffering," Ryura huffed. "You say that, but you do not share your gifts or wisdom with anyone. You are denying what you are, and I do not know if you plan to do things that way, or if you cannot be bothered with us."

The woman was deluded. "I see that we're no closer to agreeing than we ever were, Ryura. But here's a warning. If you keep trying to act as my voice with people, you'll be made to leave. And I'll hold a meeting and tell everyone why."

That seemed to worry Ryura, and she lowered her eyes. "I do not claim to speak for you," she said.

"Well, then it's even worse. Then you're acting like a *providez* yourself. And you aren't a seer of any kind. It would take you years of renunciation and you would have nine powers"—here Yevliesza paused, realizing she was entirely too worked up and speaking nonsense of her own—"and you would not be blocking my path when I'm trying to get somewhere!"

Ryura stepped back a pace, and Yevliesza swept away from the woman, feeling chagrined that she had lost her temper.

Dreiza was standing outside her tent, waiting for her.

"Come in, my dear," she said, holding the tent flap open. She didn't chastise Yevliesza, but her expression said it all: *Young woman in a job she is unequal to loses her temper and makes fool of self.*

"I meant to come to see you earlier, but I didn't want to see Ryura."

"Obviously."

Inside the small tent, the two women regarded each other. "It's so good to see you," Yevliesza said, heartfelt. Dreiza's face, only slightly lined despite her advanced years, was a welcome sight.

Dreiza grasped her hands. "And you, my dear." She turned in the direction of the young woman siting on the pallet. "As you see, Kassalya has come with me."

Kassalya was casting small stones unto a piece of cloth inked with lines forming boxes. She looked carefully as the stones fell. Yevliesza had seen this kind of scrying a few times, but she had thought it was a game. Kassalya did not play games. She wore the pale tunic and trousers of a *satvar*, a contrast to her midnight-black hair.

"Kassalya. Welcome to Haiga camp," Yevliesza said.

The girl looked up. "Blood birds fly," she said in a resigned tone.

Yevliesza glanced at Dreiza, but got no help there. "Blood birds?"

Kassalya's gaze became a stare. "Flying." She nodded sadly to herself, then picked up the stones and cast them again.

Dreiza gestured Yevliesza to a stool and took a seat on a traveling chest. "The Devi Ilsat sent us. I hope you do not mind. She thinks Kassalya might be a support to you."

If the High Mother thought that Kassalya should be in Yevliesza's counsels, she might be right. It did no harm to at least listen.

She wanted to tell Dreiza about Arrow Shaft, and would do so when they were alone. Kassalya's heart was in the right place, but she was only sixteen and emotionally fragile. Best to keep the secret from her, especially in this camp.

As she sat with Dreiza, Yevliesza let the older woman's *satvar*-calm touch her. Even though she herself wasn't a *satvar*, Yevliesza had felt at least some of that same peace. *The numin pool within.* Since her experience in the castle of Holdfast.

"How is Valenty?" Dreiza asked, breaking the silence to inquire about her former husband. "With his wound."

Yevliesza wondered the same, every day. "Healed. So we hear." His wound from an arrow during their flight down the city-palace stairs to the plain.

From the direction of the pallet, the rattle of pebbles on Kassalya's grid.

"Yarna brought all the news back from Osta Kiya," Dreiza said. Yarna, who had helped bring a cloaking fog when they took Valenty out of captivity.

"How is the High Mother?" Yevliesza asked. "We heard she collapsed during the Blossom Moon rites."

"She rests. It is what happens when a healer takes things too far."

"Too far?" Yevliesza was missing a piece. Her last glimpse of the High Mother had been when, in the courtyard of Osta Kiya, she broke the great circle to embrace Valenty. The *satvar*'s gesture had been meant to bring a touch of healing, easing the sorcerous control so that he could cooperate with his rescue.

Dreiza went on. "She exceeded the strength of her natural gift of healing. She drew upon her own bodily strength to fully banish the sorcery from him. A healer should not draw upon her own body's health that way."

The High Mother had played a greater role in Valenty's rescue than Yevliesza had realized. She had brought Valenty out of sorcerous control, not just the small degree they believed might be possible, but entirely, using a dangerous ploy.

"But the High Mother will be all right?"

Dreiza smiled. "We are taking the best care of her." She patted Yevliesza's knee. "But you have news for me, my dear." Dreiza's fore-knowing.

Yevliesza bit her lip. "Something happened yesterday. I think you and Kassalya should know." Dreiza waited to hear. Kassalya was still intent on her scrying.

Dreiza noted her glance. "It is a soothing game she plays." She smiled. "Sometimes I cast stones, too."

Yevliesza went on. "I'm trying to sabotage the crossings in some places. You know about that." Dreiza nodded. "And when I did, the Mythos quaked. The tunnels did. They rumbled and shook so hard I could hardly stand." Talking about it brought the scene vividly to mind. The sudden instability of the world.

Dreiza closed her eyes, finally murmuring, "The very thing you have been fearing." Her face was open, filled with a compassion that Yevliesza had always seen in her. An ability to know how another person felt and deeply care.

"The Mythos is the alter-world, isn't that right?" Yevliesza asked. "It may not be permanent if I tamper with it." Saying it out loud had made it more real. This was not merely a dilemma—it could be a cata-strophe.

They sat with this dark thought. She didn't expect Dreiza to know what to do next, or not do. But she had wanted to tell her what had happened. And Kassalya, if the girl knew of the future.

Yevliesza went on. "The First Ones know that I have this power—even if it was a mistake, or if the High Mother and her group *thought* it was mistake. But if they know I have it, why don't they outright tell me this isn't the way? Because the next time, I might go even further." Like a healer unwisely tapping into personal health to give it to another.

Kassalya looked up from her scrying. "They are talking to you," she blandly said. Yevliesza exchanged glances with Dreiza. "They speak. I think they do, but not to me. To you."

"Kassalya. They don't. They've never said a thing to me."

The girl looked at the pebbles in her hand. "Their timeline is separate from ours. They are without time."

"But they gave me the power because Volkia is a threat *right now*."

"They try. Maybe they will come to you long ago or someday." She looked worried. Kassalya's life was one long worry.

"Long ago or someday," Yevliesza whispered. So no help from the other side.

Dreiza took Yevliesza's hand. "We may be on our own, my dear. What does your instinct tell you?"

"To continue."

She was as afraid as she had ever been. More than when she had faced the Trespass Door and the thousand-foot fall, and Nashavety urging her, *Jump. Jump!* Because then it had only been her own life. And not everyone's.

Chapter Six

Prince Tirhan sat in a chair facing some fourteen scowling clansmen of Alfan Sih.

He felt it was not right to hold a war council in a temple. It was enough that the elders had opened the halls of the Talfyn Sid temple to bivouac the six clan lords and their lieutenants, but Elder Lodwyn had graciously said, "This is wartime. Hold your discussion in our hall, Lord Prince." He added with a smile, "But we would ask you to shed no blood."

They should be able to hold talks without using swords. But the clan lords, particularly Lord Gryffyd of Rhydwyn Clan, were not ready to unite. Gryffyd knew that such a coming together under Tirhan would move his opponent closer to the throne. But fighting as separate clans, making insurgent strikes, had accomplished little. The Volkish still held the major towns and controlled river traffic. Their one notable victory: overcoming the fortified Glenir Manor to free his imprisoned mother, Queen Gwenid, and his sisters. When the Volkish had dared to use wraith wolves as guard animals, under creature control, a thing abhorrent to Alfans.

Queen Gwenid sat at his side, dressed in an embroidered gown of deep blue linen with sleeves and hem fraying, but patched. But frayed raiment or not, her presence reminded those present that her son was the traditional choice to succeed his father. She was his father's queen, and Tirhan would choose his own. Had chosen Morwen. But he was not yet king of Alfan Sih. The clans had not agreed to meet on the matter.

Lord Gryffyd's voice came strong in the hall of quarried stone. "We strike and fade before they can marshal a response. We weaken them. Why give them a larger target?" The years had diminished the clan lord, but he stood proudly, his mostly gray hair loose and tangled around his shoulders.

No one would interrupt him if he was not finished. "Each clan knows its terrain and the best way to inflict hurt." He looked around him as the war chiefs muttered their assent.

"The tactic has served us," Tirhan conceded. "Served us up until now. But soon Volkia will storm the gates of Numinat. Perhaps tomorrow. Will we be ready to overrun their positions when they withdraw their main force? Not unless we unite."

"If we knew the day," Gryffyd countered. "Then. But we do not know. Come upon them untimely, and they have their full force to crush us. Your ambitions blind you to the reality."

"Ambitions, Lord Gryffyd? Is it not to expel the Volkish from our land?"

The two of them eyed each other. The sounds of the forest around them, visible through the pillars of the hall, were all that could be heard. The chittering of squirrels, the cries of birds in dispute over territory and mates.

"No one doubts your intentions," Gryffyd allowed. "But the wisdom can be doubted."

He would doubt Tirhan's wisdom until Tirhan agreed to make Gryffyd's daughter Anwelyth his bride, thus binding the royal house to Clan Rhydwyn. It was time to make clear that there would be no alliance through marriage.

He wished that Morwen were here. She was his lieutenant and had the right to stand in counsel, but these past six days she had gone to Pemfyndr to visit her sick father. And promised to be back by the evening's feast. He would introduce her then, making his betrothal public. That could either put an end to the delaying tactics or make Gryffyd even more determined to undermine him.

Inian, the young clan lord of Mid Daihinn stepped forward. "I will bring my clan to your side, Prince Tirhan." He looked at the scowling faces around him. "Who joins with me?"

Tirhan nodded at him, accepting him gladly. Inian's clan was small, but the support was welcome in the hostile meeting. No one else spoke.

When Queen Gwenid did, her voice carried through the hall. "Lord Inian, we knew your honorable father. He was always welcome in our halls." She smiled serenely at Rhydwyn's clan lord. "As were you, Lord Gryffyd."

An uneasy silence filled the room. For all the confusion surrounding who would be king, they did not want any disrespect shown to the wife of the king who had died fighting the invasion.

Gryffyd met Gwenid's gaze and nodded in respect, though his eyes said otherwise.

Tirhan rose, concluding the meeting. "The Talfyn Sid elders have a meal to share with us tonight. If any chief will step forward in solidarity, let him do so then."

He had not expected that at this meeting it would be easy to bring the clans together. The clan lords were afraid of Volkish retaliation for any major offensive. They faced losing their land and their holdings. If they lost.

Did no one think of winning?

❦

It was a fine evening in the courtyard of the temple, and these days a rare pleasure to have the chieftains share a feast. Tirhan anchored the head table, and the rest of the gathering sat at smaller tables facing him. At least they had not argued about the table arrangements. They would not, as long as Queen Gwenid was present.

Gwenid sat next to Tirhan, but on the other side, a place left purposely vacant. For Morwen. Tirhan's sisters, Cadris and Hanavar, sat at one end, with Tirhan's lieutenants making up the difference.

Gryffyd claimed a visible place in the courtyard, surrounded by chieftains. Seated next to him was his daughter, Anwelyth, wearing a gown of deep green velvet and a jeweled necklace that sparkled as it caught the fire from the central pit.

Morwen had not arrived as planned, but it could serve Tirhan's purpose that she was late. Let them wonder who would sit next to him. The mood of the gathering had softened. The mead from the casks of the temple elders went far toward improving moods, and bellies were full from venison, potato pies, and rabbit stew. Hanavar, just fourteen, had Gwenid's permission to help serve the ale, and the gesture was greeted warmly by the chiefs and by Anwelyth as well, who engaged her in lively conversation.

Someone made a toast to Numinat, soon to come to battle with Volkia. At this, Tirhan stood and vowed Alfan Sih support once freed from the enemy's yoke. A clamor of agreement met this pronouncement.

Elder Lodwyn poured more ale for Tirhan, saying, for his ears only, "Will we bury our fallen in another realm, then, my prince?"

"You must tell us how to honor our dead, grandfather. If you say they must be buried here, we will bring each man home."

"Or woman," Lodwyn said, looking up at someone's approach. Morwen.

She stood at the edge of the courtyard. Cadris was already crossing to greet her, and soon the whole assembly watched her as she drew near Tirhan's table. She wore a mud-splattered tunic and trousers and a vest of knives. On one cheek, a streak of blood.

Nodding to the queen, she bent down to speak to Tirhan. "An ambush near Gwerlech. There were only six of them, but they were fresh and outnumbered us." Her eyes held a story that she was not yet ready to tell. "Two of us survived, my lord." A wisp of white-blond hair fell over her face as she leaned over, and she swiped it behind her ear. Having made her report, she straightened up and took note of the hall of warriors, all of them watching her.

"Morwen," Tirhan murmured. "That is hard news. Harsh indeed. You are unhurt?"

"I took lives, and their swords did not touch me. They fled, and Cynod wanted to pursue them, but I said you would want us at Talfyn Sid."

"I did." He amended, "I do, Morwen."

At his other side, Gwenid leaned in to say, "Let Cadris attend her." Cadris, noting her mother's gaze, approached. "Morwen, my dear," the queen said, "you must join us when you are refreshed . . . and changed from battle dress."

Morwen, who had not been unduly worried about her state of dress, now became self-conscious and wiped her hands uselessly on her trousers.

"She has been fighting," Tirhan said in low voice to his mother. "Which is more than most of these clansmen have done."

Morwen shook her head. "No, she is right. I should have made myself presentable first." Then she was gone, and Tirhan made his demeanor calm, though he noted Gryffyd's expression of amusement.

After a decent interval, Gryffyd rose and introduced Anwelyth to the chieftains and bade her stand with him for a moment. She looked every inch a queen.

Gwenid noted Tirhan's darker mood and murmured at his side, "Now was not the time."

There would be no announcement of their betrothal tonight. "Well, but she must join the banquet. She has every right to be here."

"Cadris will bring her when she has bathed." Gwenid smiled at the gathering as though nothing was amiss. "Be patient, my son."

When Morwen came back to the feast, she wore fresh clothes but no gown, only a good woolen shirt and trousers. Her long hair was washed and combed and fell down her back nearly to her waist. Tirhan wanted to join her, leaving his mother to anchor the table. He wanted so much to go to her.

But now was not the time.

Sofiyana picked up the tureen of stew and shoved it at her maid. "This is rancid! Take it away!"

"But, my lady, it is the same as yesterday!"

"Then you have served this revolting dish twice," Sofiyana shrieked. The stew was tainted and her stomach roiled with it. The whole tent was filled with the odor, the hot, stinking soup. As her gut twisted, she rushed outside and fell to her knees, retching.

Attendants hurried to her side, bringing towels and making concerned noises. She sat back on her heels, weak and sweating. People nearby stopped to stare, and she hissed at her people to make them go away.

Back in her pavilion, she dismissed her attendants and took a few sips of water, trying to calm herself. In her pocket, Nashavety's amber ring was hot against her thigh. It had singed her clothes once. The best thing was to wear it on a finger, where it could stay cool, but people looked askance at the thing. They had heard stories that she talked to it, so she kept it hidden.

She had not slept last night after Nashavety visited her, when the thin, sunken form came to her, hair snapping, voice guttural, stinking of rot. She had demanded that Sofiyana immediately send soldiers to seize Yevliesza at her hideaway.

But for soldiers to enter Yevliesza's camp could mean a fight. Sofiyana feared that Yevliesza's peasant devotees would fight, and many would die. Nashavety had promised—*promised*—that no Numinasi lives need be sacrificed in the coming takeover. There would be no great battle—it had all been arranged between the two of them. And now, an armed intervention at Yevliesza's camp. Would Commander Ilyan even obey such an order?

As long as she led the army in the defense of Numinat, she was tolerated. But if her fighters killed villagers, her situation could quickly change. With Yevliesza merely an annoyance, why was this raid even necessary?

Nashavety had dismissed Sofiyana's protests. She must be obeyed. To do otherwise was unthinkable.

Perhaps the Haiga encampment would be so daunted by the arrival of a strong unit of soldiers that they would not dare to interfere. And as for Warden Kirady's men, if they tried to thwart royal orders, they could justifiably be called traitors. But if Yevliesza died in the encounter, her followers might rise up. They would fall before trained fighters, and Sofiyana would be blamed.

This morning she had lost her composure over nothing. That must not happen again. But she felt herself standing upon shifting ground, reacting, not leading. Not obeying her mistress, who would soon return to Numinat with a great army.

When she was rested, she would speak with Ilyan. But she could not face the encounter today. Retrieving the amber ring from her pocket, she absently rubbed the stone.

Chapter Seven

Yevliesza and Rusadka made their way through the woods toward the cave. Only Zander and Ostov accompanied them, no more swords than usual, even though the cave was of extraordinary value.

The problem was how to keep Arrow Shaft Gate secret and at the same time protected. Yevliesza argued that the fewer who knew about the gate, the better. She had overridden Rusadka and Kirady on this. Secrecy was the best security, but difficult. The camp was swelling, with some fifty more people from local villages just yesterday, bringing their numbers to a hundred and seventy-five.

As they reached the bottom of the scree slope leading to the cave, Rusadka brought up gate security again. "Two cannot do the job. Zander and Ostov are not enough."

"But a dozen guards? It would draw attention."

"If you had been guarded during your Mist Wall vision, Ryura would never have gotten near enough to claim you went in."

Yevliesza did listen to Rusadka. But she couldn't see the logic this time. "But anyone who follows us from camp will see nothing in the cave. Not even a whorl on the rock wall."

Rusadka remarked in a flat tone of voice, "And they will not notice that you went into a cave and disappeared?"

Yevliesza smiled at her friend. Going into the cave and disappearing would stoke the rumors of her mystical powers. "I see your point," she said. Rusadka was the one she listened to most. She spoke the truth as she saw it, not holding back.

As the four of them climbed up the scree slope, Yevliesza was thankful for her sturdy boots. Her first military lesson from Rusadka. The second was how to really ride a horse. Even more important: *there are some things one must fight for.*

"Anyway," Rusadka said mildly, "Kirady has three men trailing us, out of sight."

Damn it to hell. Yevliesza turned to Zander. "You knew?"

"Yes, ma'am," he said, his eyes hard. He was Kirady's man.

Rusadka watched her warily, but Yevliesza had never fought with Rusadka and didn't want to start now.

As they stood on the lip of the cave, she changed the subject. "When is the last time you saw Elivasa?" Elivasa had been Rusadka's lover since Anastyna's escape from Osta Kiya.

"A month." Something in her voice, and it wasn't resignation. Rusadka went on. "The princip still has her traveling."

Anastyna had sent Elivasa to make the rounds of the polities, explaining Sofiyana's alliance with Nashavety. Elivasa had proof of it from the spies she had run when Sofiyana had been a *fajatim*, head of Raven Fell Hall.

"We could use her smile around here," Yevliesza said. "Her wit. You must miss her."

"Aye." Rusadka's eyes scanning the forest below. Her mind on Elivasa.

They entered the cave. The align streaked like a flaming arrow into the wall. She and Rusadka were going into the backways to hunt for targets, men or machines. Yevliesza placed her hand on the rock face with its delicate etching of concentric rings. No gouges or ridges, but the rings were there, though Rusadka and the others couldn't see them.

Rusadka noted Yevliesza's hesitation. "Are you ready?"

As I'll ever be, Yevliesza thought. *Mythos, help me,* she beseeched who or whatever was in charge.

In response to her intense concentration, the whorl faded. A section of the wall faded. In its place, a bright shadow. It lengthened. Before them, a tunnel appeared. Faintly glowing walls illumined the way.

Rusadka murmured, "Are you sure you do not want to close it after us? If the Volkish find it . . ."

"I'm sure." Yevliesza turned to Zander and Ostov, and they nodded to her. They would be waiting for her.

Once in the tunnel, she and Rusadka walked silently. Volkish soldiers would certainly be close, in the main routes. The backways were narrow, the air clotted and stale, infused with an almost creature-like, yeasty smell of skin and hide. The crossings were not built of stone and soil, but a substance that could be made to bend and flow. The pathways were the essential mystery of the Mythos lands. She wondered how, in the mundat, the First Ones had even thought to create the crossings and thought how it would have taken great courage to leave the mundane earth and believe in the prospect of a better place.

She held up her hand in a signal to stop. Closing her eyes, she sought a clearer vision of the schematic of the routes. She perceived people at key stations along the main route, but little movement. The backways empty but for her and Rusadka.

But then something stirred in her internal map.

"Anything?" Rusadka whispered.

"Wait." Far down the main route between Volkia and Numinat, three figures moved. One of the figures wore a long gown. A woman, it must be. Behind her, two individuals carrying something. It was only a small group. But: Nashavety might be with them.

Yevliesza saw a route through the connected tunnels that would get her close to the main path. "Hurry," she whispered. "Nashavety is here." They set off at a quick pace.

At a dead end, she found the spot she had been aiming for. The group was approaching. Yevliesza moved to the wall. She decided not to create a spy hole, but to perceive the main tunnel with mind-sight.

Her internal map was not detailed enough for her to see the face of the woman approaching. But she did see what the men behind the woman were carrying. A cage. Inside it, a small, ugly creature. It was a creature like the one she had seen in Holdfast: hairless, shriveled body, with wings as well as arms and legs. The monster of the maze.

"What are you going to do?" Rusadka asked. Pulling the ceiling down had not turned out so well last time.

Yevliesza had only moment to decide. "It's Nashavety." She took a deep breath. "I'm going to bury her." Nashavety's death could be a crippling blow to Volkia. Sorcery would be dispelled from Numinat, from the woman who wore the torc. *Yes,* she told herself. *Yes.*

She waited until the party was only a few yards away, then willed the ceiling of the tunnel to fall. She closed her eyes, trying to pull the tunnel down, to press it down. It gave, slumping like warm candle wax. She dragged the full weight of the ceiling onto the woman and the cage and the men who carried it. Shouts and a throttled scream erupted. In a few seconds the group was mired in a heavy slag of tunnel material.

In her perception of the scene, she could make out that Nashavety was moving, but struggling to rise, her hair caught in the slag. She was alive. Next to her, the creature was perched on top of the ruined cage. It jumped down and ran off, scuttling into a side tunnel. It was in the backways.

"Run!" she urged Rusadka. They turned back, but with many junctions and twists in the path, Yevliesza needed to stop a few times to work out the route.

A rumble underneath their feet. A quake beginning, then increasing in magnitude. They staggered as they ran. Yevliesza's concentration on the crossing's layout faltered, replaced by panic. "Rusadka! I'm getting lost."

"No, I think it is the next left." As they ran, the quaking quieted.

Yevliesza breathed in a forced calm, and, as she did so, the map came to her, showing her location and the small, scuttling figure of the demon racing, racing toward them. She would not be able to close its path in time, and besides, it might easily take an alternate route.

Rusadka stopped, drawing her sword and facing the way they had come. "Go. Run for the gate!"

"Rusadka, no!"

She pushed Yevliesza away. "And close the gate behind you," she growled.

"No, I can still bring the ceiling down on the demon!"

"Eight dark hells, woman. I am expendable, and you are not. Tell Elivasa . . ." Yevliesza stood frozen, watching her friend. "Tell her I thought of her." Rusadka waved Yevliesza away. "Go!"

Yevliesza ran.

Rusadka would kill the demon—she was bigger, stronger. But, with a jolt, Yevliesza glimpsed more small figures scuttling toward her from several directions. There wasn't just one. There were three, spurring her to run even faster. Yevliesza's ears filled with the sounds of her footfalls and gasping breaths. She tried to anticipate which figures were on course to overtake her. It was almost impossible to predict the paths of three pursuers at once, but in her panic she made a few wild changes to her route, ignoring the need to choose paths with clear connections to the cave.

Drenched in sweat, with her visual of the crossings increasingly hard to perceive, she stopped. She had to concentrate.

Her internal map snapped back. Yes, three of the demons. And now soldiers, too. The map was startlingly clear, allowing her to see every movement, every route, every presence. She clearly discerned a way to safety. But she turned back. There was a route for Rusadka to escape, and Yevliesza was not going to leave her.

She ran back.

When she rounded a bend, she found Rusadka, standing with her bloodied sword, red gouts on her face and chest. Yevliesza ran up to her, taking her arm. "Rusadka!"

Rusadka looked down on her dead opponent. "The blood belongs to the demon." The monster lay sprawled at her feet, unmoving, nearly decapitated. She had won her fight. But it wasn't enough.

"There are more of them," Yevliesza said. "Run!"

They rushed off, Yevliesza in the lead, evading, selecting alternatives, sometimes moving more slowly lest they betray their position with noise.

When they saw a gray patch ahead, they knew they were approaching the cave. As they rushed through the gate, Yevliesza turned and, though she had vowed not to, pulled the gap shut. She and Rusadka looked at each other in stunned silence. They had made it out.

For a moment all was peaceful, and Yevliesza felt a surge of hope that closing the gate would not cause a quake.

Then the ground shook. Yevliesza felt the trembling in her feet, in her chest. The whole cave vibrated, accompanied by the scream of rock shifting.

After a short while, quiet and stability returned. Yevliesza had accomplished nothing. And those quakes. Always the quakes.

The shadowy cavern was dimly lit with a manifesting light produced by Zander. Rusadka wiped a trickle of blood out of her eye. "The demon fought hard," she said. "How many of those things from hell are there?"

"Three," Yevliesza said. "But now, two."

She and Rusadka shared a bleak look. Of course there were more.

Chapter Eight

The day after the sabotage in the crossings, Nashavety made her way through the main tunnel in silence, accompanied by Marshal Reinhart and a few soldiers hauling a wagon.

Nashavety's hand went to her hair. Long strands had been tangled so badly in the collapse that they had to be cut off to free her. Now her hair hung in ragged tendrils around her face, causing people to stare at her more than usual.

They passed the area where the bodies of the traitors hung on the wall. The St. Eustus group, the pathetic cabal that had tried to overthrow the leadership. Reinhart had wanted to display the heads on poles. A distasteful impulse, and she had not allowed it. As he walked by her side, sweeping his gaze back and forth, he watched for any movement, despite the fact that the girl of the mundat operated only from the backways. Strigo had almost caught her there—the *almosts* were becoming tedious—but one of the beasts had been killed, likely by soldiers that had come with her.

The wheels of the cart squeaked under the load. The load of bodies in their stitched bags, bodies that would be brought to the Lowgate garrison for burial. Diplomacy was a fine thing. It operated even in time of war, such that Volkia was able to offer the enemy their dead, the bodies that had been hauled out of the crossings after the victorious battle two months ago. They would be surprised by what the bags actually contained.

Meanwhile, Volkia was constantly on guard against saboteurs. *The saboteur.* Units were now patrolling the backways, but the girl—the Keeper, Yevliesza styled herself—had an uncanny way of evading pursuit. Nashavety felt her lip curl. She had been a canker amid the grace of days from the moment she had arrived in Numinat. And now she was trying her hand at assassination.

Out of range of the men's hearing, Reinhart murmured to her, "Your princip should have eliminated the saboteur by now, madam. Since she has found the hiding place, why does she not move swiftly?"

"She is timid." Nashavety glanced at Reinhart, allowing herself a small smile. "You must leave the matter to me."

"Of course, madam," he said humbly, recognizing the warning in her tone of voice.

He was eager to take Numinat. They would not wait much longer, even with the danger of sabotage during their march through the crossings. They had overwhelming numbers. But it was better to avoid hard losses if they could. They had kingdoms to keep in line, to administer.

Yet the quakes still mystified her. Was their occurrence tied to the mundat's sabotage? It gave her pause. Might it be the machines? There were times when she worried that using elemental power for battle machines was not effective in avoiding the land's intolerance of machines. She did not want to believe that she herself had destabilized her beloved land. She pushed such thoughts away, but they clung to her like cobwebs.

They neared the gate.

Numinat would take the cart and its honored load. They suspected nothing. The soldier who had volunteered to present the Numinat fallen to the garrison commander walked by the side of the cart. He alone, aside from Nashavety and Marshal Reinhart, knew what the body bags really contained: *strigoi.*

There were thirty-two of them, the full number of Strigo's pack. Volkish soldiers feared them, how they lived off the blood and not the meat of their prey. Repugnant to the common soldier. Even worse, their bodies were humanlike. The blood demons were said to have once been human. So they were not natural animals. *Natural* was highly overrated.

The leader of the beasts, Strigo, would find the Keeper—by smell—and it and its swarm would tear her apart.

Reinhart stopped at the great gate. "It is a pity that the *strigoi* will swiftly kill this Keeper," he murmured. "She deserves a slow death."

"You are welcome to have your men find her in the crossings," Nashavety threw back. "Then she is yours."

"I thank you, madam."

She approved Reinhart's keenness. A fiercer warrior than Albrecht had been. It was like having a savage thrall by her side, barely controlled by creature power. But they shared a cold and clear view undiluted by sentiment. He was most satisfyingly ruthless. A bond between them.

At the boundary gate, the heavily armed Volkish stationed there made way for them. The volunteer saluted to Reinhart and made a stiff bow to Nashavety. This captain would conduct the cart to its destination. He was exceptional in that he claimed that he had no great fear of the things in the bags. Perhaps he did not quite understand what the creatures were, what they were capable of. He would remain at the garrison long enough to exchange pleasantries with the Lowgate commander, but he must return without delay, in case the *strigoi* did not wait for dark as they had been told. If they emerged early, Captain Brandt could be mistaken for prey.

"You are ready?" Reinhart asked him.

"Yes, sir."

One of the gate sentries raised the hammer and thudded it three times against the door. After a few moments, the gate slowly began moving to one side.

It opened enough for Numinat soldiers to determine it was just one man and a cart of body bags. Nashavety had merely a brief, cramped view through to the other side, but the sight caused a lump to form in her throat. Numinat. She would soon be home.

In her mind's eye, she saw a great spire rising up from the prairie. The place where her mother had brought her when, as a young girl, the time had come to receive her gifts. Creature power came to her then. It was the lesser of her two powers. But elemental power rushed into her at that time, as well. Her noble gift.

When it entered her, she became larger than others. Deeper. She would return there to thank the Mythos. Gratitude was so often overlooked.

The Numinat garrison sent a few soldiers out to haul the cart up the incline. As they did so, Arman Brandt, messenger of Duke Tanfred Wilhoffen, accompanied them into Numinat.

SEVERAL NUMINASI OFFICERS MET ARMAN BRANDT IN THE GARRISON yard. Evening was drawing on, and torches lit the enclosures, flickering against stone and timber walls. Warriors packed the garrison, some of them with bows on the fort wall, and others in full battle dress in formation on the ground. They were prepared for treachery. But not the right sort.

He and Lowgate Commander Yaros exchanged introductions. He was a large, florid man, long past his fighting days, but armed with a sword it would take Arman two hands to wield. Arman turned to watch a few men pull the cart out of sight.

"Perhaps you would take refreshment, Captain?" Yaros asked.

It was now that Arman began his betrayal of the Volkish Army. He had been told to return immediately lest the enemy untimely discover the true contents of the cart, but that was against his purpose. He was on the other side of the gate, and he could safely disregard orders.

"Very kind. Thank you, Commander." His throat was dry as he said, "I have urgent need to talk to you."

Yaros cocked his head. "Then come with me."

In a simple cabin built against the fort wall, Yaros led him to a table, where they took chairs facing each other.

To confess that the carts held dangerous animals was a shocking, possibly fatal, thing to disclose. Arman swallowed and began. "Commander, I ask for asylum. It is no longer possible for me to serve my kingdom. And I have intelligence of import to give you, but I would beg you not to hold me responsible. I have only brought the cart because it would allow me to help Duke Tanfred Wilhoffen, who seeks to leave Volkia and bring hope to those who oppose our leadership."

Yaros frowned. "The cart? What about the cart?"

"Sir, it does not contain bodies, but animals who are intended to go free and do harm. I urge you to kill them. Immediately."

Yaros rose to his feet. "What sort of animals?"

"I know not. But they are called *strigoi* and are capable of flight. Vicious creatures. Do not open the sacks, but I urge you to use swords and destroy them while they are confined."

Yaros strode to the door, where an officer waited out of hearing range. The officer eyed Arman and drew his sword as Yaros hurriedly left. The officer demanded that Arman lay down his sword and other weapons. He had only his sword, which he placed on the floor. He stepped back, waiting. If only Yaros would do as he had asked. If only they would refrain from opening the sacks. He had meant to sound a clear warning, but he feared that—

Shouting pierced the relative silence.

"Please," Arman said to the lieutenant, who was now noting with alarm the commotion outside. "Please, I have told Commander Yaros that the cart does not hold bodies, but savage weapons. I beg you, do not count me responsible. I came to warn you."

Through the window, though dusk came on, Arman saw a black shape glide by. God in heaven, the creatures were loose. Screams punctuated the air. The *strigoi* dived, clawing and tearing, only to rise into the air again and choose another victim.

The soldier grabbed Arman's sword from the floor and rushed out, slamming the door behind him. The lieutenant was one more man among many, and he could be little help. Arman ran to the door and opened it.

The soldiers had thrown open the fort gates, and those bivouacked outside came to join the fight, some seizing torches and using them with some effect to drive the beasts off, but it was a chaotic scene, with the air full of demons swooping and killing. A sickening sight, so much more terrible than Arman had imagined.

As he watched men flayed by the swarm, he knew he had to use the attack to cloak his escape. He still owed service to Duke Tanfred, and his death here would do nothing for his cause. Even if the beasts were finally beaten off, the soldiers would certainly kill him, no matter what he pleaded, if he even had a chance to plead.

Shedding his army jacket and hat, Arman entered the mayhem of the yard, running into the thick of things and making his way to the open fort gate. Outside, he made for a ditch that held a few low thorn bushes and hunkered down to run along it. The shouts of soldiers and the clamor of the fight spilled onto the flats. With darkness now enveloping him, he climbed out of the ditch and ran. He did not know which direction to take, except away from the fort, into the plain.

After a time, he heard the sound of wings above him, and he dove to the ground near a boulder. The sound passed. But then more wing-beats, as the demons swarmed past him. Lowgate garrison had fought them off. Either that, or the creatures had other plans.

He picked himself up and hurried into the blackness of the immense prairie. The garrison would soon be looking for him. He could not blame them if they killed him. Perhaps he had not given enough warning, but it was more warning that they would have had if any other Volkish soldier had volunteered.

He kept looking at the sky, trying to discern if the creatures were still nearby, but they were not merely winged; they could also walk, so they could be anywhere. They were not merely beasts with a flocking behavior. It was known that *strigoi* could talk, and even had a kind of intelligence. He wondered if Reinhart and his sorceress had sent them with a mission other than striking at the garrison.

He walked on, putting as much distance as he could between himself and the fort.

Yevliesza, he thought. Duke Tanfred had urged him to find Yevliesza.

He stumbled on into the night.

Chapter Nine

Pyvel rubbed goose fat into the set of chain mail, cleaning and polishing so that Captain Nikander would have proper dress for the battle.

His captain was one of the officers who had been with Anastyna from the beginning. He had accepted Pyvel as his aide at Lord Valenty's recommendation. Lord Valenty. Whom he had hoped to serve, but Grigeni did instead, as was right, since he had known the lord longer. Nikander was good enough. Gruff and distant, but his horse was a fine stallion and got along well with Pyvel's roan, Kasha, even though she usually bit at stallions.

Dipping his cloth into the fat to rub at a tarnished spot, he thought about the war to come. They said it would be over in the first battle. The armies would meet on the plain, with Sofiyana's force blocking the way to Osta Kiya.

He was glad the battle would be out in the open—where exactly, no one knew, except that it would not be in the confines of the crossings, those awful tunnels where so many had died that day. His first battle, and it had been lost, badly lost. But by trickery, not valor.

In that battle he had not shown much valor. There was little enough of valor anywhere, only an overwhelming smell of blood and shit.

Machines, death, blood, and shit. He knew what the next battle would be like. He just hoped that the captain's horse and his own survived. He had never seen a horse die and thought it would be an awful thing.

He looked up as a rider approached—a woman. A few people gathered around to hear the news. Then he saw that it was Elivasa. She had been out recruiting and came in from time to time to report. He hurried over to her.

"Pyvel," she said, happily. "You have grown a hand-span since I last saw you!"

He grinned. She was always cheerful, though she looked like she had ridden hard, her skirts mud-splattered and her horse lathered.

"What news?" he asked.

"That's for the princip's ears, not for the likes of you," she cheerfully said, dismounting.

"But no fighting men are coming to join us?" Every day he expected a horde of fighters to show up at camp. Anastyna was the rightful princip. They had to come.

Elivasa smirked. "Well, she has *me*."

⚜

Valenty's spirits rose when, from the royal hilltop, he saw Elivasa climbing the slope to Anastyna's hut. Urik followed behind her with Captain Lysandry. He hoped she had succeeded in her recruitment. Even two hundred fighters would gladden the princip. And more would come once a few wardens acknowledged her.

Elivasa had been gone over two tendays and might well have reached the Agarvesky and the several polities in between.

It began to rain, and Anastyna received Elivasa in the royal quarters, a simple cabin of logs, smoky from the fire in the center pit. Valenty happily greeted Elivasa, his one-time fellow spy from Osta Kiya. Urik and Captain Lysandry joined the group in the cramped space of the hut.

By Urik's expression, he had already heard the news. Anastyna saw it too and kept her face impassive.

Elivasa glanced warily at the rafters where Anastyna's falcon *sympat* roosted. She did not like birds, and Valenty thought that the feeling might be mutual.

"My Lady Princip," she began. "I went north into the Numin foothills, first stopping in Tanaya. A force has arrived from the town?"

"It has."

Captain Lysandry said, "Tanaya sent twenty."

Elivasa frowned. "The town master promised eighty. But no one is willing to commit to us or to Sofiyana."

Anastyna interrupted. "But you have told them we possess proof that the usurper wields sorcery. They care not?"

"They noted the claim and fear it."

"Noted? They do not believe it, though you came with our imprimatur?"

"They have never heard the like. It was harsh news, and they did not want to believe it, though I think Warden Radiz at Mensk listened well and was angry to hear of it. If he comes, he will bring two hundred, among them the best archers in the outland."

"Then why," Anastyna snapped, "does he delay? With Volkia massing their men and machines even now?"

"My lady, they all wait to see what choice Dorodna makes." Elivasa paused. "There is a minor gathering around the Keeper of Wolves, who is camped by the Haiga. But they are villagers and stragglers only."

"How many?" Captain Lysandry asked.

"There are the fifteen men you sent to protect her. And some one hundred sixty peasants, many of them women who are not trained to arms."

"Two hundred," Anastyna mused, rounding the number up. "And only four days ago, it was one hundred."

"It is the polities who will swell our ranks, my lady. They wish to join you. But if Dorodna—"

Anastyna raised a hand to stop her. The falcon flapped its wings, waiting for a summons. "Yes, yes. So you have said." She looked at Urik. "What say you?"

"My lady," Urik said. "The people have not seen sorcery at work. Anyone may accuse, but so far few have seen with their own eyes."

"And so?"

"It will take time for your cause to be well known. When they see what Sofiyana truly is, they will support you."

He left unsaid that the kingdom might be lost by then. Valenty feared it. But there was still hope.

She turned to Elivasa. "Tell us of Sofiyana's strength. Who stands with her?"

"By their colors, Volrikh and Ortvala Polities. The standing army brought two thousand into the field. Her total force looks to be about three thousand."

Anastyna watched the central pit fire, and no one interrupted the silence. "Yevliesza hinders our recruitment," she finally said. "Her camp grows and soon may include fighters, bleeding off those who could come to our banner."

That was wrong, Valenty thought. There were only two factions in contention for the torc, both vying for the privilege of leading the defense of Numinat: Anastyna and Sofiyana. Yevliesza, though, worked alone, and if her camp grew, it was also bogged down with unarmed peasants.

Anastyna would soon have an additional five hundred fighters when Kirady brought the rest of his men down from Eiger Polity. But that would still mean only eight hundred for Anastyna and three thousand for Sofiyana. Anastyna had far to go, but it was not because of Yevliesza's recruitment.

The princip stood, signaling the meeting was over. Valenty stood as well, wincing, his wound feeling angry with the change in the weather. Anastyna turned to him. "You could have warned us, my lord. That the girl had pretensions to lead."

Valenty paused. This was nothing but wild imaginings. Yevliesza would never pursue the torc. Anastyna grew desperate, grew suspicious of him.

"My lady," he began, measuring his words. "Do you have confidence in me?"

Anastyna pursed her lips in annoyance. "Of course. Yet one could wish for you to be more watchful for our hopes."

"I am always watchful, Lady Princip." He did not like her new mood. Now more than ever, he worried about Yevliesza. What Anastyna might do.

The princip turned to Elivasa, smiling. "You do us great service, Elivasa. Take your rest and set out as soon as you have. There is still the south to cover. It may be that farther from the city-palace, we will find honest men."

❦

Valenty walked with Urik after hearing Elivasa's report. Rain spat down, but the fresh air was welcome after the smoky den of the royal hut.

"Be careful, Valenty," Urik said. "She did not like Elivasa's news. Someone will be found at fault."

"The princip favors me. It is a bond, despite difficulties." He had served her faithfully for years. He had led her rescue when she would have faced the Trespass Door.

Urik did not speak for a time. They walked to the end of the ridge and looked out north to the plains. Empty now. Perhaps soon filled with the machines of war.

The *harjat* said low, "With a princip, favor is always provisional."

❦

Arman Brandt had been walking for two days through a plain of golden grasses bent low by never-ending wind and creased by deer trails. Hunger gnawed at him. He had no idea of the direction he should take. Nor was there any sign of habitation where he could buy food— he carried gold coins to pay for it—and ask for information about the whereabouts of the woman named Yevliesza. But he had seen nothing but grass, sheep, and a few scouts on soaring dactyls.

At least the demon birdmen had not returned.

The land slowly rose into rumpled hills as rain came in on a freshening wind. Perhaps there would be shelter of some kind in the hills. He pushed himself onward. His plan had been to convince the commander at Lowgate to send his information to those in authority and tell him what he knew, if anything, of Yevliesza, but the escape of the *strigoi* and slaughter at the garrison finished that idea. He had barely escaped with his life, and if soldiers pursued him, he might still die. Then he would have failed Duke Tanfred and the Volkish people who suffered under the witch Nashavety. His high purpose scattered on the winds. He shivered as the rain dampened his shirt.

Onward. He must go onward.

At the crest of the first hill he found a small lake fringed with cattails. Beyond a gap in the hills he saw another lake. A flock of birds rose from it in one burst, crying, he imagined, "Follow me, follow me."

In the next moment he glimpsed a man on horseback making his way up the flank of a hill in the near distance. Was it a search party from Lowgate? The rider sat his horse like a soldier. Arman looked around for cover, but the immediate area was devoid of hiding places, and the rider could turn in his direction at any moment. Crouching low to the ground, he tried to think. The rain came harder now, pelting the lake with a thousand dents.

The lake was his only chance. He crawled through the mud at the lake's edge, entering the water, cold as a lizard's kiss. Tubular reeds grew thick in the shallows, but not enough to hide him. He saw the rider coming into the vale and two more behind him. He had to submerge.

Breaking off a reed, he snapped off the head of the plant and blew through the stem, spraying water from it. Creeping into deeper water and placing the reed stem in his mouth, he went under. The cold stung his face. Lying on his back on the pond's muddy floor, he pursed his lips close around the reed and prayed for air. It came to him. If he could keep still, he might be safe. *Breathe, breathe. Do not move.*

He concentrated on remaining still and keeping the reed from moving at the water's surface. Blind and deaf, he was shut off from the world above. It was as though he were already dead, buried in the cold ground. He would have been if he had attended that last meeting of St. Eustus, where a heavy Volkish boot crashed through the door and ended the great plan. He had been delayed by a conversation on the street in Hapsigen. An old woman who knew his mother, and how was she, and what news of the war and other things, meaningless things, the things that had saved his life. The last man.

He breathed through the reed and knew that he was alive. And for a purpose.

Something struck at him. He lurched, bringing his head up from the pond in a loud splash. A man stood in the water next to him, laughing. As Arman sputtered, he became aware of two more men, armed with swords, pikes, and lances. They kept to their mounts near the shore.

The soldier nearest him, up to his knees in the pond, pushed Arman toward the shore. "An innocent man has no reason to hide," he said. "Why did you, then?"

"I have run from my army unit," Arman said.

The soldier frowned. "Not a good answer." He put the tip of his short sword to Arman's throat. "Which army?"

"Volkia's."

His captor glanced at the nearest two riders, then turned a hard stare to Arman. "Where are the Volkish?"

"Still in the crossings. I have come with information that Numinat needs. That they will welcome." The wind lashed at his wet skin and clothes, but he felt nothing but relief. He was betting these men were not from Lowgate.

More riders were straggling into the vale. It was not a search party. It was a force of at least a hundred men, and more arriving every moment.

The soldier put a hand on his neck and pushed him toward the two mounted soldiers, one of whom had an air of authority and wore a good cloak with a silver clasp. Across his back he wore a sword.

Arman stared at him. He was one of the largest men Arman had ever seen, with a full beard braided into strands.

"Your name," this man said.

"Captain Arman Brandt, lord."

"Captain, is it?" He exchanged glances with the man at his side, a warrior dressed in mail over leather. When he turned back to Arman, he said, "You do not look like a captain. Skinny and wet, and you stink like goat shit. The Volkish are not here. Maybe you like a big tale to keep me from slitting your ugly throat."

"I come from Duke Tanfred Wilhoffen of Volkia, and if you kill me, your princip will make sure you never command troops again."

The man's face lost its good humor, but he restrained his man from urging his horse forward to retaliate.

"Which princip?" he growled, hand on the short sword at his side.

Arman had to guess which of the contending princips this chief served. But he did not know much about which contender for the torc was which. "Whichever one wants to defeat the Volkish."

"A good answer," the man said. "You speak with an accent. Maybe you are who you say you are. But any man can pretend to be Volkish."

"I have Volkish coins."

The lord held out his hand, and Arman plunged his hand into a trouser pocket and produced one. He handed it up to his interrogator, who turned it over in his hand, examining it, and then tossed it back to Arman.

"For now, you can keep your gold." The lord looked at the fighters who crowded into the vale—over two hundred men, Arman estimated. "I am on my way to Princip Anastyna. I may let you tell her your tale." Arman began to believe he would live.

"I am Warden Zergai of Nenska Polity," the big man said, looking down at him. "And at my campfire you will have only a short time to convince me of who you are." He walked his horse away, as the men around him began to make camp.

They brought Arman dry clothes and fed him, bringing a blanket to put over his shivering body. It was thick and coarse and stank of horse sweat, and he welcomed it like a rich cloak.

Before a good fire, and with the Warden Zergai and a few of his men listening, Arman began his tale.

Chapter Ten

Tirhan lifted his head, listening intensely to the woods. Something had come near. A fox, a boar? The crush of leaves under a heavy boot? Behind him, Morwen and six partisans froze in their steps. Through the heavy fog they could see little, but the mist carried sound like a river.

They waited. Some twenty paces to one side, a blur of white and brown. A stag, with a great rack of antlers. As though a spirit from the otherworld, it regarded them, its sides rippling, then sprang away, disappearing.

The band moved on. Volkish had been tracking them for a few hours, but the occupiers were not used to the forest, and the fog doubled their blindness. The intention had been to strike at a small outpost not far from Osian Gate, but now Tirhan's band must lose themselves in the wilds and wait to strike a different day.

Tirhan signaled for a rest, and they brought out water skins and took some ease, sitting on rocks fallen from the canyon wall.

Seated beside him, Morwen said, "They do not usually come so far."

So far into the woods. Volkish solders were wary of the deep woods where their machines faltered, as did their eyes and ears.

"They are learning," Tirhan said ruefully. They were becoming accustomed to Alfan Sih.

Cynod stood, ready to move on, uncomfortable with too much rest. He and Morwen had barely survived their encounter with the enemy patrol three days ago and left friends' bodies behind when they escaped. Tirhan worried about Morwen constantly. The stray arrow, the projectiles from devices, the slash of a blade. All the ways to die and only one way to live: to strike fast and disappear. There were times when love was a burden, for he wanted to keep her safe, and he could not.

The fog thinned and a shaft of sunlight pierced the forest, striking trees thick with leaves that glittered at the sun's touch.

Morwen recognized it first. "A silverwood grove," she said, pointing.

As the band approached, the fog thinned to a net of mist through which they could see a glistening tree with silver, crinkled bark. Leaves caught the sun from a thousand planes. It was beautiful.

But it was the only one.

Trees lay strewn, their trunks severed by axes. Gouged into the forest floor, tracks where some of the logs had been dragged off. Tirhan stared at the devastation. It wounded his eyes, to see such ravaging. The group moved among the fallen trees in stunned silence.

"Sacrilege," Cynod muttered, looking at Tirhan, his gaze dark.

"They take them to sell," Tirhan said. This wanton reaping would be for trade with realms like Nubiah and Arabet. Treasure to pay for their wars of conquest. They had left one tree standing. A perverse mercy.

Morwen's hand went to her knife vest, fingering one of the weapons she so skillfully used. "This grove will not recover for a hundred years."

For centuries the harvest of silverwood had been limited to careful thinning under the guidance of grove masters from the local clans. This brutal cutting felt like desecration.

The sun dampened as heavy fog returned, and they quietly made their way through the fallen trunks, following the scarred forest floor where the trees had been dragged away. The cuts in the soil were new. Tirhan and his people walked softly, following the tracks, carrying their bows, ready to attack and fade back.

When they came upon a road, they found a wagon loaded with silver-barked trees shorn of their leafy branches. Crouching behind a hedgerow, the partisans peered through the bushes, picking their targets. Only five men worked, and they were all in the open.

Tirhan gave the signal, and arrows flew all at once, each striking home. Two, only wounded, took a second arrow, and they lay twitching as Morwen went in and slit throats.

As she did so, a movement caught Tirhan's attention. Something was moving behind the wagon. Two men carried a tall shield. Morwen's back was turned to them as she began to walk back toward the hedgerow. The men held the shield in front of themselves, and Tirhan saw a tube projecting from its middle. A volley gun. They were bringing it to bear on the hedgerow.

"To ground!" Tirhan shouted.

Morwen fell as the air exploded with the sound of pellets erupting from the nozzle set into the shield. Bits of hedge shredded around Tirhan's group as the deafening sound continued. Tirhan raced to Morwen's side.

Cynod called for the archers to cover him as he ran, but the arrows came too late. The shield slowly turned in Tirhan's direction. It fired.

At the same moment, a shadow loomed in front of Tirhan. Impossibly, it was a man dressed in a helmet and mail. He held a spear, and, as he raised it, the projectiles changed direction and raced uselessly over Tirhan as he crouched by Morwen.

The partisans rushed out to flank the volley gun and killed its operators.

As Tirhan and Morwen got to their feet, silence descended on the road, the hedgerow, the partisans.

Tirhan stared at the warrior in mail, a figure that appeared half shadow, half solid.

Although Morwen stood beside him, Tirhan could not turn to her, nor move in any way.

The shadow's voice came as a lament. "A grievous mutilation, young lord."

The side pieces of his helmet covered most of his face, but Tirhan knew the voice. He knew this visitor. It was one of the forms in which a spirit had shown himself to Tirhan before, the shade from the otherworld.

He wanted Morwen to see this figure. Before, when one of his visions had cautioned against Tirhan's rash plans, she had scoffed. Morwen would have savaged the enemy. But caution, not fierceness, had been the spirit's council.

The warrior pointed to the grove where the lone silverwood tree stood. "The trees weep, and so must you."

"I do," Tirhan heard himself say, or thought he heard.

The shade spoke again, a sonorous pitch as though from the center of a great stone hall. "The dead cannot come home, Lord King. Their path is through the silverwood groves. Each soul passes through the grove nearest the place where they lay down their lives. Too far away, and they cannot find their way, nor can we welcome our Alfan sons and daughters to their rest."

He pointed to Tirhan. "You must stop them. You must throw your cloak over the silver forest. This is your task, for if they take the groves, they have taken the heart of us."

"Grandfather," Tirhan said, but whether out loud or silently, he could not tell. "We are few, and the groves are many."

"Yet that is where you must stand and fight. Fight, young lord. Fight to keep the portals open."

"Portals, grandfather?"

"To the otherworld. Once the portals are closed, it will be a hundred years until the dead find peace. Your sons and daughters will roam the world forest looking for their heart's peace and the suffering will be beyond measure."

"Should we not drive the Volkish from our land?" Tirhan asked or thought. The groves were a precious heritage, but they were not everything.

Morwen's voice came to him. "He has spoken the truth. Listen, my love, listen."

She did hear. She was sharing his vision, but now the warrior began to fade. Patches of forest appeared through his tunic and mail. "The groves. The groves," came the words. At last only the spear remained. And then the shade was gone.

Cynod called out, "No one hurt, Lord Prince." His men were safe.

The worlds did not easily mix, Tirhan knew. Spirits could come to the living, but seldom did, and then only obscurely. Yet he had been visited several times.

"Did you see the vision?" he asked Morwen.

Her voice was merely a whisper. "Oh, Tirhan."

"Did you not see it?" He turned to her and looked at her wonder-filled face.

"I did. He stood in front of you and deflected the pellets. He was from the otherworld, and he saved you."

"And you," Tirhan said, exultant that she still lived.

They made their way back to the bushes, where his men were only that moment picking themselves up from their dive behind the hedge. They had seen nothing.

Morwen leaned in to murmur, "I am sorry that I did not believe you before."

"You believed me. But you did not believe what I had been told."

"I did not want to." Her eyes narrowed as she looked at the wagon loaded with silverwood. "But I do now."

闏

In the middle of the night, the ring pulsed on Sofiyana's finger, waking her up, squeezing as though it might cut down to the bone.

She sat upright on her cot, dragging a horrid dream with her, a dream where Yevliesza, wearing the torc, had soldiers holding her down, ready to slice off her finger. A dream, only a dream.

And now a worse one. Nashavety stood at the side of her cot.

At the shock of it, Sofiyana's heart almost jumped out of her chest. Thin, impossibly thin, tendrils of her mistress's hair twisting as though alive.

The wraith's voice was low, too low: "Who do you serve?" it gargled at her. "Who?"

"My . . . my lady. You, I serve *you*."

The wraith bent close to her, breath like a long-dead beast. "No, you do not. You pretend, but you do not *serve me*."

With her head pressing against the tent wall, Sofiyana could not back up any farther on the cot. "Please, mistress!"

"Please whaaaat!" came Nashavety's voice, but the lips did not move correctly. It was as though the words came from something nested within her, deep down where it could never be extracted.

"Please have mercy!" Sofiyana cried, for she knew something terrible was about to happen. "What have I done?" But she knew, she knew. Not obeying, not fast enough, not good enough.

"Give me your hand."

No. She could not. She could not touch the creature.

"Give me your hand," the wraith whispered, terrifying Sofiyana worse than the monster voice.

Sofiyana felt tears spring to her eyes. "Which one?" Nashavety wouldn't hurt her *left* hand, surely.

"Your left hand."

Her left arm shot out from her side and presented her hand as commanded. Sofiyana, still trailing the nightmare, could not breathe; she was strangled under creature power.

A clutch of cold air swathed her hand. Sofiyana closed her eyes and heard herself begin to whimper. "Please, mistress, please." She closed her eyes tightly against the pain. Her hand was limned with a dire frost, down to the very bones.

The guttural voice again: "You will capture or kill Yevliesza. Or, sadly, your punishment will continue."

When Sofiyana opened her eyes, the dark figure slowly shrank, a horrifying transformation into a withered, doll-like simulacrum.

Oh leave, please leave, go away. . . .

The doll's high-pitched voice pierced the darkness. "You will obey me now. You will see that you must serve me."

The sending vanished, leaving Sofiyana breathless and chilled.

She lit candles to dispel the darkness, but nothing could dispel her trembling.

A servant mewed from outside, "My lady, may I enter?"

"Yes," Sofiyana whispered, then realized the maid could not hear her. "Yes! Enter."

The servant did so. "All well, My Lady Princip?"

Sofiyana looked at her hand. A black smudge tinged the fingertips of her left hand.

And it stank.

She stared at her hand. A mold was growing.

The maid brought a basin of water, and Sofiyana washed her hands. But the rot stayed, blackening her fingertips. Floating in the water, specks of black, the outer layer that she had managed to scrub off. But under her fingernails, coal-black shadows.

The tent stank of rot. Nashavety had sent a corruption into her. A punishment. And Sofiyana realized the stench was not from Nashavety, but from her own hand.

Chapter Eleven

Yevliesza walked the Haiga marshes, skirting around the potholes filled with water. Only Zander and Ostov were with her, since Rusadka was in camp with Elivasa, who had ridden in the day before. Anastyna drove her recruiter hard, but Elivasa, passing near the marshlands, could not help but stop to see Rusadka.

In the distance Yevliesza spied one of her hunting parties riding out, looking for game. With Haiga camp now feeding a new influx of men, women, and children, those who had horses were scouring the region for food and supplies. Some of the newcomers were seekers, and others came for protection, as fear of the Volkish invasion spread.

In the last six days she had been into the crossings three times, but failed to find targets, even small ones. Few Volkish units, human or machine, were coming through, and when they did, they moved swiftly, making them impossible targets. There were large numbers guarding the gates, but Yevliesza did not dare destabilize those regions. So she told herself, with only her intuition to guide her.

Yevliesza and her advisors felt that the Volkish had concluded there was a saboteur, and they had altered their movements accordingly.

Yevliesza did not need to attack soldiers and their weapons directly. She could bring down a section of the crossings, depriving the Volkish of passage for a time. But when she did so, the crossings would still react to the disturbance. She would not risk it for so little gain. The quakes did no visible damage to the crossings, but that did not mean there was no damage. Whatever bound the Mythos worlds could be tilting, on the brink of an unthinkable collapse.

For now, she was stymied.

The shrill sound of a horn pierced the stillness of the Haiga. Outriders alerting the camp of someone's approach. Ostov was quickly at her side, with Zander moving to join him.

Three riders made their way through the marshes, bearing a standard of gold and white.

"Nenska Polity," Ostov said, but he had drawn his sword anyway.

Two of the riders wore mail and bore swords, but the third man was dressed in peasant clothing.

Zander walked forward to meet them. The conversation took some time. At last Zander came back. "Anastyna sent them. They say they have a message." He handed Yevliesza a scroll of paper tied with a string.

Curious, she undid the string and read: *Greetings, and hear this man's news. May it hearten you, as it has us. Do your duty, and we shall be grateful. —Princip of Realm, Bearer of Torc, Servant of Numinat.*

And Anastyna was none of these things. *Do your duty.* Chiding her, always.

Yevliesza had no doubt the letter was from Anastyna. It was her exactly. She walked toward the newcomers, Zander and Ostov at her side. "Which of you is the messenger?"

"I am," said the man without armor. Well built and fine-featured, he had a commanding presence. His face was sunburned, his hair a light brown no one would mistake for Numinasi. And she knew the accent. Volkish.

She looked up at him as the day grew brighter. "There is news? From who?"

"Duke Tanfred Wilhoffen," he said.

THEY HAD BEEN QUESTIONING ARMAN BRANDT FOR A LONG TIME AND were no closer to certainty about him. Yevliesza, Rusadka, Kirady, and Janov listened intently to the Volkish defector. Elivasa sat with them. Though she for now worked for Anastyna, Yevliesza did not want to exclude her from the group.

Lura had brought bread and soup, but Captain Brandt had set his aside to tell his story.

He had begun with a tale of a doomed opposition group called St. Eustus. He explained his allegiance to their goal: the downfall of Reinhart and his helpmate, Nashavety. He related how he had found Duke Tanfred in hiding and been convinced to seek out Yevliesza in the hope she could guide the duke to a safe haven in Numinat.

Guide him? How was she supposed to do that?

Kirady continued his questioning. "You could be luring the Keeper into a trap. Our enemies seek to kill her."

"They do," Captain Brandt agreed. He turned to Yevliesza. "You almost killed Nashavety in the crossings. Her hair was trapped in the tunnel breakdown and she had to cut it off."

Join the club, Yevliesza thought, fingering her own short hair, hacked off as she had fled in a carriage, making for Rorrs Gate.

Kirady went on. "By your own admission, you brought demon birds with you. Thirty-four of them. Creatures which you say have already rampaged among our troops at Lowgate and are now loose in the outlands."

The blood birds Kassalya had foreseen. From Captain Brandt's description, these were the same creatures as the three that been released into the backways to attack her and Rusadka.

"What are these creatures?" Yevliesza asked.

"I do not know much," the captain said. "In Volkia, there are tales of men turned into vile beings with demonic power. In stories, they are called *strigoi* and are said to live on the blood of their prey and to have keen intelligence. They were brought out of the Breminger Forest by Marshal Reinhart's close advisor, Nashavety."

Kirady scowled. "We know of her."

Nashavety. Her power grew and grew. If only she had died in the crossings.

"The beasts can be killed," Rusadka said. "*Strigoi* are no match for a good sword."

"I saw them rampage through Lowgate garrison," Arman said. "Soldiers are not used to fighting things that fly. People say that in the wilds they have only one natural predator. Dactyls."

"The beasts might have learned some fear now," she returned. "I killed one in the crossings."

Captain Brandt looked at her, assessing the woman who wore her hair knotted and was clearly a *harjat*.

Kirady continued the interrogation. "Why did you not alert the garrison commander of the danger immediately after the gate had closed?"

The captain paused, measuring his words. "It was important for them to understand that I was defecting, and that took precious minutes. I should have raised an alarm earlier, but I thought they would kill me outright. It was not the time for me to die."

"A man never thinks it is time," Kirady muttered.

Rusadka asked, "When *is* it time, Captain?"

He held Rusadka's gaze. "When I have done honor to the eleven men of St. Eustus who died without me."

Hearing him refer to the group as St. Eustus, Yevliesza recalled from her time in Volkia that the realm had retained its Christian heritage. Duke Tanfred was certainly devout, advised by Father Ludving, whom she greatly admired.

Kirady went on. "But you did not help the garrison to fight off the beasts, though you have creature power, you have said. You only turned and ran."

"The duke sent me on the mission to find Yevliesza. I swore to him."

Kirady was not impressed. "If you mean us well, tell us where Reinhart will come through. And when."

"Volkia is ready now. The army is massed outside Rorrs Gate. But they are waiting. For what, I do not know. And as to the choice of gate, that is a secret kept even from higher-ranking officers."

"How many men does Volkia have?" Rusadka asked.

"Nine thousand, not counting occupation troops. Add those in, the ones that can be spared from their foreign duties, eleven thousand. And battle machines," the captain went on. "The command does not want to risk machines in the crossings." He looked at Yevliesza. "They are afraid of you, mistress."

Yevliesza was taken aback. "They know it's me?"

"They do. It is not clear to me how they deduced this, but yes."

Yevliesza felt stripped of something she set value on: her anonymity. Now it was gone. Strange that Nashavety had figured it out. There was no one who could have told her. Except Duke Tanfred, and he would never have done so.

"Where is Duke Tanfred now?" she asked.

"Hiding in the house of a rebel, three miles outside of Hapsigen."

She would dearly love to bring Tanfred out, but how was she to create a path that led anywhere near him? When she had created a tunnel into Alfan Sih for Prince Tirhan, they had ended up in the correct realm, but far from an ideal location.

"When you spoke with Princip Anastyna, did she believe you?" Yevliesza asked. She must have, or she would not have sent this man to them. Anastyna's endorsement was worth something.

"I believe she did," he answered. "Duke Tanfred said you are the only one."

The only one. It corroborated his story. Tanfred knew her secret and had communicated it to Captain Brandt. Tanfred knew. He had seen her make an indentation in the wall of the main crossing tunnel. He had believed that she possessed the lost power from the moment he had seen her naked back when they sat chastely on her bed at Rothsvund Palace and she had told him what she could do. The Volkish captain was not lying that he had met Tanfred.

Hope surged. If she could find a way to bring Duke Tanfred to safety, those who chafed under the repressive regime and their demonic machines could gather under a new leader. Even if it was one in exile.

And creating a tunnel was something she thought the Mythos would tolerate.

They sent Captain Brandt under guard to a rough shelter where he could rest after his long trek on foot from the garrison as well as his side trip to Anastyna's base in the Stora Hills.

When he left, Yevliesza said, "I believe him."

Janov, ever a shrewd judge of people, nodded.

Kirady said, "I do as well. There must be many who share his convictions. But how much he can inspire Volkish people to rebel, is the question."

Yevliesza knew it was a long shot. But she was desperate to do *something*.

Rusadka looked eager for it. "We should find Tanfred if it can be done. We cannot ignore any possible advantage."

Kirady did not argue. "*Can* it be done?"

Yevliesza had the same question. "Some of it can. I can't predict exactly where a crossing path will lead, but from the crossings, I know I can get to a realm. I did it once before. I got into Alfan Sih."

Rusadka added, "And, when you made a way for Prince Tirhan, there were no tremors, were there?"

"That's true, there weren't." Yevliesza thought of Tirhan and how she had taken him into Alfan Sih. It was then that she first saw the strange and beautiful silverwoods, and when the two of them finally found a group of partisans who kneeled to Tirhan as heir to the throne. The moment when she had known he was not the man she would be with. She was always falling for men who had larger concerns than her. Maybe that was why she was attracted to them, that they cared for something noble.

Kirady was intrigued. "Extending a tunnel is different from collapsing one, then."

"That's what I'm thinking." She felt it would be the right decision. "I think the creation of a path is something the Mythos tolerates."

Kirady looked at her with renewed hope.

"And maybe this time I can direct the route better." Excitement stirred. She would finally be doing something. She had never tried to pinpoint an exit, but she was learning more about primal root power each time she went into the crossings. And an idea was starting take shape in her mind.

"I'll need this Volkish captain with me," she told the group. "When I go back to the crossings."

She saw Rusadka and Elivasa exchange satisfied smiles. The warrior and the spy loved moments like this.

And right now, so did Yevliesza.

PART II
THE GATES OF VOLKIA

Chapter Twelve

From his vantage point on the knoll, Valenty gazed northwest, where the folded hills gave way to the vast basin of the outlands. Masses of blue-black cloud swelled over the plain, carrying a storm in its bowels.

"When will they come, my lord?" Pyvel asked, standing at his side.

The boy was almost a man. His fourteenth year was beginning to sculpt his body with a new leanness and muscle.

"Tomorrow, I suppose," Valenty offhandedly said.

Pyvel grinned. "And we will meet them on the plains?"

"Wherever the battle is engaged." Anastyna would join Osta Kiya then, hoping to be in time. A few more small polities had come in, swelling her fighting force to five hundred, though many of them had only pikes and hoes for weapons.

Thunder growled from the approaching storm.

Pyvel gazed into the distance as though seeing the great Volkish army marching with its thousands, with its stalking machines. "But if she goes to the battle, Sofiyana might arrest her."

"Osta Kiya will be eager for any help, even hers." Valenty shrugged. "Afterward, Anastyna must retreat. It will be a close thing."

Even with the danger of capture, Anastyna must be at the battle and be seen to fight for Numinat.

Pyvel did not ask the obvious question—what happens if the Volkish win? *We become Volkish slaves.* Because Pyvel already knew. He had been Nashavety's slave in the Breminger Forest. Under creature control, he had served her bowls of soup, the only thing she could eat in the days when she recovered from the maiming of her hand. When she turned to the dark arts to regrow it.

The Volkish officer who had defected gave everyone new hope. He had spoken with Anastyna, suggesting that there might be a way to offer the Volkish army an alternate leadership: Duke Tanfred. The captain had claimed that some in the enemy ranks were dissatisfied and would follow new leadership. But could Yevliesza find a passage to bring the duke safely past the heavily guarded crossings? It would have to be a backway path. Amazingly, she had done it once before. No wonder Anastyna wanted to control her.

But even with Duke Tanfred standing as an alternative, many of the enemy soldiers were likely to stay loyal. They believed that some blood ran finer and braver than other blood, and that the Volkish had a destiny to rule. To teach them differently with sword and shield was Numinat's destiny.

The thought of Pyvel dying on the battlefield was painful to him. But so much was uncertain. Whether Nashavety's plan was for Sofiyana to surrender. Whether Osta Kiya might fight in defiance of Sofiyana. Whether Alfan Sih and Nubiah joined them.

He yearned to see Yevliesza one last time before the fight. He had promised to find her again, a thing said out of longing, not logic. They had divergent paths. But he would not give up, even if Volkia's vast army stood between them.

A few drops of rain came in on the wind as the clouds threw sudden shadow over the hill country.

"The horse unit are fierce fighters," Pyvel said, perhaps bolstering his courage. He had been in battle and could have few delusions about it. This time he would carry his officer's extra weapons. Valenty knew that Pyvel wanted to bear a sword. His own sword.

"In the fight, you are not to expose yourself needlessly. You are there to serve Captain Nikander."

"Unless he falls?"

"Then you serve another lord. We will all be there." He waited for agreement.

"Yes, lord." Said without conviction.

Someone was coming up the trail from the camp. Grigeni, carrying something.

"You came without your cloak," he said, gasping from the climb. He shook out the cloak as the first wave of rain hit the summit.

Grigeni was fussing over Valenty. But his arrow wound was healing well, the one he received when he escaped from the city-palace. With Yevliesza's help. "I have stood in the rain before," Valenty said as he secured the cape at his neck.

"And never died of it," Grigeni allowed, smiling.

Grigeni took his duties as steward seriously. Previously, at Osta Kiya, he had been Valenty's Keeper of Books while serving in his circle of spies. Now his boots were muddy, his black hair rank with sweat, and his clothes torn and several times patched. But he still made efforts at decorum.

Together, the three of them went down the hillside, pelted by fat drops of rain.

❧

Anastyna sat with two female soldiers, plying needle craft. It almost looked like the old days at the palace, except she wore a re-sized man's shirt and a wool skirt, and her ladies wore army trousers and tunics. Her residence was a hut built of logs and thatch that was lit with thick tallow candles, sending shadows skittering whenever someone moved.

Valenty sat to keep her company. It had become her habit to sit with him in the mornings, sometimes with her women who were working on an embroidered hem for some garment or other.

"You should learn to wield a needle," Anastyna murmured,

jamming her own into the cloth and then looking annoyed that it disappeared from sight.

"Me, lady?" he asked in amusement.

"What other amusement do you have? No women, no strolls on the parapets of Osta Kiya, no gossip."

"There is always gossip."

"Then tell us the gossip." She still searched for the needle that had fallen through.

One of her attendants, the round-faced one with skin the color of mahogany, smiled at the prospect of gossip. Smiled at Valenty. He smiled back, then checked himself. Nothing was going to begin there. He was not sure if he was sworn to Yevliesza or mourned her, but the result was the same. He would not be with another.

"Someone saw nine crows on a tree limb," Valenty said, "and claims we will have victory."

Anastyna looked amused. "Did the crows speak?"

He felt a smile cut into one of his cheeks. "Apparently it was *as though* they had spoken."

"Who saw this omen?" she asked. An attendant handed her a new needle, threaded, so Anastyna could start again.

"Gavril, a helper at the iron forge. He has a fondness for his ale, ale as weak as—" He amended *horse piss* to *water*.

"Well, then," Anastyna said, putting on a forlorn expression. "You deprive us of our omen." She set her cloth aside and caught his eye. "Do you think, Valenty, that our servant in the Haiga"—how she sometimes referred to Yevliesza—"will be able to bring our friend home?" *Our friend* being Tanfred. A question that was much on everyone's mind.

"We will soon know." Yevliesza would surely try, now that they had a chance to establish Tanfred as the prince in exile. Or duke in exile.

"We have a claim on him," Anastyna said. "We gave him safe haven once. When he arrives, he must come to my side, not Sofiyana's. One might send a messenger to the Haiga making this clear."

Valenty did not want her thinking along these lines. If Tanfred chose to remain with Yevliesza, it would stoke Anastyna's hostility. "He must make his own judgment, do you not think?"

"No, I do not think! Such an ally could inspire warriors to come to my side. If polities of importance see the duke at my side, the dam will burst, and our ranks will swell." She pinned him with a gaze, asking sarcastically, "Do you not think?"

"A major ally could commit at any moment. Your reputation does not need Duke Tanfred."

Anastyna stabbed the needle down, dissatisfied with his answer. "As well, our servant of the Haiga should accompany our friend. She would find protection with us. She has too great a role to play to be camping in the marshes and eating fish." Anastyna motioned for her women to leave, and they did so after stoking the central fire, which had begun to sputter from the rain coming in from the smoke hole.

"Valenty," Anastyna began when the women had left. "You could persuade her."

She was not going to leave this. "My lady, she no longer listens to me. She knows me for your man."

"Jealous, then? Of her princip?"

"Suspicious, rather."

"Of me," Anastyna said, defiant, daring him to confirm it.

"No, my lady. Of me. We could wish her to be here. But she wants freedom to test the crossings. How much they can stand of interruption, and how much the underpinnings can bear. And if we press her too hard—"

"Then we make of her an enemy," Anastyna said, frowning.

Rain sputtered in the firepit, bringing the smell of charred wood and soggy ash.

"Perhaps," Anastyna mused, "she already is."

❧

ALL MORNING YEVLIESZA AND CAPTAIN BRANDT HAD BEEN PORING over a map showing Duke Tanfred's hiding place in Volkia. With no better material at hand, the map was sketched on deer skin.

The map showed Rothsvund Palace, the Danstree River, and the flats to the south of the city. Yevliesza knew that palace, that river. She had bleak memories of them.

The Volkish captain said, "Hapsigen was built where it was because of the Danstree River. It offers both a barrier to an attack on Rothsvund Palace and access to transport. For us, though, it is a disadvantage." He pointed at the map he had drawn with charcoal. "The ground is marshy and flat, affording few hiding places, and the mud and standing water require a circuitous route to any destination."

The captain wished to be called by his given name, and she had readily agreed. After the several hours they had spent together working out plans, she felt comfortable with him. With his obvious love of his kingdom and its people. With his determination to help Duke Tanfred and carry on the work of the brave men who had died trying to save Volkia.

Arman was sharp-featured and lanky and younger-looking than his thirty-five years, his skin very fair and his hair a shade of brown, very like the deer skin on which he had drawn the map. The blue eyes bothered her, since they were so much like Prince Albrecht's. A man could not help the color of his eyes, but neither could she avoid imagining her tormentor when she sat so close to Arman Brandt.

He pointed to the map. "Here is a grove of trees, what we call the Keider Woods."

They were working on her idea that she might determine a direction for a crossing route if she could picture in her mind the desired destination. Arman had tried his best to describe the area where Tanfred was holed up—specifically in the house of one Danzman Keller—but however fine his descriptions, they could not be sure that her own picture of the landscape was a close approximation.

Arman went on. "There is more than one stand of trees near the city. If we break through wrongly—"

The sound of voices outside signaled someone approaching.

Zander's voice at the tent flap: "Keeper, it is the Lord Warden."

When Kirady came in, she saw a stern expression on his face. She and Arman rose to greet him.

"A problem in the camp," Kirady told her, nodding at Arman. "Ryura," he said wearily. "She had a group of about a hundred gathered on the other side of the west ridge. We asked them to disperse, and she became disruptive."

"People can get together. They don't need permission," Yevliesza pointed out, though she did feel annoyed.

"She was talking about you, more of her nonsense. And she was hiding, or why go behind the ridge? Now we have a couple of mothers who are asking to see you for advice or healing, or whatever they think they can get from you." Kirady held her gaze. "It has to stop. Women and children have no place here. This is a fortified camp, not a school for pilgrims."

"What do you want to do?" Yevliesza asked, not really wanting to hear, but knowing that Kirady was accustomed to leading and was good at it.

"Escort her back to Branova," he said. "Make it clear she has lost favor."

Ryura would be unhappy, but she had brought it on herself. "It's your decision, my lord. Of course."

He left to take care of it.

"Who is this Ryura woman?" Arman asked.

"She's someone who saw that I was spending time with a wise woman, what we call a *providez*. She got it into her head that I had entered the Mist Wall and seen the dead." She caught his look. "Which I definitely did not."

"So she is rousing people to believe you can help them. Save them."

"Something like that."

Arman was silent for a moment. "I can see how people might think so. Am I not doing the same?"

Well. The difference was that Ryura had lost touch with reality. Still, she felt a pang at the thought of shaming her this way.

They went back to their map. Yevliesza tried very hard to visualize the area where Duke Tanfred was hiding, but she had never seen much of the lands around Rothsvund Palace where she had been held.

Later, she stopped by Dreiza and Kassalya's tent.

"I'm leaving tomorrow," Yevliesza said. "For a little while."

Kassalya was sitting cross-legged on the cot doing stitchery work. Dreiza gestured for Yevliesza to sit on the storage chest they had traveled with. She did not ask where Yevliesza was going. She knew where. The cave.

"You are concerned about something," Dreiza said, right as usual.

"I'd like to ask Kassalya something."

Kassalya, hearing her name, glanced up and then returned to her stitchery.

"Yes, of course," Dreiza said.

She might not receive an answer. But Yevliesza had thought of a way to ask how things would turn out. A way that might not trigger Kassalya's sometimes unbearable visions.

"Kassalya, may I ask you a question?"

"Most people do not like to know," the girl said, taking a stitch in the fabric.

"But, for me," Yevliesza insisted, "if you see something, I would like to know."

Still, the stitchery. "Ask."

"In the future, how will people judge me? Am I regarded well or badly? What do people say?" It was not a trivial question. It was a way of finding out how the use of her powers would turn out.

Yevliesza and Dreiza waited for her to answer. They could not tell whether Kassalya was trying to see the future or not. She was quite calm, and that boded well. By asking what people would say, she spared Kassalya some of the terrors of the future and might discover what her legacy would be.

"Nothing," Kassalya finally said.

"You see nothing?"

Kassalya's bright eyes flashed in the candlelight. "I see." She put down her needle and cloth. "People say nothing of you. It is as though you did not exist. Very few people will think of you."

So much for her clever question. Depending how far you looked into the future, everyone eventually was forgotten. Even heroes were buried in time. And horribly destructive people.

Dreiza's forehead wrinkled in concentration. "It is not about your death."

Or it might be. But people would still have opinions about those who—alive or not—had been at the hinge of events.

Kassalya said again, "People say nothing of you."

Dreiza looked at Yevliesza with concern. But Yevliesza squeezed her hand reassuringly. She was content. She had wanted to know if people would despise her for bringing some calamity to the Mythos. But no one would remember.

Of course, it could also mean that no one was left to condemn the past. No one was left to say anything about her.

Chapter Thirteen

Yevliesza set out the next morning for Arrow Shaft, riding into a region of moor-covered hills. Rusadka and Arman rode with her, along with five guards. The vault of the sky was a luminous blue as a hawk skimmed over the low hills, watching for prey.

Rusadka rode by Yevliesza's side, having said goodbye to Elivasa, who would continue her journey, telling of Sofiyana's ensorcellment and urging the polities to join Anastyna.

Rusadka broke a long silence. "She had to go."

Both of them apparently thinking of Ryura. "Yes." Yevliesza supposed it had to be done. "If she will stay away."

"She will. Kirady's men took her hair."

"Her hair?"

"They shaved her head. She has been shamed."

Yevliesza bit her lip in dismay.

Rusadka added, "It is our way."

Yevliesza knew that there was no answering a Numinasi who brought up *our way*.

Rusadka looked up, frowning at something in the sky. A large bird. More birds trailed behind.

"*Strigoi!*" Arman shouted.

The mass of creatures was heading straight for them. Rusadka jumped from her mount and hauled Yevliesza off Mitri. Ostov rushed to Yevliesza's side, pushing her down and casting a warding over her just as the first demon bird swooped at her. Ostov's warding held, and one of her soldiers lunged at a creature, which flapped away, avoiding his sword. The air was now full of leathery wings and screeching demons. She cowered at Ostov's feet. Her companions fought off the beasts as they repeatedly dove at Yevliesza. Flecks of blood hit the ground around them.

Rusadka, Arman, and the soldiers hacked at the creatures with swords but were hampered by the bunching *strigoi*, and only a few thrusts landed home. Yevliesza heard an enraged scream from Mitri. He rose on his hind legs and stomped on a demon bird, his huge hooves breaking open the creature's chest. He lunged at another, biting its face off.

A demon fell upon Ostov, clinging to his back. Ostov cried out and staggered away from her where she crouched. In dismay, Yevliesza tried to think of how to help, but she could do little, armed only with a knife. The sound of combat, of grunts and shouts and the screams of horses, filled the air.

She wondered if she would die, if they all would, her friends and guards. And if she had somehow brought these beasts to them. She thought of Valenty. *Valenty.*

Ostov had gone to his knees, bleeding from his head. Rusadka stepped in, straddling Yevliesza, her sword held high and back, waiting for the onslaught. "To me!" she cried.

Arman's voice: "Begone! Fly on, I conjure you! Fly on!"

He had creature control, and it might have given the *strigoi* pause. The one on Ostov's back released its hold. As a group, the *strigoi* jumped into the air—she looked up and could see them flapping wildly amid the slashing of swords, swords that struck down a few as they rose into flight. They rushed away but already were wheeling around to return.

Arman called to Zander, "Manifesting! The likeness of a dactyl!" He spun around. "Who has manifesting?"

Yevliesza saw Zander standing still, concentrating. An image wavered in the air: broad wings and a long neck with a crest on the head, scales shimmering. It was faint but unmistakably a dactyl. An enormous one. At this vision, the horses panicked and charged away.

Now the *strigoi* came again. The leading demon dove for her. She met its eyes, paralyzed by its notice, but it faltered as the dactyl image raised its head and snapped at the air. Veering away, the blood bird flapped into the air.

The rest of the swarm followed and sped down the valley.

Silence fell over the group. Yevliesza was gripping a tussock of grass, her hand the only part of her body she could feel. She looked at the grass in her fist, the handful she had pulled from the ground. Tendrils of green and yellow. She would live after all. Grass, the valley, the vault of the clear sky—it was all as it had been moments before except for six wounded and dead *strigoi*. The wounded ones were quickly dispatched.

Seven soldiers, including Rusadka and Arman, had fought off the attack. One of their soldiers was dead, and Ostov wounded. The rest of the group stood protecting Yevliesza, waiting for the next onslaught, but the *strigoi* had disappeared into the hills. The only horse that had not bolted was Mitri.

Arman and Zander had saved them.

Rusadka wiped her blade clean on her trousers. "Now I believe you, Arman Brandt," she said to the Volkish captain.

Arman gave her a curt nod in acknowledgment. *Harjat* did not apologize. Not that her comment was an apology.

As he helped Yevliesza to her feet, she shook the dust from her clothes. "You have a very loyal horse," he said.

"That's Mitri," she replied. "He's not afraid of anything."

She thought of the screams, the blood, the shrieking of the demon birds. She had known sheer terror in the attack. Terror was different from fear, somehow it was. Terror was the stoppage of time, the gripping of the good earth, the farewells.

Rusadka was at her side. "It is over," she said, almost gently. "You are well?"

"Yes," Yevliesza managed to say.

They looked into the sky in the direction of the saddle of the hills to the north. Nothing. For now, at least.

She and Rusadka went to Ostov. One of the soldiers was cutting away his shirt to examine his shoulder, which was bleeding heavily. "How bad is it?" she asked Ostov.

"Bastard bit me," he said, wincing as the soldier pulled the fabric away. Ostov added, "But I still have my arm, mistress." As though he could still fight. But he wouldn't be wielding a sword for a while.

One of the men set out on Mitri to round up the horses.

A soldier's body lay crumpled nearby. Yevliesza asked Rusadka, "What was that man's name?"

"Alaric. Sworn to Lord Kirady." His throat was ripped out, and blood pooled around him. "We will bring his body back to Haiga camp."

They had barely beaten off the demons with seven fighters. Now, two fewer would be in their group.

"I will return to camp with the body," Rusadka said.

"And bring more fighters?" Arman guessed. The *strigoi* were loose and might come back.

She nodded. "We all move quickly. I will take the chestnut mare, a light horse and fast. By the time you emerge from Arrow Shaft, forty warriors will be there to greet you."

Until then, Zander had a noble power of manifesting, and Arman had creature power, so they were not without weapons.

When the horses were herded back, the men tied the guard's body onto Rusadka's horse. Before she mounted, she turned to Yevliesza. "They came for *you*, you know."

She was right, they had. Somehow, she had attracted them. Or someone had sent them.

"How do they find me?" Yevliesza asked.

"Exactly what I am wondering," her friend said, looking into the sky. She glanced back at Yevliesza. "Try not to get into any more trouble while I am gone."

Just that much lightheartedness made all the difference. She wanted to hug Rusadka, but of course she wouldn't.

⁂

VALENTY WALKED THROUGH THE CAMP TAKING NOTE OF THE DAMAGE from the morning's windstorm. A new carpet of pine needles, deadfall from the surrounding trees, a hat stuck in a fallen branch, a bowl shattered against a firepit.

Gusts tugged at his cape, but they were stragglers compared to the storm winds.

The camp was beginning to look like an army, with a thousand trained soldiers as well as hundreds of men from towns and villages answering the call to arms. Still, Anastyna hoped for more. She wanted the polities to join her and not Sofiyana. And some had. But others did not believe the stories of sorcery, or they saw Osta Kiya's overwhelming force of nearly five thousand and would join the strongest army.

Valenty returned through the encampment to his bivouac. Arriving, he found Grigeni standing by the heap of Valenty's lean-to, a jumble of horse blankets and saplings.

He was shaking his hawklike face, thin and earnest. "Your bed, lord," he said forlornly. It had taken Grigeni days to construct it, and though it had survived the night, the morning gusts must have done it in.

"I hope the water bucket survived."

Grigeni looked at a puddle rapidly disappearing into a mud hole. "Alas."

Valenty did not ask nor expect Grigeni to act as his man under wartime conditions, but Grigeni was not cut out for a rough life, and he held firmly to his former role as steward.

"I do not need to sleep under a tent. The open air will do."

"It would not be seemly, lord, and you are recovering." Valenty's wound had created an excuse for Grigeni to get back into the life he once had: serving a high lord of Osta Kiya.

"I will fetch more water," Valenty said, picking up the bucket. He saw Grigeni open his mouth to object and stared pointedly at him. *This far and no farther.* Grigeni well understood his meaning.

As he made his way to the creek, a shout came from within the camp. A horn blew. At the sound, Valenty ran back to camp, as fighters grabbed weapons and men dashed for their horses. Stopping by his campsite, Valenty grabbed his sword. He told Grigeni to follow him, and they both ran toward the massing of their fighting force.

Captain Lysandry's defense was forming up on the slope to the ridge where Anastyna's domicile stood, with the first line arrayed on the flats in a dense half-circle composed of a hundred of the strongest fighters.

Valenty found one of the scouts standing by his horse, white with sweat. "Who is it?" he demanded.

"Hundreds, lord, flying banners, but at that distance we could not tell their symbols. They are coming fast, but still out on the plains."

"On foot or horseback?"

"Riding, lord. And foot soldiers behind."

Grigeni had caught up to him. "It may be a fight," Valenty told him.

"Your leathers!" Grigeni cried, remembering. "Still at the lean-to." At Valenty's nod, he raced back for them.

Valenty brought his horse from the paddock and joined Captain Lysandry and Urik, who were conferring.

Lysandry turned to Valenty. "They fly the banners of the towns of Dvegda, lord. But if they were sent by Osta Kiya, we will stop them."

"They are outmatched," Urik said. On the left flank of the front lines, his *harjat* unit were mounted, flying their banner of black and yellow "If they come to fight, they will parley first."

Grigeni brought Valenty's hardened leather tunic, and he shrugged into it, wincing at the movement.

Anastyna's forces waited. The fighters were silent, hoping for friends but ready for foes. Horses stomped and bridles clinked. In back of them, sunlight broke over the ridge. Out on the prairie, Valenty could see flashes of light off metal spears and helmets.

With Anastyna's forces arrayed for battle, the mass of approaching soldiers stopped well back. Two men came forward alone. Urik and Lysandry mounted their horses and rode to meet them.

Anastyna was making her way through her soldiers. She was mounted on a dappled gray mare with a decent saddle, the leather polished as bright as chicken grease could make it.

Then all four of the soldiers parleying came back together, and Valenty knew the fighters had come to join them.

Valenty accompanied Anastyna as she rode forward.

"My Lady Princip," Lysandry said as they moved forward with the two men who came to parley, "these nobles and village masters come to offer service of their combined six hundred men. To represent them, the lord Dorofey and village master Genrikh."

Anastyna nodded to them. "You are most welcome." She cocked her head at the massed soldiers behind her. "We thought Volkia had ceased their cowering and come to make trouble." She smiled at them, dazzling the two leaders. "We have little here," she admitted, "but we will gladly share what we have."

"My Lady Princip," said Dorofey, a large man with a bald head and heavy beard, "we have brought wagons of supplies, and they are at your disposal."

Anastyna accepted the title as her due and, with Valenty and Lysandry at her side, led the group into camp.

Valenty felt her optimism, saw it in the set of her shoulders and the confidence in her face. He shared it. The true princip now had thirteen hundred fighters as well as fresh food and supplies. It was little enough compared with Sofiyana, but for now, Anastyna was happy.

Chapter Fourteen

Nashavety felt a turning of events. After blockage, things were about to move. All the pieces she had put in place. Thwarted for a time and now rushing toward a triumphant culmination.

She had once been a banished citizen, stripped of honor and possessions, her left hand defiled. Now she was strong and obeyed by the leader of Volkia. Numinat had been outraged by the *strigoi* slaughter at Lowgate and vowed retaliation. They were welcome to try. She had the largest army in the Mythos. Add to all this, Strigo might have by now dispensed with the girl of the mundat. If not, Sofiyana would have her in custody. Of course one could not trust Sofiyana to contain a rabbit in a cage—the girl was adept at losing prisoners—and so the raiding party had been told to kill Yevliesza the moment they were out of sight of her followers.

She might even be dying at this moment. A satisfying prospect.

Soon there would be a great contest on the plains of Numinat. The princip would surrender, but the commander might not obey. It was even possible that Nubiah might fight its way through the crossings and add its thousands to the fray. But neither Numinat nor Nubiah had an iron army that could break through the strongest defense and mow down ranks of soldiers. Nashavety would be there to witness the greatest battle ever seen.

Of course, she would not be merely a witness.

She would wield her powers to assure victory over the erring Numinasi. Volkia would maneuver the Osta Kiyan army onto the Plain of Monuments in the great flatlands. When the kingdoms met, it would be in the place where the spire rose from the plains like the fist of a buried god awakened. It was there that she would draw upon an ancient pool of darkness and channel its strengths, amplifying her powers.

Thank you, Mother, she thought. When her birthright powers had first come into her, it had been in that place of monumental energy. Her mother had brought her there, and they had stayed for weeks, fasting in the merciless sun and sleeping under the stars. And when her powers filled her, even her mother was afraid, looking at her daughter as though she did not recognize her. Returning to Osta Kiya, she had not lived long. Perhaps she had not wanted to, seeing what she had created.

But thanks were due, and Nashavety gave them. For everything that was to come. The salvation of Numinat, rescued from ideas that sapped the strength of her people. Ideas championed by Anastyna, that weak and wretched princip. Anastyna's crowning lunacy: bringing to the kingdom Liesa of Barstow County, styled Yevliesza for a time, and then Keeper.

Yevliesza would keep nothing. And Numinat would not keep her, either.

❧

"As you see, my lady," Commander Ilyan said, nodding at the men in the front line of the massed soldiers, "our troops are the finest in the Mythos." With the man's girth, Sofiyana pitied his horse. But Ilyan was also powerfully built, with an impressive beard, and she was a little intimidated by him.

Sofiyana rode beside the commander, reviewing the assembled army. In a dazzling blue sky, clouds raced westward as though fleeing the Volkish hordes. The troops stood at attention, the only sounds the clink of bridles and the snap of standards in the wind.

Until now, she had avoided any appearance before the troops, suspecting that she was not popular and not wishing any proof of it. In her stead, she would have sent the *fajatim*, the five women who could make or depose a princip, but they had stayed at Osta Kiya. Perhaps fomenting mischief. But in a few more days it would not matter what the *fajatim* did. The kingdom would change hands; not given to the Volkish, but to Nashavety, who would rule independent of, but a friend to, Volkia.

Sofiyana nodded to the men turned out for the inspection. She would rather be in her tent, but tonight was the festival of the Horse Moon, and a measure of royal largesse was in order.

She waited for news of Yevliesza's capture, since five days ago forty soldiers had ridden for the Haiga marshes to arrest her. She hoped it would not be an occasion for bloodshed. Nashavety knew the soldiers were on their way. But still, the mold on her fingers had not subsided.

Flexing her left hand in its riding glove, she tried to convince herself that it did not hurt. If anything, a brief stab. The black growths around her nails had now moved into the tips of her fingers. Soon it would subside. When she convinced Nashavety that she was truly loyal.

Ilyan led her down the line of soldiers. They were clean-shaven, with helmets, shields, swords, and polished mail. In their midst, the pennant of Osta Kiya, red with a white circle, symbol of unity and the princip's torc. The men in front seemed proud to be under her standard, and the men in the next row as well. But behind she discerned less friendly faces. The massive group made her feel small and exposed. Her army, stretching onto the plain.

"How many of our force have swords, Commander?" She knew some of the men were nothing but farmers and laborers, bearing only truncheons, staves, and hoes.

"Half of the newcomers. But among them are archers we can deploy to great effect."

All these details Nashavety would be privy to, but Sofiyana's mistress seemed more keen on Yevliesza than the battle. Osta Kiya faced overwhelming numbers. Perhaps Nashavety could not imagine they would be much of a barrier to conquest. Even if they did fight. And if they fought, it would mean that Sofiyana had lost control. She clenched her left hand, wincing at the pain.

Ahead, someone on horseback approached. One of Ilyan's officers. He stopped beside them. "My lord," the man said to the commander. To Sofiyana, a respectful nod. "We have a report from the men who returned from the marshes, sir. They did not find the fugitive."

"What?" Sofiyana cried. Her dismay leaked out despite her effort to hide it.

"We will hear more of this," Ilyan said, his face rigid with displeasure. "In my pavilion." When the officer rode off, Ilyan said, "They were not to return without her. And they were to arrest Warden Kirady as well."

In Ilyan's tent, a man with stinking leathers and a dust-filled beard stood before them. No officer, but one of the unit sent to the marshes. An officer pushed him forward.

"Where are the people you were to apprehend?" Ilyan demanded.

"Lord Commander, the rat-scum went over to the warden of Eiger Polity. Twenty-four of them. Your sworn men stood with Warden Kirady and dared us to interfere."

The report continued, but it came from a distance. Sofiyana was far away from the words, a small animal hiding in grass as a wolf's shadow loomed. It was as though she watched the bearded man from another world.

Ilyan looked at the other soldier present, one of his captains, who asked the soldier, "You left without a fight?"

"It was sixteen of us left, sir. He outnumbered us."

Ilyan snapped, "And you did not see the girl of House Valenty?"

"She was not there. They showed us her empty tent. She may have been hiding, but we could not search for her."

Back in her tent, Sofiyana paced the confined space. The news, black and suffocating. The attempt had failed, but it was not her fault!

Yevliesza had a force of soldiers and was not even in the camp. Sofiyana could not be faulted this time, this time when she had sent a war party. But the wolf's shadow crept closer.

Her left hand grew unbearably hot inside her glove. She ripped it off. And stared. The black mildew on two of her fingers now covered the first joints, and each finger had its cap of mold. It brought a warm pulse of rot to her nose. Hiding her hand in her riding skirt, she rolled up the glove so that its smell did not pervade the tent. She must bury the glove, because surely the stench was not coming from her hand. It would not be fair. Her people had failed her, but she had tried.

Nashavety would understand, would she not? Or at least give her another chance. Yes, another chance.

৩৯৩

Yevliesza walked with her two companions in the cramped backways of the crossroads. Each of them had their role. Zander as bodyguard. Arman, the one who would enter the new tunnel. Yevliesza, the one who would create it.

They maintained silence. Yevliesza concentrated on the crossings displayed in her mind-map, scrutinizing the network as they walked.

The air was warm and close, rich with its yeasty smell, so different from a tunnel of mud and stone. It was not a tunnel, but a root. She liked to think of it as such. It grew. It lived, in some sense. And her power, her strongest power, was to cultivate it.

Zander and Arman both had short swords and knives. There would be no room for slicing with a sword, but they could stab. Yevliesza had a knife strapped to her ankle. She would be little help in a fight, but she had once used a knife efficiently against the dark prince of Volkia.

Here in the crossings, the first thing was to detect aligns. An align, she had decided, was the likely way to create a path. Maybe the only way. And there *were* aligns here, small, incandescent lines that crisscrossed the tunnels. And, as well, aligns along the paths themselves. These surged most brightly, which was probably why she had not noticed the other, tangential, lines before. When she had formed a new route to Alfan Sih for Prince Tirhan, an align must have been present. Maybe, being new to the crossings at the time, it had escaped her perception. Now she hunted the fainter lines.

"Anything?" Arman whispered. He was tense, determined to do this good thing for his country. In the twilight of the crossings, he looked sallow, with his pale Volkish skin, his light brown hair.

"I do see some. Only a few." But not only did she see aligns, with some amazement, she clearly perceived where they went. So far, none entered Volkia.

Zander squinted, trying to see the invisible things they were talking about. She wondered if anyone else who had align power could also see the destinations or if it was a property of the ninth power.

As she opened herself to detecting where the aligns went, a curious thought arose: What did the aligns pass through to arrive in one kingdom or another? What was outside of the crossings? She had never heard anyone discuss this. But . . . a distraction. For now, she must concentrate on every align she passed.

Once she found an align that went to Volkia, their hope was that she could influence its direction—bend it—toward the area near Tanfred's hiding place. She would keep Arman's map and his vivid descriptions firmly in mind. Especially the Keider Woods, which were, Arman said, very close to Tanfred's refuge. It might not be impossible to influence an align by visualizing a specific place, but Arman's optimism was infectious, and she felt it had a real chance.

Every few minutes she stopped, closing her eyes to better perceive the crossing layout. The tunnels, strangely empty except for heavy guard units at every gate. Though her internal map had never been wrong, it was still unnerving to walk in the twisting back routes. Every time she turned into another path, she felt a spike of nerves at what might be there. Thinking of the maze in Holdfast, she knew how suddenly nothing could turn into *something*.

A line snapped into view. Like a wire, hot as embers. She halted, staring. The align slanted from one wall of the pathway into the wall opposite.

"Volkia," she whispered. "This one." She met Arman's hopeful gaze. Reaching for the align with her left hand, she traced the line with her finger. Her hand twinged with gentle fire. "This one."

"Are you sure?" asked Arman.

"It's Volkia." She and Arman exchanged smiles. They had far to go, but without an align to build on, she could not create a path.

"That's one, then," she said. "We keep looking." They wanted to find at least three and hoped that she could influence one of them, since it already pointed close to the place they needed.

An hour passed, and Yevliesza found only one other Volkia align. The occurrences were rare enough that she decided they should proceed with the aligns they had.

They sat against the tunnel wall, sharing out a meal. Arman would need his strength. He'd be the one to find Tanfred and lead him to safety.

Zander refused to sit. He accepted that Yevliesza could visualize if anyone approached. However, his training was not about belief, but readiness.

When they finished their meal, Yevliesza began her work. She called to mind the way Arman had described the Keider Woods near Hapsigen. She willed a passage to come into being along the align. With a kick of excitement, she felt root power flow through her hand, throbbing and warm. No one spoke as she lost awareness of standing next to the two men.

In moments, the tunnel wall slowly sagged, then fell away. Zander reflexively touched his right hand to his chest, an ancient protective gesture.

A niche formed, then a deep indentation. She pushed on, imagining the align continuing to open. She stretched out her arm, unsure if it helped to do so. With all her heart, she willed a tunnel to form.

As she pushed, the path lengthened, and, as it did, it gained speed. The crackling noise she sometimes heard in the crossings intensified. *What trees would hear if they had that sense. Branches growing, woody stems crackling with life.*

She brought to mind the sketch of the Keider Woods, the nearby

Danstree River, the flat bogland. . . . Time disappeared. The branch grew and grew.

Suddenly, she was through. With a gasp she said, "It's there. Arman, it's open!" She lowered her arm, aching by now from having been tense so long.

He gripped her forearm, and she covered his hand with her own. She had done it. Somehow, she had broken through. And it was, she knew, Volkia.

A draft of cool air hit her face. "Feel that?" she asked her companions.

Zander nodded, proud of her. Arman whispered, "By God, fresh air."

Now they would test whether the path could be used. Whether it was close enough to Tanfred's hiding place. Yevliesza and Zander would remain there. Arman would be the one to follow the route and see where it took him.

He was soon making his way down the passageway.

No tremors. She smiled to herself. It confirmed her new understanding of the crossings. An action of creation was welcome; destruction was not. The tremors were not merely a natural adjustment of the crossing's structure. They were a warning to whoever held the ninth power: do not undercut or destroy. It might be a grand clue to the entire structure of the Mythos. And now she might have a chance to use creation in the fight against the Volkish.

Might. The tunnel could take Arman wildly off target: to the Breminger Forest or Rorrs Gate. The idea of envisioning an exit point might not be correct. They would soon know.

She and Zander silently waited. The crossings were quiet now, the air thick and warm. No convoys moving. No *strigoi* scuttling. She would have liked to talk with Zander. But he wouldn't presume to have a conversation with the Keeper who could alter the crossings and befriend a wraith wolf.

She dozed against the wall. Zander's sudden movement woke her, and she saw him standing with his sword ready.

It was Arman returning. He stepped into the path from which the new tunnel had budded.

He didn't allow himself to look disappointed, but his words dashed her hopes. "A mountainous area," he said. "I did not recognize it, but it would not be close to the duke."

Mountains? And she had worked to imagine the flat plain near Hapsigen.

Retracing their steps, they went back to the first Volkish align she had found. They would try again.

⁂

ON THE SECOND TRY, THE PATH THAT YEVLIESZA CREATED HAD LED TO a field near a large town. It was indeed in Volkia, but not near Hapsigen. It was the city of Fornich, far from their target area. As they sat on the floor of the backways resting, they considered whether to keep at it or try again the next day.

Arman's face was pale in the fey light of the crossings. He had covered miles in his scouting the two pathways, and if next time they succeeded in getting near Tanfred, Arman would need to travel fast, to bring the duke out. No time could be lost, since Volkish patrols either in the crossings or in Volkia might discover the new path. Nor could Yevliesza close any of the paths she had made because these would be acts of destruction, however well meant.

"Are you tired?" she asked Arman.

"No, not tired."

"Rest for a bit," she urged him anyway. Getting to her feet, she told Zander, "I'm going to find a place to relieve myself."

"Not alone," he said.

"Yes, Zander, alone." Reluctantly, he watched her wander off.

Bringing forward her mind-sight of the crossings, she scanned for any nearby movement and, finding none, headed for one of the niches that budded off the pathways.

As she walked back to join Arman and Zander, she rubbed her face, trying to push away her fatigue. Her attempts to visualize specific destinations were not working. It could be that her concentration was faulty, or maybe it was not possible in the first place.

She noted a faint line in the tunnel floor. So very soft, like a golden strand of spider web. Squinting at it, she tried to convince herself that it wasn't just her exhausted eyes finding aligns everywhere. But here was another one that went to Volkia. The thought struck that it should create a path to Rothsvund Palace. It was a place she knew well.

A place she knew well. She stopped to let the idea settle. It would be better to use her own memories of a place, even if they were as dangerous as Rothsvund Palace, the Volkish army headquarters. Her familiarity might not be ideal, but it was stronger than looking at Arman's map. And with any luck, the egress point would be outside the building. She knew the grounds between the palace and the river.

She rushed back. "I can do this," she blurted. "I can do it. Because I was actually there. Near the river. Wandered near the river." When she escaped from Prince Albrecht, that harrowing time when Duke Tanfred and she fled the city. "I met my *sympat* by that river, and I climbed down a vine from a tall window and walked on the rooftop of Rothsvund Palace! I looked around. I saw things!"

Zander looked at her like she was having a breakdown.

Arman slowly got to his feet. "You found a Volkia align, then?" he gently asked.

"Yes. And this time I'm going to put my intention on Rothsvund Palace. Outside it, in the environs." She smiled at Arman. "Have you got one more foray in you?"

"Ready and waiting." He looked at Zander and got a nod. They were all ready.

"Maybe I should come with you," Yevliesza said.

"No," Arman and Zander said at the same time.

"But you don't know the palace as I do. What if the path opens on Nashavety's lair?"

A smile tugged at Arman's mouth. "I pray that it does." Zander smiled wolfishly. Arman went on. "If I judge the locale will work, I'll come here and tell you before I go to the duke. So if in the end I don't make it back, you'll at least know you succeeded."

The thought of his not making it out again sobered her. But he was eager to go.

"Tell Duke Tanfred that . . . that I owe him my life and wish him Godspeed."

"I will."

She led her companions twenty paces into the backways where the tendril of neon light faintly glowed. She turned to her task. *Outside of Rothsvund palace. The sloping ground. The road beside the River Danstree. The tangle of bushes along the perimeter. The outside of the palace. The three-story palace and the great city surrounding it. Rothsvund Palace.*

☙❦❧

ARMAN HAD BEEN GONE OVER AN HOUR. YEVLIESZA PACED IN agitation. Constantly checking her mind-sight of the backways, she walked into areas she had never been before, looking for new aligns and the directions they headed in. Backups. Zander followed her, a few steps behind.

When they returned to the new tunnel, Arman was waiting for them.

"It goes to a church," he said. "A famous one. The Church of All Graces. You did so well, Yevliesza! It is very near Rothsvund Palace."

She had done it. The Church of All Graces, nearly a bullseye. How vivid her memory of that night of her escape, how her carriage raced past the church, the horses' hooves pounding, the church windows lit with the celebration of mass for the soldiers fighting on foreign soil. The church where Albrecht sat among his black-uniformed officers praying for total domination and planning to see Yevliesza in little more than an hour for a private celebration of his own.

The church was where her mind had gone when she thought of the palace environs. The most notable feature of the entire city of Hapsigen. All Graces!

Arman went on. "But it leads inside the church. In the vault below the nave. And there is a service going on at the moment."

Oh God. So very like the night of her heart-pounding flight through the city.

"There is no exit from the vault other than upstairs through the church proper," Arman said. "I will have to wait below until the service is over, and even then it may not be completely empty. Add that wait to the time for me to get the duke and make my way back."

"And the damaged crypt could be discovered," she finished. She looked at Zander.

He said, "I could bring soldiers to go with Captain Brandt."

"It is tempting," Arman told him. "But several people are more suspicious than two." He shrugged. "It is nighttime, at least."

Yevliesza had lost track of time. Night would help.

"If I am to go, it must be now."

She knew he was right. Zander handed him the last of their water in a skin.

Yevliesza nodded. "We'll wait for you."

"Near Arrow Shaft," he reminded her. "Not here." In case of Volkish sentries in the backways.

"Not here, but when I perceive you in the backways, when I see the *two* of you, I'll come and get you."

"God willing," Arman said softly. And then he was gone.

Chapter Fifteen

By moonlight, the Alfan Sih village of Abergaer looked peaceful, snug between a spine of hills and the Gwerlech river. Though small, the village thrived on river trade, cargoes of wool cloth, medicinals, and the north region's apples and pears. And now, silverwood.

"Not many cookfires," Lord Inian said as he scanned their target. He lay on the hilltop next to Tirhan and Morwen, his warriors behind them in the vale. Inian was young to be lord of Mid Daihinn clan, but he had been decisive in siding with Tirhan instead of with Tirhan's now open rival, Gryffyd.

"Many are billeted in the houses," Tirhan said.

"Our scouts say there are seventy-three soldiers," Morwen said.

With Inian's fighters, Tirhan had nearly that number, but they would not engage the Volkish in the open. Over the days since the vision of the warrior in helmet and mail, Tirhan had split his best archers into three groups and sent them to scout the nearest silverwood groves, hunting for any infested with Volkish woodcutters. It was Morwen who urged him to attack Abergaer, one of the main shipping points for silverwood logs heading for Lliatern Gate.

Demyr, Tirhan's second-in-command, had sent two men into the village in the last of the daylight to count the boats. They reported four at the single loading dock and seven more beached or secured alongside others. Attacking this dock meant firing one ship heavy with silverwood logs. The wood was so dense it would not catch fire, but the boat would, and the tree trunks would sink into the river, depriving the enemy of their value.

Tirhan would set the fires, taking only Demyr and Morwen with him. Demyr was a big man, barrel-chested and muscular, and could throw a spear farther than anyone Tirhan had ever seen. Morwen would use her strong warding power to protect them. It was a risk. But everything they did was a risk. If they wanted to protect the silverwood groves, firing their transport ships could hurt the Volkish ability to profit from the desecration.

By the light of a crescent moon, Tirhan, Demyr, and Morwen moved down the hillside toward the river. In the thick woods, they lost sight of the village. Their footfalls loomed large in Tirhan's ears. They watched for soldiers, but the Volkish would not post men so far into the woods. The only sentries were two owls, exchanging cries from one tree to another.

The three of them carried several sacks of thatch soaked in tar. Demyr would fire the first one with elemental power, and they would light the other sacks by the first one. Then all they would need was a few good throws and a true aim. With seven boats beached close together or tied alongside, not all the bundles needed to hit home, but they brought enough sacks to hurry the conflagration.

They threaded their way into the village, evading widely spaced sentries, and moved to within sight of the dock. Three guards. An even match. When Demyr and Morwen were in position near their assigned men, Morwen loosed her hair from its tie and strolled up to one of them. The guard paused just long enough to leave himself open for her knife thrust. At the same time, Tirhan and Demyr slit the throats of the other two.

The sound of a door slamming in the village. The raiding party hurriedly lit three sacks from Demyr's elemental flame. The pitch caught fast. Demyr gave a great heave of his burning sack, landing it in the farthest boat, the silverwood boat. Morwen brought her torch to the ship on the dock, while Tirhan cast his burning sack into another boat. The fires burned hot, but remained small until an explosion aboard one of the nearest boats spread the fire to the benches and whatever cargo lay athwart them.

Shouts from the village. Men were running down the narrow paths to the shore. Tirhan saw that they did not have time to fade into the woods. And now they were seen, with little chance of outrunning their pursuers.

"Here!" Morwen called. The docked boats were afire, but one less so than the others. She untied the bowline that bound the vessel to a cleat.

"With Morwen!" Tirhan cried to Demyr, and the two of them raced to the dock. Demyr severed the stern line and jumped into the belly of the boat, grabbing an oar. With Morwen and Tirhan right behind him, he gave a mighty heave of the oar against the dock.

They were now on a burning boat, but one that still had oars and oarlocks. Tirhan and Demyr sat on the bench farthest from the fire, while Morwen was pouring water on the flames with a bailing pan, but with little effect.

Behind them, the boats were fully engulfed, the fire driven by the explosion. Tirhan watched the silhouettes of men milling on the shore trying to salvage the boat with the silverwood cargo, but already its keel was eaten through, and the boat tipped stern first into the river, weighed down by the heavy logs.

It was then that Tirhan saw that the soldiers on the shore were fighting. Inian had brought the partisans to cover his escape. *No,* Tirhan thought. He had never meant them to engage the enemy sword to sword.

As he watched the fight, his boat caught the current and was underway.

The river carried them, the fire amidships lighting their way, glazing the water molten yellow. They raced into the night, expecting at any moment to have to abandon the boat as the vessel listed to one side. Tirhan and Demyr used the oars to push off from the boulders jutting up as they passed.

"Can you swim?" Tirhan shouted at Demyr. He and Morwen could.

"Yes, lord!"

The river was not broad, but it was strewn with boulders and floating logs.

Morwen clawed her way back to the two men, shrinking from the fire that had already singed her hair. She pointed toward the shore. "Sandbar!" she shouted over the fire's roar.

It was on the far side of the river from the village and provided their best chance of escape. "Swim for it!" Tirhan ordered them. Morwen stood, ready to jump.

Demyr struggled to use an oar, thrusting it into the river and using all his weight and strength to find purchase on the river bottom to swerve the boat closer. He made a last push, and Morwen jumped free of the ship. Tirhan and Demyr followed.

Morwen was the first to reach the sandbar, followed by Tirhan, who dragged Demyr with him, for the man had lied and was no swimmer. They lay on the bank of sand, gasping for breath. Their boat sailed on, now engulfed with wildly dancing flames, illuminating the fir trees on both shores with a snapping, brutish light.

They had no time to lose. At least some Volkish would be pursuing them on horseback and would easily see them where they stood. They were able to wade across the smallest arm of the river split by the sandbar and scramble up the bank, grabbing tussocks of grass to climb into a patch of brambles. They crouched, resting from the river's challenge.

Tirhan saw that Morwen's white-blond hair was blackened with soot. "Are you hurt?" he asked.

"No, my lord." She patted the knives sheathed in her leather vest. "My knife vest protected me."

"But not your hair." He pulled strands of her sodden hair behind her ears. They were alive and free. The blazing ship had managed to carry them to safety. But the men he had left behind were fighting at

Abergaer. Even if they won, it would be costly in Alfan lives. Lord Inian had made his choice against Tirhan's orders.

Tirhan embraced Morwen, stunned by the thought that he could have lost her to the Volkish or the fire or the river. She clung to him.

Demyr crouched on the edge of the bank, watching for pursuers. They did not know where a ford might be possible for horses, but at least none had yet arrived on the opposite shore. Demyr stood, urging Tirhan and Morwen to follow him. "Hurry, my lord," he said. They set out with Demyr leading them away from the river into the forest.

"We are well into Clan Rhydwyn territory," Tirhan said as they walked.

"Aye," Demyr muttered. "We could get horses if we had coin."

Gryffyd was clan lord, and horses were treasured, if the heir to the throne was not.

Thoroughly wet, they hiked through the woods well into the second quarter of the night before deciding to sleep. A bed of fir boughs would do. Demyr stayed awake long enough to ply his elemental gifts to bring warmth to the communal bed of branches. The three of them huddled together in their wet clothes and got what sleep they could.

⁂

Demyr sprang up, sword in hand, startling Tirhan awake. With dawn chasing the shadows from the woods, Tirhan could see two Alfan warriors approaching, bows strapped to their backs. Likely Gryffyd's men.

When they saw Tirhan and Morwen, they deduced who the strangers were. "My Lord Prince?" one of them asked.

"I am Prince Tirhan. You are of Rhydwyn Clan?"

They nodded to him in respect and told them that they were close to the hall of the local chief, and that Lord Gryffyd and his men had been there earlier, and were now out hunting for Volkish. After sharing a blood sausage with the three newcomers, the clansmen led the way, a long trek through a broad valley of small lakes home to hundreds of waterfowl.

One the soldiers offered Morwen his dry half-cape, and she thanked him, but refused it. Of course. She would not have a cape if Tirhan did not. Or Demyr, for that matter. Tirhan wished she had taken it, for her frame was smaller than a man's, but felt a flush of pride that she had not.

The clan hall was modest, half of stone and the upper half of wood. It was the domicile of one of the Gryffyd's chieftains, with a few outbuildings and cookfires where women and youngsters were tending kettles. A paddock with a dozen horses. Tirhan eyed them hopefully.

They entered the hall, finding warmth at a central firepit that burned hot, the smoke rising up to a hole in the peaked ceiling. As they waited for Gryffyd to return with his raiding party, a few servants brought refreshments.

Before the sun was at its peak, they heard the approach of horses, and soon the clan lord was ushered into the hall with four of his men, short swords in scabbards.

"Lord Tirhan!" Gryffyd said as he strode across the hall. "Be welcome."

Tirhan stood. "I thank you, Lord Gryffyd. We had need of rest."

Gryffyd handed his sword and belt to a servant and joined them at the fire. "We heard." He nodded to himself. "We did indeed." He nodded to Morwen and glanced at Demyr, careful to give only as much greeting as rank deserved. But he had nodded to Morwen. So he was in a mood to be gracious.

"Your losses at Abergaer were hard, Lord Tirhan." He accepted a cup of ale from a servant, while Tirhan's group demurred. "We have been in a fight as well. Yesterday my raiders took five Volkish to their graves," he said, "and we lost not one man."

"What were the losses at Abergaer, if you know?" Tirhan braced himself for the count.

"My scouts could not be sure, but fifteen or twenty." In the fire-light, Gryffyd's eyes glittered. He saw advantage in those deaths and was not loath to show it. "So you decided to bring a fight to the Volkish now that you have Lord Inian?"

"It was not my plan. Three of us went in to sink the boats used to trade in silverwood. We fired them and escaped down the river, but as we fled, Inian brought swords into it. The Volkish were fighting to preserve the ships and were at a disadvantage, so he went in. Most of his men escaped, then?"

"Enough," the old clan lord said, unwilling to call it a success. "But why fire ships? For the trees?" he asked with disbelief.

"They are killing the groves," Tirhan said. "Taking the silverwoods as timber and selling our heritage. It is an outrage against our land. And worse, Lord Gryffyd. Worse." Gryffyd narrowed his eyes, waiting. "The silverwood groves are the portals to the afterlife. Without them, the spirits of our loved ones cannot find home."

Gryffyd looked around at his lieutenants, who had drawn near to hear Tirhan's story. The clan lord did not believe it, or did not want to.

Tirhan went on. "Six days ago we found a silverwood grove laid waste. One tree left standing, because it was too small to profit from. The logs loaded on a Volkish wagon. We killed the workers, Volkish soldiers, and that day a spirit appeared to me and urged the saving of the groves. So that the shades of our ancestors could welcome the spirits of Alfans at the time of death." Tirhan held Gryffyd's gaze, hoping to see a flicker of understanding.

Gryffyd made a show of confusion. "So now it is visions that will lead us?"

"We need not have visions to protect what is rightfully ours," Tirhan threw back. "I entreat you to watch over the groves under your protection and stop the slaughter of trees. You will find the Volkish there if you care to fight."

"I care to fight. As I have done this these last days. If they know we wait in the groves, they will know to bring arms there. This is no way to harry them from our realm." Gryffyd turned to the lord of the hall, who Tirhan had met and knew to be solidly under Gryffyd's sway. "Shall we camp in a grove and kill everyone who holds an axe?" He spread his hands, waiting for someone to say that they should. No one spoke.

"My Lord Tirhan," Gryffyd went on, "this is not a tactic of war. It is . . ." He tried to think of what to say, shaking his head in consternation.

Morwen broke in. "It is a sacred duty. The silverwoods are the heart of Alfan Sih, and you would let the Volkish desecrate them?" Her eyes held fire, and she looked unflinchingly from the clan lord to each man.

Gryffyd drew himself up, his face pinched in anger.

Morwen went on. "If you forsake the groves, you will deprive your people of a decent death."

The clan lord turned a contemptuous look at Tirhan. "Common soldiers have no business in war plans."

"As you say, Lord Gryffyd," Tirhan said. "But Lady Morwen is my future wife. She will be my queen when we drive the Volkish from the kingdom. My hope is that when that day comes, there will be at least one silverwood grove left."

Gryffyd watched Tirhan for a long few moments. No one in the circle of warriors moved, but every man was watching the clan lord.

"You have lost your way," he said to Tirhan. "Lost your way." He gathered his men and left the hall.

Soon Gryffyd's warriors were mounted, and they rode away, making explicit that the fragile alliance between the two men was broken.

Morwen murmured at Tirhan's side, "You should not have told who your queen will be."

"It gave me great joy to do so," Tirhan said. His arm came around her as they watched the clansmen disappear into the forest.

Chapter Sixteen

Sofiyana stepped out of her tent, welcoming the night. She wanted to be invisible, wanted to merge with the darkness, dissolve into it. Her life, unbearable.

She had basked in Nashavety's love and trust. In her heart. She knew she had lost those things now. How had it happened? Once she had been merely a spoiled girl from a wealthy household in the outlands, come to the capital to be trained in an arcana. Then Nashavety had invited her allegiance, and Sofiyana had sworn herself to her. She rose to *fajatim* of House Raven Fell and then to princip of the realm, joining her fate to Nashavety's, who vowed to eradicate foreign influences.

And now Sofiyana had failed. Failed to punish Yevliesza, or even to find her. And her mistress could not forgive her.

"You will follow me some paces behind," she told a soldier standing at her tent flap. She wore a dark cape and pulled the hood over her head. She wanted to walk through the camp and be with other human beings, people beyond high matters and dread decisions, men who knew how to fight but also to raise sheep or pigs or sow grain. Simple things. She envied them.

As she walked, soldiers noted her. A woman in a camp mostly of men. Not merely a woman—the princip. They glanced quickly away, unused to the royal presence. Or because they were afraid of her. Or hated her. She wanted to sit with them at their campfires and listen to them talk. Share a plain meal. Reclaim her life. She walked on, her bodyguard following.

The cool air refreshed her left hand. No gloves needed as night came on, softly enfolding the prairie and lit only by flickering cook-fires. The first stars pierced the sky.

Over and over again she remembered the soldier standing in Ilyan's tent saying that Yevliesza was gone. Half their unit had defected to Warden Kirady, which was the same as saying they had gone over to Yevliesza. Envy gnawed at her. The girl of the mundat had everything: success, the love of a noble, reputation. Honor. It was almost unbearable. Tears sprang to her eyes, and she furiously wiped them away.

The camp was vast. For the first time she realized how many men comprised her forces, each of them with a weapon, a duty, a story. It was humbling to consider their lives of quiet satisfaction. She should walk more. Already she felt a whisper of peace. From the endless plain, the overarching night sky, the many campfires lit like beacons.

She came to the edges of the encampment where families of many of the men had set up camp. Women huddled over cookfires near rough tents and lean-tos and among dozens of army supply wagons.

A woman smiled at her as she sat by a cookfire with a small child. On impulse, Sofiyana walked toward her.

"Good evening," she said. The mother tended a pot over the fire, and the child, a girl of about five or six, sat watching.

"My lady," the woman said, nodding, but not rising. This was not the palace, nor did simple folk even know the protocols.

The little girl was round-faced and her hair was so ample and curly, it stuck out in every direction. She stared at the silver torc around Sofiyana's neck. Perhaps she thought it was a necklace. Crouching by the little girl's side, she asked, "What is your name, can you tell me?"

The little girl looked at her mother, who nodded.

"Ezzy," she said, looking at Sofiyana's fine cape and dress. "What is your name?"

"Sofi."

"Sofi," the child repeated. The mother's eyes grew round as she realized who the visitor was.

The little girl scooted over, allowing Sofiyana to sit. They sat together, the three of them, and, as the mother stirred the pot, they watched the stars gather in the sky.

As Sofiyana sat mesmerized by the fire, the child spoke. "Mommy," she said. "She stinks. A bad smell, mommy."

The mother spat at her, "Hush, Ezzy!"

"But she *does*."

The mother drew her hand back to slap the girl, but Sofiyana said, "Do not punish her." She rose, looking down at the child, her heart plummeting at the expression on the girl's face.

"Please pardon us, my lady," the woman said anxiously. "She is a stupid girl."

Sofiyana shook her head as she backed away. "Do not worry. Children will say things."

True things.

She left the two of them sitting by their campfire. She wanted to disappear, so great was her humiliation. The walk no longer offered a respite. The light had gone out in her heart, and she wanted only to sleep. But first she had to dig a hole.

Followed by her bodyguard, she walked out of the camp looking for a suitable tree, one that was large enough not to fall to the soldiers' axes in their need for firewood. The one she selected had a thick trunk with gnarled branches. A tree that would last.

When she found a suitable stick, she dug at its base, past fibrous roots and small rocks. It was hard work, and she was soon sweating.

Her guard must wonder at her behavior, but she could not care about such a thing. Now she cared only for one thing: peace. The peace of the silent and sturdy tree, the peace of the beetles that crawled out of the hole, the peace of night, the only time she could bear to be alive.

"My lady," her guard said, approaching the spot where she knelt, "if you need a hole dug, I will do it."

"No. Stand away." She stared at him until he retreated a few paces.

When she had dug deep enough, she pulled the amber ring from the pocket of her dress and held it for a moment. The large yellow stone flared with light as though waking up. Quickly, she dropped it in the hole.

"Care for this," she beseeched the tree. "Keep it buried and silent among your deep roots. Never let it out, I beg you."

Using her hands, even the blighted one, she dragged soil into the hole, covering the hateful ring. Placing her hand on the tree trunk, she whispered, "Forgive me." She did not know why those words came to her. There could be no forgiveness for her wretched life. She only wished she could bury her left hand in that hole. The mold was in all the fingers. But at least for as long as she had been digging, all she had smelled was wet soil and decaying leaves.

When she returned to her tent, she ordered her guard to bring her a basin of water.

She soon had the dirt washed off her filthy hands, but it was necessary to work harder at it. The black mold still remained. She continued scrubbing her left hand until it bled.

❧

The church organ was so loud it made Nashavety's chest vibrate. She thought if it went any louder, the great stained-glass windows might shatter. The candlelit altar, the soaring columns, and the ornate robes of the priests all combined to create a thrilling grandeur.

Despite herself, Nashavety was impressed.

At her side, Walthar Reinhart in his fine black uniform bedecked with silver trim and medals. In the rows surrounding them, the elegant uniforms of the officers of his high command, who sat erect and alert, the lords of the world. Behind them, a great crowd of lesser beings, soaking up remnants of glory.

Churches like this one were created by realms where a misguided theory of deity reigned. Their god did not tolerate unbelievers, in fact hated her ancestors, who had been hunted and tortured for their powers, dubbed *magic* by the faithful. Nor would he—they thought of the deity as a *he*, she remembered, beard and all—ever allow Nashavety into his presence in the afterlife. Perhaps he might be right about that. They would not get along.

But she had to admit that a church like All Graces possessed a terrifying magnificence. Who, sitting here, would dare not to believe? Who could count themselves of any importance before this display of power and dominance?

She would have to give thought to how such an experience could be brought to the masses in Numinat. She had been told how, in the mundat, there had been stadiums filled with light and the synchronized roar of enraptured crowds. Martial songs and arresting pageantry. Volkia's heritage. Giving the masses frequent doses of spectacle.

Nashavety was not above commandeering some of this grandeur for her own purposes. While the priest droned on, she allowed her mind to consider it. For one thing, Numinat had places of grandeur. Osta Kiya, of course, a palace in the clouds. Even more, though, the Plain of Monuments. And there, taking its rightful place in the hierarchy of stone monoliths, the Citadel, its two halves joined by a narrow and treacherous causeway.

It rose high on the plain, and those who saw it often quailed at its presence, never understanding why. Not because of its height, but its depths. For deep in the ground where such extrusions begin, a well of pure darkness dwelled. It had been waiting for her to release it.

How delightful that the First Ones had themselves let the darkness in. An inauspicious beginning for Numinat. The ancients belatedly came to understand that it was not only the Numinasi people that they had led into the Mythos, but the river of evil. That river being one of the heritages of Earth. Too late, the First Ones realized that a dark river had penetrated the Mythos. In a great battle against the dark powers, the ancient ones banished the dripping, hungry blackness to the roots of the pinnacle, where it had coiled restlessly for centuries.

Until her mother coaxed a thread of it upward to attend her daughter's initiation into her birthright gifts, elements and creatures.

Nashavety knew her mother's methods. She had been there to watch her use them.

It was time to summon them again.

◈

ARMAN CROSSED HIMSELF AS HE PICKED HIS WAY THROUGH THE BONES. Bones and dust and the rags of the winding cloth, shredded now by the tunnel opening. He was desecrating a sepulcher, and he spared a moment to ask God's forgiveness.

From above, the remote chords of the great Meinham Organ, muffled by the stone crypt. The dead had no need of music to give them hope. These souls were with the Father. He could have wished for the new tunnel to have led outside, in some obscure alley, field, or shore of the river. Now his challenge was to get out of a church. And during a mass being held in the nave above.

Dust from the collapse of the vault hung thick, and he moved away, stifling a cough. But if he could barely hear the chords of the great organ, no one above would be likely to hear any sound he might make.

The crypt was murky, the only light coming from the recesses of the tunnel and, as well, a few candles left burning in a niche. His first job was to find the door to an upper floor. He made his way past a sarcophagus on a wide plinth, surely the tomb of an important clergyman. The walls of the crypt, too, held buried luminaries, as testified by the embedded plaques.

A niche in one of the walls held tall candles trimmed with silver filigree. Perhaps the candles were burning in honor of someone recently interred. Taking one of them in its holder, he explored the room to find the exit.

The music above came to a thundering conclusion. He judged that the mass was beginning. So it would be some time before he could leave. Meanwhile, he held his fine candle and continued his search.

Coming to a deep recess in the wall, he found a few shelves containing missals and old books. Back in the main chamber he paused to see that he was walking over the marker for someone buried beneath the stone. *Margaret Anne of Holm.* Next, *Bishop Johnathan Vogt.* Then another recess opened to his side. Someone standing there.

With his free hand he grabbed the knife strapped to his ankle. But the person did not move. It was a statue. When he drew near, he saw it was a carved saint with an arm missing. He replaced his knife in its sheath. Here, more shelves. Dusty blankets, old candleholders, tools.

His perimeter search led back to the gaping hole in the crypt wall.

A few paces beyond broken rock fragments, he found a door. It led to a flight of narrow steps. He judged that above him was the front of the church. If the stairs led to an exposed view from the congregation, he would have to wait until the service concluded. Setting the candle in its holder on the stone steps, he climbed. The stairs came to a landing and then switched directions. At the top, he faced a large wooden door. He could not see the latch mechanism and carefully felt for it. Then he cracked the door, letting in a sliver of light from the sanctuary.

He could see a section of the nave and a few rows closely packed with people. The church was full. That might help his purpose. The more movement and noise, the less likely that anyone would take notice of a priest emerging from a door, but Arman had hoped for a less conspicuous place.

The sonorous voice of a priest came to him, followed by the answer of the congregation. From what little he could see through the cracked door, he appeared to be near to the sanctuary where the priest held forth, but at least he was tucked behind one of the great columns forming a side aisle. Now might be the time to go through, when people's attention was on the sanctuary. But what would the priests and acolytes think of a man in peasant clothing suddenly appearing amongst them?

He went back down, picking up his candle and returning to the recess with the statue. There he looked through the blankets, thinking to make a cape out of one of them. But he discovered that the shelves held more than blankets. There were a few dusty and stained black cassocks. A priest's clothes.

He laid a few of them out on the floor, selecting one that, while grease-stained and smelling strongly of mildew, had no tears. He pulled the cassock over his clothes. It fit snugly, with not much give for a fight, but it would do. From the hem of another cassock, he sliced off a length to make a cord to tie back his hair. After replacing the extra cassocks on the shelves, he went back to the other recess and took a book with a tattered cover. A book in Latin to add to his disguise.

Ascending the stairs to the sanctuary once more, he opened the door somewhat wider than he had before to better judge his moment to leave. To his dismay, he now saw army uniforms in the congregation. Many of them were officers' uniforms. His stomach coiled. Before he had time to further consider this situation, a Volkish officer walked by the door, but did not glance at it. The officer's footfalls receded.

Arman wondered if some among the congregation might be people who would recognize him. When he had not returned from Lowgate after taking the cart of *strigoi* through, Commandant Reinhart probably thought that Numinasi soldiers had killed him. Arman was a dead man if he came to Reinhart's attention. With any luck, the commandant would not be in attendance. Nor Madam Nashavety, for that matter. But she, at least, would never attend a religious service.

Soon it would be time for the second reading, when the congregation would stand. Amid that noise and movement, Arman would enter and walk in a dignified manner up the aisle to the vestibule, looking as though he belonged there. He was, after all, dressed like a priest.

At the concluding words of the priest, he waited a beat, and as the hundreds of people stood, he opened the door and softly closed it behind him, clutching his book.

The bright lights of the church assaulted his eyes. But he could see the congregation now. Filled with black uniforms toward the front, and the uniforms of lesser soldiers mixed with citizens behind. A horrid congregation. All too soon, the noise of the responses evaporated. Arman emerged from the door and began an excruciating walk toward the vestibule. He was conscious of every footfall, which seemed to echo on the stone floor and fly up to the buttressed ceiling.

The aisle stretched long before him, going through the transept and past row upon row of people to one side, some of whom looked at him as he shuffled by. He continued, barely breathing, when a piece of uneven stone floor tripped him and he stumbled, the book slamming on the floor like a thunderclap.

☙❧

MARSHAL REINHART'S HEAD JERKED TO ONE SIDE. HE FROWNED.

Nashavety had heard a soft thud, but from where she sat, she could not see what might have caused it. Even the priest noticed it, but the reading from some book or other was droning on, and the audience was paying strict attention. She tried to keep an expression of humility and appreciation on her face, but truly, it was difficult to keep from sneering.

If she had possessed a book of wisdom to guide her through the awful transformations she had endured, it could have helped, but it would never have been this incomprehensible babble of stories and sayings.

At last the reading was finished and she was able to sit again. By all the hells watching, how much longer?

☙❧

ARMAN PICKED UP THE BOOK AND STRAIGHTENED. A FEW PEOPLE WERE frowning at him, but no one raised a hue and cry.

As he passed through an archway into the vestibule with its great front door, a priest was waiting for him.

"You fell, Father," a young priest with a tonsured head said, his expression stern.

"A stumble. No harm done!"

"Except to disrupt the high service." He was looking at Arman's cassock and noting its worn condition. "We have not met."

Arman was older and decided to adopt a confident stance. "I am Father Geoffrey, priory of Eisenberg." He raised his chin, waiting for the priest's response.

It did not come. "Why have you left our Lord's service during the liturgy? Are you ill?"

"Your name, may I ask?" Arman held the man's eyes. He had been a Volkish captain, and a young priest was not going to cow him, though his stomach knotted. He avoided looking at the nave. Soldiers could come through at any moment.

"Father Johan," the priest responded. "I see you have a book."

"Yes, Father. My abbot has permission to study it, and I am waiting for his arrival, which, for some unfortunate reason, has been delayed."

"Abbot?"

"Of St. Culberg's Abbey. Abbot Paulus."

The young priest frowned. "I had not heard that the abbey had a new prelate."

Arman did not pause at this unwelcome obstacle. "Yes. A most holy man." He hoped that the priest would not ask about the book, because he did not even know the title of it. It was in Latin, which he could not read.

"Will you wait for him here or outside, Father?"

"Outside, Father Johan. I am sure his carriage will be here soon." He added in case it would be noted that a carriage never did arrive with an abbot, "Unless he was prevented from coming by some pressing matter at the priory."

"Then you must deliver your book, Father. The Lord be with you."

Arman nodded. "And with you."

He walked away, clutching the book with a claw-like hand. In a few paces he was able to open one side of the massive front doors, taking in a thankful breath of cleansing spring air. As he moved down the stairs leading from All Graces, he noted an ugly grease stain on the front of his cassock.

The sooner he disappeared, the better. He walked off at a brisk pace into the streets of Hapsigen, shrouded in helpful darkness.

It was three miles to Danzman Keller's house, where Duke Tanfred hid. Though it was spring, the night was cold, and if Arman came upon any soldiers, he thought he would look conspicuous not wearing a coat.

Before he left the city, he spent a precious half-hour on a street where taverns and a few restaurants remained open. His plan was to buy a coat off a stranger for an extravagant price. When he spied a man with a long black coat, he almost made his move. But the man looked too prosperous to be tempted to sell a fine coat. Arman's disguise as a priest had worked well at All Graces, but here in the streets, he drew attention. He retreated into the shadows to wait for a man who might sell his outer garment if the price was high enough.

The man he found was drunk, but his black coat was not torn or rank, and Arman's offer of a gold piece was persuasive. Thus attired, Arman hurried on, leaving the city center and finally the outskirts.

In open country he quickly left the lights of dwellings behind, and walked down a road poorly lit by a half moon. It was not yet ten thirty, he judged, and travelers on horseback were not uncommon this close to Volkia's largest city. At any approach, he would be able to hide in the bushes or underbrush at the side of the road. He still carried the book, though he did not know the title or its subject. It had proven useful in the church, and he decided to keep it. He tucked it into the waist of his trousers.

As he walked, he tried to think of a story to explain what he was doing out so late on a country road. He rejected several stories as being too easy to verify or too unlikely to believe.

After the sight of the church full of Volkish officers, he was acutely aware of his danger. As a soldier, he had always assumed that, if called upon, he would die bravely. But when his fellow conspirators in the St. Eustus group died in the raid, it left him feeling wrongly alive. To savor his life in any way seemed unworthy. So if he died this night, or was captured and was to die on the hangman's gallows, he would not have regrets.

It was not guilt that he felt. His escape had been due to circumstances that caused him to be far from the meeting where his friends had fought and been overcome. But his own life had lost its luster. Until he had met Duke Tanfred Wilhoffen in the house on the muddy flats. Where a young girl had inadvertently revealed that someone hid in the basement. Then he knew why God had spared him. Now he would pursue his mission until the very end.

He was startled from his thoughts by a movement in the distance.

Three men mounted on horseback headed down a road that would soon intersect with his own. A suggestion of motion near the ground. Dogs.

They were close enough that they might have seen him. If he left the road now, they would come in pursuit. But if they had not seen him . . . Without making a conscious decision, he moved swiftly into the field bordering the road. A stand of trees temporarily hid him from the riders. If he had been seen, there was no undoing his actions now. He cut diagonally across the field toward a few small structures that could mask his movements. Reaching a byre and storage shed, he looked for any sign of the men, but saw no one.

Leaving the refuge of the buildings, he headed into the marshy ground that dominated the plain around Hapsigen. His boots sank into the muck, and his vestments trailed in puddles and through muddy tussocks of grass. He could not be more a mile from his destination, but it was still a great distance if the dogs got wind of him.

They had. A distant bark reached his ears. It was faint, but for him to hear it, the dogs must be in the field.

He ran. The soldiers pursuing him might not be able to see him at this distance, but the dogs had picked up his trail. He dashed headlong through the field, trying to maintain the distance provided by his head start. Several times he almost fell, staggering as he stepped into a depression or his boots slid on a rock. But it would be the end if he broke an ankle. He slowed and then maintained a loping pace, holding his cassock and coat away from his legs. The barking came louder now, as the dogs grew excited and were pushed on by their handlers.

Arman's lips move in silent prayer. *Oh Holy Mary, Mother of God, succor me in my necessity. There are none that can withstand your power.* He splashed through potholes of water, slapped through deep mud. And ran. Ran in prayer. *Succor me in my necessity . . . Oh Holy Mary, Mother of God.*

If he could get to the duke, he could tell him where to go, and then Arman could lead the dogs away, and Tanfred could survive.

He fell. When he managed to pick himself up, his legs were weak, but he staggered on. Slower now, he weaved through the standing water of the field approaching the Keller house. Falling once more, he lay in the mud, listening for the dogs. Barking in the near distance. They would be on him before long.

Yea, though I walk through the valley of the shadow of death . . .

Dogs barking. A man shouting. But farther away? He lay in the pond of muddy water, not daring to move.

More barking, but fainter now.

The water. The puddles and the mud. The dogs had lost him. Under the half moon, for as far as he could see, the flats reflected a wan light in patches. Watery patches that had saved him.

When at last he knocked at the door, no one came for a long time. It was past midnight, and people might be awakening and putting on clothes. Perhaps calling the master of the house before opening the door to someone in the middle of the night.

Danzman Keller came, easy to recognize, being taller than most men and broad-chested.

"What is this?" he demanded. "Who are you?" He looked at Arman's filthy condition, mud covering his arms and front.

"I am the man who brings a message to Duke Tanfred from Yevliesza."

"Duke Tanfred!" Keller said in mock surprise.

"Mr. Keller, I am the soldier who found him in the basement here when my men and I came to search your house. I found him and promised to help him escape. You must let me in before the patrols find me."

Keller hesitated only a moment, checking the environs. He drew Arman inside and shut the door.

Chapter Seventeen

Inside the house, Keller led Arman into the parlor. He closed the drapes tightly and lit a small lamp.

In moments, Duke Tanfred entered the room, wearing badly wrinkled clothing in which he surely had been sleeping.

"Your Grace," Arman said. "You have a way out. It is dangerous, but using it, I got past the guarded gates between Volkia and Numinat. We can leave the same way."

"You found Yevliesza?"

"I did." He wanted to mention the path, but with Keller standing by, he refrained.

"Yevliesza," the duke said in a kind of wonderment. "She is well?"

"She is. And is waiting for you in the crossings."

"In the crossings, you say?" His face showed doubt.

"I will explain everything, sir, but first we must assemble our clothes."

Tanfred looked like a man who glimpsed salvation. "You have risked much, Captain. Please tell me your name so that I can know whom I owe so much."

"Arman Brandt, sir. But we are in the greatest hurry." He turned to Keller. "You can help."

"Anything," the big man said. "But you must leave tonight?"

"Yes. As soon as we can find His Grace something to wear. And my clothes must be cleaned." Arman turned to Tanfred. "You will be a servant to a priest." He unbuttoned his coat, revealing his priest's cassock. "Me."

⚜

ON FOOT, DANZMAN KELLER HELD THE REINS AS HE LED THE TWO MEN doubled up on the only horse he owned. They rode the mare to keep their clothes free of mud, as Keller led them. The horse's hooves slapped through the boggy ground surrounding his house, and they proceeded to the main road to the city. The moon cast a sallow light on barren fields that had not yet awakened to spring. Though it was June, it felt like March.

When Keller prepared to turn back to his dwelling, he said, "You could keep the horse."

"We will have more flexibility to hide if we are on foot," Arman said. "But my thanks."

Duke Tanfred shook hands with Keller. "I owe you my life," he said.

"The country owes you all it has, Your Grace," Keller said. "Go safely."

Arman had completed half of his mission, and he had reason to hope that the duke would be safe. But now the challenge was to avoid search parties and enter the church in the middle of the night. If the tunnel access had been discovered in his absence, the crypt would be under constant surveillance. There would be no way to return to Numinat.

Arman and Tanfred walked briskly but at a pace they could maintain for the long trek to All Graces. Tanfred wore a monk's robe, quickly cut from a brown wool blanket and sewn by Keller's wife. Adding to his disguise, his head partially shaved into a tonsure, and a thin rope as a belt. A polished wood cross hung around his neck. He carried a knapsack with apples and cheese and Arman's tattered book.

As they made their way along the muddy track, Arman told the duke how things were in Numinat, the fall of Anastyna—which he had heard of—and Yevliesza's growing command of the crossings, which, by his expression, the duke found remarkable.

"But she is learning her limitations," Arman said. "Any destruction of parts of the crossings causes the very ground to thrash. She can open ways up from inside the crossings, but closing them causes quakes, and she avoids doing so. Not everyone thinks she should be so scrupulous. But she is strong in her decision."

"That is Yevliesza," the duke said fondly. "That is her, perfectly."

An owl hooted from the thorn-hedged fields, then fell silent. In the distance, smoke from the furnaces of Hapsigen glowed in reddish disquiet. Arman no longer recognized his beloved land. It had become, under the indifferent moon, a land of angry forges and bruised skies, where men roamed with dogs to capture human prey.

"You say the new crossing destroyed a grave?" the duke asked.

Duke Tanfred, Arman remembered, was a pious man. "Yes, the crypt of All Graces now has a gaping hole."

"When they find it, they will enter to see where the pathway leads."

"Yes. But it will only take them into the crossings. The one path we do not want them to find is the new one that opens into Numinat. Because that is the gate by which Yevliesza is able to enter the crossings with impunity."

From a cottage near the road, pigs rutted in a sodden field. They were awake early. Arman judged that dawn was still an hour away.

The duke continued his thought. "Still, to desecrate a sanctified tomb . . ."

"She tried to direct the exit to Rothsvund Palace. But it is a new skill to her, to alter an align's path so greatly. The result could not be helped."

From behind them came a faint sound of horses' hooves. They were on a great stretch of flat road, and any move to evade the newcomers would be noted.

"A farmer in his cart," Arman murmured, looking back.

Duke Tanfred squinted at the shadow moving toward them on the road. "Or Volkish soldiers?"

"They would not be traveling with a cart." At least, Arman did not think so.

As the cart drew abreast of them, Arman and the duke stepped aside and nodded to the driver. He wore a Volkish uniform.

Three mounted soldiers accompanied the horse-drawn cart, and one spurred his horse forward. "Good evening," he said. His horse snorted and stomped. "Where are you bound so late at night?"

"Good evening," Arman responded. "In the Lord's work, we make our way to All Graces Church in Hapsigen."

"Your names?"

"I am Father Geoffrey, and this is Brother Emil of St. Culberg Abbey."

Tanfred bowed his head to the Volkish officer. With his robe and cross and his hair greased and tucked behind his ears, Arman hoped the duke did not look too much like the richest aristocrat in Volkia.

"Your business on this road?"

Arman shook his head in exasperation. "Therein lies a story, Major."

"Captain, rather," the officer said. "Let us hear the story."

"Sir, we were sent by the abbot at St. Culberg to discover the truth of a woman's claim that she had seen a vision in the fields near Keider Woods." Arman paused, noticing that the cart carried four people, men who looked so dispirited that they did not bother to bestir themselves. "It was said to be of the Virgin Mary, so naturally we had to investigate."

"Naturally," the officer said without conviction.

"We found that there were several others who also claimed to have seen visions, and it took all day to speak with everyone and judge for ourselves." Arman gestured at Tanfred. "Myself and Brother Emil, you see."

"And so?"

"By the time we determined to our satisfaction that the young woman was imagining what she would like to have seen rather than what she did see . . . For one thing, she said Holy Mary was wearing a green robe, which meant—"

"That she was lying," the captain interrupted. "And you are walking on the road so late, why?"

"Because it took until the end of the day, and it was too late to return to the abbey. We decided to try to walk to the Church of All Graces, but misjudged the distance, and Brother Emil developed a blister on his foot. So we have moved slowly and will welcome a warm bed if the church will provide succor."

The captain motioned one of the other mounted men to dismount. "Search his satchel."

Duke Tanfred handed the soldier their bag. The soldier rummaged through it. "Apples and cheese. And a book."

"You travel light," the captain said.

"Indeed," Arman said, "we did not expect to be detained more than a day by our mission."

The soldier paged through the book as though it might contain a suspicious item. "It is Latin," he reported.

"You are a learned priest," the captain said affably. "Read me some Latin."

Arman swallowed in dismay. He coughed, scrambling for time to collect his thoughts. "In the poor light of the moon . . . my eyes. Alas."

Duke Tanfred reached for the book and opened it. He read: "Consideravimus namque huius doctrinae novitios, quae a diversis conscripta sunt"—by God, the duke knew Latin!—"plurimum impediri. Partim quidem propter multiplicationem inutilium quaestionum—"

The captain raised his hand. "Enough."

Duke Tanfred closed the book. "The holy words of St. Thomas Aquinas."

The captain nodded, apparently satisfied.

"Before we part ways," Arman said, trying not to sound jubilant, "may I pray with the miscreants whom you convey to the city?"

"You can pray all you want. We will take you to All Graces if you do not mind a ride with traitors."

"The Lord loves sinners," Arman enthusiastically said. "He does not turn His back."

With that, he and the duke climbed into the back of the cart. As the Volkish unit got underway, Tanfred began a prayer, and the captives joined in.

The wheels squeaked as they trundled along. They had not only miraculously escaped arrest, but had a ride to their destination. The cart held three men and a boy of not more than thirteen, thin as a pole, with a shock of red hair.

"What is your name, boy?" Arman asked.

"Niko, Father," he answered in a tremulous voice. His face was mud-streaked and one eye was blackened from a soldier's fist.

"How old are you?"

"Twelve, Father."

Arman and Tanfred exchanged glances. This boy would hang with the rest of them.

"And your crime?"

"My father spoke out for the slaves at the forge." The boy glanced toward the angry clouds reflecting fire from the iron works of Hapsigen. "They killed him."

"And your mother?"

Niko's face contorted, and he could not speak.

Arman's mood sank at the boy's plight. It was an ugly fate. A sorrowful one. Oh, that his country had come to this, he thought bitterly. He took a deep breath. The sky had a trace of indigo; the dawn would not be far behind.

Tanfred asked Niko if he would like to pray. When the boy nodded, he covered Niko's hands with his own and they murmured a prayer together as the cart jostled on its way.

Hapsigen was empty as they plunged into its narrow streets. Smoke slithered through the early morning air, making Arman's eyes water, and soot lay heavy on the stone fronts of the buildings and on the cascade of roofs. The dome of the Church of All Graces loomed a few streets away. Not every church remained open all night. He hoped this one did.

The captain spurred his horse to the side of the cart. "Here is your church, Father."

Tanfred jumped down first, then extended a hand to Arman to allow him a dignified exit from the cart. "Thank you, Brother Emil," he said. He turned to the Volkish officer, still mounted. "Captain, the boy is only twelve. I beg you to let me take him, that you spare his life for the sake of the mercy of our Lord."

The captain snapped, "His crime must be answered."

"Yes, but I would put him to the discipline of the church. He would serve the monastery and its good works."

The captain's horse raised its tail and produced a pile of dung in the street, adding the stench to the already poisonous air of the city. The captain was hesitating.

"God would reward you," Arman went on. "We must all face Him one day."

The captain grimaced. "Take him." He touched heels to his horse and moved forward to join the rest of his men. Tanfred was already motioning for the boy to join them.

"Thank God for you," Tanfred murmured to Arman.

Arman, conscious of the dangers they still faced, said, "But I may be taking us all into a fight." He met Tanfred's gaze. "If the basement has been discovered."

They hustled Niko up the stairs leading to the church's great door. Tanfred pushed on the lever to release the latch, and the door opened.

Inside the vestibule, a few manifesting globes illumined the hall.

"Niko," Arman said, "we will take you to safety in Numinat. Can you trust me to do you no harm?"

"Yes, Father. But . . . Numinat?" Niko frowned. "It is allowed?"

"No, but we have a tunnel. Can you be brave and make no sound? We must walk through the church and enter the crypt where the tunnel begins."

Niko nodded. "Yes, Father."

From the church gallery housing the organ, a wan light illumined the back of the church. By its light, the three of them made their way along the aisle, with Arman leading and Duke Tanfred behind, holding Niko's hand.

No one sat in the pews at this hour, and the altar was empty, barely visible in the shadows that engulfed the front of the church. The tall windows of All Graces barely showed their colored panes. It was as though the church had no eyes to detect them. *Almost home,* Arman thought.

At that moment, a great blast of noise shattered the quiet. Tanfred cried out at the sudden grumble of sound that filled the sanctuary. They turned to see what had happened, but silence returned for a moment. Then a man peered over the edge of the gallery.

"Please pardon me if I startled you!"

Arman stared at him, trying to assess what was happening.

"I try to practice at dawn when no one is here." The man waved at something behind him. "The organ."

Finding his voice, Arman said, "The great Meinham Organ. Of course! We were momentarily surprised, that is all!" He gestured at the gallery. "Please, by all means, continue."

"Thank you, Father. You are here so early!"

"We have come to pray and shall start our devotions in the crypt at the tomb of"—Arman searched for the name of one of the tombs he had seen—"Margaret Anne of Holm. My guests have come a long way to see her resting place."

"Yes, Father. But will my practice disturb your devotions?"

"Not in the least! Please continue. We would be honored to hear the great Meinham." He paused, waiting for the organist to return to his instrument. With a nod, the man did so.

Arman looked at Tanfred, who appeared to have recovered from his shock, and the three of them slipped through the door to the crypt as the organ's thunderous chords began again. On the stairs they touched the rock wall at one side to guide their steps as they descended. A faint light streamed from the gaping hole. The crossings with their perpetual light.

Stepping over bones and chunks of shattered stone, Arman led Tanfred and Niko into the tunnel.

Once inside, Arman stopped and turned to the boy. "We are in the crossings, Niko, and we have a walk ahead of us. I promise you that at the end, we will meet friends who will welcome you. But if you want to stay in Volkia, you are free to go."

Niko was looking around, his red hair catching the crossing's light in a bright halo. After a moment, he gave Arman a suspicious look. "You are not a real priest, are you?" The boy's eyes held a lively intelligence as well as a sense of adventure.

"My disguise," Arman admitted.

Tanfred put his hand on Niko's shoulder. "And I am not a real monk. But sometimes I think I should have been."

Niko said, "I am coming with you." He looked behind them. "They could be coming after us. We should hurry."

Arman laughed. "Yes, let us hurry. Lead the way, Niko!"

☙❧

THROUGH THE LONG NIGHT, YEVLIESZA HAD PACED JUST INSIDE Arrow Shaft Gate, trying to stay awake so that she could keep the map of the backway in mind. Rusadka was with her, keeping vigil at her side.

Yevliesza had imagined every disastrous thing that could have happened to Arman. That people in the church had heard the noise below in the crypt and alerted soldiers. That Arman got out of the church but was arrested on his way to Tanfred. That he succeeded in finding Tanfred, but they encountered soldiers on the way back to Hapsigen.

When she saw shadows moving in the newly created tunnel, she knew that people had entered the pathway.

"They've come," she told Rusadka.

"The two of them?"

"No, three. And one of them is smaller than the others." A youngster, she thought.

They made their way into the backways, accompanied by a few soldiers that Kirady had insisted upon.

As they walked, Rusadka said, "You have done a fine thing. More than anyone could have hoped."

Yevliesza looked at Rusadka, surprised at the praise. Surprised that it was even true. She finally *had* done a fine thing. She smiled gratefully at her friend.

As they waited at the entrance to the new path, someone came into view, wearing a priest's robe. It was Arman Brandt. She went to meet him. "Arman!" He grinned and turned to the man behind him. Dressed in a monk's robe, his hair pulled back, was Duke Tanfred.

"Thank God!" Yevliesza whispered, approaching him.

"We do thank Him," Tanfred said. He grasped her hands and looked at her with tenderness. "You are extending the crossings. A strange and wonderful thing, Yevliesza."

Strange and wonderful. And so it was.

"A thing no one has done in a thousand years."

Rusadka came to her side, her face lit with satisfaction. The duke would give disaffected Volkish soldiers someone to hope for, to rally to. And the success would inspire Numinat in the coming days. Rusadka went back to Arrow Shaft to report to Kirady, who waited for them.

"And who is this?" Yevliesza asked Tanfred, looking at the redheaded boy who accompanied them.

Tanfred drew the boy forward. "A young man who helped us. Niko."

She smiled at him. "Welcome, Niko," she said in Volkish, much to Arman's surprise. She had learned a few words when she'd been held prisoner.

Turning to Arman, she shared a triumphant look with him. "I want to hear everything," she said. "But you should escort Tanfred and Niko to Arrow Shaft now. I'm going to close things up." He would know what she meant. Around the youngster, they wouldn't make her abilities explicit.

She said to Duke Tanfred, "Tell Niko not to worry if there's some trembling in the ground and in the walls. It will pass."

Arman, Tanfred, and Niko made their way through the tunnel.

Her soldiers waited with her at the opening to the pathway down which Arman and Tanfred had come. There was no need to close the opening. But she felt she must close the exits into Volkia, lest they be discovered. Lest the Volkish learn the true extent of her abilities. Unless they had created a detailed map of the backways, they would likely not notice the new tunnels, and if they did, they would not see the point to them.

But standing there, she could not help it—she hesitated. All her instincts went against destroying any part of the crossings. She had not behaved with perfect care toward the Mythos as she had come to understand its needs. The rule was do not destroy. The alter-world was fragile, and fragile most of all in the crossings. She knew that at a level that few, if any, other people did.

For others like Kirady and Rusadka and Valenty, the Mythos just *was*. The ground beneath their feet, the only world they had ever known, its existence unquestionable. Its disappearance unthinkable. But Yevliesza had not lived in the Mythos her whole life. She came as a stranger, and to her the Mythos had always been tinged with wonder and fragility. It had arisen from the Earth and might so easily have never come into being.

Maybe that was why the First Ones had given her this power. Not because she owed no allegiance to any one kingdom, but because she could have a clearer view of how the Mythos might be destroyed. And how to keep it safe. Maybe she finally had the answer of why she had been chosen.

If only Isha were here so that she could tell her. *I finally get it. Why I'm the one.*

She imagined Isha standing at her side, a small smile on her lips. *Let us get on with it, then, shall we?*

Now she had to close the end points of the three new pathways— those she had created only hours ago. When she did, the resulting quakes would alert the enemy that she was in the backways. Then she would have to get out in a hurry.

She closed her eyes and in her mind-map envisioned the closure of the three new exits in Volkia. *This is the last time,* she thought. *The last time I will bring down the substance of the crossings.*

The quakes came, as she knew they would. The tunnels rumbled angrily. A soldier took her arm to help her balance as they hurried on.

When she finally came through Arrow Shaft, Rusadka was waiting for her. The escort of soldiers came through behind Yevliesza, and they filed out of the cave. She and Rusadka were alone. Through the cave opening, the bright day streamed.

Rusadka glanced at the gap in the cave wall. Wondering if she would close it. But she would not. They were using that gate, and closing it each time was too destabilizing.

"There is a crowd waiting for you," Rusadka said. At Yevliesza's surprise, she went on. "We have moved camp. Warden Azry of Lukya Polity has come with five hundred swords."

"Five hundred! How can we feed them?"

"We are closer here to villages where we can buy food. It is already arriving down the Haiga River."

Kirady was generous, providing coin to supplement their food. "But to camp here!" Yevliesza said, hardly getting over her surprise. "People will figure out that there is a gate."

"They know anyway. Secrecy has been impossible in a camp of soldiers." Rusadka allowed herself a smirk. "Much less your civilians."

They aren't mine, Yevliesza thought. But then again, weren't they?

"The story is going around that you fought off the blood birds sent to destroy you."

"*You* fought them off, while I whimpered at your feet!"

Rusadka gave her a deadpan look. "That will not be the story."

A shadow at the cave's entrance. Tanfred. He was dressed in a tunic of fine wool dyed deep blue, with a thick chain of gold and a fur-trimmed cape. Kirady had wasted no time in making him look like a duke.

"I worried about the quakes. Worried for you," he said.

"They won't happen again," she said. Glancing at the cave entrance, she added, "I understand there's a gathering outside."

"They are waiting for you. But it seems that they know I have come as well."

Rusadka interjected, "We are spreading that news as far and wide as we can." She gestured for Yevliesza and Tanfred to go out.

"Stand with me?" Yevliesza asked Tanfred.

"Always."

They joined hands and walked outside onto the lip of the cave. Kirady was waiting, and Arman, with a slim, older man whom she took for the Warden of Lukya.

In the sparse wooded land stretching before the cave, hundreds of soldiers stood waiting. She saw the pilgrims on one flank, the nearly two hundred that, for some reason, were still with her. They let out a cry when they saw her, and, giving in, she waved to them. After all, they were hers.

She raised her hand joined to Tanfred's, and the resulting cheer roared through the woodland, scattering birds and making her heart stutter. These hundreds of souls looked to her for some great, good thing, something that would, perhaps, save Numinat.

"Tanfred," she said, "we have so much to work out."

"God will provide," he said, gazing out at the great crowd.

At that moment, she thought he might be right.

PART III
A TANGLE OF ALIGNS

Chapter Eighteen

In Arrow Shaft camp, Yevliesza and Tanfred watched as his personal banner took shape under the watchful eye of the seamstress. It was a representation of his gift over growing things, verdure power: a single green tree, leafy branches spreading out on a field of white.

"Your perfect symbol," Yevliesza said, watching the women stitching, the memory still vivid of the woody vine Tanfred had created for her to climb down from her imprisonment in Prince Albrecht's palace.

"My grandmother had strong verdure, too," he said. "She designed the emblem." He brushed his hand over his tonsured head, as though he hoped that his hair might have grown back already.

"I love it," she told him. "And now your gift may save Volkia."

He smiled. Self-deprecating. "Hardly that." He watched as the women stitched on the tree. "I had hopes that the resistance groups in Volkia would be stronger. But Prince Albrecht's heel remains so thoroughly on the necks of the people. And with Commandant Reinhart, the same." He smiled at her, his boyish face bearing new lines around his eyes. "Now, perhaps some good."

It was their hope that on the battlefield the Volkish might come to the banner with the green tree. "There must be a lot of common soldiers who despise what their kingdom is doing," Yevliesza said. She knew such people were everywhere in Volkia. She had met them in Rothsvund Palace, and they had tried to help her. It gave her hope that the people would rise up.

Tanfred was leaving soon to join Anastyna. Yevliesza would be sorry to see him go. During their escape from Albrecht's palace, they had shared the most harrowing hours of their lives, and it had forged a bond between them. She looked at his kind, broad face and thanked the Mythos that she had met him.

He brought up the subject of the boy he and Arman had brought out of Hapsigen. "Thank you for taking Niko into your care," he said. "The lad has no family left."

"We're completely happy to have him. Lura is devoted to him already, seeing to all his needs." Already Yevliesza's maid had begun the boy's Numinasi lessons, while spoiling him with the sort of food morsels she had formerly scrounged for the Keeper. The boy was thin as a reed, and Lura had made a project of putting weight on him.

Raised voices came from outside. Yevliesza and Tanfred stepped out to discover the cause and found two women loudly disagreeing amid the tents and makeshift huts. Dreiza and Kassalya.

Yevliesza ran to them.

"The sounds!" Kassalya cried as Yevliesza approached. She was pushing away Dreiza's attempts to comfort her. "The sounds of clunking, like thunder ripping the world!" She yanked free and ran a distance, only to stop and bend over, covering her ears.

"What's happened?" Yevliesza asked.

"An intrusion," Dreiza said, shaking her head. "Of the future. When Volkia invades."

"It's loud?" Yevliesza asked helplessly, seeing how the girl covered her ears.

Kassalya saw Yevliesza and wailed, "The machines, the machines that walk, spitting metal! The land hates them!" Then, cocking her head as though hearing another blast of noise, she ran farther off, moaning, "They come, they come."

Janov arrived. "We will bring her back to your tent," he said. "She is upsetting the camp." Many of the seekers were standing nearby, watching the commotion. A few paces away, Duke Tanfred also stood watching, joined now by Kirady.

When two soldiers gently took Kassalya's arms, she tried to yank away. "The Nine cannot bear them, do you not see? Can you not hear?"

Yevliesza asked Janov to bring Kassalya to her. She didn't want her hauled off and shoved into a tent. He went to give orders.

Dreiza told her, "It came on suddenly. It is agonizing for her. She cannot tell if it is happening right now or tomorrow or next month. I am sorry if she has upset people."

Only the seekers were upset. The soldiers already knew what was coming.

As the men took Kassalya in hand, Yevliesza said, "If we can't stand to see what's coming, how will we have the courage to fight when it does?"

A movement in the distance caught her attention. A flash of gray in the trees. Kiya was here, but he wouldn't approach. Now with the greater numbers in camp, he would likely stay away. It was midday, not a likely time for him to be there, but maybe day and night didn't occur at the same times in the spirit world as in the realm of the living. Or maybe a wraith wolf didn't need the cloaking dark to prowl, since it could cross over and disappear at will.

She wished Warden Azry had not come with his hundreds of soldiers, and not only because of Kiya. The warden was using the camp as a halfway point, ready to pivot to one or another of the princips. Hedging his bets. Anastyna would blame her for it.

When Kassalya stood before them, Yevliesza got her to sit on a log by a dead campfire, and she and Dreiza sat with her.

"Kassalya, please tell us what you see."

"You do not want to see," Kassalya said. She was only sixteen years old. Too young to bear her intense gift of foreknowing. Her skin was as smooth as fine linen, but her eyes old and haunted.

"I've seen the machines, too," Yevliesza said. "And I killed one." And she had, in the crossings. "They're not invulnerable."

Kassalya quieted, but she didn't look convinced. "I see them coming."

"Yes, they're coming. But they can't kill us with noise."

"Violent machines," Kassalya insisted.

"And we have three armies waiting for them. From Anastyna. Osta Kiya." Yevliesza spread her hands, looking around. "And us."

A smile tried itself out on Kassalya's face. It wobbled, but it was a start.

IN WARDEN AZRY'S PAVILION, ENOUGH CHAIRS HAD BEEN FOUND FOR A meeting. Azry's contingent had brought many supplies. In addition to weapons and food, a tent fit for a battle commander. Besides Yevliesza and Azry, there were Kirady, Tanfred, Rusadka, and Arman.

Kirady opened the discussion by thanking Captain Brandt for helping them bring Duke Tanfred out of Volkia. He related how in Volkia, the captain had volunteered for the assignment to accompany the *strigoi* through the gate. It being his only chance to take Yevliesza the message from the duke, that he sought to return to Numinat.

It was Yevliesza's only big success, and she savored it.

Warden Azry nodded at Captain Brandt and then at Yevliesza, acknowledging her role. The warden had been told of her unusual power, since, with Tanfred's rescue, it could hardly be kept a secret from him.

"And our thanks to Duke Tanfred Wilhoffen," Kirady went on, glancing at Tanfred, who stood next to him. The duke nodded soberly to the group. She knew that he was keenly aware of not having brought any swords to the conflict.

"I must go to Princip Anastyna," Tanfred said. "If I can beg for a few warriors to accompany me. It is a two-day ride." On the journey, he might encounter Sofiyana's scouts, who would certainly detain him. "Fifteen men bearing arms," he went on, "and we will look daunting enough."

Warden Azry had fighters to spare. In fact, he had a force of five hundred.

"Ten soldiers, then," Tanfred threw out. "It would suffice."

At last Warden Azry said, "My men of Lukya will accompany you, Your Grace."

Tanfred nodded, gratified. It would get him to Anastyna's camp. Although there were blood birds patrolling. They had been seen here and there, wheeling high in the sky like vultures, looking, looking. Looking for Yevliesza, Arman had said.

"Not ten of us," Warden Azry went on. "All of us will accompany you. So I will take my army to Anastyna. Five hundred and twenty strong."

"By the Nine, my lord," Kirady said. "The princip has need of you."

"But what of Dorodna Polity?" the warden asked. "Prince Fadimir can summon at least twelve hundred fighters from his lands. If he waits longer, they will be upon us."

Prince Fadimir was leery of actions that might amount to treason. Maybe he couldn't be faulted if he supported Sofiyana; she was the apparent princip. But he should support Anastyna if he believed the claim that the new princip used sorcery to command the *fajatim* and unlawfully take the torc.

"Osta Kiya has nearly four thousand men," Kirady went on. "And with your fighters, Anastyna will have perhaps half that. But whether Fadimir goes with Anastyna or Sofiyana, our cause will have at least six thousand men on the battleground." He made it sound impressive, even if they were still outnumbered.

Azry shrugged. "We will soon know the prince's decision. But the real question is, what will the Keeper do?" He turned to Yevliesza.

In one sentence, the focus had turned to her. She should have known it would, but she wasn't prepared to answer these men. They were the ones whose lives were on the line.

Warden Azry went on. "We are overmatched by the Volkish. But take away Lowgate access, and they must march the longer distance from Causeway Gate. Tired soldiers do not fight as well as rested ones."

Tanfred interjected, "Yevliesza is the one with the crossings affinity. She is the one to decide how to use it."

"What good is it," Azry threw back, "if she will not save us?"

His words struck Yevliesza like blows.

Rusadka spoke for the first time. "She has already done much. Tanfred may create a mutiny in the Volkish army."

Warden Azry shook his head. "If they know the banner of the duke." He spread his hands. "Pardon me, Your Grace, but there will be hundreds of flags on the battlefield. Battles are confusing, chaotic. And you cannot personally ride into the midst of it waving a banner."

Tanfred drew himself up into his I'm-a-duke-of-the-realm stance. "I would not have come, Lord Azry, if I did not think I could influence the soldiers of Volkia."

Azry couldn't out-face a duke, even if he was from another kingdom. He remained silent.

Kirady stood. "If the Keeper says the power is dangerous to the Mythos, I believe her." His look made it clear that it was the end of the discussion. The meeting was over.

Lukya Polity would go to Anastyna. And accompanying them, Duke Tanfred, proof of the alternative to Marshal Reinhart.

But Yevliesza was still stuck on Azry's words: *What good is it if she will not save us?*

Chapter Nineteen

Nashavety watched as Marshal Reinhart's senior officers assembled in his command tent. They took places in a circle around a table with a map laid flat. Nashavety sat in a back corner, observing. She would not participate. In front of his senior officers, Reinhart needed to maintain his image as a commander. Women did not rule over men. A pleasant fancy if you were a Volkish man.

They discussed the coming invasion. These oafs in fine uniforms had better know how to fight, since they knew little else. How she missed Numinasi men. While magnificent, they knew their limits, leaving governing to women.

She was in a black humor, having suffered the betrayal of the mewling girl she had raised so high. Sofiyana, Princip of Numinat. A helpless child. She was either dead or had collapsed under the pressures of high office. Who could have guessed she had so little iron?

Perhaps she had pushed the girl too hard, but these things were difficult to judge—a person's mettle, their vigor in the face of threats. Sofiyana's spirit quailed from a minor blight on her fingers. Nashavety glanced at her own gloved hand. *If she thinks that the creeping mold I sent her was bad, she has not seen* my *hand.*

Marshal Kenrick was droning on. "We will leave more than a token force behind to block any reinforcements from Alfan Sih. Prince Tirhan is no doubt waiting for us to abandon the crossings, at which time he hopes to bring through a force of clansmen. We will surprise him."

"Agreed," Reinhart said. "One hundred men inside each of the two Alfan Sih gates. As well, we encamp four hundred swords at the great gate of Nubiah."

That had always been the plan. The Lion Court in particular had ties to Numinat. Anastyna's former lover was a noble of the realm, the reason she had lost her torc. It had been Nashavety's suggestion that the *fajatim* arrest Anastyna for treason when she rushed to defend Nubiah from a Volkish invasion. One that never happened. Her downfall had been simple. A forged letter to Prince Chenua, swearing that, by her love of him, she would bring her army to his kingdom's aid.

When the Volkish forces lying in wait in the backways ambushed the Numinasi army, nearly two thousand of Anastyna's fighters died. The princip fell. A fond memory. Lately, there had been so few.

The meeting had moved on to a question of the enemy's strength. "Numinat will bring five or six thousand troops into the field," Marshal Kenrick said. "A greater number than we expected, and with Prince Fadimir, it is a thousand more." He grimaced. "If Osta Kiya would have surrendered—"

Reinhart interrupted. "That hope is gone."

Oh, gone. Sofiyana had fallen from her exalted place. Had *run* from her place. Cast aside the amber ring, refusing contact with her mistress. Nashavety was—should have been—her mistress. Nashavety was the future princip of Numinat. It was all she had ever wanted, aside from control over Raven Fell House and the *fajatim*, policy regarding foreign influence, the respect and decent fear from all who saw her, and Yevliesza's obliteration, along with the odious Valenty, the dark bitch Rusadka, and all such craven acolytes of the girl of the mundat.

The generals droned on, and Reinhart's hatchet face was tightening into that familiar rodent look. "Numinat may come to the field with six thousand, but we still have overwhelming numbers, and with our Iron Brigade, we will drive through them like a sword through water."

Another officer interjected. "But six thousand only if Anastyna joins with Osta Kiya."

"As she will certainly do," Marshal Kenrick said. "In one of two ways: either in coordination with Osta Kiya, or in a separate attempt to engage our flank or rear. Thus we hold a unit of horse in reserve, to swiftly overtake them."

They loved to hear themselves discuss tactics. But Nashavety's mind was elsewhere. Had she made mistakes? She had made Sofiyana princip in order to secure Anastyna's removal and to ensure that Osta Kiya would not fight when brought to battle. But Sofiyana had cast off the amber ring. Perhaps she had been murdered. But no, she was not dead. Nashavety could almost smell the rank odor of Sofiyana's betrayal. How it galled after everything she had done for the ringleted girl!

A Volkish officer was saying, "If we wait at Lowgate for them to engage us, they cannot outflank us."

Marshal Kenrick greeted this statement with grudging respect. He glanced at Reinhart, who finally said, "We have chosen the battlefield. It will be the Plain of Monuments."

Nashavety was suddenly listening.

"On the plain, however," the officer said, "we are vulnerable to attack from all sides."

Kenrick was nodding agreement. "And, at Lowgate, we are easily resupplied through the crossings."

"If I may suggest . . ." Nashavety said in a whisper that carried. All heads turned toward her.

"If I may," she said with all the humility she was able to muster, "the Plain of Monuments will allow me to help you." She smiled in what she hoped was an engaging manner, but one of the officers stepped back in alarm. "At Lowgate you are without recourse to"—how to put it?—"my *arsenal* of power. And you will need it."

Marshal Kenrick pulled himself up into a more commanding

posture. "We have superior numbers. We have the Iron Brigade." He smiled at his fellow officers. "It will more than suffice, I think."

Here was what he would get for trying to outthink her. She put her gloved left hand to her chin in the smallest of movements. She need not do so to bring her creature power to bear, but the gesture was insult in conversation, and Kenrick deserved the affront. As she willed him to immobility, he froze in place, his head slightly cocked, his expression still condescending. The other officers looked at him in perplexity and then concern. Kenrick began to sweat, rivulets running down the sides of his face as he struggled to reclaim his mobility. She sharpened her will, and he staggered as his breath failed.

Reinhart snapped, "Madam!"

Upset, are we? But he was quite right—she must relent. As she released Kenrick, he staggered to maintain standing, slamming a hand on the table for support.

After a few beats, the meeting resumed, the choice of battleground safe from further discussion.

I am going to the great rock monument in the prairie, Nashavety reassured herself. The Citadel. It could be seen for miles, along with the lesser formations that surrounded it in the vast flatland. She would look down on the battlefield from atop the looming mass, and, if the contest's outcome was endangered, she would release her reservoir of power. Unfold the pool of blackness from the roots of that monument. Deliver her elemental power into the midst of the Numinasi.

At the Valley of Monuments would be a great bloodletting. The army of the Numinasi would die by the thousands. She did not like it. She had hoped for it to be otherwise.

But in her present mood, she rather looked forward to a good killing.

⚜

RUSADKA ENTERED YEVLIESZA'S TENT WITHOUT THE GUARD announcing her. "Come for supper," she said when she saw Yevliesza sitting on her pallet.

"I'm not hungry."

Rusadka narrowed her eyes. She wore a leather jerkin over a shirt and trousers, and from her belt, her sword hung at her hip. Her heavy boots looked like they could be weapons themselves, and undoubtedly were. "Come anyway. Or people will think there is something wrong."

"There *is* something wrong," Yevliesza said.

"Warden Azry?" Rusadka curled her lip.

"Yes, Azry. He asked what use I am when I won't fight. What use *have* I been?"

"Same as anyone," Rusadka snapped. "You fight as you can, and so do I."

"People expect more from me. Azry does. Anastyna does. Even the camp followers!" Yevliesza finished defiantly. Even Valenty, she thought in misery.

For a moment, Rusadka let the dust settle. "What about supper?"

"Jesus," Yevliesza muttered. She kicked her feet off the bed and reached for her boots.

"Kindly swear like a Numinasi," Rusadka said, and left her to finish dressing.

Yevliesza felt chastened, but resentful. What did the First Ones make of her efforts, she wondered? Kassalya had assured her that the First Ones did speak to her. Long ago or sometime soon. Her riddles, worse than useless. Well. Maybe not useless. She had predicted that the blood birds would fly, and they had. So she was right about some things. But which things? It was the reason foreknowers were seldom used in politics or battles.

Dusk was settling in as Yevliesza walked toward an open tent set up for soldiers' meals. Zander and Arman followed her. Arman had begged to take the place of Ostov, who was recovering from his *strigoi* wound. Arman, who still meant to do his utmost against the Volkish plans. Zander barely concealed his displeasure at working with a Volkish soldier.

In the mess tent she saw Rusadka sitting with Elivasa. Rusadka's companion had likely been a persuasive witness in the halls of the polities, convincing some that sorcery had invaded Osta Kiya. Now the time for persuasion had passed, and Elivasa had asked Anastyna to release her from duty and was granted that wish. The two of them would be inseparable for the next few days. And still, Rusadka had found time to get her to supper.

Instead of entering the tent, Yevliesza turned to Arman and Zander. "Go to your own suppers."

Arman raised an eyebrow. Zander made no move to leave.

"I'm going to stroll through camp," she explained. "Collect my thoughts."

"Ma'am," Zander replied, "one of us will come with you."

It was ludicrous. All this protection and concern, and for what? So she could bring back a duke of Volkia, which would somehow convince the enemy to defect? They would just walk by Nashavety and she'd be happy to let them go? Clearly, her attitude needed adjusting.

"I'm going alone," she said with what authority she could muster. If she was not sometimes by herself, Kiya would never approach. And she missed him. He reminded her of the next world. And somehow clarified this world for her. How to be strong in it.

"Please, Arman. Zander. Do not hover." She walked away, hoping they'd allow it.

Surprisingly, they did. The camp was crowded with soldiers. Some of them cooking food over fires, others scouring mail with sand or sharpening swords. Many of the fighters called up from their homes and steadings had only staves or makeshift spears, but those were being sharpened, too. The Volkish were coming. Maybe because of Yevliesza's sabotage actions, Reinhart was waiting to lead his thousands through the crossings. But they wouldn't wait forever.

As night came on, an owl hooted from the canopy of the woods surrounding the camp. She heard a vixen cry.

Twenty yards away, in the first line of trees, she thought she saw Kiya, but it was only a deer, frozen upon seeing her. It bounded away. At that movement, a flock of birds flapped into the air from hidden perches. The black shapes moved as one, wheeling and disappearing into the distance.

Quiet descended as the forest lost the daylight. In the background, murmuring voices from camp.

She turned around to go back, but a shape blocked her path. It was too small to be a person, but too large for dog. Too thick. It had wings.

"Yeesss," it whispered. "We find she."

It talked?

Oh God, it was the monster. Behind it, no one in sight. She would scream. No, if she did, it would jump on her like it had before. She backed up.

It jumped.

But someone was running toward them, and they tackled the creature as it was about to land on Yevliesza. Both shapes fell. Someone was fighting the blood bird and screaming. A woman.

Yevliesza cried out for help, and, moving into the vicious-sounding fight, she smashed a boot against the demon, but still it clutched its prey, savaging her with tooth-filled jaws.

By God, it was Ryura. Ryura, her bald head gashed, blood streaming down her face.

Men rushed from camp. Dozens came, armed and shouting. The blood bird released Ryura and, opening its huge wings, jumped into flight.

Yevliesza sank to Ryura's side. She had been badly wounded. "A healer! A healer!" she cried.

Arman and Zander reached her first. From the camp came shouts and the sounds of fighting. More demon birds.

Yevliesza wiped the blood from Ryura's eyes. The bodice of her dress had been ripped from neck to waist, and from her side blood flowed.

Arman knelt and pressed his jerkin against Ryura's side.

"Keeper," Ryura whispered. "Keeper." She tried to get up.

"No, don't move," Yevliesza told her. She brought Ryura's head into her lap.

Ryura squinted up at her. "Keeper, is it you?"

"Yes, it's me, Ryura. I'm here. We'll take care of you."

People milled around them. Yevliesza heard mention of *"strigoi,"* and "middle of the camp." Sounds of fighting from the camp evaporated. The blood demons, driven off.

"I meant to help," Ryura weakly said.

"You did help. It was very brave."

"But it was always . . . what I wanted." She smiled crookedly. "Did it all wrong."

"No, I did it wrong," Yevliesza said, knowing it for the truth. She had pushed Ryura away, shaming her. "I'm sorry, Ryura. I have been stupid."

Ryura started to shake. Arman looked at Yevliesza and slowly shook his head. He stood, leaving them in privacy.

Ryura's voice was only a whisper. "Did you ever go in? Ever?"

The Mist Wall. "No, but you were right—I did know something. I learned something."

Ryura smiled, blood on her teeth.

"I learned that the First Ones gave me a birthright gift of control over the crossings. I've been trying to stop the Volkish with it."

"The crossings . . ." Ryura whispered.

"I couldn't tell you because I was afraid. And I never meant for them to shave your head. I'm sorry."

"You came to save us. I knew. I knew."

"Yes, you did. You knew."

Her eyes fluttered closed. "I am afraid."

"Ryura, I believe there is a life to come. I will see you again soon. Be peaceful. All will be well."

"Keeper . . ." Ryura whispered. But she did not move again.

Arman helped Yevliesza to her feet. They walked through the camp. A mangled body lay next to a cookfire.

"Ryura died to help me," she told Arman, her voice cracking. "She died, and it should have been me."

"I know how that is," he said gently.

She turned to him, and he took her into his arms. Yes, Arman knew how it was. He held her tightly, taking on some of her pain. His kindness gave her courage, and she straightened, pulling back.

He had been through worse and was surviving, making his life mean something, since his companions had taken the death he might have had.

Kirady was hurrying toward Yevliesza. Around her, the camp was growing quiet. Kirady took her arm. "Are you all right?"

How to answer. But: "I'm all right. Ryura ran at the *strigoi* and it killed her."

"Ryura?"

"She came back." There would be time later to tell the details he wanted.

They walked through the camp, taking stock of the attack. Yevliesza saw at least two bodies of villagers. Several people hurt. Four *strigoi* bodies were attracting attention.

"Monster," a woman said, looking at a blood bird. Some people looked to the woods where the beasts appeared to have flown. They were gone. But how far?

Chapter Twenty

Even in the relentless rain, people were still arriving at the village of Ailfyd for the wedding. Tirhan had sent riders out to announce his marriage to Morwen, and every house and hayloft had their share of visitors, as well as Ailfyd's only hostelry. In these hard times, people were loath to travel, but this was a royal wedding, and the groom was the son of the former king, even if he was not king himself. Not yet.

In the great hall, Tirhan's sisters and his mother, Queen Gwenid, had been sewing for days on the silks they had brought for the bride's dress.

"I do not need a fine gown," Morwen said, looking skeptically at the dress. Pale blue, with gold trim on the long, draping sleeves.

Gwenid kept stitching. "You may not need one, but everyone else needs to see you in it." She looked fondly at Morwen. "Especially me."

"And I, Mother," Tirhan said, taking Morwen's hand.

There in Ailfyd, his mother's home village, they had hoped to be married in a clearing in the woods, but the heavy rains made that impossible. Now the people of the village were making the hall ready, sweeping and laying new rushes on the floor. They bound willow branches to all the pillars and tied strips of colored cloth to the twigs.

It had been seven days since the burning of the boats. Tirhan had since reunited with his men and Lord Inian, the young clan lord who had joined his partisans. Watchful for Volkish, a dozen scouts patrolled the surrounding woods and as far as the Myrwyst River.

"I cannot wear muddy boots with that gown," Morwen concluded.

Tirhan's youngest sister, fourteen-year-old Hanavar, earnestly agreed. "You must have fine slippers!"

"But perhaps barefoot would do? It seems fitting."

"Why fitting?" Tirhan asked, thinking how beautiful she was no matter what she wore, even with her now-shorter hair, which had been cut to equal lengths after being singed on the flaming boat.

"To be under the sky and not a sooty roof. And I have not worn a dress since the Harvest Moon."

Not so long ago, Tirhan thought, yet seemingly forever, since life had been normal. "If you go barefoot, then I will as well," he said, happy to be wrestling with the issue of shoes and not the blood-spattered fight for Alfan Sih.

Morwen looked at the scuffed boots she was wearing. "A little goose grease would bring these to a fine polish."

At the cutting table where her mother and older sister Cadris worked, Hanavar reached underneath to retrieve something. She brought Morwen a pair of low, pointed shoes covered in blue silk.

"Hanavar!" her mother called. "They were to be a surprise."

Tirhan raised an eyebrow at Hanavar. She usually managed to get her way.

His sister widened her eyes, all innocence. "But we cannot keep secrets from a queen!"

THE NEXT EVENING, TIRHAN AND MORWEN WAITED OUTSIDE THE HALL as a village elder, a woman his mother had known all her life, walked the great hall's perimeter, singing a song of purification.

Dressed in her gown of blue silk, Morwen wore her white-blond hair pulled back with ribbons. Over her shoulders, a short cape of ermine fur that her family's village had sent.

Tirhan wore leather leggings and a soft wool cape trimmed in silver. Someone in the village had given him a velvet jerkin to wear over his mostly clean white shirt, and he wore a jeweled sword belt that had belonged to his father. But with Morwen on his arm, no one would be looking at him.

The sound of hoofbeats approaching broke his reverie. One of his scouts cantered in and, seeing that the ceremony was about to start, dismounted twenty paces away, holding back.

His second-in-command, Demyr, questioned the scout and, hearing the report, glanced at Tirhan.

Morwen gestured to him. "Come. The elder is still singing."

Approaching, Demyr said, "Word from Clan Rhydwyn, lord." He hesitated.

"What news?" Tirhan asked.

"A victory. Lord Gryffyd attacked the Volkish stronghold at Welfinsid. The Volkish, slaughtered, and Gryffyd's warriors took only light losses."

Tirhan was glad of it, but wary of how Gryffyd would use his victory.

Demyr's broad face held quiet anger. "Two clans have gone to his side. Angewyst and Llanaden."

So it begins, Tirhan thought. Any three clans could call for an assembly of the clan lords. "They have put out the call, then?"

"Aye. To choose a king. At Clan Rhydwyn, in eight days."

Tirhan could not be surprised. Gryffyd had been sowing discontent ever since Tirhan's father fell in the Volkish invasion. Now Gryffyd recklessly seized the opportunity of his victory to bring all the chieftains together to decide on the succession. At the assembly he would be seen as a leader who won battles.

"The man counts bodies," Morwen said to Demyr, "and claims a town he cannot hold. Our path is the finer: saving the silverwoods."

"As you say, Morwen." Demyr added, "My lady," uncertain now that titles were being bandied about.

Gryffyd's attack against the Volkish outpost made clear his position: he would not deploy insurgency as Tirhan had asked, but battle. The price would be high if Gryffyd lost next time. But another victory would certainly gain him the Silverwood Throne.

With a creak of oaken doors, the elder came from the hall. Light streamed out from many candles and manifesting lights. Morwen beckoned the two of them, and the crowd inside turned to catch a glimpse of the couple.

She leaned in to Tirhan. "Let nothing dim our hearts."

As Tirhan looked at her, the thoughts of kingship and war fell away. The wonder of her: her strength, her beauty. That she had chosen him and would let nothing dim her heart.

The elder stepped between them, taking their hands and leading them forward. As they passed through the throng, someone shouted, "Lord Prince!" Someone else: "King!"

Tirhan saw that all his fellow partisans were there, those who were not keeping watch outside. Cynod, still recovering from his wound at the battle of Glenir; Osric, a man with the eyes of a falcon whose arrows always found their mark; Lord Inian and his men, the first clan to come to his side. Most of the village was there as well, and one of them shouted, "Lady Morwen!" Others took up the cry.

It sent chills through him. This acclaim, this love for Morwen in people's voices, in their faces. The kingdom needed a queen. Women's power went beyond contests and swords, for it was they who completed the circle of family, of throne, of hope for the future. As he stood beside her in the front of the hall, he saw the world anew. The power of the gathering, the candles giving their light, his beautiful and brave Morwen, a gift beyond understanding.

The elder stepped back from her position between them. The hall quieted. Then she brought their hands together. Times before when Tirhan had held her body, held her hand, but this touch was life itself. Here and now, he and her, among their people.

"In this world," the elder said, her face glowing. "And in the next."

Morwen's gaze transfixed him. "In this world," she said.

He answered, "And in the next."

Cheers erupted, filling the great hall. A few startled birds that had been watching from the rafters flew in exuberant circles over the heads of the crowd, as though nature itself bestowed its blessing.

❦

LATE INTO THE NIGHT, WITH ONLY THE YOUNGEST FIGHTERS STILL celebrating in the hall downstairs, Tirhan left Morwen as she slept. He went outside, hoping for a walk to clear his worries, but the rain came hard, chilling him. Hugging his cape around him, he entered the stables.

The smell of hay and horseflesh met him. A stomp of a horse's hoof. The stable boys were asleep in a corner, piled together like farm cats. A few rush lights still burned, and by their faint glow he went to his stallion. Nightwing tossed his head.

As Tirhan stroked the horse's muscled flank, he let his worries settle. All he could do was go on. He had his mission, and yet tonight it was hard to believe in its truth: preserve the silverwoods at all costs. The idea that the groves sheltered the spirits of the dead was for some a closely held belief. Others considered it a story. Tirhan ought not to doubt, because a spirit visitor had told him that it was so.

Leaving Nightwing, he checked that Morwen's mare was well stabled. The stable hands had done well. The harness with its silver mountings hung on the stall, glinting in the rush light. He rubbed the metal with the edge of his cape, burnishing it. His new wife did not care about becoming queen. If Gryffyd was to be leader, they would still find contentment. The clans would choose, and might well choose the man who brought outright victory.

Someone slipped in the stable door. As Tirhan reflexively moved his hand to his belt where his knife hung, the man approached Tirhan across the darkened barn. "You could not sleep, my lord."

Tirhan did not immediately recognize his voice.

"Good evening to you," Tirhan said.

"Ah, evening. I remember how it was." The man was lanky but all muscle, with white in his beard. He wore a leather jerkin and trousers tucked into boots.

Tirhan moved out of the horse stall. "Do I know you?"

"I was called Gethin," the stranger said. "In the old days."

The back of Tirhan's neck prickled. "And now?"

"Now? I do not remember, Lord King."

In the next moment, all feeling left Tirhan's limbs. He could not move. He and the spirit—for that is what this surely was—were in a space unto themselves, and only one of them was at home there.

"You protect the silverwood groves," the spirit said.

Tirhan saw specks of light floating in the air, but the barn remained shadowed. Lights that gave no light. "I do, grandfather," he managed to respond, using a term of respect for an older man. Possibly *much* older. "My warriors do the best we are able."

Around him, the horses still moved in their stalls, and the stable boys stirred in their sleep, but in the envelope of Tirhan and the spirit, everything held unnaturally still.

This shade—who, unlike Tirhan's last visitor, wore no armor— looked at him with approval. "You and your warriors have already won that battle, my prince. The men with axes have left."

Was that so? That the Volkish had withdrawn from the silver- woods? Tirhan's heart swelled with relief.

"The dead thank you," the spirit said, "for they cannot find peace if the place where they die lacks an ancestral grove. The men who kill the silverwoods have fled. But more is required of you, my son. For the realm of Numinat."

"I am eager to go," Tirhan said. "My people are eager." The clans had vowed that when the Volkish abandoned the tunnels for the inva- sion, they would assist Numinat.

"Yes, you will go," the spirit said. "But it is a far kingdom."

"Is it, grandfather?" Tirhan had been taught all the realms were near.

"Oh, far. Far indeed. A journey to harrow the soul. It will require not only courage, but faith."

"The crossings will be hard, then?"

"Ah, the crossings," the spirit said, sounding wistful. "When the path to Alfan Sih arose, I was there. It is like a story to me, but I was the one who found the align. They called me Gethin, the name of my father before me. We were in the river valley, and the churchmen stalked us, and they brought torches into the moors and would have burned us."

By the Deep, Tirhan thought, *this shade is one of the ancients.*

"Sioned was at my side," the spirit said, looking over Tirhan's head as though seeing a history there. "She and I had been looking for a good align, one that left the river valley and traveled to far places. When we saw a strong align, we perceived how it left the valley—and not only the valley. The world.

"We discovered our align only moments before the raiders came running with fire. Our people had been hiding in the woods, and when they saw the churchmen entering the valley, they streamed down the hill to join us. And Sioned spread wide the align, forming a path. A corridor sprang into being before us, rounded on all sides like a tunnel. Ahead, we saw the shimmering land of Alfan Sih, or so I remember. I added my power to Sioned's, and the tunnel grew wider."

"You were the first," Tirhan whispered. By the Nine, this man had forged the first crossing to Alfan Sih.

"But it was not easy. Seeing the opening, our people were afraid and would not enter. We heard their screams as the churchmen cut them down. Sioned bade me go ahead, so that others would follow, and she would remain behind to urge our people on. They followed me. Enough of them. Sioned died in that field. But she is all right now."

Tirhan listened, rapt. Gethin. The first person to set foot in the realm.

"We saw how our path was not the first. Others were entwined in that site. Other paths crossed ours, following their strong aligns. Because before we came, different peoples had forged paths to the places of their hearts' longing. To Arabet, Numinat, the Jade Pavilion, the Indigene kingdoms, Norslad. It was the crossroads of the great aligns. Beyond the origin world, beyond the hills and forests we had known. The paths to the arisen worlds."

He held out his hand, spreading his fingers wide. "The aligns are everywhere." He closed his hand into a fist. "But in the great well of the crossings, they bend together into a knot of attraction. Not all aligns on the origin world extend into the void. Those that do come into proximity, and we saw those other corridors, but we followed our own bright path."

It was already dawn. Light crept through the barn door that sat ajar.

"My noble son, is the tale not told here of Sioned and Gethin?"

"I am sorry, grandfather. No."

"Lord King, we were there. It is a story you will tell your son and daughter, and they will tell their children after you have come to dwell at my side."

The vision started to fade as the morning brightened. Morning already, although moments before it had been darkest night.

Tirhan could see through the spirit's form, as thin as silk. "I will have a son and daughter?" Tirhan felt a wondrous opening in his heart, in his mind. His children. A son and a daughter.

A rattle at the barn door. Someone was coming.

Gethin's voice came from an echoing distance. "Your people must not let fear sap their strength. For what is coming. Have faith, you and your lady. Show no fear. . . ."

The barn's gloom dissolved as the door came fully open.

"No fear," came a faint echo.

Morwen stood in the doorway. As she came to join Tirhan, the stable boys stirred. They sat up, rubbing their eyes. Tirhan found that he could move again and took her hand.

"My love?" she asked, seeing some wondrous expression on his face.

"A visitor," he said, his voice hoarse. "Morwen, it was from the otherworld. One of the First Ones," he whispered.

Morwen nodded gravely. "What do they say we must do?" She had seen one such spirit in the silverwood grove, and she knew that sometimes a visitor from the next world came to him.

"He said we—we and our fighters—when we go to the aid of Numinat, it will be a journey to harrow the soul." He looked at

Morwen, her hair disheveled, wearing her worn soldier's cape. She was listening carefully. "He said we will need to have faith."

"But in what?"

Tirhan was still mesmerized by all that he had heard. "I do not know. But for what is coming, we must have faith."

"It will be a brutal fight, then," Morwen murmured.

Tirhan wondered why the shade had been worried about his courage and that of his fighters. Had they not shown that they did not fear death?

He considered these things throughout the morning. Finally, he sent for Demyr.

"Ride out," he told him, "and find a partisan who speaks Volkish. Go to Welfinsid and take a uniform from one of the fallen enemy."

Demyr nodded.

"Go without delay, and take a fast horse."

The battle in Numinat was imminent. Tirhan needed to know how strongly the enemy was fortifying the crossings. Was Gethin saying that if the numbers were overwhelming, they must enter the crossings no matter the odds?

Demyr said, "You are sending someone into the crossings, then." Tirhan acknowledged it. "But how is he to pass through a gate?"

"I know a way, Demyr." He smiled at his second-in-command. "Have faith."

Chapter Twenty-One

Arrow Shaft cave was lit with torches as Yevliesza secured the knife in its sheath at her ankle. She would know if any soldiers came into the backways in pursuit, and she could outrun them. But to please Kirady, a bodyguard of two. Rusadka and Arman. Rusadka stood below on the slope saying goodbye to Elivasa. A formal leave-taking. Everyone accepted Elivasa as Rusadka's mate, but a *harjat* did not publicly show affection.

Yevliesza was returning to the backways after several days. This time, not to destroy, but to confuse. Ryura's final words as she had died in Yevliesza's arms spurred her to do more. And she had a few ideas.

The crunch of gravel alerted her that someone was approaching, climbing the short slope to the cave. A soldier's voice came to her from the cave ledge, announcing Kirady.

He entered. "You are still here. Good." Kirady noted Rusadka and Arman, armed for a fight. "You are going in."

"Yes." Yevliesza had told him her plan: a few things that would not cause quakes, but might help their cause.

"Go carefully," he said, looking at her with a fatherly expression.

She smiled. "I have protection. And I can see anyone coming." It was hard for others to believe that she saw more than a map. It was what the mundat would call a real-time view. Difficult to explain to a Numinasi.

"Keeper," he said more formally, "you know that I sent for my remaining men from Eiger Polity. They began arriving this morning."

She knew what that meant. He would go to Anastyna with this final band of soldiers, the remaining men from the farms and steadings that owed him service. It had always been his plan that his full force would join the princip. He had committed to Anastyna when she first fled Osta Kiya, and it was time to go to her side. But Kirady's leaving distressed Yevliesza.

"Fifteen of my men will remain with you," Kirady said.

That wasn't right. "You shouldn't leave a bodyguard. I'm no longer . . ." She hesitated to put it into words. "I'm no longer central to your purpose."

Kirady gave her a pointed look. "Fifteen will stay," he repeated. "I hope I will be here when you return. But if not, I will see you soon, I hope." He nodded to her, a kind of bow, and it greatly moved her.

"You will, my lord. I'm sure you will."

"So now you have foreknowing?" he said good-naturedly.

"Yes. Didn't I tell you?" She tried to make the goodbye light-hearted, but her throat constricted. It signaled what was to come. The invading force. The bloodshed. "Tell Anastyna . . ." She didn't know what she wanted him to tell her. "Tell her what you think she wants to hear from me."

A silent laugh. "I will do my best." He cocked his head toward the forest, the camp. "Promise me that in camp you will always be with your guards."

The blood demons knew where she was. Sometimes Yevliesza saw their shadows on the sky, wheeling together, watching.

"I will. I promise."

Rusadka had joined them, and Kirady looked at her to emphasize his concern.

"Fewer of them than before," Rusadka said. They had killed five of them in the valley before Zander's inspired manifestation of the dactyl had driven them away. Several more were cut down during the attack on the camp.

"There is still the problem of the girl from the *satvary*," Kirady said. "She has been running about and upsetting people again. Janov had to round her up twice. Perhaps you should send her home."

He had suggested this before. But the High Mother had seen fit to attach Kassalya and Dreiza to this camp. Yevliesza wouldn't muzzle the girl.

Kirady saw that she hadn't changed her mind. "Well. Dreiza has prepared a potion to calm her."

"A potion?"

"A soothing drink." He shrugged. "She calls for you, but her words stray here and there. Janov says she is suffering a commotion of the mind and has confined her to her tent."

Yevliesza had hoped that Kassalya's visions would become less terrifying to her, but clearly they were not.

When Kirady left, she was eager to be on her way. They entered the gate.

They called it a gate. It *was* a gate. But here, people had not yet built a door of wood and iron. Someday it would have a garrison and a metal-studded door, but in this remote place they had no means to construct one.

As they penetrated the backways farther, Yevliesza stayed alert for any sign of blood demons scuttling toward them. Or any patrols in the backways. Or, in the main tunnels, any woman in a long dress with evil leaking out her pores.

Ryura's words kept returning to her. *You came to save us.* Ryura, to whom she owed her life. In the two days since the *strigoi* attack, Yevliesza had found herself reexamining her vow not to destroy any part of the crossings. She still held to that, but gradually a new idea had formed. She still had to take care. Be, in effect, the Keeper of the crossings. But some actions would be more like bruises than wounds. Actions that could hurt the Volkish even more than slumped tunnels. Yevliesza had been stymied until now. Until Ryura. There was still something she could do. She could weaken the Volkish by sapping their courage. She could show the Volkish army that the Mythos was angry with them.

Arman cut a look at her when she stopped for a moment. His question, obvious: *Do you perceive anything out there in the larger tunnels?* She shook her head.

As they walked on, Rusadka spoke, keeping her voice low. "I am glad you changed your mind about coming back here."

"Small cuts," Yevliesza said, "instead of big ones."

"With small cuts, an enemy can still bleed out," Rusadka said.

"I don't know about bleeding out, but I have to do *something*. For Ryura."

"That was not your fault." Not exactly her fault. But she hadn't treated Ryura well. "She kept trying to hold on to you," her friend went on. "She liked the power."

"I don't think it was power, Rusadka. Ryura saw that my life had meaning. She knew I took instruction from the seer, and she wanted instruction, too. I pushed her away. From the very beginning, I criticized her and pushed her away." Yevliesza thought that Isha might have been wrong. People didn't always come to a seer for help when they wished for things to be better. Sometimes they wished for themselves to be better.

"But still, it was not your fault," Rusadka said. Arman was listening, looking concerned.

Yevliesza turned to them. "I'm not discouraged. Don't think I'm beating myself up."

Rusadka pursed her lips. "A mundat expression?"

"Yes, a good one. But I'm not discouraged. I'd just like to do better." She led them on through the tunnel.

Bright threads sometimes crossed the path. If at eye level, she waved her hand through them as though they were spider webs, golden ones.

Aligns. But because of her rare power, they could become paths. She saw where all of them went. Some of them went to Nubiah. She and her advisors had dismissed that manner of bringing Nubiah's fighters to Numinat. If she forged a path from the backways to Nubiah, the route would bring the fighters into the crossings, where they would be vulnerable to the Volkish army. They were bivouacked at all the gates, and they also could draw thousands from the camp at Rorrs Gate. Nubiah wouldn't march headlong into the crossings full of Volkish.

As they continued, conversation fell away. For most people, the tunnels of this region-between-the-worlds were utterly silent. Yevliesza, however, heard them growing as they enlarged with use. The crackling sounds. The sound of roots probing into the black surround.

She could perceive a real-time layout, but not a detailed one. Not detailed enough to find the bodies. The bodies of the St. Eustus group hanging on the wall. At Arman's urging, she was going to cut them down. Arman considered these men heroes, and although she judged him to be one also, she knew he would not agree. She wished she could convince him that it was not wrong to survive.

She noted that small numbers of soldiers were on the main paths. Volkish officers and messengers moved between the garrisons of the gates, supplies were carried from Rorrs Gate to replenish the camps, and troops were changed out. To frustrate any sabotage, they always moved swiftly, but they couldn't know that she had a clear sight of their movements.

Apparently the Volkish command had decided to create as few targets as possible. No machines, no long lines of soldiers preparing to stream through the Numinasi gate of their choice. They might know there was a saboteur. But Arman said the common soldiers believed the slumps and the quakes were omens. That the shuddering of the crossings showed the anger of the Mythos at the presence of diabolic machines. And discouraged fighters lost battles.

She was going to feed their worries.

At least an hour had passed when Yevliesza finally came upon the awful line of bodies hung from the walls by ropes. From in back of that wall she quickly softened the places where stakes had been driven in to fasten the ropes. She released the bodies.

Arman went to one knee. She and Rusadka stood by his side, paying their silent respects.

What she had done was only a small thing, but they hoped word would spread. What conclusions soldiers would draw from that, they couldn't know. Maybe *The Mythos released the bodies.* And maybe they would blame those who had ordered the bodies displayed: Reinhart and Nashavety. That marriage of lost and cruel beings.

Now came the small strikes Yevliesza and her group had planned.

She watched for the passage of soldiers through the main tunnels. She and her companions knew that even a small attack would bring soldiers into the backways. They were prepared to move fast at the first sign of pursuit.

After a brief wait, Yevliesza noted a group of four soldiers coming through the main tunnel from Volkia. When they approached the place where she lay in wait, she confidently willed and created a minor slump of the crossing wall. When the soldiers saw the tunnel distort, they stopped. They began backing up, no doubt thinking more was to come.

"They're running," Yevliesza whispered. Seconds later, a quake answered this affront, but only a slight one. *No destruction, only alteration,* Yevliesza silently told the Mythos.

Arman looked around as the soft rumble passed through the walls. Rusadka, more prepared for the phenomenon, did not react. "The shaking won't grow," Yevliesza whispered to Arman.

She led them to another place in the backways where they shared a wall with the main tunnel to Volkia. Someone was coming. She was going to get their attention.

It was only one soldier this time, but she couldn't delay, because pursuit might already be organizing. This time she summoned a bulge in the floor ahead of the soldier. He didn't see it at first, but as she developed the ridge, he stopped. Then she pushed the bulge back down. Tremors began. Looking wildly around, the soldier ran past where the ridge had been.

Yevliesza and her team quickly retreated. She perceived that a band of soldiers was entering the backways. They spread out but were not even close to finding the correct route. Yevliesza easily led her group back the way they had come, losing them.

She felt the exhilaration of success and saw it on Rusadka and Arman's faces. Even though every time she did this, the crossings would tremble. But enemy soldiers would tremble, too. And spread the rumors of the danger throughout the army. Danger, and maybe the displeasure of the Mythos. Displeasure at forbidden machines. At campaigns of murder and domination.

❧

MEETING DREIZA OUTSIDE THE TENT WHERE KASSALYA RESTED, Yevliesza asked, "How is she?"

"It is bad now," Dreiza said. "She has waking nightmares and cries out in her sleep." She shook her head. "She does not sleep without a potion."

"But she's sleeping now?" It was midday.

"She must rest, but she does wish to talk to you. Later, perhaps."

"What will happen to her?" Yevliesza asked. Dreiza also had the gift of foreknowing, but it was a small power. She wondered if Kassalya would always see the troubling things. The terrible things of the world.

"My gift does not foretell," Dreiza said. "But since the world is a terror to her, she will live her days at Zolvina." She smiled. "Our youngest *satvar*."

"But you do not see *me* at Zolvina," Yevliesza said, fairly certain it was true, but wondering what would become of her if Volkia was defeated. Sometimes she thought she might return to the Agarvesky Forest and stay with Isha. If Valenty came back to her, then she would go with him. She still hoped for him, if they both survived what was coming.

She shoved such thoughts aside. Every time she allowed them, her heart fell into shadow.

Dreiza looked at her fondly. "Alas, I do not see you at Zolvina. Perhaps someday you will come and take my place."

How strange, Yevliesza thought, to see herself as an elder. She could barely imagine tomorrow, much less decades from then.

She broached the thing she had come to say. "It troubles me that Kassalya is given potions."

"Well. Lord Kirady has said to keep her calm. So as not to let her upset you."

"Kirady is leaving. He's taking all the new arrivals to Anastyna. So we can decide."

"I have not liked it, either." Yevliesza saw Dreiza's conviction form. "Very well," Dreiza said, "no more potions. If her spells will not upset you?"

"Everyone is already upset," Yevliesza said, looking around at the camp with its tents and makeshift shelters and people soberly going through their day. "I don't see how any of us can fear what she says. We're already afraid."

Chapter Twenty-Two

Valenty watched as Anastyna's advisors gathered on the ridge overlooking the camp. The knoll was getting crowded. It held not only Anastyna's hut and her guards' shack, but the tents of the new polity leaders who had joined them.

Since none of the tents was large enough for all the leaders to assemble, they met in a circle outside the royal hovel, with Anastyna seated on the only chair and the others on logs. Besides Valenty, there was Captain Lysandry, Urik, Lord Dorofey, and Warden Genrikh.

"When the battle is engaged," Captain Lysandry said, "we will join the ranks of the Osta Kiya army. However they are arrayed, we will form the flanks. Agreed?"

He watched as each man nodded.

It had taken all of first-quarter day to get that far. Everyone's mind was on defeating the Volkish and, when that was done, how to respond if Sofiyana's army then turned on Anastyna. The polity chiefs said they would come to her side to defend her; promises were made, for what they were worth.

"Numinat is sorely outnumbered," Anastyna said. "Unless Nubiah and Alfan Sih come swiftly, our task is hard." *Hard.* Showing bravery in front of these men, she would not use a stronger word.

"And," she went on, "we have seen their diabolic weapons." All of these men had been at the battle of the crossings when Osta Kiya had tried to go to Nubiah's aid. "We know what the mechanicals can do. Our fighters must not waver. They are prepared?"

Warden Genrikh answered. "They do not fear death in battle. But they fear the dark machines. They disturb the Mythos lands." His expression was dark. "Our people thought we had left machines behind when we left the mundat."

Lord Dorofey said, "If we kill the men who power the devices, their machines are useless."

Valenty was heartened to hear him speak optimistically. At the battle of the crossings, Dorofey had lost a hundred men to the great iron cladders.

"My foreknowers say the mechanicals have massed at Rorrs Gate," Anastyna said. "The men who power them are standing at their sides. We must do more than wait."

Valenty wondered what she meant by *more*.

Dorofey interjected, "But if Nubiah does come, with their numbers, we can overwhelm the machines."

"If, *if*," Anastyna scoffed. "With the crossings controlled by the Volkish, their fighters will be picked off as they enter through Okavezi Gate. And if they come later, it may be too late. We must choose another way. We do have a way."

Valenty noted how she had turned the conversation. How she refused to meet his eyes.

Anastyna went on. "We must destroy Lowgate. The gate where they will surely come through. And if they choose Causeway Gate, then it must be destroyed as well."

"So, this is the Keeper that we have heard of," Lord Dorofey said, glancing at Lysandry, who had told them of primal root power and who possessed it.

Anastyna nodded. "Yes, the Keeper, as she styles herself. And in these fateful times, her betters must decide how to save Numinat."

Valenty barely controlled his anger. "She has your word, my lady, that you would not compel her."

"My word?" Anastyna turned to him, her face harsh. "The kingdom may lie in ruins in the next few days, and *my word* is now paramount?"

As they locked gazes, she dared him to oppose her.

"As a practical matter, my lady," he evenly said, "we have no means to force her. The power lies only with her."

Anastyna settled back in her chair, a smile edging at her lips. "Perhaps not force. But first we bring her before us. To answer how her inaction can be right. When so many will die," she added, looking from Dorofey to Genrikh.

And if, as was likely, Yevliesza refused? Valenty feared Anastyna would not be above using any force necessary.

"And so?" Anastyna demanded of the group. "What say you?"

Valenty and Urik would have no vote. Lysandry would have to support her. It was only the wardens whom Anastyna wanted to hear from.

Everyone watched them. Dorofey finally spoke. "Let her come to our council."

Genrikh swiftly concurred. "She is your subject—she must agree."

Valenty looked at Urik, but his friend did not notice his glance, or would not notice.

"The girl will be sent for," Anastyna said. The words sliced the air. She would be sent for.

Valenty stayed in the circle when the others had left. Anastyna softly said, "You are against this, it would seem."

"I am. To bring down the gates. A fateful decision, one that Yevliesza says could shake the core of the world."

"The world is already shaken." Anastyna slowly shook her head. "You love her, and it blinds you to the truth."

"She will not obey, my lady. She fears our destruction will be complete. Not just Numinat. All."

Anastyna cocked her head as though mystified. "Not obey?" She looked out at the great encampment. She was swelling with confidence; she had an army, she had the allegiance of important wardens. "Yevliesza will obey."

Valenty saw there was no persuading her. But his silence told Anastyna all she needed to know.

She considered him carefully. "You were never a soldier."

That was true. Her spy. Her advisor. Her savior, when Sofiyana would have executed her.

"You were never stern enough to be a soldier."

He held her gaze, seeing his influence with Anastyna dissolve.

She left him, walking back to her hut.

VALENTY PACED THE LENGTH OF THE RIDGE WHERE THE COMMAND tents stood. At the farthest end, the outcropping dropped away sheer to the valley floor. He looked north in the direction of Yevliesza's new camp. *Run,* he urged her.

Anastyna's decision had shaken him. Her recklessness, her cunning charm and bearing that had knocked over the lords Dorofey and Genrikh like cups on a table.

He stared northward. Somewhere out there, the armies would meet. Strangely, it was not the worst thing that could happen. The worst was collapsing the gates.

Returning to his bivouac, he passed by the backside of Anastyna's hovel. He heard a voice outside the door. Someone talking to Anastyna, he guessed.

". . . three days at the most," the person was saying.

"Bring her bound if you have to," Anastyna said. "Choose twenty warriors. Use what means you have to and bring her with all speed."

"At your command, my lady." Urik's voice. She was sending Urik. And twenty *harjat.*

SOFIYANA WOKE AS THE DAWN LEAKED INTO HER TENT. SHE WINCED AS a flash of light caught her gaze. Not from outside but from the middle of the tent.

Disoriented, she staggered from the cot, grabbing her cloak from its pile. She approached the square of light that should not be there, could not be there. By the Mythos, it was a mirror. It rested upon her great trunk that served as a dressing table.

She recoiled. Mirrors were never used, since it was a simple matter for a manifester to send an unpleasant image into mirrors. How could it even be there? Sofiyana slowly reached for the frame, reached for it with her right hand, since her left was black and throbbing with pain.

Bringing the mirror up to look within, all she saw was her reflection.

A thin, haggard face, but her own. She had grown thin—she had known this—but now, the proof. Her skin, taut over her cheekbones, crinkled with small lines. Her nose and chin jutted unnaturally large. Her eyes, dark and sorrowful, like trapped animals.

Slapping the mirror on the chest, Sofiyana turned away, cupping her hands to her face, feeling the truth of what had been revealed. Her skin like parchment, her plump cheeks hollowed.

Fleeing the tent, she stepped out. No guards attended her.

The camp was awake, with cookfires tended here and there and soldiers rising from their rest.

Someone had placed a mirror in her tent. A mirror, eschewed by Numinasi for causing mischief of sendings. But this mirror was not for mischief. It was a rebuke, as though someone would have her look at herself and see a hideous revelation. And they had help. The guards, leaving their posts. Her attendants, curiously absent.

Sofiyana laughed. The sound drew the attention of a few soldiers nearby.

You cannot hurt me, she thought. Her life was over. All the tasks, the expectations, the terror, the folly of it all. The thought lifted her heart: she could be done with it.

None of you can hurt me.

Her world had turned against her. The farther she had stepped into the world of high affairs, the more despised, the more ruined, she had become. Until there was nothing left. No one in the mirror. No one she recognized.

She was done with things. *You cannot hurt me.*

⚜

AS HER ATTENDANTS—SUDDENLY APPEARING—HELPED HER TO DRESS, she ignored their stiff behavior, their furtive glances at each other. She chose a fine dress of brown velvet trimmed in black fur and rubbed a soft cloth over the torc to bring out its shine. Her hair, tamed with fragrant oil and secured in its net. Black leather gloves for both hands, not just the ruined one.

Her steward brought her horse, and she rode to the top of the hill where she saw Commander Ilyan mounted on his horse with other officers nearby. She had not pressed him to make further efforts to arrest Yevliesza. Now that she had failed, the black rot grew worse, even though she had buried the ring. It was in her skin now, and it was spreading.

Ilyan looked surprised to see her after so many days of her keeping to her tent. "My Lady Princip," he said in a flat tone when she drew near.

"Commander." There was one last thing she had to say to him. He hardly glanced at her, sitting on his horse like a great block of stone, draped in the red and white of Osta Kiya. "What news?" she asked.

"News of?"

A rude response. She no longer deserved his respect. She almost smiled at how such things once had mattered. "Of the war."

He looked out at the prospect before him. The camp with its tents, wagons, and horses. Its thousands of soldiers. "The enemy is coming, and their numbers will be vast. They control the crossings, so we do not look for help from Nubiah. Not in time."

"Or from Alfan Sih."

"Or Alfan Sih."

"How do the troops fare?"

He cut a glance at her, perhaps wondering why she suddenly cared. "They are hungry. We are months away from harvest, and winter stores run low."

"But you will still fight," she said. Under Ilyan, the men would fight. No surrender.

"When they come."

She stared far into the plains, where the sunrise ripened along the horizon in an orange smear. "Do we have a chance?"

Ilyan rubbed the jowls under his beard as he considered how truthful to be. "We are overmatched, my lady. Three to one unless Anastyna comes. Then almost two to one."

As she gazed out, she tried to imagine the first sight of the invaders, leading with their machines, the stalking iron monsters she had heard of, the shields that spat iron.

"If you move forward from this position now," she said, "and meet them halfway, our fighters will be rested, and theirs will not."

He snorted. "Halfway to where?"

"The Plain of Monuments."

He stared at her. "The Plain of Monuments?"

A hawk swooped in front of them, spooking his horse. He patted its neck, calming it. She watched him as the idea took hold that she knew the enemy's plans. He must despise her, but he also needed her information. "Coming through which gate?"

"Perhaps both," she murmured. "Coming at you from the north and the south."

He watched her closely, his expression outraged, barely restrained. "North and south."

"Of course, no one can be sure how they will come," she said. Nashavety's plans could change. But she would leave it at that. If he thought she spoke to the enemy, then he might believe her. The breeze in her face and across her body felt cleansing.

There was nothing more to say. As she turned her horse, Ilyan quietly spoke: "It is not too late, my lady."

Oh, it had been too late long ago.

"You can stand with us," he said.

That was not to be. She felt a smile try to form, but it only tightened her face. "Commander, it is not too late to win. Or nobly try."

Nobly? She wished she had not allowed that word past her lips. Ironic, coming from such as she.

Her horse knew the way back to the tent.

There, she had an attendant summon the Lord High Steward from his tent among the gathered functionaries of Osta Kiya. He possessed the key to the torc, to take it from her neck.

The wind off the plains blew through her. She did not believe in redemption, not for such as her. She could not think what to do with her wretched self, except to leave the torc behind. Leave the camp and its world. To leave behind the burden and terror. To leave herself entirely.

Chapter Twenty-Three

In the shadow light of predawn, Valenty walked toward the camp paddock. The smell of incipient rain came to him with its gray promise. He passed the newly erected pavilion of Duke Tanfred, pennant flapping in the sporadic breeze like a one-winged bird. It was an odd standard, a lone tree on a white field.

As he passed the tent, a voice halted him. "Lord Valenty." Duke Tanfred approached him, merely a shadow in the gloaming.

"Your Grace," Valenty said. "You have either stayed up late or arisen early."

"A little of both, I think."

Valenty had met Duke Tanfred when he briefly stayed at Osta Kiya after helping Yevliesza escape from Volkia. He liked the man—a Volkish noble who disdained his kingdom's leadership, and who had given heart to the army camped here.

As they stood, the duke absently twisted a large ring on his finger. "I cannot speak freely, my lord, but I am troubled." Valenty waited for him to go on, suspecting why he was disturbed. "I helped a woman once. I fear she may need help again, God forbid."

The Volkish, Valenty remembered, believed in a deity. If their god could forbid something, he wondered, why did he not prevent it from happening? "Yevliesza is called to answer for herself," he cautiously said. Called to answer why she did not close the gates. Anastyna well knew what her answer was.

Tanfred regarded him, waiting for him to go on. Things that could not be said hovered in the air.

"You have some influence," Tanfred finally said. "More than I."

"Not in this matter." It was an abrupt response, and Valenty, regretting it, decided to trust him. "I have spoken plainly"—he glanced at the hilltop—"to no effect."

"I see." The duke's disappointment was well masked. In his latter days in Volkia, he must have learned how to keep his opinions hidden.

"You may yet know more of my intention, as the day unfolds." Valenty had said too much already, and he was in a hurry. "I bid you good day, Your Grace."

As Valenty left, he wondered if Duke Tanfred had more than a kindly concern for Yevliesza. If so, he did not think Yevliesza returned his interest. When she had come back from Volkia, she had become Valenty's lover. Not the actions of a woman who pined for another. But then, only a few days ago Yevliesza had rescued Tanfred in turn, taking him through a passage she had forged. Surely only for the good of Numinat and no other reason.

But Valenty had relinquished any right to be jealous. She had invited him to be with her as she went north to establish her own camp. And he had stayed with Anastyna.

At the paddock, the sentries recognized him and did not stir from their posts. No one else was there, but soon the *harjat* would arrive to mount up and leave for Arrow Shaft camp, as Yevliesza had started to call it. Their mission: to force Yevliesza to return. Then she would be compelled to obey, the very thing she had feared since her strange power had come to her months ago.

So much had changed since then. Yevliesza had been tried for treason, acquitted, become his lover, and left him—unless he had left her. Closer to the truth. Anastyna had been deposed, lost her army then gained an army, becoming the princip in exile. The princip who would now yoke Yevliesza—the Keeper, as she liked to be known—to her will. As Prince Albrecht had tried to do.

Valenty searched for his place in this cascade of events. Tried to find himself blameless. Failed.

Was it too late for Yevliesza to live as a free woman? Was it too late for her to find the goodness she sought, the proper use of the power she had been vouchsafed—or, as she would frame it, had stumbled into by accident. A mistake made by the First Ones, who had looked for a worthy vessel and, finding none, settled on her?

Circling back, he tried to sort out what mischance had placed him in Anastyna's camp instead of the Keeper's. It was not hard to reckon. Duty. Duty to the princip whom he had served for the six years of her reign, as his father had served Princip Lisbetha before him. The princip's knower, listener, spy, and first sword.

How had he not seen the woman's true nature? She had been the new princip, learning her way, trying to do good. The noble ruler. But nobility had slipped into dilemma and then into misjudgment. Suspicion and paranoia were not far behind.

Whether it was too late for Yevliesza or not, he was going to salvage what he could of his true duty. He did not know where it would end. But it would begin now.

The *harjat* had arrived to saddle their mounts. They carried swords and small shields. Prepared for defiance.

There were twenty warriors, Urik among them. Urik, who not long ago had accompanied him on the fraught mission to Volkia. Who had helped Valenty rescue Pyvel from the demented house in the forest. Urik, who, with keen manifesting power, had enabled their escape from the Volkish-held crossings. Urik, without whom Valenty would not have survived the mission.

The *harjat* warriors noted him, and Urik separated himself from the group to join him at the fence. "My lord," he said, meeting Valenty's gaze with a neutral face. Assessing him. Guessing his purpose.

"You go north," Valenty began. "Perhaps she will not be there."

"Then we will find her elsewhere."

Valenty looked at the elite fighters who had orders to take her into custody and would surely succeed. Who did Yevliesza have to protect her besides a few of Warden Kirady's men?

"You were there," Valenty said, "at the camp by the Yanuri River, when she revealed her birthright power." He had been imprisoned at Osta Kiya at the time, but he knew of the meeting when Yevliesza had tried to reconcile with Anastyna. Telling her of the lost, saving power. Which must be used for all the Mythos, not just Numinat.

"I was there." Urik waited. His men were affixing small shields to their saddles, pointedly not looking at the two men conferring over the fence.

Valenty went on. "She told the princip that she could not be under the control of any kingdom. You know why. For the Mythos?"

"So she said."

He was going to make Valenty say the words. And he did. "You can stand down. If you find her, stand down. For the Mythos."

Urik put his hand on the hilt of his sword.

Valenty noted it, wary.

Urik said, "When I came to Anastyna's side on the plains of Osta Kiya, I believed the new princip was under sorcerous control." His voice was low, out of hearing of his men. "But Anastyna is not infected with sorcery, and I am sworn to her."

He would not break ranks.

"As are you, Lord Valenty," Urik reminded him.

"No longer," Valenty said. Urik raised an eyebrow. "Today I will ask her to release me from service."

Urik's gaze became less friendly. "You should have waited to speak to me until you had been released." He walked away a few paces but then turned back. "I will forget this meeting."

❧

Anastyna's attendants made him wait. A low cloud blanketed the ridge. Rain spat down like stones. The two guards stationed at her door appeared not to notice.

One of Anastyna's women came out to retrieve firewood and curtsied to him as though they were in the royal quarters of the palace. The trappings of power. Anastyna would have her warm hovel and was showing displeasure by leaving him in the rain. It was petty, and he refused to be bothered by it.

At last the door opened, and an attendant ushered him inside.

Anastyna sat in a wooden chair covered by a striped horse blanket. Over her plain bodice and skirt she wore the only fine thing she had, a cape with an ermine collar. She liked to cover her neck where the torc should have been. Her face was wan and pinched. He wondered how he had ever thought her handsome.

"My Lord Valenty," she softly said. Not asking him to sit in one of the other two chairs. Her attendants stood against the wall. All to make a statement. This was to be an audience with the princip, not a conversation.

"My Lady Princip." He glanced at the two attendants. They had hastily dressed, and one had not had time to pin up her hair. It fell long in back, gathered with a thong. Anastyna's hair was properly nesting in a crocheted hair net.

She thought she knew why he had come: that he would ask her to retract the order to seize Yevliesza.

Instead he went to one knee in front of her. "My lady, I beg to be released from duty. It has been my honor to serve you. But now I ask your permission to retire."

In the long silence that followed, his heart was heavy. Sparks flew upward from the surging fire, up toward the hole in the roof. Stars fleeing the world, in a sky where they could only be short-lived.

"Valenty," came Anastyna's subdued voice.

He saw that she was trying to smile, a tender smile. Perhaps she wished to charm him, to show him a gentler disposition than he had lately seen.

"This is not necessary."

He still knelt. "I do ask it, My Lady Princip."

"What would you do?"

"Become a simple soldier." He would not say *her* soldier. He hoped she would not ask.

"I do not see this, Valenty. A simple soldier! Please stand. It is not necessary."

"Am I refused, then?" Valenty said, meeting her disturbed gaze.

Anastyna sat very still. The moments dragged on. She would not beg him to reconsider, not in front of the attendants. Perhaps not in any case.

Then: "I release you, my lord." She gestured for him to stand, and he did so. "What will you do, Valenty?"

"I will find a unit that will have me. And fight." Not the complete truth, but truth enough.

The princip nodded, her face stony. Pointedly, she glanced at the door, and, taking this as a dismissal, he left the audience hut.

He would fight. But first it would be against Urik, if he could catch him.

Before he left the camp, there was someone else who should be released from duty.

Grigeni was waiting for Valenty, having built a morning fire and laid out a portion of hard bread and the last of a rind of cheese. Valenty placed the food in a saddlebag that he had packed the night before.

Grigeni raised his eyebrows, questioning. The camp was stirring now, the sentries changing places with fresh men, cookfires smoking and spitting in a fading rain.

He hoisted his saddlebag over his shoulder and faced Grigeni. "Anastyna has released me from service."

A stunned look.

"Grigeni, my friend." Valenty hated to dismiss him, but he had no choice. "I am leaving to find service elsewhere. I will miss you."

"My lord—" Grigeni's voice broke as he uttered the words. "Why? You have earned her respect, done everything that—"

"Grigeni. I asked leave to go. I cannot serve her in good faith. But her actions are always for the best of Numinat. Trust her, as I have. And as I no longer can."

Grigeni struggled for what to say. "She said yes?"

"She did. Would you tell Pyvel?"

Grigeni looked beyond Valenty's shoulder, and Valenty turned. Pyvel.

The lad spoke. "I did not mean to overhear."

Valenty went to him. "I have to leave, but it is with the princip's permission."

"Can I go, too?"

He could not. The boy was with the army. Attached to Captain Nikander in the horse unit. "You must fight honorably for Anastyna. As I know you will." He put out his hand. Pyvel stared at it, then clasped it with his own.

Turning back to Grigeni, Valenty heard Pyvel ask, "But why do you have to go?"

Standing between the two of him, he gave up on discretion. "For the love of Yevliesza," he said. "Which I tell only you. No one else." He gazed pointedly at Grigeni and then Pyvel.

Pyvel nodded, and Grigeni said, "I would come with you."

Valenty did not think his mission would end well and did not want Grigeni there to share what would happen.

"No, Grigeni, but I thank you."

With that, he went to the paddock to find his saddle and one of his horses from Osta Kiya, one of those that a month ago had carried the princip and her rescuers who fled from the city-palace.

Dawn crept soddenly over the plain as he set out. The rain stuttered on in fits. He found the trail of the *harjat* and followed it.

❦

HE TOOK A SMALL, FAST HORSE. VALENTY'S ONLY HOPE TO WARN Yevliesza would be to outride the *harjat* unit and get to Arrow Shaft camp first. It was a two-day journey. One, if he did not sleep. Urik would not use up his horses by moving fast and would rest them at night. Valenty would not.

As he set out, his plan was to circle around the riders, keeping out of sight, and, when they stopped to camp, continue on as well as he could by the light of a nearly full moon. If the rain cleared.

Twenty riders had left the paddock that morning. Coming upon the party, he counted them. Twenty still. Urik was not using outriders to scout.

For the first-quarter day, the undulating landscape gave him cover in the ravines. It was the season when deep gullies bore streams. This saved his water supply and provided new green fodder for his mount. The piebald mare was young and muscular, a mount he knew well from Osta Kiya days. The rain came in erratic pulses, sometimes merely splatters riding on gusts and other times drenching him and the mare. Except for those times, they moved fast, seeing little of settlements, only the occasional farm and herd of sheep. Twice a dactyl soared overhead, once close enough to see the mounted scout who appeared not to notice him. He—or, more likely, she—was watching for an army, not a lone rider. Dactyls preferred female riders, for what reason, no one knew.

He thought of Kirjanichka, the dactyl he had gifted to his former wife, Dreiza, and how the creature was old enough to have borne Dreiza's mother before her on journeys. Kirjanichka still lived, taken back into army service when Dreiza went for a *satvar*.

His former fellow spy, Elivasa, in her wanderings, had told him how Dreiza was now at Arrow Shaft camp in company with a young woman whose gift of foretelling had unbalanced her mind. Kassalya, her name was. Hardly more than a girl. He remembered seeing her, wild-eyed and reclusive, at Zolvina.

These thoughts hovered like gnats around him, but riding his shoulders was the constant fear for Yevliesza and her jeopardy should she be brought before Anastyna. Who was running out of time to save her kingdom. The gates must fall, the princip believed. Yevliesza would be forced to it, Anastyna being in a hurry and believing that the coming battle would be a massacre.

Chapter Twenty-Four

At first her goal was to ride to her home in Karsk Polity. Her
mother still lived there and would take her in. No doubt with
dismay. It seemed a lifetime ago when Sofiyana would have
cared about her mother's disapproval. Now it would feel like a blessing, so long as her mother was not sending her nightmares and asking
her to murder people.

The family hall was no palace: a dozen rooms, a few servants. The
distant mountains with its snow-fed streams fed the river that watered
the crops. Their land included the apple orchards where, as a child, she
had loved the rows of blossoming trees that formed corridors to
adventure.

If only she had never left.

Her horse had stopped to graze. Dismounting, she tied its reins to a
fallen log. She had remembered to bring grain for it, but it was all gone
now, two days into her journey. It was a stupid animal, but she needed
it for her journey to Karsk. Ahead, the Numin Mountains were a
purple, lumpen shape on the horizon. She rode northward to put
distance between her and the torc. Her and the amber ring. Her and
Nashavety, who was coming to take the realm.

She remembered the resounding click when the Lord High Steward turned the key to remove the torc from her neck. Ah, the lightness as the torc fell away! Like manacles struck from the ankles of a prisoner grown accustomed to their weight. While she was still princip two days ago, she had ordered the high steward to delay a few hours before he told anyone that she had set aside the torc. Soldiers could still come after her. But why would they? They would be happy to be rid of her and her short reign of eighty-two days.

Mounted again, she rode on. Her only food, a hunk of bread and a winter pear left over from her breakfast. Every day she let herself have three bites of each.

When she came to the confluence of rivers and the way home was to the west, her horse plodded on northward. It knew she was not going home. She could not remember having decided; perhaps she had always known the true end of her journey. Her destination called to her with harsh but valiant words. *Come to your rest. Leave all your burden behind. It will not be so bad.*

❧

Sofiyana's legs ached from the saddle, her thighs locked in iron pain. She had grown to appreciate pain. To expiate her ruinous stupidity. She still hated Yevliesza—she could not get past that—but saw it for the envy it was, so another reason for the pain of riding the horse. She needed some pain, but she was not above wishing for respite. Moments when the great flatlands lay in the exalted shadows of dusk, or a bird soared in a kingdom of light. At times like that, she knew the secret of happiness. Not being inside yourself. The prison of her self, where all bad things unfolded. Wanting to be first in the arcana; wanting Prince Tirhan to admire her; wanting Nashavety to stop hating her; and, finally, wishing for Yevliesza to fall from grace. The end of the journey of wanting.

❧

North to the mountains. The silvery, cold breath of winter-still-clinging. The clean white ice and snow.

She came to a village in the foothills. She had hoped to reach the snows during the daylight, but in the heavy cloak of darkness, the horse could not pick its way. A pallet of straw and several dusty blankets, paid for by a piece of silver from her purse.

The next day, weak from hunger, she allowed herself a morning meal of bread and blood sausage. She had hardly eaten on her journey, and the rich food was soon lost as she fell to her knees and retched.

Then she rode on.

The mountains were not all one spine. There were ranges upon ranges, each one taller than the last. Somewhere up there—she had asked the tavern-keeper's wife—was the Zolvina Sanctuary. Her horse could not manage the snows surrounding Zolvina, and she felt remorse taking it into the mountains, but she could not think how to save the beast. The villagers would not let her walk into the snows; they would easily find her and bring her back, perhaps inviting her to earn her keep by cleaning the inn floor or shaking the blankets. But such a peaceful life was not for her.

Peaceful life. Not for her. Peaceful anything.

❧

Sofiyana lay on her back squinting at the light. Her body, aching and pierced by spears of pain. Everything clouded over, but the sun, still dazzling.

Death coming. Painful and bright. Or death already, brightly painful, if one's body lay in the sun, one's bones littering the rocks.

A murmuring. A face appearing, then fading. She was still able to close her eyes and did, but still, the brightness. So not dead yet. Faces and sounds. The image came to her, of fire and snow. She tried to speak, but nothing came out. How hard it was to speak when only bones were left. It was something to think on, and she tucked it away for later.

Someone was near. A blur, a presence.

"Am I dead?" she asked in a throaty whisper.

"No, Sofiyana."

That name. It had been hers. "Am I still her?" she asked.

The figure murmured, "Perhaps not now, but you will be."

She opened her eyes a little more. A shaft of sun was falling across her shrouded form. Lying on a cot. Above her, a woman's face, a stranger.

"Are you warm enough?" the woman asked.

"Cold."

A heavy weight fell across her body. An edge of it touched her face. Wool blanket.

"Who?" she asked. If they must drag her back from the peace of snows, she wanted to know who.

"I am Yarna. Of the *satvary*."

"I died?"

"You are healing, my daughter. The inn sent word to us that a great lady had fallen on the road and that the woman had been taken in, but with injuries. The snows are no barrier to me. My gift of the elements."

"Your gift," Sofiyana repeated. There were gifts, she remembered. "Mine was aligns."

"Yes, we know. You will be welcome at Zolvina. I came to take you the rest of the way."

"I cannot be a *satvar*. I have ruined things." *Everything.*

"Ruined things can be rebuilt."

They could?

She didn't think she had spoken, but the *satvar* answered. "It may take some time, but yes."

Yes. It had been so long since she had heard that word. "I will try. But my hand . . ."

"There is a great healer at Zolvina. She is waiting for you."

Sleep pulled on her, but Sofiyana remembered the horse. She could begin there. He was only a beast, but he deserved his life.

"He has been gifted to the inn-keeper, who refused it, but said he will keep it for Zolvina. Occasionally we go forth into the world."

Go forth into the world. Not a good idea.

Then she heard, "What did you do with the torc?"

Torc? Oh, the metal collar. "In my tent. Do you want it?" People seemed to want it. Hard to know why. It was very heavy.

"No, my daughter. But the High Mother would like to keep track of it."

"She cares?"

"In her way. *From a distance,* she likes to say."

⁂

THE LAND GRADUALLY ROSE INTO A REGION OF FOREST. VALENTY LET his mount pick its way through the underbrush, slow progress except when they found a deer path.

In the first-quarter night the weather worsened, and to go on risked a broken leg or other injury to his horse. They camped in a clearing that held the remnants of a log charcoal kiln, and Valenty took cover under a giant cedar where the overhanging branches made a roof.

The moon had not yet risen. He would sleep for a short while and move on when the storm front passed.

He woke to find the clearing silvered by the nearly full moon. Standing next to the charcoal pit, a man. Valenty sprang to his feet, grabbing the sword that lay next to him. The man was warrior, leather-clad and broad-shouldered, a short sword at his hip.

Urik.

"I guessed it was you who followed us," Urik said. "But my men said you would not be so foolish."

"Followed you?" Valenty asked in mock confusion. "Last I noticed, you were far behind me." Valenty walked toward him but kept a few paces away.

"Where are you going, Valenty?" Urik asked. No pretense of friendship. No deference to a lord of Osta Kiya.

"That is my own business. But Anastyna has released me from service."

"Yet you still owe her a subject's loyalty." Urik's right hand was resting on his sword belt instead of the weapon's pommel. Not threatening. But not relaxed.

"I have business with my wife at Arrow Shaft camp."

"The wife you abandoned. I wonder what a man says to such a woman. And how many would ride so far to say it."

Urik was not going to let him go. How could he when it was clear Valenty was trying to warn Yevliesza? Urik appeared to be alone. He might stand a chance.

"If you want to stop me, you will have to kill me," Valenty said. "Or the other way around." He and Urik were about the same height, but the *harjat* had the strength of two courtiers and was the better swordsman. Once, they had been friends.

"Valenty," Urik softly said. "Go in a different direction while you are still able."

Valenty stood with his sword, ready to fight. Urik unbuckled his sword belt, flinging it away along with his weapon. It would be hand-to-hand. Valenty cast aside his sword and advanced on Urik, moving to the right, Urik's left and weaker side.

Urik moved in fast, ready to punch. Valenty's hands were clenched in front of his face, but Urik's jabs got through, hitting him in the mouth and cheek. Not giving ground, Valenty sprang forward, slapping Urik in the side of the head and bringing up an elbow to follow the blow, but Urik ducked away. He swung around to land a punch under Valenty's chin that sent his head backward.

Urik moved forward, grabbing him by the shoulders and ramming a knee into his chest, but Valenty was already stepping backward, draining the force of the blow. A kick to Valenty's hip sent him sprawling.

Knowing that he was finished if he stayed down, he rolled onto his side and started to rise, but Urik landed a full-booted kick to his stomach, knocking the wind out of him. Valenty managed to stagger upright, bringing his fists up to block the next assault.

Urik punched him in the ribs, a hard blow this time. The other punches and kicks had been to find his measure.

Valenty might have brought his warding to bear. But it would have been cowardly. And it would have only prolonged the fight.

Urik's men had come to watch at the edge of the clearing. There was no point to the fight now. But he had to finish this, one way or the other. Nothing to gain, but rage needed satisfying, no matter the battering he might take. Urik was the lackey of a half-crazed monarch and had misplaced his honor.

Valenty rushed at him, delivering a high kick to his chest that landed solidly, getting a satisfied grunt from a man who so far had hardly broken a sweat. Valenty closed on him, fists up, but Urik slapped his hands down and swiped an elbow into the side of his face. The world tilted. Dazed, he saw the ground come up to meet him.

Stepping back, Urik waited for him to rise. He could not.

"Brave to fight without your warding," Urik said.

Valenty made it to his feet, swaying. Had he even touched his opponent? He remembered a good kick he had delivered. It pleased him. It also pleased him that Urik had not killed him.

"I am taking your horse," Urik said. Of course he was. Without the horse, Valenty could not interfere.

In another moment the clearing held only Valenty and the charcoal pit. A dark sky diluted by moonlight shed a fey light on the clearing and the surrounding woods.

By the place where he had slept, he found his water skin and drank. He could not see much beyond the perimeter of the clearing. Had he not been in this state for a long time? His sight, always incomplete. No wonder he had misjudged his duty and the devotion that he owed the only woman he had ever loved for herself alone.

He did not think he could bear what was coming.

❧

THE NEXT DAY HE SET OUT AGAIN TO FIND YEVLIESZA, FOLLOWING THE clear footprints of twenty horses heading north. The day was warm, and he stopped to drink from his skin of water.

He could not thwart Anastyna's intention, but he would go to Yevliesza, wherever she was. When Urik returned with her to Anastyna's camp, he could see them coming and would meet them on the way. He had nothing else to hang on to, no goal, no fine thing to accomplish. But a man could walk and see what the world brought to him.

It brought him Grigeni.

His servant crested a hill on a fine gray gelding. He approached, sitting uneasily in the saddle, bumping along as though he had never seen a horse before, much less ridden one.

Valenty helped him dismount. "Did the army dispatch you to seize me?"

"No, my lord!" Grigeni looked at Valenty's swollen face in dismay.

"Then you have deserted." Valenty looked at his erstwhile steward, his narrow face and keen eyes, his thin frame better suited to caring for shelves of books than wielding a sword. A man who nevertheless had helped Anastyna escape Osta Kiya one desperate night when the world went mad.

"I came to serve you, my lord." Grigeni looked bewildered by Valenty's condition. His torn shirt, his badgered face. "Where is your horse?"

Valenty ignored the question. "Grigeni, you serve the princip. Go back, or you will be a fugitive, never again welcome in Osta Kiya."

"I will not be a Keeper of Books anymore," Grigeni fiercely said. "Or a soldier." In his face, a challenge. "I have my own life."

"The cost, Grigeni. The cost." This man used to serve a lord. Valenty now had no status and could not provide for him.

Grigeni held his ground. "But do we belong to Anastyna?"

Valenty used to think so. He patted the horse's neck as it pawed the ground.

"It is one of your horses, lord," Grigeni assured him, as though Valenty could not distinguish one horse from another.

"I well know it, Grigeni." He glanced in the general direction of Anastyna's camp, murmuring bitterly, "She does not own everything."

Chapter Twenty-Five

Lura shook Yevliesza awake as dawn crept into the tent, infusing the walls with a dull glow. "Rusadka is here, mistress." Her maid wore only a shift, and her unruly hair framed her face in curly tangles.

Shaking herself awake, Yevliesza saw Rusadka standing at the tent entrance. "Riders," she said. "Get dressed."

Yevliesza hurried to do so, worried by Rusadka's tone of voice. She shed her night shift, and Lura handed over a shirt and leggings.

As Yevliesza shrugged into her clothes, Rusadka said, "Twenty of them. *Harjat*."

"Maybe friends?" Yevliesza pulled on her boots. "Bringing word of something?"

"One *harjat* can bear a message. Five make up a bodyguard. Twenty are coming for a fight. And Urik is with them. Anastyna's *harjat*."

Anastyna. Yevliesza bit her lip. The wretched woman had done it again, was trying to use her. "How close are they?"

"The sentries say they will be here any moment."

Lura held Yevliesza's knife, offering it, but Yevliesza waved it away. What good would a knife do her?

"Take it," Rusadka said. "You will look weak without a weapon."

"Watch them cower," Yevliesza murmured.

They left the tent, and when Zander spotted them, he approached. "Keeper?"

Rusadka said, "We are going to take refuge in the cave."

Captain Vadik, charged with Yevliesza's protection, approached with his men. "Zander, you will meet with the warriors. But do not try to stop them." Though the camp's size was reduced now to a hundred and twenty people, mostly peasants, there could be trouble if people saw that the camp was under threat. Vadik went on. "If there is a fight, it will be at the cave. My men will accompany the Keeper."

The fifteen trained soldiers that Kirady had left to guard Yevliesza fell in with her and Rusadka as they hurried off. At Yevliesza's side, Captain Vadik said, "You will have time to lose yourself in the crossings, mistress. We will hold them off at the base."

When they arrived at the cave, she and Rusadka scrambled up the rock-strewn slope and stood on the outcropping in front of the entrance. Vadik and his men took up positions on the lower slope.

Yevliesza saw that, some two hundred yards away at the edge of the camp, the band of *harjat* had ridden in. An impressive display of mounted warriors.

"We can't win against them," Yevliesza said.

"But we can," Rusadka said. "Go into the crossings." She cut a glance at her. "And close the miserable gate behind you."

Rusadka's face stiffened as a tumult began around the newcomers. She told Yevliesza, "Go."

"They are fighting?"

Rusadka had keener eyes than Yevliesza did, and reported, "The fight is over. Go!" Since Captain Vadik couldn't see from his position what had happened, Rusadka went down the slope to tell him.

Chest tight, her breathing shallow, Yevliesza waited to see if she could talk to Urik. She didn't know him well, but she wanted to be sure what was happening. If he was determined to take her by force, she could easily disappear into the backways.

As the warriors approached the cave, Rusadka climbed back up to join Yevliesza, unhappy to see her still outside the cave. She drew her sword.

Urik and his men assembled some twenty paces from Captain Vadik's soldiers.

"Mistress Yevliesza," Urik said in a strong voice, looking up at her, "Princip Anastyna sends for you."

Yevliesza called back to him, "What does she want, Urik?" She thought her voice sounded weak, like a girl's. She rested her hand on the knife she had stuck in her belt. Using a broom against a bear.

"She has not told me," Urik answered, his voice carrying well, no need to shout. Behind him, the band of *harjat* stood relaxed. Alert. Too alert. They had not drawn weapons, but stood with hands at their sides, wisps of their long hair catching the wind. Their mounts with narrow streamers fluttering from their saddles, the *harjat* color of yellow and black.

"Go," Rusadka harshly whispered at Yevliesza.

Instead, she called out, "Did you kill any of my people?"

"One has a broken rib or two. The others stood down."

"But you will fight the men here?" She looked at Vadik's troop.

"Not if you come willingly."

"Miserable hells, go!" Rusadka spat at her.

Urik was speaking again. "I know that you can go into the backways. I cannot stop you. But I will wait. You will need food and water. Eventually, you will come with me."

The very thing she had been thinking. She couldn't stay in the crossings forever. What Urik didn't realize was that, once inside the backways, she could forge an escape to somewhere far away from Arrow Shaft. "How long do I have to decide?"

"I would give you all the hours you want, Mistress Yevliesza," Urik gravely said. "But it is not my mission."

"But how long?"

"You must come now." He looked at the soldiers arrayed against the slope. "These fifteen men will fall. There will be blood on the rocks, and nothing will have changed for you."

She couldn't avoid the conflict by giving herself up. Anastyna would compel her to pull down the Numinat gates, using whatever torture she could devise. Yevliesza would be the one who ruined the world.

Movement in the camp caught her attention. Many people were walking through the forest clearing toward the cave. Her people in the camp, some with staves and hoes for weapons. Her seekers. The ones who had come to her, hoping to learn truths or be saved, or to learn to be brave. They were already brave.

She was afraid for them. People were going to die here. Either people from the camp or Vadik's men. Maybe both. Was her life worth more than theirs? Her usefulness was no longer critical. The ugly truth began to come into focus. She could not be responsible for ending these lives, the lives of people who mistakenly thought she was supremely valuable.

There might be a way out, but she was having a hard time resolving to do it.

She turned to Rusadka. "Will you go down and speak to Urik? Tell him that the people who are coming are peasants, mostly women, and we don't want them hurt."

"I am not going to leave you."

"Rusadka. If it comes to a fight, another sword will do no good. But you can save these people." She looked at her friend. Rusadka hated to miss a fight, and if she went down, Urik might not allow her to rejoin the soldiers. "Quickly, please."

Finally Rusadka sheathed her weapon and left the shelf of the cave, picking her way down the slope toward Urik.

Yevliesza hated to deceive Rusadka. But it was the only way.

As Rusadka spoke with Urik, Yevliesza sat, her back against the rock wall. Vadik and his men stood in place on the flat and some on the lower slope, weapons drawn.

A *harjat* called out to the approaching villagers. He held a lance perpendicular to his body and thrust it forward, clearly telling them to stop. The crowd hesitated. They looked up at Yevliesza for direction. She waved her hand at them in a pushing motion.

The sun rose over the trees, its light reaching first the cave entrance and then inching down the rock slope. As she considered what had to be done, her skin prickled. A cold shiver snaked across her arms and chest. She had always been a visitor here. That is all anyone was in the world. The space around her grew quiet and overbright.

Still seated, she drew her blade, resting her knife hand on one knee. "Urik, you see that I have a knife."

"I do."

"If you come up this slope, if you kill any of these soldiers standing in front of the cave, or even if you push past them doing no harm and come up the slope, I will use this knife on myself."

A moan from the crowd.

"There is no need for anyone to die," Urik said. He walked closer to the slope.

She put the knife to her neck.

"Stop," Urik said. "I'm coming closer so that I do not have to shout."

A lie. He hadn't been shouting. She kept the knife poised.

"Yevliesza," he said. "All this is for Numinat, the land that took you in. All for Numinat."

The noble partial truth. The entire truth was that it was not only about Numinat. She responded: "The Mythos will die, Urik. It can. Anything can die."

A movement caught her attention. One of the villagers, a man, rushed forward with his stave. A *harjat* kicked it from his grasp, then blocked a feeble attack from one of the women. The rest of the band ranged out to each side of their fellow warrior, presenting a wall of fighting power. The crowd quieted.

Yevliesza called out to Vadik, "Captain, please go to my people and persuade them that they're distracting me from my purpose. That I'm asking them to return to their campsites and wait for me."

Vadik sent one of his men. Meanwhile, Urik and his warriors stood waiting.

Now she was growing afraid. She tested the blade's edge, hoping to find it sharp. It would have to be, to make the action quick.

It was very sharp.

The crowd began to disperse. Rusadka started to climb the slope.

"Rusadka! Stop." Yevliesza hardened her heart. "Anyone who climbs the slope kills me."

Rusadka hesitated. She had come farther than any of Vadik's soldiers, but now she stood still. No one moved.

Yevliesza suspected this would be a long wait. She wanted to ask the Mythos, *If this is how it's going to end, didn't you see it? Didn't you see I was never the person who should have had this power? Didn't you think the whole godawful thing through?*

The sun rose in the sky. It fell on Yevliesza's face like a mother's hand, warm, reassuring. The day was cloudless, the blue of the sky infused with light. The trees reached for the sun, their mossy hue slowly brightening to a drenched velvet green. Everyone below her, standing still. A raven swept across the lip of the cave. An omen. Of something.

Urik ordered his *harjat* to sit. He did as well. His signal that they would wait.

At first Vadik didn't allow his soldiers to sit. But he must have known that it was a way of agreeing to stand down, at least for now. Then no one was standing except Rusadka.

The sun rose high. Yevliesza was grateful for the cloak, because of the wind and the rock ledge that still held the night's cold.

A small movement below. Vadik had a skin of water on a strap and stood to throw it to her. A *harjat* sprang up and stretched out a forbidding hand. Vadik looked up at her, and she shook her head. No one was going to die over a drink of water. He could have died if he had thrown the water to her. Because of honor. There was a code, invisible but powerful. You give your word. You know your duty, and you do it.

The same as her. She hadn't sworn to anyone, but she knew her duty. Anyone would know if they were in her place. But still: *I swear,* she said to whoever or whatever was listening.

The standoff with Urik was a game of chicken, as they said in the mundat. Who would give up first? She was no use dead, but they would have to believe her threat. She could cut off the small finger of her left hand and accomplish the same thing, but she wasn't sure how long it would take to saw through the bone and if they could grab her before she succeeded. And she worried that her other fingers would get in the way, and that she couldn't cut off any of the others fast enough. The knife at her throat, more reliable.

Rusadka tried to speak with her from time to time. She didn't answer. Words weakened her resolve. Words couldn't carry the load of meaning she clung to. Having sworn.

The best time for them to come for her would be at night. Vadik's men would fight. If she fell asleep, the noise would wake her. If they waited for her to weaken from lack of food and water, the Volkish might already be on the plains, and Urik's *harjat* would be far from the battle. When they figured that out, they would leave. If she could keep her courage.

The sun fell on her face and hands. The wind stirred the tree tops. Her cloak tented around her shoulders and thighs. Her mind quieted. Somewhere in the background thoughts jumped around, but never caught her attention.

The sun sank behind the rock outcropping. Sometimes she shifted her position to soothe her aching muscles and make clear that she was alert.

Nighttime. Wind harder now, thrashing the trees, grabbing at her cloak. She considered inching into the cave opening out of the wind, but no. Sitting on the ledge with the knife was her whole strategy. They had to see her to know she wasn't sleeping. Fear kept her awake. If she nodded off, the *harjat* would come, killing the soldiers in their path. Even if she woke up in time to use the knife, many would die. A thought to keep you awake.

A noise inside the cave sent shivers of alarm over her skin. Someone in there? She scrambled to her knees, knife ready, before she saw that it was Kiya.

He came to her side, his fur smelling of evergreens and gray dew. *Oh, Kiya.* Could he lead her to safety? As he had in the Castle of Holdfast, could he show her some mysterious way? She sat again, waiting for him to show her what to do, the impulse strong to throw her arms around him. Which you did not do with a wraith wolf. He stood at her side, looking out on the midnight scene below, his deep green eyes seeing things she could not. She inched back to rest against the rock slab. Kiya was with her. He lay down. Settling in.

Did he know she had a knife?

Then she had a thought of why he was there. He was here to accompany her to the place she was going. A tide of emotion rushed through her. Caught in her throat. So there was someplace to go at the end. Who could be afraid with a wraith wolf at their side?

They waited. She rested her left hand on his back. He allowed this.

Isha had introduced her to Kiya. When she had earned him. *All you have to do is poke your head out of the fog. To know your depths. Then nothing can touch you.* Yevliesza had pushed back. So she was supposed to give up everything? If that was all she had to do, why didn't Isha just say so? *Because it depends on what you want. What lasting, immutable, certain, and noble thing?* Well, a lasting thing. What lasted? Love of the world and all its creatures. Who could not want to protect that—who wouldn't die for it?

The call of an owl. The moon rose and she watched as it silvered Kiya's fur, his dark muzzle. The knife caught a sliver of moon. She rested her head against the rock wall, her thoughts on Valenty.

She jerked her head up. She had been sleeping! Loud noises below. Heart pounding, her limbs so stiff she couldn't get the knife up to her neck. Arms dead. Legs frozen. Kiya, gone. Or in the cave?

Shouts from below. Scuffling on the rocky slope. By the light of the false dawn, shadows moving below.

Rusadka called up. "Yevliesza, they are leaving! Do not move! Urik is leaving!"

Yevliesza had scrambled to a standing position, gripping the knife. Blackness below. They could be holding a knife to Rusadka's throat, forcing her to say it. Her heart, a drumbeat in her chest. She listened for any approach.

Vadik's voice. "Mistress! The *harjat* are leaving."

Were they truly? They would not leave; they were *harjat*. But a spark of hope somewhere in the depths. Leaving.

Rusadka spoke. "May I approach?"

"What?"

"Can I come closer to speak to you?"

"Only a little closer."

The crunch of boot on rocks. "How is this?"

Yevliesza stepped a short distance into the cave to look for Kiya. Nothing. No shadows in the backways behind the gate.

Rusadka was speaking to her. "Yevliesza, I am here, but will come no closer."

Yevliesza stepped back onto the ledge. "All right."

Shadows of Vadik's men were still arrayed in front of the slope. They were not dead. She was savagely alert, but her brain was cold and slow.

"Prince Fadimir is coming, Yevliesza."

"Who?"

"Prince of Dorodna Polity. With a thousand men."

She tried to imagine this. "How do you know?"

"Advance riders came into camp. Fadimir's men said that he has come to see the Keeper. Urik's scouts went out to confirm it."

"Come to see *me*?"

A beat. "Come down, Yevliesza. It is over."

Chapter Twenty-Six

She was in a crowd of people, Vadik and Rusadka at her side. Trying to make their way to her tent, they had to part the masses of people who pressed around her. Faces happy, relieved. Yevliesza stumbled. Vadik's hand shot out to catch her by the elbow. She had been sitting for hours, and now her legs felt like taffy in the sun.

Prince Fadimir had arrived in camp, and that had changed everything. Urik had heard that the prince had come to see the Keeper. He might have concluded that Fadimir was a friend to Yevliesza—in which case he must give in—or he had used it as an excuse to abort his mission. He was Valenty's friend. Maybe he hadn't savored his assignment.

A woman holding a youngster reached out to touch her hand. Yevliesza took it, gave her a solid grip.

"Keeper!" someone called out. Then more shouts. *Keeper, Keeper.*

"Thank you," she kept repeating. *Thank you.* Everything was vivid, the trees leaning in as though sharing in the procession. A square-faced man with a braided beard. His work-blackened hands. A stout woman with most of her teeth missing smiling in delight. A child of seven or eight with the deepest violet eyes she had ever seen.

They approached her tent. Several men, most of them strangers, waited for her. Zander came forward to lead her to them, saying, "Keeper. Thank the Mythos." He could not meet her eyes.

"You were right to avoid bloodshed," Yevliesza said. "It's what I wanted."

A small nod. Not what he had wanted.

In front of her tent they found a richly dressed man waiting for them. Fadimir, she assumed. Short and barrel-chested, elegant in an embroidered jerkin with a heavy gold chain around his neck. His fur-trimmed cloak was dyed blue to match his gold and blue banners. The Dorodna army formed a long column through the middle of the camp.

Zander said, "Mistress, this is Prince Fadimir of Dorodna Polity."

"My lord," she said, noting how he regarded her, his eyes hard. His lieutenants in fine cloaks and good leather boots. She needed water. Asked for some. Fadimir glanced at one of his men, a young man with a velvet doublet and a silver chain securing the front of his cloak. He handed her a skin of water.

Like nectar. She handed back the water skin, realizing that she was supposed to take charge, but too dazed to come up with words. She glanced at Rusadka.

"My lord," Rusadka said, "we can talk inside." She gestured to the tent where Lura stood, eyes wide and hands fretting with nervousness. At her side, young Niko, obviously dazzled by the sudden appearance of a prince and his entourage.

"Bread and ale," Rusadka told Lura.

The young lord drew the tent flap aside, and, with Rusadka's hand in her back, Yevliesza went in first. "Vadik too," she murmured. "And Janov."

"Janov is a commoner," Rusadka said.

"So am I."

They found seats and faced Fadimir and the young man, his son.

Everyone waited for Yevliesza to say something, but words skittered away. Fadimir's arrival had saved her, but he could also be a danger to her. If he was going to join Anastyna, he was the princip's man.

Rusadka finally said, "You are welcome among us, lord."

Prince Fadimir acknowledged this with a nod.

Yevliesza knew she had to manage Fadimir. She had to lie to him. Or at least not tell him much. *No, I have to lie.*

Fadimir was saying, "I have come to see for myself, what to make of a . . . seer among us." An insincere smile jabbed at his cheeks. "Mistress Keeper."

"Then here I am," Yevliesza said. "No *providez*, though." Her mind was getting into gear, slowly.

Fadimir watched her, probing his teeth with his tongue. "With your permission, we rest here for the night and go on to join the princip." He glanced at Vadik in some impatience, as it must seem to him that no one was in charge.

"An honor, lord," Vadik said.

"Which princip?" Yevliesza abruptly asked. "Everyone wants to know."

Fadimir snorted. "I am sure they do. The true princip. Anastyna."

So now they knew that he *was* a danger. Anastyna's man.

"There was trouble in the camp when I arrived," Fadimir said.

"Yes," Yevliesza said. She had to lay out a plausible story. "I support Princip Anastyna, whose torc was stolen by traitors. I've been on missions for her and given her my service. But she doesn't control me."

Fadimir raised his eyebrows. "If she is your princip?"

"She's not, though."

Fadimir cut a glance at his son, who frowned. Learning politics at his father's side.

"Have you heard the rumors, Lord Prince," she continued, "that a woman named Yevliesza came to Numinat from the mundat?"

"Rumors, were they?"

"No, the truth. I'm her. I'm of Earth, and I don't owe Anastyna allegiance. I'm a foreigner. I was born of Numinasi parents when they were envoys from Princip Lisbetha. Raised on Earth. I was grateful for the welcome I received here. But I'm not sworn to Anastyna, and I don't follow her orders. Not all of them."

"Were the *harjat* here to enforce an order?" the prince asked. "What were her orders?"

"I'm sorry, my lord, I can't tell you that. I mean, I can tell you that I refused. Then, after waiting overnight for me to change my mind, they left."

"I see." He waited for her to say more, but she left this improbable, but mostly true, story hanging in the air. "The Lady Princip indulges you, eh? Since the *harjat* could have required compliance."

"I hope she indulges me. It might end one day."

"And if it does?"

"Then I go back. Where I came from." And would she? She didn't know. All she wanted now was for him to leave and not take her with him.

But Fadimir had visibly relaxed. At first, he might have merely seen an unimpressive young woman with grimy hair and old clothes, but now he seemed more comfortable. He knew she was at least loyal to the realm. Or loyal enough.

He said, "I have been told that you speak to the dead."

"Well. Somebody's making up stories. Because no."

She saw his disappointment. "So you do not have more than a natural allotment of gifts?"

Yevliesza shrugged. "I know that sometimes a seer has several affinities. Or they claim they do. Not me."

"What are your birthright gifts, Keeper?" he asked, now seeming genuinely curious.

"I mean no disrespect, my lord. But I keep some things private."

He chewed on his lip, scowling. Then, in a softer voice, said, "My wife died last month. Alyshia, her name was."

"I'm sorry, lord," she murmured, knowing what was coming.

He glanced at his son. "A sad thing, to be deprived of his mother."

"And you miss her," Yevliesza quietly said, seeing the ordinary, suffering person he was, despite the gold chain and the thousand warriors. Seeing the boy's crushed hopes of hearing words from his mother.

"I do," Fadimir said. "I do miss her."

Yevliesza went on. "If it was possible for me—for anyone—to contact her, I would do all I could to help you. But I cannot speak to the dead, my lord." She had spoken to her mother, dead these past twenty-one years. A thing she could not admit. If it *had* been her mother, that figure in the small cabin in Holdfast, who told her daughter that she already had everything she needed.

Fadimir nodded slowly, accepting her statement. "People should stop saying these things about you."

"If only they would."

Fadimir sighed. He put his hands on his knees, preparing to leave. "Then—"

The tent flap was pulled aside as several people entered with trays of food and tankards of ale.

It was only polite to share a meal. And Yevliesza felt more comfortable with the prince, now that she knew a little of his story and he had heard some of hers.

She wolfed down a piece of bread and took another. Vadik asked the prince about the war, and Janov shared information on their best water source and the stored victuals they could spare. Rusadka asked about their numbers. Twelve hundred men, half of whom bore arms and the rest untrained but owing service.

Lura stood ready to pour more ale, looking anxiously at Yevliesza, who clearly needed attending to. Her maid would be fussing over her when Fadimir left the tent.

The bread was delicious. Yevliesza paced herself with the ale. Fadimir would leave things be, she felt. After all, he had deniability; no need to get involved. She was a foreigner.

Being a foreigner was the source of every terrible and wonderful thing that had ever happened to her. And in the end, that she was a foreigner wasn't even true.

⚜

IN THE HEIGHTS, THE DAY WAS FAIR, SCOURED WITH WIND. PRINCE Tirhan and a dozen riders, including Morwen, led their mounts up a steep path into the hills above the Myrwyst River and the home village of Clan Rhydwyn.

It was a region of rock outcroppings towering over lowlands studded with gem-like lakes. They approached a small field where Tirhan's men would wait for him. Even though only clan lords were invited to the assembly, he would have Morwen at his side and did not think anyone would forbid it. The two of them climbed the path to the Giant's Shield, the towering, sloping rock that jutted from the hillside. Behind it, a broad, flat stone where sacred rituals were conducted, sheltered from sight and wind.

Gryffyd and the chiefs of two other clans had called the assembly, and it was within their right to choose a place. But that it was at his own holdings, Clan Rhydwyn, made Gryffyd's hope for the kingship clear.

Most of the clan lords were there already, including Lord Inian, who had sworn to Tirhan and fought at his side. The lords were dressed more for battle than discussion, as they must be in this time of war. The Volkish threat was why they had chosen this barren height to assemble; enemies could be seen approaching from afar, and they would be facing uphill for any assault on the Alfan position.

"They will not like to see me here," Morwen said, her sturdy boots crunching on the rock-strewn path. "A provocation."

"I mean it to be." Tirhan glanced at her, noting how she wore her hair severely back, held with a leather thong. Much of it had burned in the fire ship, and he liked that the clan lords would have heard of that and be reminded she was a warrior like them. "You will not speak. Not this time."

"I know."

"But you will not be silenced once you are queen."

"Queens may speak?" she goaded him in good humor.

He smiled at her. "And they are listened to."

The platform behind the Giant's Shield lay in a depression just off the path. He and Morwen made their way down the slope as the gathered clansmen watched.

Gryffyd moved forward to welcome them, looking kingly in

leathers studded with silver and a short cape of fox fur, a heavy gold chain draped over it like a circlet that need only be placed on his head to serve as a crown.

"That gold chain," Morwen muttered as they approached.

Gryffyd stood before them, his glance flitting to Morwen as he nodded to Tirhan. "Be welcome to the assembly, my lord."

"I thank you, Lord Gryffyd." Tirhan turned to the others. "Queen Gwenid sends her greetings to you and wishes us wisdom for our deliberations." At least for the few hours more she was still called queen. Until a new king was chosen.

The posturing at an end for now, an elder of the shrine of Belfour tapped his staff on the great, flat rock and raised a hand to the sky, his long robes flapping in the wind. He reminded the assembly of their high duty, invoked the power of the shield rock and the spirits of Alfan Sih to guide their discussions. No sword could be drawn amongst them, nor any except a clan lord speak except by permission of the assembly.

"Nor wives," Gryffyd said, giving Morwen a pointed look. She held his gaze, her face placid as any warrior who was being reminded of things he well knew.

The clan lord of Llanaden, one of the three that had called for the assembly, began by asking if there were any names that should be considered for the empty throne, the Silverwood Throne, besides Lord Gryffyd and Lord Tirhan. He would not call Tirhan prince, being in Gryffyd's camp. No one suggested another candidate.

Gryffyd stepped forward. "The choice is between experience and youth." His gray hair lifted in the gusts. "We respect the long lineage of Lord Tirhan, but in these dark times, we need more forceful action." Some of the men murmured agreement. Gryffyd had led the attack on Welfinsid, freeing it from Volkish occupation. Several of the clans had joined him there, and the fight was still clearly in their minds.

After a decent pause, when Tirhan had not spoken, Lord Inian said, "We rejoice in the victory at Welfinsid. Yet, overall, we are greatly outnumbered. It is more prudent to strike quickly and preserve our fighters for the larger battle."

"Which will come when?" Gryffyd asked. "While we wait, the Volkish become stronger, sinking their roots deep into Alfan soil." He looked at Tirhan with contempt. "We chase them out of Silverwood groves, but they spring back when we move on. This is no way to break the enemy."

Inian found himself defending Tirhan, since he would not speak for himself. "We preserve our numbers in order to unite with Numinat. It is the only way to rid the Mythos of the Volkish blight. Join with a larger army."

"But when do we join Numinat?" Gryffyd responded. "We wait for the enemy to abandon the gates and devote themselves to the invasion. But it does not come." He raised a hand to gesture at the great rock looming over the assembly. "Like waiting for the wind to whittle down the Giant's Shield!"

Tirhan finally spoke. "The gates are garrisoned more strongly than ever. We have you to thank for that, Lord Gryffyd."

Gryffyd looked at him incredulously. He made a gesture of impatience toward the assembly.

"I have a man who has lately come from the crossings," Tirhan said. "I ask you to hear his report. It is news of the utmost importance."

"This dilutes our purpose!" Gryffyd said. "We know what must be done. We must gather our courage and take out their strongholds one after the other. When the Volkish withdraw from the gates, or draw down their numbers, we join Numinat."

Tirhan turned on him. "But since we came here to discuss, let us speak."

A clan lord spoke up. "Who is this man who went? And how could he have been in the crossings?"

"His name," Tirhan said, "is Birach of clan Mid Daihinn. And he entered the crossings from the gate in forests of the Daihinn uplands."

Gryffyd's face grew wary. He knew, everyone knew, that when Tirhan entered Alfan Sih months ago, he came through that gate. Up until now, in its remote location, it had never been used.

"Let the man speak!" one of the gathered said. Other voices joined him.

Tirhan turned from the group and waved to a man who waited on the path.

The group fell silent, some grumbling, while young Birach came down the hillside to the slab.

Birach, slim but muscled, wore a leather tunic and coarse leggings, his bow strung over his back. For his mission, he had cut his hair, shaving it close on the sides, as low-ranking Volkish did.

"Tell them what you found," Tirhan said.

"Prince Tirhan told me the way, and Demyr rode with me to the deep forest where a vale hides the gate. It is a half-day ride from here, but from my village, three days. It is a place few would ever go, so no enemy have yet found it. Once through the gate, I went a long way and came out of the passageway into the main crossing route."

"You walked right into the crossings, riddled with Volkish, did you?" Gryffyd asked.

"Yes, lord."

"Without being seized." Gryffyd snorted in disbelief, looking at his fellow clan lords in bewilderment.

"Yes, lord. I speak Volkish from my grandmom, and my brothers, too. And I took a uniform off an enemy soldier at Welfinsid, one that was not buried in the pit." Seeing that he had wandered, Birach blurted, "And I learned that the invasion has begun."

At this, everyone began talking at once, shouting questions, a confusion of voices that effectively silenced the lad, who was not going to respond to an assembly of agitated clan lords.

Tirhan held up his hand and, as the assembly finally quieted, asked the scout, "How do you know the army went through to Numinat?"

"A Volkish soldier told me. Said the devices went first, and then the army."

"When?" someone shouted.

"Yesterday, lord."

"Why was this soldier you spoke to not with the main army?" Tirhan asked.

"Because he is with the forces occupying the crossings, lord. The Volkish want to keep everybody else out of the fight. Especially Alfan

Sih, and they have strong forces at our Osian Gate, on both sides. And the other Alfan Sih gates. He said they suffered a big loss at some village. He tried to pronounce the name. But it was Welfinsid. He said that now, since the Alfans had such an army, they need to keep us off the battlefield."

Tirhan took in the group of clan lords. "We exposed our strength. Made them wary that the clans would unite. Now that they see we have changed our tactics, it reminds them that other kingdoms may be willing to do the same. Unite. Attack."

Gryffyd had turned to his supporters, of Llanaden and Angewyst, but the clan lord of Llanaden avoided his gaze. Someone growled, "Gryffyd won at Welfinsid."

Tirhan turned to the speaker. "It was a rash enterprise and taken, not for the sake of Alfan Sih, but for the throne."

He let the thought catch hold and glanced at Morwen, whose face was shining. She nodded at him to say the thing he had come to say.

"I am the heir to the Silverwood Throne, but I will support any man you choose. If I am your choice, I would lead you in the strong and steady way of my father. When the time is right, I would lead you in battle. I would give my life for your right to be free." He looked at Lord Gryffyd. "I would welcome each of you as brothers in arms in times of war. And in peace, as respected Alfan leaders."

He turned and motioned Morwen to his side. When she came, he took her hand. "And when we march to Numinat," he said, "I will lead you to victory."

The elder's staff hit the floor with a resounding thump. "Do you each wish to speak your choice, or is there agreement?"

The Llanaden clan lord said, "Let it be by acclamation."

"Tirhan!" someone called out. And then they all did.

Chapter Twenty-Seven

Valenty stood on a small rise and looked down on a clearing with dozens of tents and crude huts. A few wagons served as shelters, with rushes lashed together for roofs. This was the Keeper's supposed force of fighters to rival Anastyna: perhaps a hundred peasants and a handful of soldiers. A wood surrounded it. Backing up to it, an outcropping of rock that must contain the new gate she had opened. That *Yevliesza* had opened.

At Valenty's side, Grigeni said, "It looks peaceful enough."

A scout at the perimeter had not told them much. He would not say where the Keeper was, or even if she had ever been in the encampment.

Presuming that Urik had already taken Yevliesza, Valenty's only recourse would be to get a fresh horse and ride back to Anastyna's camp. But he needed to find out what had happened. When he returned to Anastyna, he could do little, if anything, to prevent the princip from forcing Yevliesza to destroy the gates, but he would try. He hoped to share her fate, and that he might not be able to dragged at his heart.

As he and Grigeni led their horse into camp, he named himself to the soldiers who met him, and they bade him wait as they summoned someone to greet him. When the person arrived, it was a man named Janov, a broad-chested fellow of middle years.

Valenty introduced himself and Grigeni, not explaining how they came to share a horse. "Has the *harjat* party been here? And left?"

"Yes, lord," Janov said. "They are gone."

Well. He had known they would be. "A fresh horse, and a swift one, Master Janov. In exchange, my own mount." Grigeni would stay here.

"Of course, lord." Though friendly enough, Janov made note of Valenty's condition. Ripped tunic and trousers, bruised face. Valenty could imagine his curiosity.

"You are welcome to food and any comfort we can offer," the man said. "We have not much, but we can provide you a tent." With a simple, quick efficiency, he explained how a meal might be gotten and whom to see for further needs.

A woman was approaching. A familiar face. She stopped a few paces away.

"By the almighty Deep," she said, grinning. "Lord Valenty."

Elivasa stood before him. Dressed in traveling garb and armed with a short sword, he almost did not recognize her. "Elivasa," he said, glad to see a friend, very glad. The spy of the Osta Kiya court who for years had charmed and gossiped her way to vital information on his behalf.

She taunted him, "I can imagine you did not come all this way to see *me*." Though for many months she and Valenty had pretended to be lovers, their late-night trysts had only been to share plans and information. But that she could say such a thing to him when the circumstances were so fraught surprised him.

"I am glad to see you."

As Janov excused himself, Grigeni took the horse to see to its needs.

"When did Urik leave?" Valenty asked.

Still in high spirits, Elivasa said, "Yesterday, thankfully. But it was a close thing!"

"A close thing?"

"That Yevliesza was not stolen from us." Her eyes narrowed at his startled reaction. "Oh. You did not know. Forgive me, Valenty. I would not have prolonged your concern. The *harjat* troop came for her, but with the presence of Lord Fadimir's army, they departed. Without her."

"She is here?" he said, keeping his voice steady. Elivasa confirmed that she was. "And unharmed?"

"Tired, but unhurt. She is sleeping after her night-long vigil."

Vigil. Prince Fadimir's army. Missing pieces, but: Yevliesza was here. By the Mythos, she was here.

"You look hungry." Elivasa gestured in another direction. "Come to my tent. Let her have a little more rest, and I will tell you everything."

"Tell me now," he said.

Elivasa sighed. "The *harjat* came upon us shortly before dawn yesterday and found us as you see, a camp of untrained villagers and few soldiers. Urik led a group of twenty, and there was no opposing them. Yevliesza ran to the cave, where we thought she would attempt to flee into the crossings. Urik knew that in the crossings she could cut off any pursuit, so he said that he would wait for her to grow thirsty, and then, when she came down, she must go to Anastyna." She paused. "She threatened to hurt herself."

Valenty frowned. "Hurt herself?"

Elivasa pinned him with a hard look. "She had a knife."

To kill herself. His mind reeled. But he kept a steady gaze on Elivasa to keep her talking.

"She had fifteen soldiers standing on the rock slope between her and Urik's men. She had her *sympat* at her side—"

"*Sympat?*"

"Please, Valenty. It is not my story. Let her tell you."

"At least inform me where Fadimir's men are now. Why did he come?"

"He was on his way to reinforce Anastyna. He stopped here. To speak to the dead." She took a deep breath. "A complicated tale."

"Speak to the dead?" He and Anastyna had heard that Yevliesza's followers believed that she had some usual abilities. But speaking to the dead . . .

"It is nonsense. But some people began saying it when she first came out of the Agarvesky. When she had spent time with a *providez*."

He was acutely aware of how long he had been separated from Yevliesza. If he had not chosen to keep service to Anastyna, he would have known all these things about her: the rumor of speaking to the dead, the *sympat*. He would have been with her.

"My lord, before you fall down, a bit of food and a cup of ale?" An impish smile on Elivasa's face. The woman loved seeing him confused about such happy things.

"When can I wake her?" he said, not rising to the bait.

With barely concealed mirth: "When Dreiza allows it."

He had forgotten that his former wife was here. The woman could entangle herself with more things than a lord high steward.

Elivasa took him by the arm and led him to the tent she and Rusadka shared. "Also—you may not have heard—Rusadka and I are vowed to each other."

He finally allowed himself to smile. "Pray, no more disclosures until I sit down." But: *Rusadka was in love?*

❦

AFTER A MEAL, A BASIN OF WATER FOR CLEANING, VALENTY PEELED off his jerkin and sweat-stained shirt, taking a look at the blackening welts on his ribcage. Grigeni bound his torso in strips of cloth he had somehow managed to find. He had also brought an only slightly ripped tunic as well as clean, coarse leggings. After these ministrations, he set to cleaning Valenty's unacceptably muddy boots, which a noble should not be seen in, Grigeni declared, even in the field.

Valenty, impatient to see Yevliesza, allowed his man to do one pass over the boots. His man. But Grigeni had always been more than a steward. He had been Valenty's spy. He had been helpful in the rescue of Anastyna when she was forced to become the princip in exile. And he was a friend, his future now tied with Valenty's.

A noise outside the tent, and Rusadka entered. Fully armed and carrying an extra sword. She gave him a reasonably good-natured nod. And to Grigeni.

"Good day to you," Valenty said in greeting, glancing at the sword she held, wondering for a moment if she intended to challenge him and finally put their differences to rest.

"Urik spoke to me when he left," she said without preamble. She handed him the sword. "Yours. Somehow, Urik was in possession of it." Her expression showed what she thought of a fighter who lost his sword. "How fares the princip?"

"She has two thousand fighters. Three thousand when Fadimir joins her." Beyond that, he had nothing to say about Anastyna. Nothing he would say to most people.

"Anastyna may be a danger to us," Rusadka said, "now that Urik has gone back empty-handed."

"Empty-handed. But her mind will be on the invasion."

"Delayed, it appears."

Volkia could afford to wait, and Numinat could do nothing but brace itself. "Delayed. But we will know when they come." Dactyl riders would see them. Or the garrison manning the gate would send word by mirror, if a manifester survived among them. The Osta Kiya army would know, but word would not reach this camp. Nor Anastyna's. To be wisely deployed, Anastyna's army would have to join Osta Kiya very soon. But he was no longer privy to those decisions.

Grigeni gave him his boots. As he pulled them on, he asked Rusadka, "Do you think Urik left his task undone on purpose?"

"No."

Valenty waited for her to say more, but nothing. Well. She would not accuse a fellow *harjat* of deceiving the princip. Let it stand at no, then.

He thanked her for the sword and left to find Dreiza and coax his way past her.

Approaching Yevliesza's tent, he saw three women standing in front of it.

One in pale *satvar* garb. Dreiza. One young woman who he thought might be the Keeper's attendant. And Yevliesza. Yevliesza, dressed in leather trousers and a short tunic, a belt with scabbard and knife. Raven-haired, tall and slim, her face so beautiful it almost hurt to look at it. She did not smile.

Valenty stopped a few paces away. It would be a formal meeting. A maid and a *satvar* in attendance and people in the camp turning to watch.

"Keeper," he said, nodding his respects. Drinking her in. Heart in his throat. And: "My lady Dreiza."

Dreiza smiled at him, her eyes kindly. Kinder than Yevliesza's.

"Valenty," Yevliesza said. A smile, so quick it might not have really been there. "My lord."

"You both have much to discuss," Dreiza easily said, leading Lura away. A backward glance, to assure herself the meeting would not deteriorate. Dreiza, ever watchful that other people were happy. And he was. Completely so.

Yevliesza looked well. Tired, but vivid, and oddly calm. He waited. No invitation to enter the tent. He had wondered what his reception might be. Cool, then, until he explained himself, and he did not blame her. "I have left Anastyna's service."

The words settled around her. "She allowed it?"

"She did."

"I'm surprised." Valenty started to respond, but she put up her hand, smiling. "And so very glad."

An opening. He would give much to hear more of the same. How glad? Glad because she wanted him, or glad because no one should serve an overreaching and misguided ruler?

The sun lowered toward the hills. High clouds, sheared flat by the wind, caught the first gilding of the sunset. And still no going into the tent where they could speak in private.

"I have been such an utter fool," he said. It seemed to move her, and, for some reason, that made him feel even more the idiot. "When I learned of Urik's mission, I tried to stop him. I was overmatched."

She gave a silent laugh. "By only twenty *harjat*?"

An ironic laugh, but it gave Valenty hope. "He fought me himself. And left me alive." He would not pretend more honor than he had. He hoped he would not have to grovel, but he would if she wanted it.

"I heard you rode in sharing a horse with Grigeni."

Apparently she did want it. "It was my shame to lose the contest. And, in the process, my sword and my horse."

"Your warding failed you?"

People were watching them. Had word gotten around so quickly that he had come to beg Yevliesza's pardon? Or was everything the woman did of interest in this camp?

He shrugged. "I did not use it. So he left me my sword belt."

So much to say, but he could not find a way in. He tried, "I do not blame you if—"

Yevliesza stepped forward, taking his hand. "No, don't speak." He saw in her eyes something like concern. Or trust. It disarmed him, flooding him with relief.

"I love you," she said. "Forever. Don't doubt me. I couldn't bear it."

That was all it took. He stepped forward and embraced her so hard he felt her intake of breath. "Please say you forgive me," he whispered.

She pulled back, a flash of violet in her eyes. "I won't say it. You followed what you believed was your honor." He started to respond, but she mouthed the word *no*. "Valenty, I almost died." She glanced over his shoulder, toward the rock outcropping. "I'm different now. I don't blame you for anything." She saw him struggling to understand. "The fog is gone," she said, not very helpfully.

He did not know what she meant, and yet he did. Soldiers who came back from dire wounds spoke of being different. Seeing more. Or perhaps less. Less of outsized worry and perceived slights. When he looked into her eyes, he knew she was different. And yet the same, that remarkable, strong, and loyal love of his life.

He glanced at the tent flap. She gestured for him to go in.

Once in the privacy of the tent, they went into each other's arms again. He could not get enough of her, could not hold her close enough. "I thought you were lost to me."

"I thought that, too. I've said goodbye to you lots of times."

He knew how that was.

She looked so desperately tired. "Lie down with me," he said. They lay on the cot, his arms enfolding her, the knot that had been cinched tight in his heart dissolving.

"I had no chance to help you," he murmured into her hair. "But I still believed I could." He smiled to himself. "I do not think you need me to protect you."

She gripped him more tightly. "I do. That's where you're wrong."

"You have warriors who appear willing to die in your service. A whole camp watching out for you."

"Valenty," she softly said. "Just be quiet."

They rested, listening to the sounds outside, muted voices, the distant cries of birds, the footfalls of people passing by.

Yevliesza was asleep. He watched over her.

A young woman ducked her head inside the tent—Yevliesza's maid, he remembered—and quickly backed out. Voices near the tent. Valenty disentangled himself from Yevliesza and laid her back onto the cot.

Stepping out of the tent, he found that the sun had dipped behind the low hills, throwing the camp into calm shadow. Grigeni was there. Dreiza as well. The man who had welcomed him: Janov. As well, two serious-looking guards, one of them sandy-haired, a rare look in Numinat.

Janov saw his look. "That is Arman Brandt. Who brought us Duke Tanfred, my lord."

The Volkish officer who had defected from the enemy. Valenty nodded to him, eager to hear his story.

Dreiza approached. "She is sleeping?" When Valenty nodded, she said, "Then we should not wake her. But . . ."

"Something, Dreiza?"

"Well. Kassalya. A young woman who stays at the *satvary*." He knew of Kassalya, the girl with the unbearable foreknowing. "She begs to speak to the Keeper. It calms her, sometimes. But it can wait."

Hearing this, Janov said, "My lord, she is half-crazed. We try to keep her from harming herself. And others."

Dreiza looked at the tent flap, weighing what to do.

Valenty noted that Grigeni was standing next to Yevliesza's maid, an attractive girl with a face framed by curls. By the Deep, he was smiling at her. The maid—Lura was her name—made a noise that sounded very like a simper. Valenty raised an eyebrow at him, and Grigeni reddened.

The tent flap was drawn back and Yevliesza emerged. She noted that the group had a discussion underway and walked past them to Kassalya's tent.

Dreiza said, "Lord Kirady always tried to keep the two of them apart. He thinks Kassalya makes too much trouble, but these days Yevliesza does as she pleases."

"Dreiza. She has always done that." He exchanged knowing looks with her. Still a handsome woman. Now wasted as a *satvar*. Well, "wasted." She was probably happier than most people.

Soon Yevliesza ducked back out of the tent, gesturing for Dreiza and Valenty to join her. "She is calm," she said as they came out. "But she wants me to go into the woods."

Arman, the Volkish captain, had come to stand beside the tent with Janov and, having heard Yevliesza mention the woods, spoke to Janov. "*Strigoi*, Master Janov."

Valenty saw the concern on the group's faces.

Dreiza explained, "Demons. Out of the deep woods of Volkia's Breminger Forest. They feed off animals in the woods around here, but they always look for Yevliesza."

Demons were following her? He and Dreiza ducked into the tent. Kassalya was putting on her boots and stopped when she saw Valenty.

Yevliesza was quick to say, "You said he could come in."

Kassalya looked at him with great, soulful eyes. "He may. But we have to hurry." She glanced at the tent wall, apparently toward the woods.

"My dear," Dreiza began, "to go into the woods is very dangerous."

Kassalya turned to Yevliesza. "Hurry." To Dreiza, she said, "You stay here."

"Where in the woods?" Yevliesza asked.

"To the top of the rock. The rock with the gate." Kassalya fastened a cape around her shoulders.

"I think this is something urgent," Yevliesza said to Valenty and Dreiza. "We have to go."

"Kassalya," Valenty said, "soldiers will have to go with you."

"Only around the rock. Not the top." Kassalya turned to Dreiza. "Dreiza. Goodbye."

"*Goodbye*, my dear?"

The girl nodded. "For now. Goodbye." She turned and walked out of the tent. Yevliesza and Valenty followed.

Chapter Twenty-Eight

Yevliesza had never been to the top of the rock outcropping. It protruded from the spine of the low ridge and was steep on all sides. There could not be much room at the summit.

She had to go with Kassalya, though she was preoccupied with Valenty, the shock of seeing him, the understanding that he had tried to protect her. That he was actually here with her. Each time she looked at him, she felt stunned by her turn of fortune. He was a handsome man. Dark-complected, his face perfect in its planes and sharp features. His body strong and lean. She had come to Mythos to find him. Not true, but she liked the thought. Loved the thought.

Dusk was coming on. It could be dark by the time they came down from the ridge. Janov and Arman, who were coming along, would not like that. Nor Captain Vadik, who brought his men to wait for her at the foot of the outcropping. Rusadka would not have allowed it, but she had not been there to know they were going.

Kassalya took them around to the back of the outcropping. As they looked up at the rock wall, they could discern crevices and hand holds. A possible route.

Kassalya looked at Yevliesza. "Do not be afraid."

"I'm not. The climb might do me good."

"Do not be afraid of the war." The girl looked up the side of the great rock extrusion. "The Volkish are here."

A jolt of alarm. "What do you mean, *here*?" Yevliesza said.

"This morning, here in Numinat. With their army."

Valenty had overheard. "What do you see? They have entered Numinat?"

Arman was at his side, listening intently.

"Yes, into Numinat," Kassalya said, looking into Valenty's eyes for the first time. "You will need courage." She turned to Arman. "And you. Have faith, Arman."

The invasion had come. Although they often ignored Kassalya, the conviction settled on them that she saw truly. Word passed through the group. Janov. Captain Vadik. Kassalya looked at them but, at the same time, did not seem to notice them.

Yevliesza gripped Valenty's hand. She had almost forgotten about the war. Now it was here.

"Which gate, Kassalya?" Valenty asked. "Do you see which one?"

She ignored him. "I have to go now. Up." She began to climb.

Valenty gripped Yevliesza's hand. "Everything changes if she is right."

"What will you do?" she asked him.

"I will go to the fight," he softly said.

They would all go. Arman, Rusadka, everyone. If Kassalya was right. Wasn't this why Kassalya was so calm, because the waiting was over? Now, the doing. Except the doing wasn't a calm thing, but a terrifying, bloody, and inescapable thing.

Kassalya began climbing.

Arman spoke up. "Some of us should go up with you."

Kassalya heard him and called down, "Only you, then."

Arman insisted on going first and began the climb, Yevliesza and Valenty following. The dusk was heavy on this side of the outcropping, mirroring Yevliesza's dark thoughts. Something was at the top of this hill, but she couldn't imagine what it might be. What she could imagine was another goodbye to Valenty. He would go to the fight. The day was slipping away, and with it, Valenty.

At the top, Arman gripped her hand to help her up. She saw something fierce in his eyes. The confrontation was coming. He would be in the battle, needed to be. And it would be soon.

She saw that the summit area was larger than she had guessed. Though Kassalya had said she was taking them to the woods, up here there were only two stunted trees hugging the edge of the main slab of rock. The camp looked small from this perch. People starting cookfires; children racing; soldiers at the foot of the outcropping. The forest darkening as the sun sank farther into tomorrow.

Kassalya was looking out on the encampment. "Now she comes."

Yevliesza went to her side. "Who comes?"

Kassalya did not answer, only smiled. Yevliesza realized she had never seen the girl smile. Her unbearable gift of knowing was at least, for now, not terrorizing. The Devi Ilsat had taken her in out of compassion for her suffering. Kassalya bore the pain of every horror to come. But now, a smile.

"All well?" came a shout from below.

"We are," Arman called back.

Kassalya took Yevliesza's hands in her own. "They have been speaking to you, but it might have been some time ago."

Long ago and someday, she had told Yevliesza before. Then she knew who was coming. A spirit was coming to speak to them. "Valenty, sit by my side."

She felt better sitting. Valenty beside her.

Kassalya seated herself on the rock platform. "I will tell you a thing," she said, looking past the three of them. A tear slipped down her cheek.

"Kassalya?" Yevliesza asked in concern.

"I cannot stay," Kassalya said. "You must listen."

The back of Yevliesza's neck prickled. This wasn't Kassalya. It was her body, but not her essence.

"Do you see what's coming?" she murmured to Valenty.

"No. Do you?"

"A spirit. Speaking through Kassalya. They were always trying to speak to me, but I was never there. Because their hours are different from ours. Now I have to listen."

"We will listen, then," Valenty said, and she was glad of his steadiness.

Kassalya spoke again, but not meeting their gazes. Looking over their heads. "I can speak of these things because I was one who had root power like you."

Had root power? She knew, then. It was a First One speaking. Someone from long ago. From the beginning.

Kassalya softly said, "You have done well, Yevliesza. But not perfectly. You did not see the crossings as they are, but who could have done better? Now you have very little time, so I believe. It is hard to know."

"Can you hear her?" Yevliesza whispered to Valenty.

"Yes, I hear her."

She took his hand, gripping it hard. Arman stood behind them, watching. Listening.

They had all thought the girl was mentally unseated, as they put it. Giving her potions to keep her quiet. She was the perfect conduit, though. If they couldn't reach Yevliesza one way, they would try another. The First Ones.

"Here is the truth," she said. "The crossings cannot be removed. To cut away at them is to destroy them. You made mistakes."

You might have told me sooner.

"This is soon. It is you who have been late, never listening, enclosed in the boundaries of yourself. But leave that be. The crossings cannot be knocked down like a child with colored blocks. They are the threads of the world. They are aligns. Great aligns. Listen: you may be able to create a crossing."

I did. The ones to Volkia. Yevliesza could not help herself from speaking—or thinking—to the spirit.

"Now you will do better. Here is the truth. The crossings that we found, they were clustered together. They bent toward each other in the great blackness. We do not know why. Because of this, when we found our path, we also saw all the other routes. They had been enlarged by people who came before us, finding their way to different kingdoms. Who first found the crossings? We do not know. But we came. Those with root power built a bridge to Numinat along a great align.

"But some aligns do not bend to the middle, to the knot in the blackness. A few are too far away to join the gathered aligns in the region where things endure. But if you have courage, you can make a path along some of those few." Kassalya shook her head almost mockingly. "To where, to where? I hear you. Always questions."

But this time Yevliesza hadn't thought anything. No, she *had* thought it: *to where?*

"Think, my daughter. What two realms must connect for the Mythos to survive?"

"Nubiah and Numinat," Valenty whispered.

"Yes, that is so," the spirit said. "If you can find such an align."

One outside the middle, too distant to make the bend.

"Also Alfan Sih?" Yevliesza asked.

"And Alfan Sih."

If she had really poked her head out of the fog, she might have thought of this herself. Create a path outside the crossings. It was a strange thought. Aligns outside the crossings.

Yevliesza asked, "How?"

Behind her, Arman whispered, "You did it before." To Volkia.

"But that was *from* the crossings."

Kassalya closed her eyes. "From anywhere," she murmured. "Make a gate."

But why didn't you tell me?

"You were not listening. Not everything is the fault of the dead. But you know how to do these things. Find a good align. Make a path."

Yevliesza was trying to imagine all this. How to perceive an align that went to Nubiah but began . . . maybe in the camp below? Or the Haiga. Or the Agarvesky. How could she find it?

"There is a problem, though," the spirit whispered. "A grave problem." Kassalya began to moan. "Oh, oh, it dissolves! Dissolves." She hung her head for a moment. It seemed that the spirit had lost Kassalya, and the girl's terrors were coming back to her.

When she lifted her head again, she whispered, "I am leaving."

"No! Kassalya, you said there is a grave problem. What is the problem?" Yevliesza desperately asked.

"The distant aligns are different. They can become paths, for a time. But they fade."

"Fade?"

"Form your path. But it may fade. And everyone lost therein."

Her heart sank. Such paths weren't reliable. They faded. "Can't I make it strong?"

"There are some things no one can do. Those who go in must have courage. Do not fear to die. I do not. Valenty and Arman, watch me. I am going now."

Kassalya slowly lay down as though the rock slab were a bed.

Yevliesza scrambled to her feet, hurrying to her. She knelt by the girl's side, finding that Kassalya lay still. No breath filled her chest. No breath. Yevliesza remembered then. The goodbye to Dreiza. The hurry. Maybe so that the spirit would be there to guide her home, to whatever peace lay beyond the world.

She put her hand on Kassalya's brow, her cheek. Cool already, as though she had barely been alive as she spoke to them. Valenty put a hand on Yevliesza's shoulder. Arman stood next to him.

Kassalya was gone. Dissolved.

Distant aligns could become paths. But they faded. *And everyone lost therein.*

They were looking at Kassalya when they should have been looking up. Shadows did not precede them, because the sun had set. The blood birds came.

They fell upon the three of them, claws grabbing and clutching. A *strigoi* swooped in at Yevliesza, lacing its talons into her hair, throwing her forward, over Kassalya's inert form. Then, in a shower of blood, it collapsed, covering her with its body. Throwing it off and grabbing her knife, Yevliesza staggered to her feet and drove it into the neck of a blood bird on Arman's back. It shrieked and jumped away.

"Stay low, Yevliesza!" Valenty shouted. She crouched by his knees, and he kept close to her, swinging his sword in protective arcs, and once clanging his blade against Arman's. They stood close together, giving her what shelter they could.

The demons, wary now, separated and came again, this time from all directions. "Kill she! Kill she!" A voice she had heard before.

The other soldiers had made it to the summit, and swords and blood thickened the air.

Men bellowed and lunged. Any beast driven off wheeled in the air and came again. There were so many, the air full of them. Raising their wings high to fall upon a victim, the blood birds reached with clawed feet, tearing and slicing. But they were overmatched now, and *strigoi* bodies littered the rock slab.

Then, moving as one, they lurched from the fight and jumped into the air, heading back into the forest.

Valenty went to his knees, holding himself up with his sword. Yevliesza crawled to him. "Are you wounded?"

"It is hard to say." His face drenched in blood.

She looked for Arman. Saw him tending to the wounded.

Valenty put out his hand, and she took it. "Are you all right?"

"One of them ruined my hair," she said, smiling grimly. She felt the back of her head where the demon had clawed her. A little blood stained her hand.

Valenty gently turned her head, looking at the damage. "It came away with a little of your hair."

"Someone killed it." She looked at the dead *strigoi* lying next to Kassalya's body.

"Arman," Valenty said. "We could have so easily lost you." His arm went around her. Her scalp was on fire with pain.

Looking around, she counted bodies. Three demon birds dead. A soldier thrust a sword into a dying *strigoi's* chest. Four. All the soldiers at least moving. The plateau lay drenched in scarlet; gouts of blood stained every soldier, unnaturally so.

"All the blood," she murmured.

"The creatures are always full of blood. From their recent meals." Valenty hugged her close once more and helped her to her feet.

As they made their way down the side of the rock, Yevliesza kept hearing in her mind, *Kill she, kill she.*

PART IV
THE WAY OF THE WOLF

Chapter Twenty-Nine

A brisk wind brought the scent of bloodshed and lifted the hair of the dead. Nashavety had come home. Her mind was spacious and clear. How she had hated Volkia with its dense forests, cold rivers, and demon birds! *Home to Numinat.*

Bodies lay around her like fallen branches after a storm. And a storm it had been. After the army's battering rams at the gate, the iron cladders came. They thundered through the doors, cutting a path into the soldiers who fell and fell. So she imagined it, from her position farther back in the file of the Volkish forces. Behind the cladders, the men carrying shields with tubes protruding, spitting metal. The rattling of the guns and the screams of wounded men pierced the crossings, echoing.

A Volkish officer had demanded surrender. Refused, and so the slaughter continued. The killing distressed her. These were Numinasi, poorly ruled, set on a degrading path by no fault of their own, but there was no other way. Some must die that others might thrive.

The other half of the army was already entering at Lowgate. The iron devices and five thousand men. It would all soon be over.

Causeway Gate had fallen quickly. Volkish soldiers had marched in after the Iron Brigade, finishing off the wounded. Her half of the army had streamed through and spread out onto the long causeway over the lake and into the fields beyond. They had feared sabotage, but the crossings remained clear. Likely Yevliesza had been eliminated. The girl. The saboteur. The one whom Anastyna had welcomed into their midst and who, in ten short months, had wreaked such havoc.

She hoped that Strigo would come to his mistress now and confirm the mundat's death. Nashavety looked to the sky, hoping to see her lovely swarm of killers. But a doubt nagged at her.

Captain Brandt had not returned from escorting the wagon into the fort. The demons might have ripped out of their shrouds immediately and attacked him. Or the garrison soldiers, knowing he had tricked them, had slit his throat. But she did not actually know what had happened.

Nashavety stood in the fort's yard, Marshal Kenrick at her side. The stench of offal and blood, the ghastly wounds. Death was worse than many people imagined. What had been living—now decaying meat.

The garrison commander was brought forward by two Volkish soldiers. He looked at Nashavety with contempt, noting her black gown, her Numinasi features.

"Yes," Nashavety said. "I am she. Come to deliver Numinat from grievous error."

The man took in the garrison yard. "By massacre?"

"You could have surrendered."

His lip curled. "It was our honor to die."

Hard to bear, this superior attitude. She turned to Marshal Kenrick. "Set him free. Let it be known that he is to be left in peace." She savored the thought of how his life would be. Not to have died with his troops. Forfeited Causeway Gate. No honor.

They led him away and pushed him out of the fort. He walked down the causeway into the new Numinat. His surviving men were grouped along the farthest shore, watching him.

Her army would rest for a day, waiting for the wagons to lumber through the crossings. Hundreds of wagons, of supply, of weaponry; the housings of the iron cladders, the shields of the volley guns. When the march to the plains began, no units would be left behind to guard the prisoners. Nashavety would quiet them in her own way.

Escorted by Kenrick and his lieutenants, she walked onto the causeway. The lake waters on either side rippled in the wind, distorting the reflected blue sky where the sun wobbled and birds shuddered through the air. The Numinasi soldiers waited on the far bank where they had been herded. They must wonder what their fate would be. Perhaps they guessed who she was: the noblewoman who had been brought low and banished by a ruinous princip. *I am back, my dears.*

She paused at a spot near the far end of the causeway where she had a clear view of the prisoners. With the Numinasi soldiers in clear sight, she raised her left hand and summoned her creature power, pushing forth her will to bind them. They began to crumple. Many fell or sat, falling into a stupor. There were too many to curtail. But enough. The Volkish troops watched, as had been her plan. Observing her true strength, it would give them heart to fight.

Most of the garrison survivors would live. When her control faded, they would be weak and comprise no threat to attack the Volkish rear.

After all, these men were Numinasi, soon to be her subjects. And she was merciful.

❦

THEY LEFT ARROW SHAFT CAMP AT FIRST LIGHT, YEVLIESZA AND nineteen others, including soldiers and her companions. They rode through the evergreen woods heading for the prairie. Slow going now, but on the flats their mounts would move faster. They were in a hurry. The invasion had begun.

She rode with Rusadka, Valenty, Arman, Elivasa, and Janov. Seven of her soldiers in front with Captain Vadik, seven others in the rear. After yesterday's *strigoi* attack, she wore a bandana around her head to protect her scalp wound. A small thing. But a reminder to look up.

Yevliesza was in pursuit of aligns, the right ones. Rusadka, with her affinity for aligns and arcana trained, could point out any she missed, but only Yevliesza could see where they went. As they traveled, her escort of soldiers remained watchful for *strigoi*. Yevliesza, watchful, too. For one blood bird in particular, which she had first encountered in the mysterious plane of Holdfast. The demon that Nashavety had sent to kill her, specifically, and not merely random others.

"Along the gully," Rusadka said, drawing her attention to the left.

"Yes." Yevliesza had seen the thread of molten light, but it didn't leave Numinat. Nor did it penetrate to Nubiah or Alfan Sih. She concentrated, trying to determine whether any align extended to another realm. And to the right one.

They hoped for reinforcements. Surely the two kingdoms would come to their aid. Volkia was spreading their control, poisoning the Mythos with machines and conquest. No land would be safe from their predations. But even if she found an align to one of the realms, would its exit point be somewhere in the wilderness, hopelessly remote? She would not have several aligns to choose from. Any route to Nubiah might have to do. Any route to Alfan Sih. So many contingencies, but they had to try.

Valenty and Janov would be the messengers to the Lion Court and its leader, King Jawara. Valenty would go, because he knew Prince Chenua of the royal court, formerly emissary to Numinat. Yevliesza deeply wished it did not have to be him. After so much separation, another goodbye.

Elivasa and Arman would go to Alfan Sih. Elivasa, because she had met Prince Tirhan when he was the Alfan envoy to Osta Kiya. They all hoped that the brief contact would provide enough credibility that Tirhan would trust the new path. Arman volunteered to accompany Elivasa. It was no surprise to Yevliesza. He wanted to earn his way. To be exonerated for living.

Rusadka and the others had decided that any gate Yevliesza opened for the armies of Alfan Sih and Nubiah should be well south of their camp near the Haiga River. Using any align that far north would deliver reinforcements days away from the likely battlefield.

The sun climbed high, a smear behind a gray swath of clouds, as they rode south, moving as efficiently as the rocky terrain allowed. The two sets of messengers would need time to make contact with their allies. Hopefully, not too much time.

Yevliesza and her group forded a shallow river, their horses up to their fetlocks in cold, rock-strewn water. No one spoke unnecessarily. Yevliesza concentrated on perceiving aligns, but always in the background: the coming battle. The diabolic weapons, powered by elementalists enslaved to their machines. The Volkish force, said to be ten thousand strong, all well armed, unlike the men called up from Numinasi polities.

Never far from her mind, the goodbye to Valenty. He was most suited to go, but Yevliesza hated it. Kassalya's warning about the instability of any path outside the crossings. *Everyone lost therein.*

"Along the ridgeline," Rusadka said, pointing.

"Yes, thank you." It had escaped Yevliesza that an align cut across the top of the hills.

The align on the ridge traveled into central Karsk Polity, of all places. Sofiyana's home region. She remembered Nashavety introducing Sofiyana, her pet, to the other members of the training arcana. Nashavety, when she had still been the honored head of Raven Fell Hall. Sofiyana, when she had still been human. The arcana seemed so long ago. Before the war, before Yevliesza's imprisonment in Albrecht's palace, before she knew that the ninth power was marking the skin on her back. Before Isha and her tough and clear teachings. Before she knew who Valenty truly was.

The land, which had been sloping from a rugged place of forest and rocks, was now flattening onto the great central plain of Numinat. Somewhere to the east, Causeway Gate. Now they watched for any sign of the Volkish army on the march, though it wasn't likely they would encounter the invading troops. If the enemy had come through Causeway Gate, they would almost certainly have already marched west toward their chosen battlefield. Her group might come across the supply wagons trailing the main army. But even if they were seen by outriders, the Volkish might not bother with so small a group. And if

Volkia came through Lowgate, the enemy forces would be far to the south.

Captain Vadik sent scouts ahead on the fastest horses to assure that they did not encounter the army. If they had come through that gate.

They had been riding for half a day and so far no saving aligns, no aligns that left Numinat and traveled outside the crossings. They stopped to rest the horses and let them forage.

After she had seen to Mitri, Yevliesza joined her team in a field of rocks. They broke out their simple provisions: hard bread and cheese, dried apples.

Rusadka sat next to Elivasa. Rusadka silent as usual and Elivasa eager to converse. "Those army dactyl patrols are doing an extra job," she said, through a mouthful. "Keeping *strigoi* out of the sky." That was at least possible. Kirady might have informed Commander Ilyan about the blood birds. And even if not, *strigoi* and dactyls were archenemies.

"I would love to see a dactyl take on the demons," Arman said.

Rusadka smirked. "As would I." She looked overhead, maybe imagining bodies falling from the sky.

One of the soldiers, his face creased by the sun and wind, glanced upward. "Dactyl scouts will not let their mounts fight. But if they did, it would be a short battle."

Arman leaned against a boulder, drinking from his skin of water. Elivasa was watching him. "You will like Prince Tirhan," she told him. "Itching for a fight, that one. Back when he was at Osta Kiya."

Rusadka looked up, approving the sound of *itching for a fight*. Yevliesza felt she could interpret expressions on her friend's face even when they were hardly there.

"He is eager for it," Valenty agreed. "But he may resent how he begged Osta Kiya to come to Alfan Sih's aid when Volkia first invaded. And was refused." He glanced at Yevliesza, and a smile passed between them, both thinking how she had taken Tirhan back to his country to join the insurgency.

"I hope Tirhan will believe a Volkish officer," Arman said. "Remember how suspicious you all were of me at first."

"Oh," Elivasa merrily said, "he will be suspicious, but he and I knew each other from Osta Kiya. I think he will be pleased to see me." Janov gave her a disparaging look, never one to like someone with a puffed-up opinion of themselves.

Oblivious, Elivasa continued, "And he is wickedly handsome. He had an eye for Yevliesza, you know."

As they prepared to mount up again, Arman came to Yevliesza's side. "We are going to find the aligns," he confidently said. "They know it can be done, or they would not have sent you to do it."

They. The spirit world. A person from the first age, who might have had an even greater align power than she possessed. *Go. Open a gate and go.* Making it sound simple.

She knew Arman badly wanted to bring the leaders of Volkia to a reckoning. He could not imagine that Numinat would fail. "We'll keep looking," she told him. "I promise. Even after the battle, if we're overcome, I won't ever leave them in peace."

"Thank God for you," he said. She had to look away, embarrassed.

If there was a God, she wanted him to be proud of her. Or for the Mythos to think she had done well. Or at least her companions. She was meant to do a great thing. The albatross hanging around her neck. She had used the expression, but no one in Numinat knew what it meant.

As they rode out again, Valenty came to her side. "Had an eye for you, did he?" he said, amused. His mind still on what Elivasa had said about Tirhan.

Yevliesza shrugged. "Maybe a little."

"It is never just a little. You are either all in, or not."

She liked to hear him say that. It meant he was all in. She let her eyes rest on him, admiring him. How he sat his horse, as though he had been born to ride. He was a man graceful in all things, and she loved to look at him. And she was delighted to see him a little jealous.

"For you," she said, "it was just a little. At the beginning."

"No. All the way from the very first."

"You hid it well."

"I was a spy. I hid everything." He noted Rusadka walking her horse toward them. "Do you think she likes me better now?"

Yevliesza smiled. "For my sake, yes."

Valenty sighed extravagantly. Turning his horse away, he left the two women to ride together.

Chapter Thirty

At the camp's meandering stream, Pyvel filled a wooden bucket for Hunter, the captain's horse. The wind blew chill off the prairie, rippling the water. It was not yet dawn, and, as he made his way into camp, he took care with his steps among the rocks and deadfall. Heading for the horse pasture, Pyvel passed among the tents and sod huts of Anastyna's camp. A few cookfires flared in the dark.

Three riders had come in, their mounts gray with sweat. They must have been riding all night. Saddles creaked as the men dismounted. One of them was older and carried a package. They gave their horses' reins to one of the soldiers.

Two of the riders wore the red tunic of Osta Kiya, the other, clothes of a nobleman. A camp officer had joined them and, after a discussion, led them toward to the ridge. Anastyna would be awakened early.

Soldiers began to gather in small clusters, watching the ridge as though they hoped to see something in the gloaming or hear the tidings the newcomers brought.

He saw Duke Tanfred emerge from his tent. A friend to Numinat, though Volkish. Outside his tent flew his standard of a green tree on white. A man that Yevliesza knew, who had helped her when she had been unfairly held in Volkia. He, too, was looking toward the ridge.

Soldiers of Osta Kiya had come, and everyone waited to hear what it meant.

Hunter and Kasha, Pyvel's horse, were waiting for their water and hay. Pyvel hurried through his groom duties so that he could get to Captain Nikander's tent in good time. Had Volkia attacked? The idea darted through him. The war had begun. Or maybe Sofiyana was leading a great force to arrest Anastyna. But why else would a soldier of Osta Kiya be here except to invite Anastyna's army to join the main force—because Volkia had come?

Back at his captain's tent, Nikander was dressed with sword buckled on. He stood with a fellow officer, calmly talking.

Heart racing, Pyvel remained out of hearing range, but made sure Nikander saw him. If they were to fight today, Pyvel would be wherever Nikander was. On his own horse, in the midst of the fight, carrying extra weapons and water.

Pyvel had seen battle. That day in the crossings, thinking the army was going to the aid of Nubiah and finding the tunnels full of Volkish who streamed from the backways and hacked them down. His lord dead, his fellow messengers dead. Somehow he had ended up with a sword in his hand. He had walked back to Numinat with Urik, through the groaning, crying wounded and the silent dead. He knew how it would be. Battle was terrible to see, but in the pitch of fighting, the world was never more vivid.

Nikander beckoned him, removing his sword from its scabbard and handing it to him. "Sharpen," he said.

"News, sir?" Pyvel could not keep from asking.

Nikander's lips flattened. "He bore the white ring of the palace on his tunic."

Pyvel waited for more, but Nikander had already turned away.

He went to his lean-to, where he kept the sharpening stone, and squatted down to work. Nikander's sword held a good edge from the last sharpening, but Pyvel stroked the whetstone along the blade anyway, glancing constantly at the command ridge to see what was happening. Nothing yet.

If Lord Valenty were here, he would have it figured out by now. Well. He would be with Anastyna and hear the news at the same time she did. And now he had left royal service. For the love of Yevliesza, he had said. Meaning what, though?

And Grigeni had left as well, going to join Valenty. The camp commander had allowed it because Grigeni would be of doubtful use in a fight, and because he had been Valenty's man. Pyvel missed them both. He had been part of House Valenty and its retainers. Not officially. But Valenty had treated him as his own, and Grigeni had been teaching him numbers and history. Also, he missed Yevliesza. He prided himself on having been her first friend, back when nobody wanted her to be at the palace, back when she first discovered that she could make her way through the Nethers without a map. Her affinity for aligns.

A shout went up. Someone was bringing Anastyna's dappled gray mare through the camp from the field. Anastyna would be coming. A crowd started to form in the center of camp, waiting for her.

A soldier led the horse up the path to a flat bench gouged from the side of the ridge some distance from the top. After a time, Pyvel saw that a few people were escorting Anastyna down a steep path to the ledge where her horse waited.

For all the excitement of the moment, the crowd was quiet, waiting. Pyvel found Nikander in the crowd and gave him his sword, which he slid into his fleeced scabbard.

When Anastyna reached the flats, she was accompanied by her officers and the wardens of the polities. The crowd parted to allow the mounted procession to come through. He recognized Lord Azry of Lukya and Kirady of Eiger Polity, lean and dignified, with beard white and close-cropped; and others he could not remember, but each looking important with gold or silver chains around their necks, their horses' bridles paneled with silver. People began shouting. Cheers and shouts of "Anastyna! Anastyna!" greeted her as she rode through the gathered throng. Her followers loved her, but these cheers? As though they knew already some happy piece of news. And when she got closer, Pyvel realized that they *did* know.

She wore the silver torc.

When she reached the center of the crowd, the man in court dress who was one of the three arrivals raised a hand and called out: "Hear me!" He looked around, waiting for the crowd to fall silent. "Hear me."

As the throng quieted, Anastyna sat her horse with confident grace. Behind her, looking pleased, the lords of the polities sat their horses. "As Lord High Steward," the messenger called out, "I am commanded by the *fajatim* to proclaim the words and decision of the speakers of the five houses. Hear me. The torc, being set aside by one who bore it through misadventure and stealth—the *fajatim* have declared that it shall be conveyed to the proper, honored, and true Princip of Numinat: Anastyna—" Here, wild cheers so loud the chancellor's words were drowned out as he went on to name her house, her accolades, and her titles.

Anastyna spoke some words, but nothing could be heard except the eruptions of shouting that jumped through the crowd as the words of the high steward were passed along. People rushed to the princip on her horse, touching her skirt, reaching their hands up as she lowered hers to touch her people. A party of soldiers spurred their mounts to her side, separating her from the press of bodies.

Anastyna dismounted. Her escort kept up with her on foot, but she pressed into the crowd, greeting people, acknowledging a kneeling subject by placing her hand on a shoulder. She spoke to a low-ranking soldier with an old but terrible scar on the hairless side of his head, and he began to kneel, but she said something, and he stayed upright.

She approached Nikander. "Captain," she said. "You have my thanks." Looking around, she said, "You all have my thanks for unswerving loyalty. Never forgotten!" Her eyes fell on Pyvel, and she recognized him as one of those who had helped her escape from the palace. "Pyvel," she fondly said. Placing her hand on his shoulder, she turned to the crowd. "My youngest soldier!" Her eyes shone as she looked at him, and at that moment he would have died for her.

"My loyal subjects," she called out, "we go to battle, and, with your courage, we cannot fail! This is our land. The plains, the Numin Mountains, the great Yanuri River, the polities where we raise our families and tend our fields! For a thousand years we have lived and loved on this land, and no diabolic army will take it from us!" The crowd roared its approval and continued to shout. She went on. "We go to fight! To drive them back through the gates! To bring peace and victory!"

Her soldiers had brought the gray mare, shying from the noise and the pressing throng. Anastyna patted its flank, calming it. Once in the saddle, she called out, "By the Mythos, victory will be ours!" Shouts of "By the Mythos, by the Mythos" followed her.

Nikander watched as Anastyna continued her progress through the camp. "Get something to eat," he told Pyvel. "The Volkish have come through Lowgate."

Pyvel felt a chill sweep over him. "Lowgate, sir?"

The captain was already striding off but turned to say, "And Causeway Gate. Both."

◈

IN THE AFTERNOON OF THE SECOND DAY OF THEIR SEARCH, YEVLIESZA and her escort were in a region of small lakes filled with cattails. At their approach, a flock of ducks clattered into the sky from a small pond, causing the whole party to reach for their swords. One of the soldiers had strong manifesting and spurred toward Yevliesza, ready to cast the image of a dactyl into the air. The ducks circled once and skimmed back to the pond. Everyone was on edge.

The horses had been ridden hard, and Captain Vadik proposed making an early camp to give them a rest. Mitri, always a strong horse, was holding up valiantly, but Vadik, nominally in charge, was right to have a care for the horses.

So far they had found nothing. No potential bridge to Nubiah. No align reaching to Alfan Sih. Yevliesza might be misjudging the trajectories. It had not been that long ago that she had learned how to perceive the route of an align—its destination. Whether it went to

Volkia or not. After that, she had taught herself to picture an exact destination, if she had ever been there, and to find those aligns. She was inexperienced and might not yet have the skill to discern which aligns traveled outside of the crossings. She needed help; a new approach. And there was one that might work.

When they gathered to take stock, Yevliesza told them her idea.

"My *sympat* might show me." Kiya had helped her before. Bringing his pack to kill the men that followed her in the Numin Mountains. Showing her the way out of Holdfast.

She met Valenty's gaze. He had not yet met Kiya and was eager to see this creature that lived half in the spirit world, or so it was said.

"He might lead me to the right align," Yevliesza said. "If it's right, I'll open it."

Elivasa spoke up. "We have not seen Kiya since he came to you on the ledge at Arrow Shaft."

Yevliesza hadn't told anyone why he had been there. To take her if she died. "I had been seeing him at Arrow Shaft camp," Yevliesza said, "in the woods. But he's more likely to show himself if I'm alone. So you all should hold well back."

Because of the danger from *strigoi*, Valenty wanted to be at her side. Rusadka did. Captain Vadik. But no one was going to be. Yevliesza might not have a useful opinion about conducting a battle, but she knew wraith wolves. She knew Kiya. In the end, they agreed.

⁂

KIYA CAME TO HER LATE IN THE AFTERNOON. SHE WAS MOUNTED ON Mitri, the steadiest horse in the Mythos. One who never shied at the sudden appearance of a fox or a blood bird.

Dismounting, Yevliesza looked back at her companions. Still forty yards back. Within sight of her, but leaving room for a wraith wolf to be comfortable. She shared a meal with Kiya, giving him the salted meat while she ate a winter apple. Wraith wolves weren't spirits, not entirely. They were predators that could easily take down a person and, in a pack, even a horse. Yevliesza had seen Kiya's pack a time or two and always wondered if they would suffer her for Kiya's sake. But usually he was alone.

After the food was gone, Kiya brushed heavily by her, his fur redolent of wind and sage. She lightly touched the fur on his back. He allowed this, but soon walked off, turning to see if she was following. She was. He headed into a shallow ravine filled with great and small rounded stones. Leading Mitri and watching for aligns out of habit, she followed him. Her nineteen fellow travelers matched her and Kiya's pace. They crossed an align, not recognizing its golden path in the sandy ground. Most of them did not.

The light drained from the ravine as the sun sank behind the hills.

She and Kiya passed a waterfall cascading down a ridge. An underground stream, one of several that fed this region of tiny lakes and ponds.

Here, Kiya paused. The align he stood upon ran perpendicular to the direction of the ravine, coming from one hillside and passing into the jumbled hillside opposite. It was in front of the jumbled hillside that Kiya turned to look at her. His green eyes seeming to say, *Are you paying attention?*

Yevliesza's mouth was dry. She took a long drink from her water skin, steeling herself to take a close look.

She sat on a rock to concentrate on the align's trajectory. "If this is the one," she whispered to Kiya, "don't leave. We will still need one more." She could not help but think that he understood her. Nearby, Mitri stamped a hoof. The waterfall splashed endlessly against rock.

Then she saw. The map in her mind became clear. It was Nubiah. Rounded hills, tufts of long grass following a stream bed, a far horizon stained red and orange in the sunset. Her breath caught in her throat. The scene spoke to her of Nubiah. But she might be imagining it was Nubiah.

Kiya came to sit beside her, and his presence brought certainty to her. This was a route to Nubiah. She went to her knees to rest her legs and began to work her power on the path. Dusk shaded the ravine as she delved the path. She urged it to widen and grow like a giant root, large enough for two men and their horses to pass. Strong enough to hold them; strong enough for the thousands of soldiers. The long line of them that would come into this land of ponds and lakes and gentle gullies.

The align wanted to expand. At her suggestion, it bloomed, the channel rushing ahead, becoming the great passageway connecting here to there. Numinat to Nubiah.

How much time had passed, she could not tell. Kiya beside her. Her back aching. Her mind exhausted.

It was done. Daylight had vanished. No moon. Her companions, however, were enveloped in a soft glow from manifesting lights. She came to her feet and walked toward them, closing the gap. "It's Nubiah," she told her companions. Valenty and Janov's mission would be the first, and it would begin here.

She grasped Janov's hands. "We have a path, and it's strong. But are you sure about going?"

"I am," he said. "If that wolf thinks it is right." He looked steady, as always. She had never met a man of such calm and unassuming authority.

Looking back, she saw that Kiya was gone. But he might be right next to her at that moment even if she couldn't see him.

She turned to Valenty. "It goes to a broad plain, a lot like this one. It's sunset there. I see a stream running down a low hillside." In creating the path, she hadn't visualized a specific location. She had never been to Nubiah. It had been dead reckoning, relying on her instinct. She had intended the path to reach Nubiah at ground level, because some rare aligns were in the sky.

"You are brilliant," he gently said. "We will be there and back again. There and back." He smiled. "Wait for me?"

"Yes," she said, her throat swelling. "Always."

She led the two men and their mounts to the gate she had opened. It looked like a cave entrance in the hillside.

They mounted their horses and Valenty looked down on her and nodded, holding her gaze for a moment. Then the two men entered the tunnel. She watched until they vanished around a bend.

Chapter Thirty-One

Behind Nashavety, a great cloud of dust engulfed the Volkish army. They were strung out in a line stretching into the distance, horses at the front, followed by foot soldiers, some carrying the Volkish battle standard, the black three-sided banner with a white star. Carts and wagons came last, full of weapons, kegs of water, ale, and dried meats, fodder for the horses, and tents for the men.

Some wagons, pulled by oxen, carried the battle machines, the metal hot under the sun. The volley shields that could hurl streams of iron pellets. The iron cladders, twice the height of a man, they lay on their backs in repose, like sleeping giants. The lovely mechanicals of her brilliant design. The Mythos forbade machines driven by offensive fuels, those being the foul legacy of the mundat. But her machines were driven by a power the Mythos itself bestowed: elemental power. It was not trespass—it was an inspiration. The elementalists coming behind traveled in comfortable wagons so that they would be rested when their duties called them.

Nashavety's mount was a strong gray mare, a blanket covering it from pommel to haunches, its tail and mane braided with black ribbons and the sidesaddle and bridle trimmed in silver. She wore a proper

Numinasi black dress and, over the bodice, a vest of dyed black leather, cinched closed with silver ties.

Marshal Kenrick, commander of the northern army, rode at Nashavety's side, barrel-chested and bedecked with silver braid. His black uniform, like that of the other officers, making a powerful impression. Far away, but marching toward them even now, Reinhart led the southern army from Lowgate. Lowgate was the closest gate to Osta Kiya, but it was the same distance as Causeway Gate from the Plain of Monuments. There Numinat would for the first time see an army of eleven thousand.

If they did not surrender, they would be crippled by fear. Though Sofiyana would have surrendered, Nashavety doubted Anastyna would. By now she had certainly been reinstated as princip. When she saw this army, she might regret having to preside over the slaughter.

She looked out at the never-ending plain under a sky slashed with narrow clouds stretched long by the wind, her heart thick with longing. She was home, but she did not possess it. The battle to come would settle that, and it would be gruesome. A necessary bloodbath.

Marshal Kenrick swiped at a fly near his face. "A dreary landscape —does it ever end?" He expected no answer, and she gave none. "You will be queen of sand."

She stiffened at the comment. The man was brutish and arrogant, being Volkish and unworthy to set foot upon such a land as this. Worshipping a god who could not prevent being nailed to a cross. Hanging traitors' bodies on a wall. Albrecht's habit of using creature power on his bed slaves. He had been a handsome man and had no need to force women. A Numinasi man would not only never dare such a thing; he would never think it.

Her Volkish helpers thought they would rule Numinat. Through her, of course. They believed her allegiance would be to Hapsigen, to Volkia. It would be the other way around. In time, they would learn this.

One of her joys out on the vast plain that day was that the land recognized her. She felt that it knew her, as well it might. It held the abysmal well of darkness. When she was young, that well had spoken to her, had infused her blood with its heat. Lying at the roots of the great outcropping called the Citadel was a wellspring that amplified her powers, both of creatures and elements.

Few beside her knew about the deep lake. Those that did know were afraid of it, never daring to disturb its sleep. How convenient for the First Ones to believe that they had transcended the world from which Numinat arose. How comforting to reflect that, while people of the mundat lived in error, banishing magic from their land, the Numinasi lived in a better world. They did, but it was not shining with goodness as they had thought. The First Ones had unwittingly brought the foul ways of Earth with them. The darkness had followed them into the crossings because men and women always brought evil with them wherever they went.

When the First Ones saw what had followed them, they combined their powers—a feat only made possible by their desperation—and buried the darkness at the foot of the first large rock they saw.

The Citadel.

The magic—call it by its mundat term, since it was of the mundat —would relish a little freedom. She would fulfill that desire.

But to do so, she had to be standing upon the rock. She soon would be.

◈

At dawn, Yevliesza rose from her bed of saddle and horse blanket to look for Rusadka. She found her standing by her horse, saying goodbye to Elivasa.

Yevliesza gave the two of them privacy. Both of them were going to meet their separate dangers. Elivasa to Alfan Sih if a way could be found. Rusadka to join her unit for the battle. Of course she would go back to join her *harjat* contingent; she had told Urik she would return.

To Yevliesza's surprise, Rusadka and Elivasa were laughing. Something funny about facing death? But, around Elivasa, laughter always seemed possible.

Rusadka saw Yevliesza and gave her horse's reins to Elivasa.

"I thought you would sleep until midday," Rusadka said, looking refreshed, even eager to be gone.

"Who can sleep when there's laughter at the crack of dawn?" Another goodbye. It was becoming routine.

Rusadka smirked. "It happens." She wore her sword on her back, her hair pulled into a bun, with two small knives crisscrossed through it.

She must have seen dismay on Yevliesza's face, because she said, "Do not worry. We will drive them out of Numinat." Rusadka glanced at the sky. Thick clouds smeared the faint sunrise into a blade of gray. "Where will you be when it is over?"

"Branova." The village Yevliesza had first gone to when she emerged from Holdfast. Where Janov had been the village master, and might be again when he got back from Nubiah.

"Good." Rusadka looked around the ravine. "The wolf?"

"Gone for now." Yevliesza sighed. "I would tell you to be careful, but that's stupid, isn't it."

"I am careful in my way."

Elivasa brought Rusadka's mare. A good horse in a battle, Rusadka had said. It took too much energy to control a stallion.

Arman came forward to bid Rusadka goodbye. "I dearly wish I could fight with you in the coming battle."

"You already are," she said. "Bring Alfan Sih to us." She mounted her horse. Elivasa smiled brilliantly at her.

Love in the midst of war. It was a good thought to hold on to as Rusadka rode down the gully.

Arman and Elivasa stood together, watching her leave. The next ones who Yevliesza would be saying goodbye to. With any luck.

After a cold breakfast, Yevliesza hoisted her water skin and went looking for Kiya.

Pyvel, on his chestnut mare in the horse unit, rode in front of

Anastyna's foot soldiers, close enough to see the princip with Prince Fadimir and the lord wardens.

Today Pyvel had the honor of being one of those who bore the princip's standard: nine red circles forming a circle on a field of white. They had been able to secure enough cloth for only three pennants, but they were large. Many standards of blue and gold flew—Prince Fadimir's Dorodna banner. Also the brown and yellow of Eiger Polity, and the blue and white of Lukya. Three thousand soldiers.

Yesterday, on the way to meet the army of Osta Kiya, they had met Prince Fadimir's army coming to join them, and now it seemed to Pyvel that nothing could defeat them. They said that Osta Kiya had almost four thousand more. They would win. Who could defeat an army like this?

Captain Nikander kept Pyvel close to the front of the horse unit, by his side. He wanted to look behind, to savor the numbers following, but no one else did, and he thought it more proper to keep his gaze forward. Forward, for the first glimpse of the Plain of Monuments.

The great formations would at first be merely specks and then grow larger and soon would loom over the massed armies of Osta Kiya. Though Pyvel had never been there before, he was sure it would be a glorious place for a battle to decide the fate of the realm. He would not bear a standard in the battle. His job would be to carry Nikander's extra sword and spears. To be ready to hand over his helmet, with its wicked cheek pieces, or a new sword. He would be in the midst of any charge of horses, and, on Kasha, he had been practicing holding a spear while at full gallop.

A group of riders was approaching them from the direction of the Plain of Monuments. As they got closer, Pyvel counted thirty soldiers, and they bore the standard of Osta Kiya, the white circle on a red field. Prince Fadimir, whom Anastyna had appointed her commander, called a halt, and the word was passed down the line of march.

Pyvel heard Nikander say to his lieutenant that Commander Ilyan was among the party.

Urik, who had been riding with Anastyna, now came back to have a few words with Captain Nikander, and soon Urik was leading Pyvel and his mount to a position some forty paces down the princip's right flank.

"Now watch," Urik said.

The soldiers set up a small, open-sided pavilion, barely large enough for three or four people.

"What is happening, sir?" Pyvel asked.

"Commander Ilyan." Urik nodded at the burly officer, who dismounted and stood by his stallion. "He chose to recognize the usurper."

"But it was not his fault. The *fajatim* voted for her."

Pyvel did not expect Urik to respond, since his comment was obvious and also possibly not respectful.

But Urik muttered, "The world has to be put right."

Anastyna was walking to the pavilion. The ranks of soldiers fell quiet. The only sounds, the creak of saddles and the occasional hoof clattering on a rock. The fluttering of pennants.

Anastyna wore a white cape lined in red and trimmed in fur. One side was folded over her shoulder, clearly revealing her torc of office. Commander Ilyan came forward, followed by a soldier. Outside the pavilion, Ilyan removed his sword from his scabbard and handed it to the soldier, who stood back.

Ilyan entered the pavilion and dropped to one knee. Receiving a nod from Anastyna, the soldier came forward and handed her Ilyan's sword. She held it for a moment, saying something to the commander. Then she gestured for him to rise and handed him the sword. Ilyan stood before her and slid the blade into its scabbard.

When they emerged from the pavilion, they stood together in solidarity. Anastyna looked like the only one who could ever be Princip of Numinat. The massed soldiers broke into shouts and then thunderous cheering. The sweeping cries of "Anastyna! Numinat!" flowed through the line of march into the distance.

Urik glanced at Pyvel. "Something to tell your grandchildren." The corners of his mouth moved up slightly, if it was not Pyvel's imagination.

Pyvel could imagine himself telling the story, of the vast army watching the pavilion, the princip standing before a man kneeling and receiving full exoneration. The world put right.

⚜

VALENTY AND JANOV RODE THROUGH THE TUNNEL TOWARD NUBIAH. Tall and wide, the corridor looked like a crossing that had been used for hundreds of years, but Yevliesza had created it in hours. It was still very strange to him. That and her wraith wolf. A *sympat* no one had thought possible. Yevliesza, who had come to Numinat already a grown woman and without her birthright power. She was, they all thought, beyond any kind of normal life. But not only one power had come to her: two. Aligns and the lost power, an affinity for the connections between realms.

Valenty and Arman were making their way though an unknown corridor. They did not know how long the journey might be. It was a path that did not share the region of the crossings and might be unreliable. It could disappear, the girl with the unbearable foreknowing had said. Yet they and their mounts were traveling in what appeared to be a normal crossing.

Janov, who had never been in a crossing path, marveled at the cavern, as he called it, as though they were deep in a cave with passages between vaulted halls.

"Light everywhere," he said. "What causes it?"

"We do not know." The walls were not bright, yet the light must emanate from them.

There were unusual sounds. The horses shied at them. Normally, the crossings made no sounds, not that most people could hear. But here, a faint thudding, like the wind hitting the outside walls. It brought to mind what the tunnel was passing through. Someplace wild and unknown. It was beyond understanding. Conjecture, useless.

"You hear that?" Janov asked.

"It may be the wind in Nubiah." If they were close, it might be.

"Sometimes a high-pitched humming," Janov said. He did not say *moaning*. But Valenty heard that, too.

The memory came to him of how, in the crossings, when a gate opened to one of the realms, fresh air swept into the corridor, reminding travelers that they had been breathing stale air. The farther end of the pathway would not be closed off with a gate. Fresh air would be their first signal that they had arrived.

They continued, often trotting the horses, which seemed to calm them. He wondered greatly where they would emerge in Nubiah and if they could reach the Lion Court in time. But no good to wonder. It was much like asking what one man could do on a battleground of thousands. What could be done must be done.

Yevliesza's image came to him. Her short hair disheveled, her expression of vulnerability and mastery. How had he deserved her? Perhaps today he would earn her regard.

"There it comes again," Janov said. "That high whine."

"The wind of Nubiah," Valenty answered. Hoping.

❧

TIRHAN ROUSED MORWEN FROM SLEEP SHORTLY BEFORE DAWN. THE tent was wet with condensation, and a few drips fell on her face.

"My lord?" She sat up, brushing the sleep from her eyes.

"Do not call me that," Tirhan said, kneeling beside her.

She smiled. "Are you not king?"

"I am. But I forbid it. Severe punishment can be meted out."

She brought her hand around his neck. "Such as?"

As he looked at her, all disheveled from sleep, he almost justified staying another hour. But: "Alas, we must ride."

"Where?" she asked as she pulled on her boots.

"Talfyn Syd. A dream came to me, and I learned we must go." He watched her as she tied back her hair and laced her leather vest. "But it was not a dream."

She stopped, meeting his gaze. "A visitor?"

"It was the spirit who came to me the day after our wedding. The one called Gethin. He said we must go to the grove at Talfyn Syd."

"The silverwood grove."

"And quickly." There had been urgency in his dream-time message. *Come to Talfyn Syd, bringing all with you. Hurry, Lord King.*

Morwen did not press for details, but gathered their few things into a sack and went out to make sure the camp left no evidence of their presence. Tirhan kept his forces dispersed. Only thirty-two warriors with him, since a larger company would draw attention. Volkish hunted them, so they stayed on the move through the woodlands, never staying more than one night in any one place.

Tirhan possessed few trappings of kingship. He had a gift of a fine velvet jerkin. His sword belt was paneled with silver and the scabbard studded with amber. But his cloak was ragged at the edges, his shirt and trousers patched. He possessed a circlet of brass someone had fashioned, but did not wear it unless they visited a steading or a village.

Demyr quickly had everyone packed and sharing a cold meal. Soon they were headed out and riding hard for Talfyn Syd, a day and a half's ride away.

Chapter Thirty-Two

Pyvel's heart lifted at the sight of the Plain of Monuments. In and around it, the army of Numinat, spreading over the plain like one massive creature. Smoke rose from thousands of cookfires, shrouding the sky. Framing the battleground, the enormous stone formations rising from the plain.

Closest to the massed troops, a gigantic butte with a flat top like an anvil. Nearby, three other strangely shaped formations. One, a spire thrusting up from a massive base; another that rose in layers to a peak; and the largest, a butte separated from a great spire by a narrow causeway.

The army of Osta Kiya waited for Anastyna and her three thousand fighters. Together, the armies would wait for the Volkish. They knew by now—everyone knew—that the Volkish were coming from two sides: from Causeway and from Lowgate. Eleven thousand fighters, it was said, a number Pyvel could not imagine.

Looking behind, he reassured himself of the strength of Anastyna's army. The column of fighters stretched out of sight. Together with Osta Kiya, they would have over seven thousand.

He wished Valenty was there with him. He did not know where the lord was, but expected to see him at any moment. He would not shirk a fight.

Anastyna and her wardens spurred forward toward the butte they called Gray Fort. There, they would make camp while the leaders agreed on strategy and positions on the field. "Jostling for prominence," Nikander grumbled within hearing. But Commander Ilyan would lead. Even Prince Fadimir would submit himself to the larger strategy.

As Anastyna's army entered the camp, massive shadows from the monuments fell over the plain, making the great rocks look even more imposing. Commander Ilyan was said to have picked this battleground. The large butte protected the army's rear, and a ledge partway up would give the officers a view of the battlefield.

In the camp they passed men of every sort, many of them wearing short armor or boiled leather. Standards were secured in the ground bearing flags of the polities. Many white and red banners, those of Osta Kiya, and others of blue and white from the Lukya region, and more that he could not identify.

He spied Urik and his *harjat* on horseback approaching a larger group—the *harjat* of Osta Kiya, the ones who had remained loyal to Sofiyana. He wondered what kind of reunion *that* would be.

Not all the men had proper weapons, Pyvel saw to his disappointment. More than half had no armor, not even leather, nor weapons other than axes, hoes, and, if lucky, spears. These were fighters who owed service to their wardens. They had been pulled from their work in fields, smithies, and taverns. They had the right spirit, though. Shouts of welcome went up as Pyvel's unit passed by, and he proudly held Anastyna's exile standard.

Anastyna's soldiers picketed their horses in an area near the great walls of Gray Fort. Nearby, wagons loaded with firewood and peat for cookfires. Pyvel took charge of Hunter and Kasha.

Once he had seen to the horses, he found a spot to settle in near Nikander's tent. A group of soldiers stood nearby, men with upper arms like hams and rugged faces creased by the sun. He heard them talking about an align. They said there was one that passed through the plain at a diagonal to Gray Fort. It could be used by a unit of their aligners to form a strong line of defense if the fight came close to the align.

One of them said that maybe the iron machines could draw power there as well, but others said only aligners could draw strength from aligns. Pyvel remembered it was elementalists who powered the cladders and the volley shields. For himself, if he got to fight at all, it would only be with what weapon he could find; his affinity for manifesting would be no help at all.

The soldiers looked up, noting a disturbance around them. Men were staring east, though there was nothing to see except one of the rock formations in the distance.

But soon word came. The Volkish army. One of them.

Shock jolted through Pyvel. He had thought they would not arrive so soon. He hurried to the horses, noting that soldiers were preparing, but not panicking. They had known the armies were close; Commander Ilyan had been receiving reports from scouts on dactyls for days. The second Volkish army was also near, converging on the Plain of Monuments.

The battle was coming.

❧

THEY HAD BEEN TRAVELING HALF A DAY, HEADING EAST. YEVLIESZA rode with Arman and Elivasa at her side. Far ahead, Kiya trotted, tolerating the party of horses as long as they stayed well back of him. Mitri plodded on, the sound of his hooves soft on the sandy ground.

In the distance, the gray mass of the Mist Wall, a hand's-breadth high. It grew, as though it was advancing. Here the primordial lands began, the soil bearing patchy grasses and saplings. Closer, there would be nothing but hard, caked ground.

"I saw the Mist Wall once when I was small," Elivasa said. "My father told me it was a dust storm far away. If he had told me it was the wall of the world, I would never have slept again."

Yevliesza squinted at the wall. The engine of the world, someone had once called it. "Hard for me to believe you were ever afraid of anything."

Elivasa laughed. "That, and birds."

"Birds?" Arman asked, with feigned incredulity.

"Yes, birds. I always hated it when Anastyna called her miserable falcon to her wrist." She smirked at Arman. "What are you afraid of? I suppose nothing, being Volkish."

"Nothing I will admit to," he said dryly. "Being Volkish."

Kiya had disappeared again. Yevliesza always tried to catch him fading into the next world. It was surprisingly difficult to spy him at the exact moment. She rode on, watching for aligns, even if she was counting on Kiya to find the *one*.

They were still too far away from the Mist Wall to hear the suppressed thunder of the great storm. The never-arriving storm. She remembered that there were aligns in the Mist Wall. She had seen them that day when she and Isha walked through the primordial lands. Lightning, she first thought, as she had looked at the towering wall, shifting, sometimes revealing shallow nodes or deep canyons. No, her teacher had said. Aligns.

Kiya wasn't taking them to the Mist Wall, was he? She reined in Mitri.

Everyone stopped with her, waiting silently, not wanting to distract her if she was investigating an align.

Yevliesza turned to her companions. "If he's going to the Mist Wall, that will be a problem. Horses won't approach it."

Kiya appeared again, now heading south, parallel to the wall. He was heading for a stand of stunted trees.

A few of the mounts were tossing their heads and stamping nervously. Captain Vadik nudged his horse next to her. "Any farther, and we should picket the horses."

Everyone agreed, and the horses' reins were soon tied to stakes pounded into the ground. Elivasa and Arman packed satchels with food and water for their mission. In case there would be one.

Yevliesza stroked between Mitri's ears, telling him, "I will be back soon." He was still a handsome animal, with his dappled gray coat, his black mane and tail. "Tell the others not to worry." Talking to animals. Stranger things had happened, she thought, smiling to herself.

They left two soldiers behind with the horses.

⚜

KIYA STOOD ON THE EDGE OF THE PATCH OF TREES, THE MIST WALL coiling in the distance. Turning around, he looked at Yevliesza to be sure she was paying attention. Seeing that she was, he disappeared into the trees.

Following Kiya in, she immediately saw it. A bright scar on the ground amid the stunted trees. It was a molten fissure, a thread of the Deep. She probed it with her affinity. An align pointing to Alfan Sih.

She looked up to find Kiya and—there!—his pelt began to blur, became a fog. In the next instant, her wraith wolf vanished. It stirred her. The next world was that close. And Kiya had allowed her to see him go.

He had done his job. Now it was up to her.

She called on her companions to join her then sat next to the align. Neither Arman nor Elivasa—nor any of the soldiers—had the birthright power of aligns, but they believed that she saw one. The right one. She identified that the exit point of the align was in Alfan Sih, though she could not say how she knew it. It was Alfan Sih as clear as any knowing could make it. Since the few trees around them limited their view of the sky, Captain Vadik set half of his remaining men to take positions on the perimeter of the grove to watch for *strigoi*.

Elivasa and Arman rested against a couple of trees while Yevliesza concentrated on the bright line. She was sitting on the ground, her left hand on the align. Probing with her thoughts, she pushed at it. A throbbing in her small finger spread to her hand. A rush of blood, or the Deep. Running up her forearm. *Grow,* she silently urged the align. She eased her will into it. It grew.

Soon she was oblivious of sitting in a grove of trees, unaware of people nearby, her hearing diminished. *Grow,* she silently told the line of neon. *Be the path. Grow and be the path to Alfan Sih.* There were no magic words, but saying her intention helped with concentration.

She was staring without seeing. But she perceived a deep valley covered by a profusion of leafy trees. A profound woods, but not high in the hills. That was good, she thought. With luck, not too long a journey.

Arman and Elivasa shook hands with the soldiers. They knew what Arman and Elivasa might face, what their purpose was. Bring another army and attack the flank of the Volkish invasion force.

Yevliesza said her goodbyes. Elivasa's demeanor showed her determination: she was not a woman to underestimate. Yevliesza had seen her fight.

Arman was eager to go. Not only would he bring numbers to the battlefield, he would be in the fight itself. If the Alfan forces could arrive in time.

When they walked into the pathway, Yevliesza thought she caught the smell of fresh air threading through the crossing. Alfan Sih of the endless forests, of the silverwoods. *Tirhan,* she passionately thought. *We are coming. Watch for us.*

❦

AT THE FOOT OF GRAY FORT ROCK, PYVEL OUTFITTED HIS HORSE WITH everything he would need in the fight: his captain's extra helmet, sword, and spears. Kasha stamped and snorted as she restlessly waited. Nikander would ride with his spear, but he would use other weapons as well and depended on Pyvel to have them near.

"Eat something," a voice said.

Pyvel looked up to see Rusadka standing beside him.

"You cannot fight on an empty stomach."

Pyvel thought she looked fierce in her short armor, sturdy boots, and two swords, one of them long, and her armband of black and yellow. "Where are the *harjat* stationed, ma'am?" he asked.

"Where do you think?" she said, friendlier than usual. "In the center of our line." Her eyes traveled over his horse, approving. "We have some surprises for them. Be confident."

He nodded as she went on her way, wishing he had said something more. *The Mythos be with you,* maybe. But he never knew what to say to Rusadka that would not seem foolish.

He dug in his satchel for a piece of dried meat, chewing it and trying to swallow. His throat dry, his skin prickling every time he thought of the waiting Volkish. This was how fear was: quiet and lurking.

Gray Fort loomed over him, a comforting presence when he was not imagining being pinned against it by the enemy horde. Here, at the foot of the butte, the horse unit would be held well back, in reserve for times of need. Next to the horses, the healers stood ready to take the wounded, those that could make it back on their own or be helped back.

They did not know when the attack would come, but the second Volkish army had already joined the first. Someone said that the wagons carrying iron mechanicals had arrived as well.

Men dressed for the fight. Those that had armor pulled it on over leather undercoats. Pyvel saw a unit of archers coming through. The archers of Mensk were well known, with their tradition of longbows that could send an arrow a great distance.

The units were moving into positions, with fighters under the immediate command of their home wardens, except for the Osta Kiya permanent army. The forces assembled in a broad line to prevent the Volkish from flanking them. By their pennants, the trained soldiers of Osta Kiya stood in the center, Dorodna on the right under Prince Fadimir and Orfeyiv and Lukya on the left, with ranks behind filled by men from other polities and cities that had responded to the call. In the third rank, the Mensk archers.

Pyvel learned that they would meet the Volkish in the middle of the semicircle formed by Gray Fort, First Ones Pillar, and the Citadel, with its towering spire.

Sometimes through the ranks of the army, Pyvel caught a glimpse of the enemy forces. They were still well back at Castle Rock, massing on three sides of it, looking like a gray sea that could surge forward at any moment. At seven thousand, Osta Kiya's army was badly outnumbered. But they had the *harjat*. And unlike the Volkish, they had longbow archers. They had the align. And Duke Tanfred's banner.

How could it ever be enough?

Chapter Thirty-Three

Yevliesza and her fifteen guards had traveled away from the Mist Wall into a region of rocky hills.

By midmorning they were watering their horses at a well. It was the steading of a sheep herder living with his large family in a hovel of wood and straw. When the family saw the soldiers coming, they had hidden in the nearby rocky hills, but gradually came out when they saw a woman in the group.

The herder used a crutch to hobble on his only leg, clearly a long-time condition, and he spoke with satisfaction that he would not be in the coming battle. Nor sharing food with the travelers, since he had done so too many times the last fiveday and their larder was thin. The herder and his wife eyed Yevliesza, curious, while relating what they knew of the war.

The Volkish horde had passed by the steading two days before, taking his herd, all but the strays that his sons had chased into the hills when they saw the army coming. In previous days, Numinasi scouts had told him that the battleground would be at the Plain of Monuments. And, to Yevliesza's amazement, that Sofiyana had abandoned the torc and fled, no one knew where. Anastyna was reinstated.

She couldn't imagine Sofiyana giving up the throne of Numinat. Who wouldn't wish to be princip of the realm? Well, Yevliesza wouldn't. Dreiza would never wish for the torc. Nor, actually, any woman Yevliesza had met in the realm. It didn't speak well for those that did, those who coveted power enough to bear the weight around their neck. Maybe Sofiyana had found it a chain. Or she had been driven from her post by others. Yevliesza would have to wait to hear more. Sofiyana would certainly be tried for trespass, sorcery being the worst form of it: compelling others, trespass of persons. She would die in that terrible Numinat spectacle of punishment. It gave Yevliesza no satisfaction to think of it.

The troop greeted the news of Anastyna's return with excitement. They looked in the direction of the battleground, eager to be there. It was time to release them. Their purpose had been to keep Yevliesza safe while she had a mission to sabotage the Volkish. That was over now.

"Captain," she told Vadik, "you and your men should go to your unit."

"Is there more you would have from us, mistress?"

Truly, there wasn't, and she said so. There was still the danger of the blood birds, but she would have to take her chances.

"Warden Kirady would not have me leave you unguarded," Vadik said. "I will leave three men with you."

After a brief rest, most of the party rode west. She had wanted to go with them, but she had no role there. But it seemed wrong to seek safety somewhere, leaving events to unfold. And she would not go into hiding, not yet. She had one more thing to do.

She needed an align that reached backways. There, she could at least disturb the Volkish supply line, if there was one still coming through. She knew the army was pillaging as it traveled, a better source of provisions than Volkia. But she would go in and see.

She wandered into the hills with her escort, alert for Kiya, alert for aligns. Now that she didn't need an established gate. Now that she had realized she could make her own.

On the rises, she looked west, imagining the gathered armies under the shadows of the great formations she had once seen on her way to visit Anastyna. That day when she had first met Kirady. When she had ridden with him, Rusadka, Janov, and Elivasa. One by one they had gone to the fight.

Low hills covered in sagebrush and stunted trees rippled into the distance. She had never felt more alone. In the two months since the Blossom Moon—May, in mundat terms—she had been among close friends and sometimes hundreds of soldiers and villagers. Now three guards remained, and she knew they wanted to join their warden at the monuments. She thought of Arman and Elivasa in the new path she had fashioned to Alfan Sih. Always in her mind, Valenty and Janov on the mission to Nubiah. She had sent four friends into paths that crossed through a dangerous place. Had sent Valenty. If he was lost, she didn't think she could bear it. *Wait for me,* he had said. *Wait for me.* Imagining him coming back kept anxiety at bay.

Rusadka had asked where Yevliesza would be after the war. She really had no place to go. There was Osta Kiya, the city-palace, but she could not be happy there. Branova, she had told her friend. The village on the outskirts of the great Agarvesky Forest. *Not Earth?* a small voice inquired, that part of her that sometimes thought she belonged there. No, not Earth. Even when she had lived there with her father, she had not really belonged, her isolation complete, being miles from a town, being a *witch*, as the locals called her.

⁂

AS ARMAN AND ELIVASA RODE ALONG THE PATHWAY, THE WALLS shuddered. To Arman, the sound was not like the quakes he had experienced before in the backways. It was a lighter, thudding sound, as though something was outside the walls, knocking against them.

This corridor was very different from any others. It did not share the region where the paths clustered like various streams forced into a deep valley. This path was far outside. Its nature was bound to be different.

The banging sounds grew louder.

They stopped for a moment as a new sound, a piercing whine, rang through the tunnel. Arman's horse stepped nervously to the side, and Arman patted him.

Elivasa frowned. "We should move faster."

Arman agreed, and they urged the horses into a trot. Ahead, a banging sound pounded the walls.

"It's getting worse," Elivasa said over the noise.

As a percussive clatter joined the clamor, Arman's horse reared. "The horses will bolt," he said. "We should dismount."

They did so, struggling with the horses, trying without success to calm them. She leaned in to make herself heard. "Let them go!" They did, and the horses, rearing and wild-eyed, galloped back the way they had come. As the floor began to tremble, Arman looked around, wondering how the tunnel could stay intact.

They waited, desperately hoping for the storm outside to pass, to weaken its rage. But it continued, now sending buckling shudders through the path.

Elivasa took his hand, gripping it. "It cannot hold," he heard her say.

As the crossing walls began to dim, he whispered, "God have mercy."

A dusk fell upon them.

"No regrets," Arman said, looking at his companion. He faced what was coming. It was not as difficult. The end. Not so very hard.

Next to him, he heard Elivasa respond, "No regrets."

It was no shame to fail. His fellow conspirators in Volkia had failed, but had the courage to try. When the soldiers' boots crashed through the door, they had moments to live, and he hoped their last thoughts were noble ones, accepting what was to come. At last he was going to join them, as he had wanted to from that day. He had done his best.

"Be of good courage," Arman said to Elivasa, and to his amazement, he saw her smile.

"For the Mythos," she fiercely said.

Another quake came through, ripping the substance of the tunnel as though it were thinnest silk.

⚜

YEVLIESZA WANDERED IN THE HILLS WITH HER GUARDS. LOYALLY, THEY accepted her task of finding one more align. This time she wanted to get into the crossings. She might not be able to carry a sword, but she could still fight. At least a little.

When she had found Arrow Shaft, the whorls on the wall of the cave had shown her the way in. But, as she mastered her power of primal roots, she saw that a plain align with the right trajectory was all she had ever needed.

On a tree-studded ridge she found a bright fissure in the ground. It flowed toward its fellow aligns in the backways. She looked at it as though seeing an align for the first time. Seeing it truly. Was it so easy, then, to just go in?

Not easy, but possible. Kiya had found a difficult align, one of the rare ones that traveled outside the confluence of aligns. All Yevliesza had to do was find a common one.

On this ridge, she had discerned one of that sort, one that penetrated the backways. She made a gate, no more than a shimmering oval that blurred the fallen tree trunk in its path.

She left Mitri in the care of her guards, promising to return in a few hours.

She walked through.

The glow of the crossings surrounded her, as well as the not-unpleasant yeasty smell of something living, living in a verdure way. As always, the sounds of crinkling, which was the root enlarging, as all the crossings slowly expanded, responding to the flow of people through them.

The walls gave slightly to her touch, as though greeting her. If she pressed, a niche would appear. If she concentrated on the faint whorls in the walls, she could create an opening to an adjacent tunnel, doing so more easily than otherwise. She knew the crossings at last and was at home in them.

Bringing to mind the map of the labyrinth, she saw units of soldiers clustered at the gates to the realms. Volkia, Nubiah, Alfan Sih, Jade Pavilion, Norslad, Arabet, and, more faintly, the closed gates of the Indigene nations. And Numinat. The Volkish were guarding against any reinforcements arriving. How surprised they would be if they ever learned they had been bypassed.

The solution had been within her grasp all along, but the First Ones had left her to discover it on her own. Kassalya had said they had tried to reach her. The girl had been certain of that, even before she became their spokesperson. Had Yevliesza really not listened? Preoccupied with herself, Kassalya said. Preoccupied with her own limitations, Isha would say. So not listening. *By the great, almighty Deep,* she thought, *they might have spoken louder.*

But if the armies came through—if they came through in time— then she would have done what she was meant to. Her part in a thing so much larger than herself.

However, the main paths were not filled with wagons to sabotage. Soldiers patrolled; messengers strode through on their missions; in the large cavern near Lowgate, food and water lay stored for the soldiers garrisoned there. No targets worth even a small disruption of the crossings.

She had been wandering in the backways, watching, probing for a target. And then movement.

Shapes moving toward her through the backways. Shapes scuttling. Wings flapping.

Blood birds.

How could they be here? Frantically, she took stock of her possible routes, seeing her path to avoid them. Rushing away from the closest of the *strigoi,* she struggled to maintain a clear real-time map in her mind. The backways comprised a maze, and some of the paths were dead ends. She avoided those, but her way out of the backway was blocked. She looked for a route around the demons, at last seeing one, but now the demons were closing in. If she could get to the bypass route, she could close the access behind her. Ah, but there was more than one entry into that route. Panic grabbed at her chest like talons closing.

She broke into a run. She knew how to get to the route. She *knew*.

Two blood birds emerged from a side path behind her. Flapping wings, moaning with hunger.

She charged for the opening to the bypass. A scuttling noise filled her ears. Diving for the opening, she dashed through, shouting, *Shut, shut,* shut, in her mind. As the access closed, a skinny hand came through from the other side, talons slowly extruding. The hand yanked back as the opening closed.

Her heart beat like it would leap from her chest.

Bringing the map into awareness again, she picked her route and ran headlong down it, but in her panic, she passed some turns that might have been the best ones. Stopping to concentrate, she saw the labyrinth in her mind once more. Saw that something was standing right behind her.

Swiveling, she saw large yellow eyes, a misshapen, almost circular mouth, like a lamprey. A sucking mouth. A *strigoi*. "Finding she," it said in a high-pitched voice. "Wo-min with root power, yesss."

The thing was close enough to jump on her. She backed up. It took a step closer.

There was a split second of a crouch, so quick, she barely had time to raise her hands to protect herself. It jumped. She twisted hard to one side, and the *strigoi* slammed into the wall, tearing her shirt, grazing her chest with its talons as it passed. *Grab it,* she commanded the wall. *Flow and hold, flow and keep!*

Yanking away from the creature, she stepped back far enough to see that one wing and the back of its head were sunk a few inches into the wall's material. The blood bird shrieked and struggled, but the wall held.

Imprisoned by the wall, the *strigoi* regarded her with a wide, fearful look. Slowly, the wall extruded farther around its head.

Stop, hold firm, she willed the wall. *Keep it, keep it.*

Small, staccato mews came from the demon's scrawny throat. She stared at it, hating and fearing it. But before it died, she wanted to know something.

"Why did you come after me?" she said, her own voice barely recognizable, shredded and breathless.

"Must kill she." As it spoke, its breath like a sewer. "Wo-min say." The mouth curved a little, as though it were thinking how good it would have been to kill her.

"A woman in a long black dress?"

It had given up struggling to pull its wing free and hung there, trapped. "Yesss. Take my kin and kill she." It stared at her in a way that, ridiculously, appeared to be pleading. As though she would release it so it could kill she.

"Kin?" Curiosity, despite having almost been torn apart by a gang of *strigoi.*

"We go hooome," it sang in its falsetto voice, "wo-min of rooot power can."

Woman of root power. It knew what she was. Nashavety knew, so her demons knew.

"Why did you release me in the maze?" It, or one of its brothers, had grabbed her in the maze at Holdfast. And let her go.

"Smell roooots. Flow in she." Again, the pathetic, longing stare.

She stared at it. Once, this *strigoi,* the one that had jumped on her, had let her go. "But you want to kill me this time?"

It hung limp in its prison on the wall. "Must kill, wo-min say." He stared at her, repeating the very thing that would condemn it. "Kill she. If kill, fly hooome. Loovely hooome."

That startled her. That it could say such a thing. "Where is home?"

"Yesss. Great, loovely forest."

"In Volkia?" It gazed at her, silent, almost sad. It didn't know the name people gave to its home. "The world where the woman in the long dress found you?"

"Wo-min in house. Aliiive house."

The house that Valenty had told her about. In Volkia's Breminger

Forest. This creature and its kin were sent to kill her. On the promise that they could go home. A Nashavety promise, never to be fulfilled.

An idea was forming. She could release the blood birds. It was a stupid idea.

"If I let you go, the others will kill me."

"Nooo! To open door so we freeee. For loovely—" His eyes grew round in fear, as the wall crept over the side of his face.

"For lovely forest," she whispered. "Will your kin follow you, or will they attack me?"

"We go forest, sweeet dark." Its voice grew faint as more of its face sank into the wall.

A weight of sadness fell over her. The striving, the separations, the blood to come. The worst thing of all, that sentient creatures were compelled. The dark madness of forcing the will of others. She was so tired of evil.

The blood bird wanted to go home. It was as if it knew the very thing to say. That would pierce her armor. Going home. The great, lovely forest.

She walked along the tunnel until she found a thread leading to Volkia. She had no memory of the Breminger Forest, never having been there, but the blood birds would have to find their own way once in Volkia. She opened the path.

The blood birds could kill her now. Nothing was a given, but she was going to send this *strigoi* and its kin home.

She went back to the imprisoned creature and released it. It fell from the wall's stranglehold, hitting the floor of the tunnel. It limped toward the smell of freshening air. Her internal map revealed that the blood birds were flying, converging on the door to Volkia. Her *strigoi* went first, walking unsteadily along the tunnel, then taking flight and leading its fellows down the twisty length of the pathway.

As she watched them disappear, her mind went wide, looking at all the paths. The Volkish-owned tunnels, the hundreds of them. The backways. Also, separate from the main crossings, the vivid tunnel stretching from Numinat to Nubiah, near but separate from the crossings.

And one bright thread, detached and snarled. Floating in darkness. A failed path. She stood in shocked awareness. It was a filament of the path to Alfan Sih. Ruined, dissolved.

Sinking to the floor, she leaned against the wall, probing for another path, surely out there somewhere. Her path to Alfan Sih. Straining her perceptions to the limit, she tried to perceive the tunnel that once had seemed so real. But it was gone.

Drawing up her knees, she crossed her arms on them, resting her forehead with its crushing load of sadness. *All lost therein.*

She wanted to believe in the great, lovely hereafter. The final home after all the doing and striving. Whatever that place was, it was hard to believe it could be as sweet as life. Kassalya believed it was. She had been eager to go. Maybe now Kassalya had her answer. *But for the rest of us,* Yevliesza thought, *we mourn people's loss. Nothing makes it better.*

When she regained some strength of will, she rose and slowly walked back to Numinat.

Chapter Thirty-Four

Standing next to Captain Nikander and his officers, Pyvel peered into the distance toward Castle Rock. He tried to make out the iron cladders, those great, manlike warriors, carrying their operators within, but they were too far away.

Around him, milling soldiers, waiting, talking of anything but the coming battle. One of them, a hulking man with a long scar gouged into one side of his face, wore an impressive war axe strapped to his back. Others carried their long swords on their backs, preferring to use short blades in close fighting, but having a bigger one when needed.

Everyone stirred when a group of riders came out from Castle Rock, their standards flying pennants of white.

"The parley," Nikander said. There were five Volkish, and one of them looked like a woman.

Commander Ilyan rode out to meet them accompanied by Princip Anastyna and her personal guards. The enemy would demand surrender and offer terms. Anastyna, of course, would refuse.

One of the officers pointed at the Volkish party.

"Nashavety," someone muttered. And someone else: "Sorcerer." The sight of her, the former *fajatim* of Raven Fell House, made Pyvel's stomach clench into a cold fist.

NASHAVETY RODE BESIDE MARSHAL KENRICK. SHE KEPT HER HORSE A few paces back so as not to usurp his status as army commander. She noted the approach of the Osta Kiya leaders on horseback. Ilyan, whom she knew from the old days, wearing a blood-red tunic and riding a nasty-looking stallion. Next to him, Anastyna on her own horse. She had managed to find a silver hunting dress with a fancy cloak. The torc looked so wrong on her neck.

The great mesa of the Citadel now loomed on Nashavety's right, the butte with its spire of power. The spire pulled on her, sending hot waves down her left arm and into her burning small finger. She glanced at her hand to reassure herself that her leather glove was not disintegrating. As they rode, they approached the rock of the Citadel more closely. It anchored the broad arena, as it did her heart. Fanning out in a semicircle, Gray Fort lay straight ahead of her, with the First Ones Pillar on her left. Behind, Castle Rock, where the Volkish thousands waited.

This was the day she had waited for ever since she left the city-palace of Osta Kiya on horseback with one servant and a small purse of coin. Holding the reins with her right hand, cradling her left hand, once maimed, now resurgent, in her lap. Soon she would maim the people who had humiliated her.

Kenrick curbed his horse, waiting for the Osta Kiya delegation. Anastyna's troops massed in the distance, their backs to Gray Fort, their spears glinting in the second-quarter-day sun.

Ilyan and Anastyna approached.

"Lord Ilyan," Kenrick said, according him a nod. Another nod to Anastyna. "Princip Anastyna. It is *princip* again, so we heard."

Ilyan bristled. "Always the princip, as you well know, Marshal Kenrick."

"But we also heard that Lady Anastyna hid in a sod hovel in the hills these last months. Am I mistaken?"

Anastyna spoke up. "You are dreadfully mistaken." She turned her gaze to Nashavety. "Led to ruin by the woman who practices dark arts.

Who lost her powers for dishonorable trespass and brought them back by sorcery."

Nashavety stared in bemusement at the woman. Playing the high and righteous leader. Wearing a silver gown to preside over the slaughter of her people. Nashavety remained silent. Time later to list Anastyna's crimes and listen to her squeal.

"Despite our different views of the conflict," Marshal Kenrick interjected, "we have no wish to destroy your army unnecessarily. We have eleven thousand well-armed men. If you surrender, we will let your soldiers live. Most of them can return to their villages and forests rather than die on these flats. We would allow Princip Anastyna to take her household to the city of Tanaya and remain in safety so long as she does not foment unrest. Your army to disperse and Osta Kiya forfeit, as well as the three gates of Numinat."

That, Nashavety thought, was not exactly how it would turn out. She allowed herself a small smile. First the woman who called herself princip would lose the small finger on her left hand. They would begin with that. Then, after a suitable debriefing, the tower door. It would be the fall of a weak, foolish, and ruinous woman who did not deserve to inherit the torc after the great Princip Lisbetha.

"Your answer?" Marshal Kenrick demanded.

"We refuse," Anastyna said. She looked at Nashavety. "Why did you order the death of Lord High Steward Michai? He had served two princips and was no enemy of yours."

Kenrick answered, knowing Nashavety would not. "It pleased Princip Sofiyana to do so. Was he not one of your vast system of spies you used against your citizens?"

Anastyna's expression hardened. The insult had struck home, Nashavety was pleased to note.

At that moment, a flash of sunlight caught her attention from Gray Fort. The air shimmered above the flat top of the butte, and a massive flag appeared in the air. A white banner and, at its center, a green tree, spreading its branches. An impressive display of sky painting from what must be a group of manifesters working together. So that it could be seen by the Volkish army.

A murmur arose from the Volkish troops. Kenrick looked up at the butte, frowning. He knew as well as Nashavety what that banner was. It was the standard of House Wilhoffen. The emblem of Duke Tanfred. But how, Nashavety wondered, had he come to Numinat? How had he passed through the crossings with its hundreds of soldiers all watching for him?

In front of the banner, which appeared to be rippling in the wind, a figure could be seen sitting a horse. The traitor himself, no doubt. He raised his arm into the air, and the Numinat army cheered him.

Anastyna had been watching the display with satisfaction and now turned back to Kenrick. "We will fight you with all that we have," she said, and turned her mare away, Ilyan and her men following.

"And you will die," Kenrick called after her.

Nashavety's chest constricted in cold anger. Part of her wanted to lash out, but she was glad she had used restraint. Because blood needed to run. Numinat had to pass through a crucible of iron and steel. And Anastyna had to be seen to bring it upon her own people.

Nashavety and Kenrick returned to the Volkish troops, who cheered them in a great uproar. They thumped swords on the ground, creating a drumming. The battle would begin.

The standing order for the entire army was that Anastyna would be captured alive.

❦

As Yevliesza rode, Kiya kept pace at her side, never slipping into the next world. Maybe he wanted to protect her, now that her guards were dead.

When she had emerged from the backways a few hours ago, she had found the bodies of her guards. They and their mounts killed by the *strigoi*. The blood birds had attacked them and then entered the backways to find her. A terrible scene. The three men. Their mounts.

Stunned by events, her mind reeling, she rode northward. She thought of Arman, gone because the path had failed. Elivasa, beloved of Rusadka, gone. They all had tried not to think of the path dissolving.

But knowing the danger, Arman and Elivasa had gone anyway. Her throat swelled to think of them.

Sometimes she regretted setting the *strigoi* free. They lived on blood, which wasn't their fault. They were enslaved by Nashavety. When she thought of that, she didn't regret giving them a path home. She tried to stop thinking about whether she had been right or wrong. She had been balancing right from wrong for too long. A wearying exercise.

At midmorning she saw smoke rising in the distance. Soon she came upon people hiding in vales and groves of trees. They emerged to ask if she knew where the Volkish were, whether it was safe to go back to their farms and villages. She had no answers for them. Smoke in the west. The Volkish were not merely stealing food; they were burning as they went. One of the groups invited her to share a meal, but she noted a few men looking appraisingly at Mitri and decided to keep moving. Kiya would deter them, but for the moment he was invisible. She felt him close by, an uncanny knowledge that might be pure imagination, but could also be exactly right.

Her destination was the gate to Nubiah. There she would wait for Valenty, on the chance that he had reached Nubiah's leaders. On the chance that he would come home. In the backways she had seen the destroyed remains of the path to Alfan Sih. But the crossing to Nubiah had lain bright in her mind, in that map of the paths that was a legacy of the ninth power.

Mitri took Yevliesza north, passing homes and barns burned to the ground. Kiya, back now, put his nose into the air, smelling what had died in these places. They detoured around the ruined farms. Yevliesza knew the way to the gate to Nubiah, remembering the align patterns in the land.

As they ascended a grassy hillside, Kiya suddenly lay down, keeping still, his ears forward. Yevliesza curbed Mitri and searched the ridgeline. Trouble ahead, maybe. Dismounting, she tied Mitri's reins to a log to prevent him from wandering into the field.

At the crest of the hill, she saw before her a broad field of grass and erratic boulders.

An enormous dactyl rested there, its scales flashing with a thousand glints of sun. At its side, a rider in leathers staring into the distance, hand on the dactyl's saddle. In the still breeze, the rider's long hair whipped out from edges of a leather helmet.

The rider turned to her as she drew near. "You are a long way from your hearth," the woman said, regarding Yevliesza closely. Her voice was as coarse as the leathers she wore, her face round, one eyebrow pierced by a metal ring, the mark of an army dactyl rider.

"Yes. A long way out. Scouting, like you." Yevliesza noted the rider's sword belt and scabbard for a knife. Knives strapped to both boots.

The dactyl turned to look at her, its great head ponderous with its skull crest. Yellow eyes regarded her with an ancient knowledge. A shiver poured over her skin.

"What service?" the rider asked, wary. Maybe the woman thought she was a spy.

"On business of Lord Warden Kirady." A person of rank who could vouch for her purpose. Yevliesza added, "And Princip Anastyna."

The dactyl continued to gaze at her, but now its scaled hide rippled with some mood. Yevliesza stepped back.

"Kirjanichka is sizing you up," the rider unhelpfully explained. "Most people do not come this close, so she wonders what you have in mind."

So this was Dreiza's Kirjanichka. "Am I too close?"

The rider shrugged. "She is tolerating you."

Yevliesza tried to be encouraged by that. A privilege to be tolerated. And by Kirjanichka, the dactyl Dreiza had given up to join the *satvary*. Being so near a dactyl brought to mind how, when she had first arrived in Numinat, she had ridden a dactyl across the plains of Numinat to Osta Kiya. How the dactyl had died from the lightning strike. Its death, mourned by the whole palace. She had never learned its name, because back when she was a stranger in the realm, back when she thought she could have an undisturbed life, she thought that knowing the poor creature's name would be more painful than if it were anonymous.

The scout looked at the crest of the hill Yevliesza had come down. "Who is with you back there? Kirjanichka knows you have company."

"My horse. There's a wolf back there, too."

A long, appraising gaze. Maybe she shouldn't have mentioned the wolf.

The rider let the wolf comment go. "You will not find the Volkish in these parts. They came through two days ago from Causeway, pillaging as they went." She looked west. "Gone now." Turning back, she said, "Strange that you are still scouting here, when they have already passed."

"I'm looking for other things," Yevliesza said.

"You can keep your secrets," the rider said, unoffended. "Do you have a message for our commander?"

What was there to say? Help may be coming. Was that useful? "Tell him there may be a path for Nubiah to come."

The woman raised a pierced eyebrow. "It must be soon."

"Yes."

The scout pulled on her outsize riding gloves, preparing to leave. A brief smile crossed her face. She nodded a goodbye. "I will tell him, Keeper."

A shrewd guess. Yevliesza was not going to deny it. "Good luck to you."

"And you. Go by the light of the Deep."

Yevliesza backed away until she was a fair distance from Kirjanichka. The rider mounted and secured herself into the saddle with straps. The dactyl heaved itself onto its great, sturdy legs and lumbered away, spreading its wings, its fine scales the color of tarnished silver. Like silverwood leaves, Yevliesza thought, thinking of the magical trees of Alfan Sih.

The dactyl moved swiftly for a dozen steps, then flapped its great wings and lifted from the ground, beating into the sky. It circled overhead, graceful in the air above the field of grass, circling higher and smaller to become a silhouette, black against the sun. The emblem of the Mythos, she thought.

Yevliesza and Mitri went on, at last entering the narrow valley where Valenty and Janov had entered the path. She found the place empty. Letting Mitri graze, she hesitated in front of the gate. She wanted to find out whether the path endured. If she went in a few steps she would clearly see whether or not it did, and her courage almost failed her.

She went in.

Chapter Thirty-Five

The army of Numinat waited, formed up in ranks spread wide on the plain. It was second-quarter day, and some of the men said that the enemy would wait for morning. But Captain Nikander said they would come now. The fight, he said, would begin with arrows. The Volkish had only a few bowman, and with their short bows they could not reach far, unlike the archers from Mensk with their longbows.

Warders stood among the Numinat front ranks, the soldiers that would take the first assault of the dreaded volley guns. In the forth and fifth rank, the archers, who would try to pick off the enemy soldiers with the shields bearing the protruding barrels of the volley guns.

Pyvel hoped the officers knew what the Volkish were really like. They used trickery and ploys. Like they had in the battle of the crossings, pretending they were invading Nubiah. Hiding in the backways. They would not fight honorably in real combat.

Banners flew straight out in a stiff breeze. The red and white of Osta Kiya. The blue and gold of Prince Fadimir, holding the left flank. On the right flank, Lord Kirady's brown and yellow. Many other pennants streamed from standards. He hoped Duke Tanfred's green tree would be shown again atop Gray Fort. That display had shown the

Volkish they could come over to the Numinat side and stand with the duke. No one had yet, though.

A horn sounded nearby, and he saw soldiers milling around someone on horseback. It was Anastyna, riding through the massed troops. He mounted Kasha to get a better view. She wore her white wool cape draping long over her mare's haunches. Some of the men cheered as she passed through and rode out to the front line, Commander Ilyan and Duke Tanfred with her.

She spoke to the men, but he could not hear what she said. Every now and then, a round of cheers. The long shadow of the enemy's monument, Castle Rock, appeared on the plain behind her as the sun rose. The enemy still lay in shadow, but he imagined the Volkish commander was speaking to them at the same time.

Anastyna lifted a sword. She held it high and her voice rose, setting off a roar of approval. He found himself shouting, too: "Numinat!" he hollered. "Numinat!" He wanted to see the enemy beaten back. They were invaders, cowards who hid behind terrible machines. He shouted until he was hoarse.

Two blasts of the horn. *Forward.* The front rank stepped forward carrying small shields. On the other side of the battleground, Volkia advanced. As Numinat's front ranks moved, other units filled in behind to take their places if they fell. He saw the elite soldiers of Osta Kiya in the center, dressed in armor and helmets and, deeper in the ranks, the Mensk archers with their longbows in their hands, quivers on their backs.

The armies marched within a hundred and fifty paces of each other, their flanks stretched out far on each side. The enemy ranks seemed endless. Some of the Volkish troops were still in the shadow of Castle Rock, but the entire Numinat force stood in the morning light, thousands of spear points and helmets flashing in the sun.

Out from the front Volkish rank came a towering iron cladder. The Numinat army quieted, watching it. Somewhere inside that hulking body was a human soldier commanding the iron body with elemental power. Pyvel's heart winced at the sight of the monster. It walked to the middle ground between the two armies and began to pace along it toward the Volkish right flank, its great feet pounding on the hardpan. As the cladder trudged down the enemy line, the enemy soldiers cheered and thumped swords against shields. The cladder turned in a surprisingly fast pivot and strode in the other direction, bringing fresh eruptions of Volkish shouting. By showing itself, it was trying to raise fear in the Numinat troops.

Pivoting once more, it came back to the center. Slowly it brought up its left hand as though offering to shake hands. But its deadly purpose soon became clear. Fire erupted from the fingers. Pyvel heard stuttering, cracking noises. The fingers shot out metal! Around the front lines, the distorted air of warding blurred Pyvel's sight. But men fell, the warding having little or no effect upon iron pellets. The center of the line collapsed as screams tore the air. With the center caved in, other ranks pushed their way forward, filling in.

Raising its other hand, the cladder sprayed fire again. Another stream of iron drove into the ranks as sprays of blood colored the air and men screamed. The barrage continued, each moment of slaughter taking a horrifying toll and filling the ranks with terror. The cladder was killing the army all by itself.

Meanwhile, the Mensk archers rained arrows on the cladder, but they fell as though against stone. The archers turned their aim on fighters of flesh and blood, both at the front and deep into their midst, but the enemy carried shields and lifted them, forming a ceiling to protect themselves. The cladder stomped back to the Volkish ranks, its supply of iron and fire exhausted, but Volkia's first attack had gutted the best soldiers of Osta Kiya.

Now Volkish bowmen darkened the sky with arrows, but these reached only the foremost ranks of Numinat, the ones who had stepped forward to take the place of those felled by the cladder. Against the assault of the archers, Numinat's front ranks raised their shields above their heads, and the clatter of the arrows against the iron-bound fir shields battered the air.

A flurry in front of the enemy front rank, and Pyvel noted several dozen long shields had moved into position.

As the Osta Kiya soldiers held their shields high against the onslaught of arrows, the shields began to hurl pellets at their unprotected lower bodies. Across the empty space between the two armies, the volley guns had a clear path. The pellets swept through the middle of their line and down the flanks.

Some of the Volkish behind the volley shields fell to Numinat arrows, but many of the demonic shields remained upright, still firing. Sickened, Pyvel watched the slaughter continue.

"To me!" Nikander shouted to his unit of horsemen. Pyvel followed him on Kasha, trembling and sometimes rearing amid the noise and the smell of blood. The captain led his unit at a trot in the direction of the enemy's left flank. When the group was in position, they kicked their mounts into a gallop. The faster horses left Pyvel behind, but he could see the men lowering spears as they charged into the Volkish foot soldiers. Pyvel followed, trying to keep Nikander in view. He saw him lean forward, spearing a man through his belly so hard the blade stuck. The captain stepped his horse back to yank the spear free, as around him, his horsemen thrust and swiped against the soldiers in gray. Trained to ignore noise and fight, the war stallions reared, hooves crashing down on the enemy. Using long swords, Volkish soldiers fought back, screaming in rage, parrying the attackers' lances and also striking at the horses.

Pyvel was dazed by the incoherent bellows, the clash of metal, the screams of enraged horses. The attacking horses were magnificent, maneuvering as their riders positioned themselves for strikes. One of them bit at a man's face, leaving a bloody gouge behind.

Pyvel managed to keep his captain in view. He saw Nikander turn and shout something to him, the words lost in the clamor, but he saw that the captain had lost his sword. He kicked Kasha forward, bringing the extra sword and giving it to Nikander.

Near him, a horse fell screaming, falling on his rider. A soldier in gray rushed forward and thrust his sword into the pinned man's neck in a spray of blood. Blades glinted in the sun as the mounted men raised them to strike at soldiers on the ground, some of whom brought warding to deflect the blades. But the Volkish soldiers not yet engaged backed off from the furious charge.

A horn called Nikander's unit back before they drove too far into the enemy's mass. Seeing Nikander turn his horse, Pyvel followed him, spying as he went a man in red and white, limping, holding his stomach. Reaching down, Pyvel pulled him into the saddle behind him. The smell of blood and torn flesh washed over him as they sped back to the Numinat line. Once clear of the battle, Pyvel took Kasha and the wounded soldier to the healers' area. The strength had left his body and spirit. They had struck at the enemy—he had seen men die under the swords of the horse unit—but it was a small victory. Numinat had suffered dreadful losses from the machines.

As he brought his mount into their holding area, he saw the wounded lying on the ground, writhing in pain or lying still, men with limbs missing, healers frantically working. Hundreds of men, the smell of blood and bowels soaking the air. He dismounted and helped the wounded soldier to do so, taking him to a free spot on the healing ground.

Nikander came through and handed his horse's reins to Pyvel, noting his dismay. "It would have been worse if we had not attacked. We charged to confuse the warders who protected the volley guns. So our men could rush in and take some of them out. And they did."

"But another soldier just takes the long shield?" Pyvel asked, not wanting to be consoled.

"No, boy. Only elementalists can employ them. All the rest"—he sneered in the direction of the fight—"have to fight like men."

In the distance, the sounds of the battle came like a dream remembered.

"My helmet," Nikander said. Pyvel noticed the captain's was missing. He handed over the new helmet and laced its cheek pieces under Nikander's chin. Nikander did not pull the helmet cheek pieces around when fighting on horseback, not liking how they obscured his line of sight. But pulling the pieces around now to protect his face meant they were going to fight on foot.

"Sir, no horses?"

"They are no match for volley guns. We must overwhelm them on foot."

Nikander led them back into the fight. Pyvel, carrying an extra sword and spear, followed. They ran to join the aligners who had occupied the align. Off to the side, Pyvel saw an iron cladder, wading through a sea of Numinasi fighters, swinging its arms and widening its path. He hoped by all the Nine that it did not turn in his direction.

More aligners, wearing white streamers on their upper arms, threaded their way through the battle toward the line of power. It would augment their strength, quickness, and accuracy. Pyvel and his unit found the align, made obvious by the line of soldiers with white streamers, some of whom were *harjat*.

Other Numinasi soldiers saw the align wall forming up and began to form a line three ranks deep to fight off any enemy soldiers that attempted to attack the aligners' rear. Pyvel stood far back, but within shouting distance, should Nikander need him.

He saw Rusadka in the wall. As she fought, she held her ground, swinging and thrusting her sword with terrible effect, but always returning to the power spot. Nikander's men stood behind, laying into Volkish who tried to penetrate from in back. Some Volkish, seeing the pile of bodies in front of Rusadka, and judging her a warrior to be dealt with, rushed at her, bellowing. They quickly fell to her wicked sword strikes and those of her fellow *harjat*, who fought like demons. As dusk came on, more *harjat*, those with aligns, came in to replace fallen aligners, and the furious line held, finally giving the Volkish pause as they saw the carnage in front of the wall.

Light began to fade from the sky and still the fight raged. Although the Volkish had slain far more than had their enemy, many of the Volkish were shying away from the align wall, turning their swords toward one or other of the flanks. They got no help from the volley guns, which could not operate amid chaotic fighting. A horn sounded, a Volkish horn, and the enemy at last retreated.

As night fell, the armies separated, leaving a ghastly litter of dead and wounded behind. Volkia had created a terrible slaughter, Pyvel thought. Now they were content with their day's success. Confident they could finish the work tomorrow.

Pyvel stood beside Nikander, stunned by the dead and even more so by the groaning and crying wounded. They left the field, and Pyvel saw to the mounts.

The armies having retreated by mutual consent, healers from both sides picked their way onto the battlefield.

Everywhere Pyvel saw beaten men. Men who knew that tomorrow would bring more of the same. And that the enemy still had fresh troops, whereas Numinat had used all they had. Men feared they would face more volley guns the next day. And iron cladders.

Pyvel lay awake that night, his mind alight with battle. He watched the moon rise over the Citadel, that strange outcropping with the rocky isthmus leading from the butte to a tall spire.

The moon cast the spire's shadow unto the plain like a black finger pointing at him. He wondered how he would make it through the next day if he stayed awake all night. He wondered if they would all die tomorrow. If his horse would be speared in the fight and if he would have to kill him. Then, after that awful duty, how he would die.

Before the finger reached him, he slept.

In the predawn he woke at a great screaming noise. An attack! He staggered to his feet and frantically looked around, but no one was running or buckling on a sword belt. A shout went up. Nearby, the big soldier with the scarred face was cheering.

Pyvel figured he had earned the right to talk to even a soldier of such power. "Sir, what is happening?"

The man looked down at him from what seemed a cladder's height. "Boy, a thousand of 'em came to the duke's standard. Came in the night, threw their weapons on the ground."

"Volkish?" Pyvel witlessly asked.

"Aye, Volkish."

A miracle. A thousand men! Pyvel felt his heart lift in his ribcage. "Will they fight on our side, then?"

Scar-Face snorted.

"But if they came over."

Shaking his head, he walked off saying, "We would not trust the turds."

Pyvel saw Duke Tanfred on his horse, parading his standard back and forth in front of Gray Fort, giving Volkia an eyeful of what was going to bring them down: Duke Tanfred, the new ruler of Volkia. Men were beating swords on their shields. *Thump, thump, thump.* "Numinat!" *Thump, thump, thump.* "Numinat!" Pyvel was shouting with them, all fear and dread forgotten.

Nikander beckoned him to come to the officers' campfire for a hot breakfast. Pyvel did not dare sit, but stood eating a roasted potato at Nikander's side. The captain returned the skeptical look of his officers with a beady stare. "Pyvel saved one of our wounded from the field and joined in two assaults. He was at the fight of the align. By the eight hells, he will soon be my next lieutenant." That put them right. Pyvel realized what Nikander said about the fight was true. He had been at the fight of the aligns!

After the potato, Pyvel made his way through the camp, past soldiers stroking whetstones along blades and eating their meals of stale bread. He saddled Hunter and Kasha and tied the extra weapons securely. Then he crossed over to the healers' ground, looking for Rusadka. She was not there, but other *harjat* were, some lying silently. The sight of such warriors lying dead snatched away the joy of the campfire and Nikander's praise. He quickly left.

Chapter Thirty-Six

Tirhan and his escort rode through the sodden woods as the sun struggled into a sky laden with a heavy fog. Their cloaks were waterlogged and clung heavily to them. But they were rested after the difficult and rain-soaked ride the day before, having found shelter in a sheep herder's stone hut and storage crofts. Morwen rode beside him. Close behind, Demyr, his second-in-command, looking bearlike in his drenched cape. A man of great size, impressive in a fight.

Go to the silverwood grove at Talfyn Sid. Hurry, Lord King. The summons had come to him in a dream, and doubts assailed him about bringing Morwen and his men on what might be a hard, pointless ride. But he had learned to follow his instincts and visions and even his dreams.

In the woods his party rode along a broad path rutted by wagon wheels, the horses stepping carefully through the uneven, muddy ground. If any Volkish unit on horseback had come through here, evidence of their passage had been dissolved by the rain. He and his partisans carried bows and swords, all except Morwen, who wore her vest of knives.

Osric and Cynod had ridden ahead to scout, and now Tirhan saw them threading toward him through the woods. As Tirhan reined Nightwing to a stop, Osric came onto the path next to him.

"In the valley ahead, Lord King," Osric said in excitement. "A vast horde of riders, ours."

"Ours?"

"The clans, lord. At least nine hundred by Cynod's count."

Tirhan exchanged glances with Demyr and Morwen. A gathering? Why did they assemble, and why was he not informed?

Demyr, wary of clan lord Gryffyd's loyalty, wanted to discover their purpose before Tirhan exposed himself. He rode off with the scouts, while Tirhan held back in the cover of the woods.

"Talfyn Sid lies ahead," Morwen said. At his look, she went on. "In the heavy fog, we must have come farther than we realized."

Tirhan's curiosity grew. Nightwing tossed his head, and he patted the muscled neck, settling him. Nine hundred men. They would be gathered for only one purpose. A battle. If a Volkish force was approaching, then Gryffyd would have his wish for a decisive fight.

When Demyr and the scouts returned, Tirhan's men moved forward to hear the report.

"Lord King," Demyr said, "the clan lords say they were commanded to come to Talfyn Sid. Lord Inian and Lord Gryffyd both say that a voice spoke to them in a dream."

"The clan lords all have dreamt this thing?" Tirhan asked.

Demyr flattened his mouth, not liking something that sounded so unreliable as dreams. "So Lord Inian said, lord."

"Then we are close to the shrine?"

"Aye, and the silverwood grove lies just beyond the low eastern hill."

Tirhan and his party emerged from the trees, coming in view of a wide water meadow. Tirhan curbed his mount at the sight of the gathered army. "This is the battle for Numinat," he told Morwen. He did not know why the spirit called them to this place, but he felt certain it was to attack the forces invading Numinat. But since the nearest gate was Lliatern, why had they not been asked to go there?

Demyr was thinking the same thing. "Lliatern is a far ride."

As they rode into the meadow, Gryffyd met them. "We have been waiting, Lord King. It is well to see you."

Morwen bristled at the curt welcome, but Tirhan was hardened to the man's arrogance.

"I will go to the grove, Lord Gryffyd," Tirhan said.

"We have already sent men ahead, Lord King."

Ignoring this, Tirhan turned to three of his men and sent them to tell the clan lords to come to his side. Together they would go to the grove.

While he waited, a man on foot approached him, carrying a staff. A man of size with a rough-hewn face. It was an elder of the temple at Talfyn Sid, Lodwyn, a man who had helped in the raid on Glenir Manor to free the queen and his sisters.

"Lord King," the elder said, grinning broadly.

"Lodwyn," Tirhan said with pleasure. "It seems we have been summoned."

The elder looked around himself. "Indeed, Lord King. We of the temple are greatly amazed. It was quiet in our world before." He shrugged. "Now the wildlife has fled."

Tirhan smiled. "Perhaps they are hiding in the fog. Come with us, grandfather. We will go to the silverwood grove and discover what we are meant to do."

The clan lords and four of Tirhan's men, including Demyr and Osric, skirted the low hill commanding one end of the meadow, Morwen accompanying them. The fog thickened, moving around them in swirls and causing the party to move slowly, picking their way through a landscape of mud and standing water.

"If we go to the fight," Tirhan told Morwen, "you must stay behind." Her face hardened. "The battle will be no place for anyone without a sword."

"I could wear a sword," she said.

"Morwen." He did not want to command her. "Do this for me."

"I will not stay behind. But I will ride in back if I must."

"With men to guard you."

"Yes, five."

He could not deny her. "Ten," he said.

At the edge of the water meadow, the land rose into forest again. The sound of water cascading over stone. Lodwyn, riding behind Osric, said, "The grove is just past the creek, Lord King."

As Tirhan stepped his horse through the shallow brook, he spied a silverwood tree. As he drew closer, he saw its branches clotted with fog, leaves catching a silvered light. In a few more steps, the grove lay before them. He dismounted, giving Nightwing's reins to Osric.

Lord Inian joined him. "You do not suspect an ambush, Lord King?" he asked, watchful.

"No. But we will see a messenger." Tirhan nodded as Gryffyd came to join them. "Since our summons arrived in dreams, we will see a being of that world."

"The otherworld, you mean," Gryffyd said. "It will be one of the spirits who came to you before?"

"So I believe. But I do not know." The clan lords had heard of his visitations, then. Tirhan detected Gryffyd's tone of disbelief, but he did not care. "Watch and listen."

The stamping of horses and the clinking of bridles stirred in the background. The rustle of wind brushing past the silverwood branches. Morwen stood by his side, her cloak thrown back over a shoulder to leave her arm free to use her knives.

A few paces away, a bruise in the fog. Inian pointed. "There." A dark shape formed. Behind him, Tirhan heard swords sliding from scabbards.

He raised his hand, keeping the clan lords in their places.

The shape drew closer, revealing itself as Gethin. He was dressed in a simple jerkin, boots, and trousers, unarmed. Though Tirhan had been in a spirit's presence more than a few times, his breath went shallow.

The shade stopped ten paces away. "So you have come. And bring brave men, my son?"

Tirhan tried to answer, but he could not move his lips. *Yes, grandfather. These are the lords of the clans of Alfan Sih. Ready for a fight.*

Behind him, he heard Gryffyd say, "By the Nine, a spirit?"

Honored Gethin, Tirhan said inwardly. *Let my people hear your voice. Let me speak.*

"Those who have ears to hear," the spirit said, "shall hear. Not all."

"His name," Tirhan said, attempting to speak to his men, and, he thought, succeeding. "His name is Gethin. I know this messenger. Once he was a man of renown. We must listen well."

Gethin's form wavered for a moment. He spoke again. "The dark kingdom is at battle with Numinat. You must go quickly, Lord King. Lead your army, and do not quail."

"We are ready, grandfather," Tirhan said, his voice echoing strangely in his ears. "Lliatern Gate?"

"Listen, my son. You were meant to travel a far path, one that probed the great dark. But that has vanished forever. Now you have a harder path. Have you courage?"

"We do. We are ready."

Gethin nodded. "That is well. Because I will lead you down another path, one that leads deep into the silverwoods. Where the fallen of Alfan Sih find their welcome."

Deep into the silverwoods. The groves harbored the portals to the next world. Those openings were the reason Tirhan had been told to guard them against the Volkish.

Gethin continued. "We do not need the crossings, Lord King, if your army has the mettle. In death there are no boundaries. To enter Numinat, you can pass through the otherworld."

Hearing this, the men behind him stirred. Gryffyd swore under his breath.

Demyr said, "My lord, he means us to die."

"Demyr, no. We must have faith."

"To go into the realm of death is to die, lord."

As the clan lords muttered amongst themselves, Tirhan saw Osric's expression of fear.

The spirit spread his arms. "I hold the door open. Who will come to save the Mythos from darkness?"

So this, Tirhan thought, was the faith that Gethin had urged on him when he visited him in the barn at Ailfyd. Faith that one could pass through the realm of the dead and yet live.

Behind him, Tirhan heard Morwen say, "I will go." And then louder, to reach the clan lords, "I am ready."

Tirhan reached for her hand and found that he could. Gethin had faded to a blur in the fog, but did not disappear. Tirhan turned to look at the assembled men. "As your king, I swear that this messenger sends us into honorable battle. It is the only way. Who will come?"

Silence met this pronouncement.

Behind him, he heard Gethin's distant voice saying, "It must be now."

Lord Gryffyd came to stand with Tirhan and Morwen. "I will go with you, Lord King. I and all my men." His voice carried into the woods. "Bring my horse," he told one of the men.

The clan lord of Angewyst said, "Angewyst will go." Followed by silence.

Tirhan spoke up. "For ten months we have suffered the Volkish boot on our necks." His voice strengthened. "They took our king's life, stole our homes, desecrated the silverwoods! We have watched as they took Norslad, declared war on Numinat, and threw their yoke over the crossings. Our lands groan under their crimes, under their machines. The very Mythos cries out for release! The First Ones offer us this chance to cut them down in battle. Who can refuse? This is the great day of our people. Today is the day we fight for our land, our families, our clans. Today is the day, the great day of our righteous cause. Today we fight!"

A clan chief shouted, "Llanaden will fight!"

"Angewyst!" came the cry. "Mid Daihinn!"

One by one, the clans joined in. Cries of "Alfan Sih!" joined the shouts. Alfan Sih was ready to go. To the realm of the dead and the battle beyond.

Tirhan motioned Demyr to his side. "Bring our men forward. We will go first." He pinned Demyr with a questioning look.

"I am at your side, Lord King."

"Go into the meadows and bring our fighters. Go quickly."

Turning around, Tirhan noted Gethin's indistinct form still waiting. Behind him, a vast shadow dimpled with specks of light. The portal, looming in all its dread and mystery.

Tirhan went to Osric and put a hand on his shoulder. "We will be in the battle soon. Let us crush the Volkish at last."

Osric nodded, his face determined. He handed Nightwing's reins to him. Tirhan mounted.

Morwen did as well. "I must come with you," she said.

"But when we engage the enemy, hold back," Tirhan said. "Find safety and wait for me." She nodded her understanding.

Demyr led Tirhan's company out of the meadows. Behind them, the whole force of the clans. They rode forward, and Tirhan turned to lead them into the darkling portal.

They entered the dark space in the silverwood grove. Once inside, Gethin's form was distinct. Tirhan rode in front on a great black stallion.

"Now we ride hard and fast, Lord King!"

The world fell away, dissolving in a heartbeat. In the next instant, the grove was filled with silver light. They thundered through. The sounds of battle came distantly to their ears.

Chapter Thirty-Seven

With the potato sitting in his stomach like a rock, Pyvel stood back in the ranks with his unit now on foot and waiting for the call to move out. The morning sun had risen over Castle Rock, dissolving the shadows on the battleground, lighting up the spire of the Citadel on their left flank, some four hundred paces away. It looked like the blade of a giant come to join in the fight.

Ilyan had spoken to the massed troops shortly before dawn. It was a good speech, reminding them that a thousand Volkish had laid down their weapons. Men cheered and the mood was more confident. Anastyna rode with him, adding her encouragement and crying, "For Numinat! For Numinat!" Cheers broke out and the chant of "Numinat!" spread through the army.

When Ilyan and Anastyna left for their perch on the ledge partway up Gray Fort, a horn sounded and the ranks began to move forward. There were fewer white and red banners of Osta Kiya now, but Fadimir's blue and gold flowed like a river. Sprinkled throughout, the yellow and black of the *harjat*. Any man that found himself standing next to a *harjat* in the fight was lucky, and the soldiers knew it. But as they waited for the enemy, the ranks grew quiet.

Soon they could hear the tread of thousands of feet approaching.

A coldness pressed on Pyvel's chest, producing an almost-paralyzing fear as the advance of the front lines gave room for his rank to move forward. He tried to swallow, failing. Many of the men around him had axes and hoes for weapons. No armor and some of them not even leather, but they stomped forward, following the rank ahead. Nikander stood some distance to his left, carrying a shield and his sword. On the captain's far side, Scar-Face, a hand-span taller and carrying his axe. They advanced.

A distant horn sounded and the enemy charged, bellowing insults in their strange language. Unlike the Numinasi, many of the Volkish wore mail over their grayish-green uniforms, making them look iron-strong.

As though in reply, Numinat's horn sounded again, and at that the ranks surged forward with cries of "Numinat! Numinat!"

The two armies met, screams erupting and the crashing of swords on shields. For a while, it was only the front ranks, but soon the biggest Volkish fighters were breaking into their midst, and men threw themselves at each other with clangs of blades and the crack of sword against shield. In front of Pyvel, a Volkish blow split a soldier's shield in two. The attacker stepped forward as the man stumbled and drew his blade across his neck. He instantly pivoted to take on the next Numinasi soldier.

Pyvel watched as Nikander lunged with his sword, gutting a man. Stepping back, the captain hacked down a man who had staggered. A Volkish fighter came at Nikander from behind, but Scar-Face's axe crashed into the man's shield, pushing it down as his next blow took off the side of the soldier's head. The clamor of the fight was so loud, Pyvel's ears went muffled, making the sound seem farther away. But all around him, men were fighting, dying, screaming from terrible wounds. A riderless horse ran wildly through the battleground, stirrups flapping.

"Back!" an officer shouted. "And back again!" Numinat fighters stepped back to force the enemy to walk through the fallen bodies, hindering their advance. But some of the Volkish had penetrated deeply, and now they came from each side. Volkish soldiers fell, but there were always three to replace him. Then, worse, Pyvel saw a cladder some fifty paces away. It crashed through the men in its path, swinging great fists. The enemy crowded behind it, staying clear of its massive thrusts and letting it open a path.

The Numinasi tried to claim the align as they had the day before, Rusadka and Urik in the lead. They reached their goal, but other aligners with their white streamers had not yet come, and the enemy, seeing two strong fighters fighting with deadly effect, converged on them. Rusadka was driven back by the assault, but swung her sword viciously, connecting. One of her attackers was tall and built like a bull. He deflected her blows with his shield and, moving in, slammed the edge of his sword against her head. Numinasi were surging to protect the align wall. They beat the wedge of Volkish back, but he saw with dismay that Rusadka had fallen.

When Pyvel turned in the other direction, he saw Nikander grappling with a fighter, their blades useless as they tried to drive elbows or pommels of swords into each other's faces. Pyvel ran toward them, thinking to come at the Volkish soldier from behind with the extra sword he carried, but he saw the man spin around, swinging his sword arm and drawing his blade across Nikander's shoulder. Nikander screamed and dropped his sword. In a swift motion, his assailant sliced the blade down on the back of his neck in a fan of blood.

The Volkish soldier spied him and advanced. Pyvel stopped, frozen.

Around him, the fight raged, but all he saw was a man in short mail, helmet-less, his face and shaven head flecked with blood, coming toward him with a sword. Two-handed, Pyvel raised the sword he carried.

The man grinned. Lightning fast, he slashed his sword against Pyvel's, knocking it out of his hands. In a moment of terror, a moment that seemed to stop the sun in the sky and Pyvel's heart in his chest, the man drew back his blade and stepped in to strike. Nowhere to run, Pyvel was facing the end.

A shadow in his peripheral vision. Scar-Face loomed. He slammed his axe into the man's head, taking off the back of it. The Volkish soldier's sword—the strike meant for Pyvel—went wide as the man fell, but not before it sliced across Pyvel's arm. A searing pain. Pyvel fell backward, slamming his head on the hard ground. He lay helpless, his arm raging with pain.

The sky darkened. In the midst of the battlefield, a black cloud loomed. The day was bright, but a darkness had opened in their midst like an impossible wall. Men looked up, startled. The tall form shimmered darkly as though reflecting the sun from a thousand broken mirrors. Some combatants continued to fight, but others watched in consternation as, from inside the dark and sparkling hole, men charged on horses. It was impossible, but on they came, plowing into the battlefield, hundreds of swords raised, yelling, "Alfan Sih, Alfan Sih!"

Alfan Sih had come! The horsemen swept into the field, slashing swords down on soldiers in gray. Nearby, among their own troops, men took up the cry of "Alfan Sih!" The cry reverberated on the battlefield.

Pyvel had forgotten his pain for a few moments, but now it claimed him again. He was afraid to look. Had his arm been severed? There was no end to horror. Nikander was dead; everywhere, men were dying.

Somehow, Scar-Face was kneeling next to him. He wrapped something around Pyvel's lower arm. The soldier's face, grim but confident. Mercy in the midst of battle. Pyvel tried to repay him by remaining bravely silent, but groans came up his throat.

Meanwhile, a new movement on the battlefield. The enemy was falling back in a mass exodus. The Alfans pursued the retreating soldiers, and the Numinasi followed in their wake.

Scar-Face left. The sound of the fight receded. Pyvel was lying on the ground, staring at the sky. A few clouds rode on the winds. Birds circled, waiting for their meals. Pain swept in waves through his body. The sun mounted higher in the sky. He began to shake.

A healer was moving him. He felt himself being pulled along the ground on a length of cloth. He cried out as he hit bumps and rocks.

At the healing ground, he lay for some time, trying not to moan. Others around him had terrible wounds, and he would not clamor for attention. Still, a man approached him and tended to his wound, saying, "This will heal. Be comforted." After bandaging him properly, he laid his hands on Pyvel's arm. On his chest. On his brow.

After a time, a woman came with a cup of water. "Have we won?" he asked her.

"The fight goes on. There are many Volkish." She looked in the direction of Castle Rock. "Still many. But now we have a chance."

A chance. Hope spread through him, a current of sweet hope that calmed his mind and his pain.

The sun was at its zenith. Pyvel managed to get up and walk through the ranks of the wounded. He made his way to the path leading to the outcropping on Gray Fort. He desperately wanted to know what was happening. At the ledge, he saw Ilyan and his officers. Anastyna. Seeing Pyvel moving up the path, one of the soldiers barred his way, but the princip said he should be allowed. She brought him to a corner of the ledge.

"The wound, is it bad?" she asked.

"Nothing much, the healer said. My lady."

"You may stay if you are silent."

He looked across the plain, but all he could see was a confused mass of roiling armies, some of whom were on horseback. Alfans. Somehow, Alfan Sih had come. The sparkling dark cloud had vanished. He saw the shape of a cladder in the distance, but Numinat was still in the fight.

Officers came and went, conferring with Ilyan. Anastyna brought Pyvel a cup of ale. It greatly helped.

When the sun threw a shadow across the ledge, Pyvel saw the officers pointing at something. Anastyna, who had been resting against the back of the ledge, stood and came forward to see.

Someone said, "Nubiah!"

the battle raged beside them, and she furiously kicked it to race faster to the rock formation. The spire. Her spire, always calling her. Now, relentlessly.

On the battlefield, the Volkish fought on two fronts: Numinat to the west, Nubiah to the east. Somehow, Nubiah had forced its way through the crossings, though hundreds of armed soldiers, past battle wagons aimed at the gates. How many of Nubiah's warriors had survived this gauntlet? Enough. Enough to be subduing her army in the field.

From the top of Gray Fort, the white and green flag of Duke Tanfred, urging the Volkish to defect. She saw waves of soldiers in gray-green uniforms streaming toward the great traitor. Those men would pay dearly for their betrayal. But later, time for all things later. For now, only the Citadel and its spire.

Reaching the foot of the monument, she looked up at the hulking formation with its butte, isthmus, and spire. She left her horse behind and began the climb up the butte on the zigzagging path.

Chapter Thirty-Eight

The warriors of Nubiah charged into the fray. Valenty curbed his horse next to Yevliesza's. "Circle wide and go to Gray Fort!" He pointed to a large butte in the distance.

She had been riding with Valenty from the eastern portal with the Nubiah thousands, and it was time for them to separate. "I will!" she shouted over the clamor of the fight.

Valenty's horse wanted to race with the others, but he reined it in and reached toward Yevliesza. They touched. For a brief moment he gripped her hand, their eyes locking. No words. They had already said everything when they had met at the portal. Seeing him emerge, relief had filled her chest like cleansing waters. The passage had held. He had survived. Janov had survived. And Nubiah had brought numbers to defeat Volkia.

As Valenty kicked his horse into a gallop, he slid his sword from its scabbard and raced off to join the charge.

Yevliesza felt Mitri's flanks rippling, impatient for a good run. In the distance she saw the formation that Valenty had identified as Gray Fort, anchoring the Numinasi side of the battle. Positioned on the Volkish right flank, she had a clear path toward it. She urged Mitri into a thunderous run.

⚜

RUSADKA SAT CROSS-LEGGED ON THE HEALING GROUND, EARS RINGING, spikes of pain leaving her breathless. Around her, healers bound wounds, dug arrows from muscle and bone, and comforted those in pain, those dying. Rusadka had taken a hard blow to the head, but her wits were clearing. She tried to get to her feet and staggered. Not good, but not terrible.

She dearly wanted to be part of the victory. Nubiah had come. Alfan Sih had come. In the thick of it, she had seen Tirhan, leader of the Alfan, fighting with lethal effect.

As she tried to walk off her unsteadiness, she saw a few people on the command ledge of the monument: Ilyan and Anastyna watching and, she hoped, seeing the battle turn. Looking to the north, she saw the largest of the formations, the butte with the spire and a ridge connecting the two pieces. Beyond it, barely a smudge on the horizon, the Numin Mountains.

On the neighboring monument, a movement drew her attention. Strangely, someone was moving up the side. She squinted. It looked like . . . it *was* . . . someone in a dress. There were only two women who could possibly be wearing a long gown on this plain. One was Anastyna, who stood on the command ledge. The other was Nashavety.

Her mind cleared. She rushed to the horse paddock, weaving only a little, and took a mount that was still saddled and looked fast. Climbing into the saddle, she leaned forward and dug her heels into the mare's sides, spurring it into a gallop.

Nashavety thought she could slip away from the fight. That was not going to happen.

⚜

YEVLIESZA LENGTHENED THE REINS, GIVING MITRI HIS HEAD, AND THEY raced toward Gray Fort. At her side, the battle spread so large she couldn't see the other side of it. She and Mitri were in complete synchrony, rushing as one toward the Numinasi encampment.

In the distance, she saw a lone rider galloping away from the butte. They appeared to be heading toward the monument with the spire. Someone with hair pulled back in a knot. Sword on the back.

Rusadka.

Curious, she turned Mitri to intercept her.

⚜

NASHAVETY REMEMBERED THE PATH TO THE TOP OF THE BUTTE. It hugged the side of the formation, a mostly continuous rock ledge. There was a section requiring a jump over a gap.

As she climbed, fury gathered within her at Reinhart's inept command of the Volkish army; at the sudden appearance of Alfan Sih; at Duke Tanfred and the hellish army of Nubiah. Anger made her strong, strong so that she could accept into herself the coiling blackness living at the base of the spire. A blackness full of infinite loathing and hunger. As it infused her, it would flow into her hand, augmenting her already-keen affinity for elements.

It was an energy that had arisen on the Earth and had flowed into Numinat when the First Ones opened the way. Not a power for the weak. A power for her. She believed it had been waiting for her. And now she had come.

Once she was infused with that great power, she would turn her elemental gift to opening up a cavity in the very ground under the army of Osta Kiya. They would fall into the gap, and she would bury them. Bury them if she had to demolish Gray Fort to do it. Then her soldiers would dominate the field and capture those enemies still standing, forcing them to their knees. They would be her servants.

She scrambled upward, along the path, her eyes on the spire.

Panting hard at the exertion, she kept her anger stoked. If she weakened, the flow from the black well would consume her. Hate would be her armor. The spire of adamantine rock had kept the malevolence buried for a thousand years. The First Ones had banished it there, choosing the spire because it was like a stake in the heart of the land that could pin the blackness down.

Time to rise up.

RUSADKA LEFT BEHIND HER SWORD IN ITS SWORD BELT AND, ARMED only with a knife in a scabbard, started the climb. The path up the butte was narrow, barely wide enough for her to pass.

Why was Nashavety climbing the butte? Perhaps looking for a hiding place. But then, why leave her mount at the base, showing that someone had come there? As Rusadka made her way up, she came into view of Nashavety on the path above her, almost at the summit. She hastened her pace, steadying herself with a hand against the rock face, warm in the afternoon sun. A gap opened up before her where the ledge in the side of the butte had fallen away. She jumped the gap. Grasping the wall on the other side, she stared down the sheer side, dizziness flickering.

YEVLIESZA LOST SIGHT OF RUSADKA. HER FRIEND HAD RIDDEN INTO the shadow of one of the formations, a large butte with a monolith protruding at the end of a narrow spine of rock.

Riding closer, she saw two horses at the foot of the butte. Looking up, she saw Rusadka making her way up the side. She hesitated to call out, not wanting to distract her on the ledge. Then she saw another shape moving along the path. Black hair whipping in the breeze, a long dress. Oh God, it was Nashavety.

The malwitch was alone. Desperation must have driven her to climb this rock, but if she hoped to escape, she would find both Yevliesza and Rusadka standing in her way.

STILL CLIMBING, RUSADKA SAW THAT NASHAVETY WAS STARTING TO cross the narrow land bridge that linked the butte to the pinnacle at the formation's edge. For the first time she considered whether Nashavety knew of some advantage that lay there. Some advantage that made her risk crossing that bridge. On the narrow ridge her fighting skills would be curtailed. And with the steep, almost vertical sides, her balance could falter. This was going to be harder than she had expected.

Once at the top of the butte, Rusadka approached the span of narrow rock with as much silence as she could muster. She drew out her knife. Nashavety had not yet seen her. The woman walked with slow, sure steps, her skirts flapping in the wind as though trying to take flight. Silence was Rusadka's ally. If she made a noise, Nashavety would see her and turn her creature power at her.

Within five paces of the woman, loose gravel beneath Rusadka's feet clattered down the sheer sides. Nashavety turned. In a slicing motion, she brought up her hand, and Rusadka dove for her, knocking her flat on the path. Rusadka brought her knee onto Nashavety's chest as she thrashed under her. She was no match for Rusadka. The sorceress's head was not resting on the narrow path, but jutted over the long drop to the plain. Her ghastly thin, shocked face. Her brutal eyes, flashing with lavender, flashing with creature power.

In moments Rusadka's arms grew tired, and her sight blurred, her strength draining under the onslaught of creature power. Nashavety struggled to wrench away, and Rusadka knew she must act before she was helpless. As she grabbed Nashavety's arm to stop it from beating on her face, her mind went dreamlike. But: Nashavety's left hand. She had to smash it. Pinning it with one hand, she wondered what had happened to her knife. She had nothing but her own fists. Raising her other arm, with all her strength she slammed her fist into Nashavety's hand. A piercing scream. Another blow to the hand. Pounding, pounding. Then the demon twisted underneath her with such force that Rusadka fell off her. Looking down, she saw the ground far below. One must be careful not to fall.

The woman pushed her. She slipped down, down. She plummeted. Down.

Almost to the top of the butte, Yevliesza rounded a jutting edge of the rock wall and saw someone crossing the land bridge. Nashavety, hunched and lurching, looking like she might topple at any moment. Where was Rusadka?

By the time Yevliesza made it to the ridge, Nashavety had made it across and stood next to the enormous spire. She stood with arms outstretched as though praying. Whatever she was doing, it was not an attempt to hide. Something was going to happen. Something was up here, and it was going to be ugly.

Yevliesza walked onto the isthmus. Looking neither right nor left, she walked along it, her skin prickling with a deep-seated fear. In the middle of the causeway she saw a knife. Unbloodied. Nashavety's. Or Rusadka's?

The path ended in a small extrusion of flat rock. Nashavety should be there, but she had disappeared. Yevliesza looked wildly around her, fearful that the woman could be near, even though on that small platform there was nowhere to hide. Forcing herself to approach the spire, she saw steps winding up. Nashavety could have gone only in that direction. But why?

Looking back at the ridge, she desperately hoped to see Rusadka joining her. But it was empty. The butte on the other side, empty. On the plain below, the armies still fought, the sound of the battle faint in her ears.

She looked at the stairs cut into the pillar of rock. She could wait for Nashavety to come down. The woman would *have* to come down. But she would have accomplished her purpose, whatever it was. She could not allow that. Sometime, someplace, Nashavety had to be stopped. After all that had transpired since Yevliesza had first come to the Mythos; after her fateful ride on the dactyl, her detention at Raven Fell, Nashavety's repeated attempts to kill her and control the realm of Numinat; after all this, she had to stop her.

She looked up the side of the pillar. Who had cut steps? What in the name of the Mythos was at the top?

Yevliesza wanted her knife in her hand when she reached the top, but, in order to climb, she had to keep it sheathed. Removing her cloak to keep it from hampering her climb, she edged out from the small rock platform and hugged the gently rounded sides of the spire. She placed a foot on the first stair. Clinging to the vertical rock, she took another step up. Below her, the vast plain. She climbed. Wind yanked at her hair. The pillar, hot against her arms. Why hot?

She dared not look down. Her heart beat like a trapped bird in her chest. *Mythos help me. Mythos help me,* she silently repeated to keep from thinking, to keep from falling. Up, up, securing each step, arms spread out on the hot, hot stone.

As she came to the top, she swept her gaze over the summit. Four paces wide. A woman in a black gown facing the plains. To pull herself over the edge onto the flat space, she had to be so very quiet.

Nashavety was chanting. It would help to cover Yevliesza's lurch onto the summit.

☙✻❧

TEARS STREAMED DOWN NASHAVETY'S FACE. HER ARMY WAS DYING. Her heart was dying. The dark well had tried to reach her, it had surged for a time, but her left hand, broken. Mutilated. The bones crushed. Blood dripping from her hand, like the blood of her army falling into the sands. Through her feet, she felt the boiling dark power. It had been coiling at her feet, but it had been unable to rise into her hand.

At a sound, she turned. Yevliesza stood there. Of course, Yevliesza. It was not enough to have killed the black *harjat* demon on the ridge, the woman who maimed her. It had to be Yevliesza at the last.

"You have lost," the girl said. "It's all at an end. All of it."

As Yevliesza looked at Nashavety, she did not see the queen of the Volkish, the powerful woman who had created so much evil. She saw a shrunken old woman, her hair hanging in filth around her hatchet-thin face. Sorrow leaking out of her eyes. "It's all at an end now," Yevliesza repeated.

She saw Nashavety glance down as though she longed to fall.

It was time, past time, for her to fall.

"Jump," she urged her. "Jump, Nashavety. Jump."

The woman's hair lifted in a gust of wind, as though she were surprised at the order. "Yes," came Nashavety's ragged voice. "It is time." Her eyes narrowed. "But you will come with me."

She lunged, slamming Yevliesza onto the stone ledge with a hard crack of her tailbone. Lying under Nashavety, Yevliesza wildly pummeled her face and shoved at Nashavety's shoulders. She sensed Nashavety weakening and, with a last shove at the woman, scrambled to her knees. Nashavety was trying to rise to her feet. With all her strength Yevliesza pushed at her, pushed again, until Nashavety suddenly rolled over the side of the spire. As she tipped, she grabbed Yevliesza's wrist. Her hand, gripping like iron. Her hand, a claw around Yevliesza's wrist. Dangling.

The weight dragged Yevliesza closer to the edge. Another jerk of her body. She lay on the very edge of the rock. Nashavety was hanging on, somehow clinging to what little purchase her feet might be finding on the side of the spire.

Yevliesza's shoulder slid over the edge. The gravel beneath her, moving, sliding her toward the long fall.

Something latched on to her other arm. A strong hand clutched her mightily.

Rusadka. God, Rusadka.

But she would fall as well. "Let go!" Yevliesza pleaded with her. "Let me go!"

"No," came Rusadka's voice. Yevliesza saw Rusadka's boot heels dug into the ground, holding, holding. But then one boot slid an inch toward the edge. "Let the hellish bitch go," Rusadka spat. "Shake her free."

Yevliesza tried to move her trapped arm, but it was pressed hard against the stone. "I can't move!"

"By the Nine," Rusadka growled, "try harder!"

Yevliesza summoned everything she had, willing her arm to thrash its way free. Nothing. She was pinned in place, Rusadka in back of her, trying to hold two bodies at once. Yevliesza had to do the job.

She heard herself scream in rage, in desperation. Throwing her hips to one side to help pull her arm away, she jerked her shoulder in a violent motion, yanking her wrist free of Nashavety's grip. The hand released her wrist.

The malwitch fell. Silent as a falcon's stoop she fell down, down forever.

Yevliesza clawed away from the edge. The stone against her hip, against her shoulder. Solid stone, warm like a mother's embrace. Her life seeping back into her. The sound of her own gasping breath. The sound of Rusadka's breath.

The sounds of the battle far, far away.

Chapter Thirty-Nine

The moonrise bathed the plain in a soft, ghostly blanket as Yevliesza rode slowly to the army camp, aching in every bone of her body. The battle was over, but figures still moved over the killing ground, manifesting lights hovering like the lost souls of the dead. Soldiers looking for friends, healers plying their skills.

She prayed Valenty still lived. How she would find him among the confusion of the two armies, she didn't know. She walked Mitri slowly, settled into the saddle in the way that Rusadka had taught her.

The two of them had made their way to the foot of the butte, but at the bottom, Rusadka could go no farther. Whether it was her injury from her fall from the ridge—down to a ledge far enough below to jar —or from the blow she had taken in battle, they didn't know. But she could not sit a horse, even behind Yevliesza on Mitri, so Yevliesza would send help to bring her back to camp.

As they had rested, propped against the great rock wall, Yevliesza thought how it was that Rusadka had saved them from Nashavety's last act of terror. Whatever Nashavety had planned, both Yevliesza and Rusadka believed it was something she thought could win the battle. Maybe it was to use her element power to bring a storm and lightning. Hardly reliable weapons, Rusadka had said. When Rusadka grappled with Nashavety on the ridge, she had crushed Nashavety's left hand. With the last of her will, as creature power crept over her, she had raised her fist, striking Nashavety's left hand in repeated blows.

"If you hadn't done that," Yevliesza had said as they rested, "she would have invoked some ugly power, I'm sure of it. But when I found her at the top, she was already beaten."

"Perhaps," Rusadka doubtfully said. "But she had the strength to push me off the ridge." Not the way Rusadka wanted a fight to end. An untrained woman against a *harjat*.

Playing over and over in Yevliesza's mind, the sight of Nashavety standing at the top of that wind-swept pillar. Her skeletal form. The gaze full of hate. Skirts lifting in the wind. Lunging for her.

It would have been a long fall. How unbearable it would have been to die hand in hand with the malwitch.

"You brought Nubiah," Rusadka said, staring into the prairie, maybe trying to take comfort in the decisive victory over the Volkish. But her mind was likely on Elivasa, having learned of the disaster only now. Lost in that dreadful way. Yevliesza wanted to comfort her, but Rusadka had drawn inside herself, doubly wounded.

As Yevliesza rode, a shape crossed her path. Kiya, she thought. No, a coyote. Then another. Come to the feast between the monuments. Mitri plodded on.

Nashavety lay dead at the bottom of the rock pinnacle. When they built the pyres for the fallen Volkish, they would place her body in the stack. Nashavety must go to ashes. Yevliesza would tell Anastyna to make sure of it, and thought that for once the princip would listen. And that would be end of it. *Only the good live on,* the Devi Ilsat had once told her.

There would be no burial for Arman, lost in the aborted tunnel. She had prayed for him, unsure if there was anyone left in Volkia who would do so. Duke Tanfred would surely ask Father Ludving to pray for Arman. Ludving, the priest with whom Tanfred had been so close and who had assisted in Yevliesza's escape from Volkia. When he brought the *satvars* to the crossings pretending to be healers and when, instead, they took Yevliesza home.

The stars emerged from hiding as night advanced. In the wide plains, Yevliesza was alone. Though thousands of soldiers were close, she saw herself journeying alone, looking for home. Somewhere out there was the life she was meant to have. Beyond kingdoms and wars and the clash of desires. She struggled to imagine the world finally free of Nashavety. She had been pushing against her so long that now she felt off balance. It was not a bad feeling, but it was exceedingly strange.

A dark shape approached her. Someone on horseback. She rode forward but then reined in Mitri. A rider in a cloak. A tall horse, the clink of a bridle. Valenty.

He curbed his horse. Then he was dismounting, striding toward her. She struggled to get out of the saddle gracefully, but ended up staggering out of the stirrups. He reached up for her, and she went into his arms. His embrace so tight, breath left her. Bringing her hands up to his face, she pressed her hands against his cheeks, his brow, reassuring herself it was he and not someone else, not a spirit come to say goodbye.

"Yevliesza," he murmured. "No one knew where you were, no one had seen you. I thought the worst." He pulled back to look at her. "Are you well? You are not hurt?"

"No, I am well," she said, relief flooding through her.

"Where by the eight hells, my love, have you been?"

She paused. How to say it? "A thing happened."

"A thing?"

"I killed Nashavety."

He was holding her by the shoulders, and for a moment there was only silence. It did not sound possible, she knew. And when she had fought Nashavety, it had, in fact, seemed impossible.

Valenty was still struck dumb. She went on. "I met her on the big spire and told her to jump. She did, but she grabbed me so that I would go with her."

"Yevliesza . . ." he groaned.

"I shook her loose. She fell." The short version.

"You killed her," he said, trying to take it in.

"Well. Me and Rusadka."

He looked out at the monument behind her. "The Citadel. That spire?"

"There's a flat space at the top."

He ran his hands though her hair and brought her close again. "She is dead?" he asked uselessly.

"Pretty sure." There were no ledges on that spire. Nashavety was dead.

"I told you to go and be safe," he said with weary affection. It seemed he was always trying to protect her and had so often failed. She hoped he didn't feel slighted.

"I meant to go to the camp," she assured him. "But then I saw Rusadka." She told him the whole story then as Mitri nudged her from time to time, impatient with all the talk, looking forward to a well-earned meal.

"Valenty," she finally said, "let's go into camp. There's someone I have to see."

ॐ

AFTER VALENTY LEFT TO FIND A WAGON TO BRING RUSADKA BACK, Yevliesza found Prince Tirhan at a campfire and sat with him. No, not prince. Now, king. Tirhan's wife, Morwen, was assisting at the healing ground.

His people stood back, giving them privacy. She had heard how the Alfan army had appeared on the battleground, giving new hope to the Numinasi fighters.

"I tried to reach you," she told Tirhan. "I made a new crossing to Alfan Sih, but it . . . it collapsed."

Tirhan frowned. He knew of her ability, had seen her make a path once before.

"Elivasa and her companion died. A man named Arman Brandt, a

Volkish officer who had defected. They took the new route in order to find you, to show you how to join us. You remember Elivasa?"

"I do. And I am sorry for those deaths, Yevliesza. I think I was meant to take that path."

"Meant to?"

"A messenger came to me. He said the clans would go to battle, but would need courage. I wondered if it had to do with you, if you were going to get into the crossings and forge a new path."

"But what messenger?" she asked, wondering how word could possibly have reached him about any of it.

"A vision. A messenger from the otherworld."

Time was when Yevliesza would have strongly doubted that. But she had learned to believe in spirits. She was on this whole journey because of such messengers.

Tirhan went on. "I had experienced such visitations before. Lately, I had. I came to understand that the spirit world was guiding me." He smiled. "Some people thought I was wrong to believe dreams and visitations."

The spirits helped him, but they had certainly kept their distance from her! The salvation of Numinat had been in her hands. But she had made mistakes. Kassalya had told her that she was too preoccupied to listen. The spirits had no idea how hard it could be to hear them.

Tirhan continued. "The last one told me that I had been meant to go through on a path but that I would not be able to. I assumed it was because the crossings were still controlled by the Volkish. We learned that the only way to reach the battle at that point was by a fearsome path: through the land of the dead. My men did not like it, and many would have held back. But Morwen said she would go. After that, everyone followed."

Morwen. Yevliesza remembered the blond-white hair hanging to the small of her back. Wearing a vest of knives. She was not surprised that Morwen had been the most willing to go.

She learned how the Alfan Sih partisans had been harrowing the Volkish and how the clans finally united under Tirhan. As he sat beside her, she thought he looked like a king. His cloak was covered in dust, his face streaked with dirt. But still, the manner of a ruler. She remembered his kindness to her when she had been under Nashavety's control at Osta Kiya. How he had commandeered a dactyl to escape the city-palace.

"Thank you, King Tirhan," she said. He made an expression. She need not call him that, but she said, "I wanted to try out saying it to you. I'm so glad I could." More soberly, she went on. "Thank you for daring to bring your people . . . the way that you did."

One of Tirhan's men approached, saying that Princip Anastyna awaited him.

Kings and princips. Yevliesza smiled to herself, glad she was no longer concerned with royal matters.

One did not hug a king, but he had taken her hand, gripping it.

She murmured, "When I think of what could have happened if you and your people had entered that path . . ."

"Do not think of it, Yevliesza," he said softly, but almost like a royal command. "We are here now."

She stayed at the fire for a time. Someone brought her a portion of dried meat and a cup of ale. Not a good meal, but she needed every bit of it. After a time, she noted a stirring in the camp and saw that someone was drawing attention as they walked among the troops.

A woman strolling and talking to soldiers. She wore a good dress and a torc. By her side, Prince Chenua, tall and striking, shaking hands with the common soldiers. She heard cries of "Nubiah!" She had only seen the man a few times in the halls of Osta Kiya. Most memorably during her first audience with Anastyna, when Chenua had disapproved how a soldier had been ordered to strike her. So she had liked the man, a foreigner in the court who spoke for her. But it had not been a good beginning with Anastyna. Nor had things ended well, how she had sent Urik to compel her to come to the camp where she would not have accepted a *no*.

Anastyna and Chenua disappeared into the throng.

Someone had come up to the campfire, but turned away. A soldier, by the axe strapped to his back.

"Please sit if you want," Yevliesza told him. "It's not my fire."

The soldier hesitated. He was tall and solidly built, with a great healed scar reaching from hairline to chin. He sat down heavily, turning his hands in the warmth of the fire.

Exhausted and taciturn, he said little, but she asked him about the battle, and eventually he said in a gravelly voice, "It was Nubiah that struck the final blow. They fought like demons. The Volkish lost hope. Died like roaches under their boots."

"Brave soldiers," she said, thinking of Valenty in their midst. "To come to help us."

He stared at the fire. "They fought their way through the crossings. Full of Volkish, it was. The bastards lurking there."

"The crossings?"

"Aye. Had to go through to get here, right enough. Met with Volkish swords, but they won through."

So that was what people thought, that Nubiah had come through the crossings. But what else could they think? "We owe them much," she said. "And their king."

He shrugged. "We would 'ave done the same."

It was best this way. She didn't want to be known. Her taste of fame, of notoriety, had first come in the village of Branova, when people thought that she talked to the dead. That she had been in the Mist Wall. What she actually had done was every bit as strange, but it was good that no one—or very few—knew about creating a crossing from anywhere to anywhere. She didn't want a following. There had been enough of that to last a lifetime.

She rose. "Can you tell me where the wounded are? I'm looking for a fourteen-year-old."

"Ah, that one. He tried to take on a swordsman. Something to see."

"He lives?"

"Aye." He gestured toward at Gray Fort.

At the foot of the formation, she found Pyvel in a space among other wounded, his arm in a sling. He seemed overjoyed to see her.

Kneeling by his side, she said, "Word among the soldiers is that you were very brave."

His eyes rounded. "They said that?"

"Yes. But I would not have wanted to see you face off with a Volkish swordsman."

"Battle is not for women," he said as though he'd seen a number of them. He winced at having said so. "Sorry, mistress."

"But maybe," she gently said, "it is for some women." She smiled at him, thinking how everyone imagined they knew things, but how it was often only a partial view and sometimes dead wrong.

She looked in the direction of the spire, vowing that she would never tell that story. Let the tales of the battle arise as they would, piecemeal, from the many views of those who saw the fight in moments of horror, moments of victory. Let them have their truths. And she and Rusadka would have theirs.

Chapter Forty

It was the seventh month and coming into full summer, which meant that the Numins were losing some of their ermine mantle. Dreiza looked out at the ranges of snow-capped peaks thinking, as always, of how pure and simple they looked.

Pure and simple—she liked the sound of it.

"What is pure and simple?" her helper, Ana, asked.

Dreiza had not realized she had spoken aloud. She turned back to repairing the willow fence that had suffered from the winter's ice. "The snow, my daughter. No matter the storms, it is always serene." Oh dear, she was starting to sound like the High Mother. She had promised herself that she would not start using homilies.

The girl looked to the southern range. "To me, it looks cold and forbidding."

That perception would change, but it was best not to say some things, things that people were not ready to hear. "Hand me a few sturdy ones," Dreiza said, looking for good anchor branches to shore up the smaller ones.

"We could fashion a solid wood door. What good does a door of willow branches do?"

"Well, to begin with, where would we get planks? And then, if someone is determined to come in, they could just climb over the courtyard wall."

The girl sighed. The former princip—renamed Ana to preserve her anonymity—was not used to be being contradicted. Yet she was a hard worker. Even in her weakened condition, she was willing to take on menial tasks. Dreiza believed she was doing . . . What was that word that churchmen used? Penance. Self-imposed, to be sure. Something she needed to do to come back from the hopeless place she had been.

The girl bent over the pile of willows searching for straight ones. Since her left hand was bandaged, she could only work with her right. The High Mother said she would heal, and already the rot was fading.

A lock of violet hair spilled out of the cloth cap that Ana used to keep it in place. "Eight miserable hells," she muttered, tucking it back in. She glanced up at Dreiza. "Please excuse me. I hate my hair."

What would Dreiza not have given to have had hair like that when she was young! But Ana's hair did always seem to want to spring free.

At last she chose a suitable branch and handed it to Dreiza. A small smile crossed her face. This was the first smile Dreiza had seen from her in the tenday since Sofiyana had arrived. When Yarna had brought her to the *satvary* that day, she certainly had not looked like a former princip. Thus it was easy to hide her identity from the *satvars* who, though well meaning, did not need to be talking about her.

"If you like," Dreiza said, "we can cut it short. Many of the *satvars* do. For simplicity." She was quite enjoying teaching the girl without seeming to. She hoped she did not seem to.

Ana immediately brightened. "Could we?" She stood straight, arching her back in a good stretch. "Could we do it now?"

They could. Dreiza led her inside the compound to the loom room, where a pair of scissors might be found. One of the *satvars* made a face about using a good pair of scissors for hair, but soon Dreiza was cutting off Ana's curly sprigs. They fluttered to the floor in a violet pile.

As Dreiza worked, the High Mother chanced by the door and paused, raising an eyebrow at her.

"For simplicity, Ana thinks," Dreiza told her.

"Ah," the High Mother said, nodding happily. She continued on her way. She often showed up where one least expected it and managed to keep all needful things moving along and everyone's needs tended to, even the needs of those who dabbled in sorcery, murdered no small number of people, and had once sent thugs to spy on the *satvary*.

Of course, all this was behind the girl.

Ana ran her hands over her head, now shorn close, and Dreiza saw a tear escape an eye.

Replacing her cloth cap, Ana whispered, "I do not suppose that I would ever be allowed to be a *satvar*?"

A few of the women smiled knowingly as they spun wool.

"All things are possible," Dreiza said, thinking of how her own life had changed so much in the past year. Her cordial parting with Valenty; the more difficult parting with Kirjanichka; her apprenticeship under the High Mother's strict standards and her sudden elevation into the inner circle of her closest advisors. Befriending the haunted Kassalya and losing her. Helping Sofiyana to reclaim her heart and her honor. Above all, the way her life had touched Yevliesza's, the girl who had fallen into their midst in the most extraordinary manner and who had, despite everything, done all that had been asked of her.

"All things are possible, my daughter," she said again, knowing it to be true.

৩৵৩

Shortly after dawn, their horses were saddled and carrying packs with provisions for the journey. Yevliesza petted Mitri's dappled gray forehead, silently promising him a good run or two that day.

Valenty was seeing to a fine black horse he had somehow acquired. They were readying for the ride north to Branova. Janov was going with them and had said they were welcome to stay at his cabin, which, as he had been master of the village, was a rather comfortable one. It was a three-day ride, and Yevliesza was anxious to be on the way. After Branova, they had no clear intentions. Valenty had lands, but they needed time to think through what came next. Besides finally being together. Somewhere to make a home. A family, even. A dream that was, at long last, a possibility.

She had said goodbye to people she knew and hoped to see again. Pyvel, when he had recovered, would stay with them, having been given leave from the army. He would soon be taken to the nearby town of Odniv, where a complex was being set up to care for the wounded who could not travel.

Inquiring after Duke Tanfred, Yevliesza learned that he had gone to Odniv to help with the injured Volkish. It would be work he had done before. Yevliesza recalled that part of his Volkish estate had been dedicated to a hospital.

Kirady was well and attending Anastyna in some of her postwar tasks. Captain Vadik, who had accompanied her south from the Haiga, had survived unscathed. Her former guard, Zander, was among the fallen, as was Carlaty, who had gone with Yevliesza in disguise to Osta Kiya's festival of the Blossom Moon. Other lost ones included Lysandry, one-time commander of Anastyna's forces in exile, and Prince Fadimir, who had died bravely in the last hours of battle. And in the same hour, Marshal Walthar Reinhart, when his own troops had fallen on him.

A group of officers approached the paddock. They accompanied Anastyna. She could go nowhere without an entourage, even if it was a private goodbye. She drew near, with her retinue standing back.

Valenty bowed, and Yevliesza did as well, less pronounced. Neither one of them were exactly in her good graces.

"Valenty," Anastyna said, ice in her voice. "And Yevliesza." A stiff smile. Turning back to Valenty, she asked, "Where will you go? Perhaps to your lodge in Merkasy?"

"That may be where we settle, My Lady Princip," he said, "but we cannot decide so soon."

"No, we expect not. Know that you go with our good wishes." After years of service, now there was only good wishes. But Anastyna had been abandoned by her closest advisor, and she felt such things keenly. Add to that, Anastyna might know that Valenty had tried to stop her unit of *harjat* from capturing Yevliesza. They didn't know how much Urik had told Anastyna of that failed mission. Maybe only that Prince Fadimir's army had come, and since it appeared that the prince favored Yevliesza, the *harjat* had to retreat.

Anastyna turned to Yevliesza. They shared a moment's gaze where each of them harbored their feelings, not to be expressed.

Anastyna said, "You have our thanks for bringing Nubiah to our aid." It sounded practiced. Succinct and proper. "The timing . . . precise."

God, was she saying *barely in time*? She could complain to Yevliesza's face? Scrambling for a suitable response, Yevliesza blurted out, "Better late than never." Stupid, but she couldn't leave *precise timing* alone.

"Ah!" Anastyna sighed. "So well uttered. Yes, we are thankful it was not *never*. Yet we are mindful of how you helped us to win our desperate struggle. And then the traitor who worked with Volkia was finally brought low." Rusadka had reported those events to Anastyna, and apparently Anastyna was leaving the description vague when discussing it in public. She would not want to burnish Yevliesza's reputation.

She went on. "As token of these services, we wish to honor you with a gift from your princip and from Numinat." She held out her hand without looking at her attendants, and an officer came forward with a small box, placing it in Anastyna's hand.

Yevliesza accepted it from Anastyna. She received a nod to open it.

Inside lay a gold bracelet studded with sapphires. It was worth a fortune.

Despite herself, Yevliesza shivered. "Thank you, My Lady Princip. I am greatly surprised."

The princip gave a tolerant smile. "We acknowledge that there have been difficulties between us. Let us consider them a storm that, having passed, leaves no trace." She looked at both of her former servants as they stood with their horses. "And so."

Nodding to them, Anastyna turned away, moving on to her next duty. And the next.

Yevliesza looked at the bracelet, brilliant in the sun. A thank-you gift, heavy and expensive, and one she would never wear. Of all the things she had ever hoped for from Anastyna. Now this ornate bracelet. For some reason, she felt like laughing.

Yevliesza showed the bracelet to Valenty. "It's worth a ton of money."

"A ton?"

"Bushels," Yevliesza said, letting a laugh escape.

Valenty smiled knowingly. His arm came around her waist, drawing her close for a moment. Anastyna was the past, though she still directed royal events. The two of them were eager to leave royal events behind.

Yevliesza tucked the bracelet into her saddlebag, and they walked out of the paddock. Janov followed, leading his horse.

As the three of them left the trampled battleground, they passed one of the cremation pyres loaded with tinder of sticks and straw. They stopped for a moment. From a cart soldiers carried a body wrapped in cloth and bound with rope. They tossed it on a heap of kindling. A length of black material escaped at one end of the body.

"Let us go," Valenty said. They would not honor Nashavety by attending her immolation.

They turned in the direction of Castle Rock and beyond, the Numin Mountains. From behind them, a loud whump as fire ignited the pyre.

⁂

AT THE VILLAGE OF ODNIV, IN A VAST, FLAT LANDSCAPE, YEVLIESZA looked at a field crowded with makeshift tents. It didn't seem promising as a place to convalesce, but it would take time for shelters to be built, with trees needing to be felled and planked, more healers recruited, and supplies brought in.

For now, hundreds of patients were settling into the temporary quarters. The villagers had taken the most severely wounded into their homes, and some would be billeted in stables once they were cleaned out. It was an enormous undertaking, managed by army officers and, on the Volkish side, by Duke Tanfred. The villagers were wary of him and especially of the enemy soldiers. Some of the locals had lost loved ones in the battle, and forgiveness would take time.

Anastyna had already sent her people in to repair the village granary and build a smithy, and had decreed that all buildings built for convalescence would in future belong to the village.

Valenty put his arm around Yevliesza's waist as they walked. His hand was often in hers, or on her shoulder. Or she reached for him. Each time she touched him, she was reassured. He was here. They were together. But it wouldn't do to hold hands in front of Rusadka. He found an excuse to leave her as she entered a hayloft where Rusadka was billeted with other wounded.

Yevliesza found her friend sitting on the floor in a long line of resting soldiers. She sat on a mattress of hay covered with a blanket and was paring her nails with a wicked-looking blade.

"Be careful with that knife," Yevliesza said by way of announcing herself.

Rusadka looked up. "You are here. Good. Now I can leave." Her belongings were still stuffed into a sack, as though she really did plan to leave despite having a serious concussion.

A large bruise adorned Rusadka's forehead and was turning a peculiar shade of green. Her nose had a claw mark snaking down the middle, and the side of her head was shaved and bandaged.

"Looking good," Yevliesza said.

Ignoring the gibe, Rusadka said, "You have not come for me, I take it."

Yevliesza sat on the bare dirt floor, facing her. "They say you aren't well enough to travel. How are you feeling?"

"Good. Having to argue with healers is the worst of it."

It hadn't occurred to Yevliesza that Rusadka was going to be a terrible patient. They sat in silence for a time. A healer stopped at Rusadka's pallet for a moment but, meeting a scowl, quickly moved on.

"Valenty is with you?"

"And Janov."

"I like Janov," Rusadka said.

Yevliesza let that go. "What will you do now?" The question seemed to be the one on everyone's mind. *What now?*

"Go back to my billet at Osta Kiya." Rusadka pinned Yevliesza with a determined look. "I am a warrior."

"Maybe there will be no more wars," Yevliesza said.

"Then why live?" A smile jabbed for a second at the corner of Rusadka's mouth.

Oh God, had Rusadka made a joke? Yevliesza smiled back, looking at the woman who had brought Nashavety to her ruin. Who had saved Yevliesza's life. *Try harder,* she had snapped, suggesting that Nashavety hanging off Yevliesza's wrist was likely to bring all three of them to their doom.

She put her hand on Rusadka's arm. "I'm going to Branova."

"A long ride, Branova."

"I wish you could come with us."

Rusadka's voice went gentle. "Time for you two to be alone."

Yevliesza lowered her voice. "I'm not telling anyone I pushed her." Not wanting to say the malwitch's name. "And nothing about the path to Nubiah."

"Well, but there is a rumor going around of the Keeper opening up strange doorways."

Oh, no. Not more stories. She had wondered if the word would get out, since she had traveled in search of aligns with a dozen soldiers. They, at least, all knew.

"Go to the Agarvesky," Rusadka suggested. "Put it all behind you. People will never find you."

It was her permission to leave. Rusadka did not need tending, or wouldn't allow it in any case.

A brief nod, and Rusadka gave her an encouraging smile. Small, but it was large in Yevliesza's mind.

Out on the field behind the village, they met Duke Tanfred making the rounds of the injured Volkish. His green and white flag was planted in the center of hundreds of men who were sequestered behind a line of stones that separated them from Osta Kiya wounded. Guards were stationed at points along the perimeter, but they didn't seem to be taking their job seriously, many of them chatting with the Volkish, or trying to.

Tanfred came up to the three of them, shaking hands, looking energized. "We have so far to go," he said, looking around at the misshapen tents and lean-tos.

"So long as they are not fighting each other, I count it a success," Valenty said, with Tanfred nodding his eager agreement.

Yevliesza was glad to see the duke. Despite all he had been though, he still had those boyish good looks. An optimism that made him handsome.

"Arman," Duke Tanfred said suddenly. His expression serious.

"I'm sorry," Yevliesza said. "He was a hero. He brought you to us. And died trying to do so much more. The path. I couldn't sustain it."

Tanfred held up his hand. "You did the right thing. You had to try. Arman gave his life for the future of Volkia. As he wished to do."

Valenty said, "I think you are that future, Your Grace."

Tanfred shook his head. "That will depend on what the people of Volkia want. I would be happy to go back to Wilhoff Manor and tend my garden. Believe me." That boyish smile.

Anastyna was sending Commander Ilyan to Volkia along with an occupation force to shore up the decimated government. No soldiers were allowed back through the Numinat Gates yet. Volkia was a broken nation. It would take time for a government to form, one that Numinat trusted.

They took their leave of Tanfred. "No more goodbyes," Yevliesza said as they went back to their horses.

Janov nodded. "Aye. Just greetings now. In Branova."

❧

ON THEIR SECOND MORNING OUT, CLOUDS RACED OVER THE SKY AND wind bent the grasses flat. A light rain fell at intervals, dampening their wool cloaks. The land sloped gently upward, sometimes cut by glimmering creeks fed by the Haiga River still miles away. The three of them plodded on, following a track going north.

That night they found hospitality at a steading that for a few coins was taking travelers in. They bedded down with a half-dozen others in a barn and counted themselves lucky to be out of the rain.

Mounted again in the morning and eager to arrive at Branova by nightfall, they raced the horses. As the weather worsened, bringing a stinging rain, Yevliesza was soaked and uncomfortable but fiercely happy. Every time she looked at Valenty, she felt an amazement that he loved her, that they had found each other. He looked so very handsome, even soaked by rain, and when their eyes met, she was stirred and longed to be alone with him.

As they crossed a meadow, sheet lightning ignited the air, followed by a monstrous crack of thunder. Janov's horse reared, and even Mitri flinched. The temperature was dropping amid a pelting downpour. The rain continued all day, as though the storm was following them to the Agarvesky.

Valenty leaned over from his saddle to speak to her. "Shall we take shelter? We can find a place out of the wind, at least."

"No, let's go on." They would not fare much worse in the storm by riding on than by hunkering beneath a tree.

Janov stepped his mount close to her and handed her a blanket he had had dug from his saddlebag. She drew it over her shoulders, and a steamy warmth soon eased her chilled skin.

It was a rain-sodden group that arrived in Branova at dusk. Janov had a villager take their horses to the barn and see to their needs. He opened his cabin, ushering them into the great room, and insisted that Valenty and Yevliesza take the larger sleeping quarters.

Valenty built a fire while Janov brought barley ale for the two of them. Yevliesza could not drink at the best of times and now could not face ale, but soon Janov brought her a cup of fresh milk from a neighbor, who also sent along hot soup and bread.

When they finished the meal, they sought their beds.

Valenty brought the packs in as Yevliesza pawed through the fresh clothes Janov had left in a pile on the bed.

Valenty moved close behind her and slid his arms around her waist. "You are not thinking of changing, I hope."

She turned to him, looking at his well-loved face, his dark eyes with their slash of violet. "So you like me soaking wet?"

He murmured, "No, but would it not suit you better to take these things off?" Without waiting for an answer, he began to pull away her jacket.

She helped him do so.

"Was that a yes?" he asked, speaking so softly it felt like they were the only two people in the world.

"Yes, it was a yes."

He pulled the shirt over her head. Her clothes stuck to her, unwilling participants in the disrobing, but Valenty was methodical, removing her leggings and casting off the half-shift she wore close to her skin. Their hands got in each other's way as she undressed him at the same time.

They crawled into bed and, unwilling to cover themselves with blankets, held each other against the cold. Enough light still filled the small window for her to trace the beautiful lines of his face, his perfect body. To see him want her.

As his hands explored her, he murmured, "I am dying for you. Will you make me wait?"

"No, please do not wait. Not another moment."

He pulled himself on top of her, stroking her hair away from her face. "I love you forever."

"Why have you waited so long?" she accused him with a smile.

"You had journeys to make. Other things on your mind."

"I don't anymore," she said. Then he gently took her, and she took him, trying not to cry out, but then not caring.

Late in the night she came wide awake, unused to anyone in her bed. She reached for Valenty to assure herself he was still there. Ran her hand over his back as he lay on his side, breathing deeply.

A howl came from the forest. It might have been a wolf. Her wolf. Or a coyote. An answering howl.

She thought of the great Agarvesky with its fathoms of green, its realm of seers and pilgrims, its looming Mist Wall embracing the trackless depths and encompassing all things. It was—Numinat was—home.

Not the usual home, but one where magic ran through the land and through the hands of her lover and where both had accepted her completely.

Thinking of the forest so close, Valenty so close, she almost could not sleep.

And then she did.

Epilogue

"We do not have enough books." Grigeni stood at the kitchen door, arms folded in front of him.

Yevliesza looked up from shelling peas, the cook counter strewn with pods.

"Not nearly enough," Grigeni said, looking flustered.

"How many children this morning?" Yevliesza asked, wiping her hands on her apron.

"Seven."

"And books?"

"Three."

"Then we will have to send for more." Grigeni had set himself to improving Pyvel and Niko, both apparently needing better mastery of arithmetic, history, and writing. At the same time, Niko was teaching Grigeni and Pyvel some Volkish. Grigeni approved this, as languages, he felt, were the mark of a good upbringing, his own having lacked the niceties.

"I will write to Osta Kiya," he said, shaking his head. "It may take months."

Lura came in from the garden with another basket of tomatoes. The two of them had spent a tenday drying, stewing, and pickling tomatoes, which, with Lura's verdure gift, seemed inexhaustible. Grigeni took the basket from her and carried it to the planked table. Behind him Lura made a quasi-exasperated face at Yevliesza. Grigeni was always wanting to carry things for his wife, as though she needed him to. As though he was flat-out in love.

"I can help you in the schoolroom," Lura said, beaming at him.

Grigeni looked to Yevliesza for permission, and, receiving a nod, they left the main house for the schoolroom cottage where Grigeni was tutoring Pyvel and Niko. Word having got out about his lessons, children from nearby villages sometimes showed up and were welcome.

Yevliesza had been working in the kitchen since early morning. She removed her apron and stepped out of the house to take in the warmth of the day. It was the ninth month. September, in the mundat calendar. Sometimes the old words came back to her. The old ways and memories. But increasingly, Numinat was her whole world, making Earth a receding land, seen through a soft mist.

She looked to the courtyard gate, watching for the visitors Janov had said were coming. He had a knowing that there would be two of them, and she was eager to see who it might be.

A fine rock wall at waist height surrounded the courtyard, a climbing yellow rose hugging it. In the center, a well with a bench. Behind the house, three detached cottages, as well as a garden surrounded by a stick fence.

Valenty's family had built the compound for a country estate and hunting lodge back when his father and grandfather had ridden into the Agarvesky to hunt elk and boar. Valenty had expanded the original stables for the several horses he'd been acquiring. Among these prize animals was Mitri, who seemed unimpressed to be among his betters. His adventures over, in the past year his muzzle, if not his heart, had further whitened with age.

The main house, the former hunting lodge, possessed a spacious great room and a deep fireplace of river stone. Mullions divided the thick glass of the windows. In the mornings, the sun threw warm, moving squares of light on the flagstone floor.

She loved the place, lively with two boys—one nearly a man, she had to remind herself. Lura tended to Yevliesza's personal needs as well as most of the cooking. Grigeni was Valenty's man and the schoolmaster. Janov had management of the estate along with four helpers, sturdy men who had been soldiers. Valenty kept them for household guards, even if they were usually working in the stables or the potato field. Not that they expected trouble. Someone named the Keeper was known to live near the forest, a local legend replete with secret passageways, mystical experiences in the Mist Wall, control over the weather, and speaking with the dead.

No one suspected that she was the Keeper. Had been. Or if they did, they kept her secret.

Woven into that secret was her affinity for the crossings. Her ninth power would always be a hidden one. Altering the crossings was in her past and would remain so. That dangerous power should never be invoked again. So many reasons. The quakes. The fragility of the Mythos. And making an align a route of travel between somewhere and somewhere else: never again. Such paths could dissolve, as she knew from heartbreaking experience.

She remembered Kassalya's prophecy: in the future, no one would remember her. She would leave no trace when she was gone. Well. She put her hand on her stomach, only slightly rounded. Like anyone else, her legacy would be her children. The baby would come in the second month of the new year, the wonder of it always present these days.

She thought lovingly of her and Valenty's steading. It was everything she could ever want. It was complete in so many ways, including that, by good fortune, each of the nine powers infused their lives. Yevliesza's aligns and undisclosed power. Valenty's warding; Grigeni's manifesting; Lura's verdure. Janov had two gifts, foreknowing and a small affinity for elements. Young Niko had a treasured combination of gifts, healing and creatures. Predictably, he was always tending an injured bird or squirrel in a cage and once even a fox. He had not yet lost a patient.

The steading was some three miles from Merkasy, a settlement where they purchased supplies and sometimes received mail. Yevliesza often heard from Rusadka, who had been promoted to *harjat* second rank. There was room at the top with Urik having left the service, and Yevliesza thought how much Rusadka deserved to rise to Urik's old rank.

The latest letter from Duke Tanfred revealed that he still had hope for an easy transition from military rule and a succession in the old monarchy that did not include him. But he was demonstrating a knack for managing things. She doubted that he would return anytime soon to Wilhoff Manor and his gardens.

She saw dust on the track south. Valenty had been out riding and was returning—as Janov had foreknown, with two more riders. As they drew closer, she saw with pleasure that one of then was Kirady. The other, to her surprise, was Urik. He wore his hair cut short now, a crushed hat to keep the sun out of his eyes, tight-fitting riding clothes, and a cape trimmed in the yellow and brown of Eiger Polity.

Entering the arched gate of the courtyard, Valenty swung off his horse and came to embrace her. "Met them on the road," he told her.

Delighted, Yevliesza went to greet them. Anastyna had bestowed on Kirady a large grant of lands. He was now warden of a much larger polity than before. And Urik had been appointed warden of Eiger Polity, Kirady's old turf.

Yevliesza thought of Urik as something like the Sheriff of Nottingham. He patrolled the district and met in villages to pass judgment on issues and land claims, sometimes gathering men of the village to round up miscreants. Troublemakers had no chance under Urik's regime.

"Kirady," she said in greeting. "Urik. You are so welcome!" She saw Lura coming round the side of the house. She waited to see if there would be two more for midday meal. "You can stay?" she asked Kirady.

"A drink of water in the yard," he said, dismounting. "We must be in Merkasy soon." He took Yevliesza's hand, pressing it in his own. With his clipped white beard and lined face, she thought of him in the role of a father. He had been happy to take that role at her and Valenty's wedding.

"Trouble?" Valenty asked. He stood at the well drawing up the bucket, and Lura came out with cups.

Valenty and Urik clasped hands. Yevliesza was glad to see it. They had fought once, and she had been the reason. She suspected it was why Urik left Anastyna's service. Once you saw royal dealings up close, it was easy to let go of it. Her eyes met Urik's, and he nodded to her, his face impassive, but not harsh. An old scar near his temple.

"Is there trouble at Merkasy?" Valenty asked again. "I can ride with you."

"No, it is only the Ninth Moon fair." Kirady made a wry face. "I am to give a speech."

Valenty grinned. "Then we must all come to hear it."

"If you have a keen interest in the harvest and the princip's taxes." Kirady sighed. Yevliesza thought he might miss his small polity.

The children had come out of the schoolroom to look over the new arrivals. At a nod from Valenty, Pyvel came forward to greet the newcomers.

Valenty murmured to Yevliesza, "Now is the time. Urik does not often come."

Yevliesza took a calming breath. Pyvel was like a son to her, despite the fact that she was only seven years older than he. She did not want him to leave. Though he could not apply for *harjat* training for another year, his hope was to win a place a year early as an apprentice.

Valenty took her hand, squeezing it. "Master Urik, we would ask a favor." Urik's recommendation would assure Pyvel a place among the *harjat*.

Urik gazed at Pyvel. "Still want the *harjat*'s life, do you?"

Urik knew him well. He had traveled through Volkia with Pyvel and Valenty and had seen him well placed in the battle at the Plain of Monuments.

"Yes, sir," Pyvel responded with a steady gaze, his voice strong, acting older than his fourteen years. Urik took a walk with him around the courtyard. The seasoned warrior and the young aspirant.

Yevliesza needed a breath of fresh air. While Valenty and Kirady talked, she went to the courtyard gate to look out. The forest was a vast green wall not far away. Not far into its depths, Yevliesza knew, an align slashed through, burning with its uncanny light. She liked that an align was near and felt, without any evidence whatsoever, that it consecrated her home.

They had chosen this place, and she thought it perfect. Remote, but not isolated, suited to a woman who wanted—who needed—to stay far from great matters. Valenty loved the place. His family's estate, with many things of his father's. Good horses to ride. Children to wait for and treasure.

Gazing across the meadow, she saw a shape emerge from nowhere. A wolf. It padded in her direction, silver fur catching the morning light.

She turned and caught Valenty's eye. "Kiya!" she said. "I'll go out."

He waved in acknowledgment, walking forward to watch her from the gate.

Her spirits restored, she left the courtyard behind and went out to meet her wraith wolf. Whatever changes happened in her life, she would not be alone. Kiya would always be nearby. In one way or another, he would always be there. Even at the end, she thought. Which was a long time away.

Acknowledgments

Writing a series is a big undertaking made possible, or at least more sure-footed and enjoyable, with the advice of early readers and mentors as well as support from family, friends, and fans. I am exceptionally lucky to have had an abundance of such help during my two years of working on The Arisen Worlds quartet.

I am so pleased to acknowledge this help here. Thank you to my husband, Thomas Overcast, my first reader and patient, encouraging, and unflagging supporter during the creation of these four books.

Sharing the journey of the writing life with other authors is one of my greatest pleasures. Thank you to Melody Kreimes, Sharon Shinn, Louise Marley, and Theresa Monsey for assistance, encouragement, and laughs. Thank you to my advance readers Janice Bogstad, Michele L. Casteel, Charles Hirst, Marilyn Holt, Morgan Mead, Marisa Miller, Lisa Montoya, Eric Morris, Veronica Rood, Janet Smith, and Leeann Smith.

Finally, thank you to Anthea Sharp, fantasy author and friend, who was the first to hear my idea for this series and who cheered me on, advising me through the ups and downs of the rich and twisty world of indie publishing.